PART TIME GIRL

Adriaan Brae

Renaissance
Diverse Canadian Voices

PressesRenaissancePress.ca

First edition 2025

Cover art and design by Nathan Fréchette.
Interior design by Éric Desmarais.
Edited by Molly Desson, Lashanda Forsberg, Alicia Murray, and Lorenzo Carrera

Legal deposit, Library and Archives Canada, November 2025.

Paperback ISBN: 978-1-990086-92-2
Ebook ISBN: 978-1-997721-02-4

Renaissance Press - pressesrenaissancepress.ca

Renaissance acknowledges that it is hosted on the traditional, unceded land of the Anishinabek, the Kanien'kehá:ka, and the Omàmìwininìwag. We acknowledge the privileges and comforts that colonialism has granted us and vow to use this privilege to disrupt colonialism by lifting up the voices of marginalized humans who continue to suffer the effects of ongoing colonialism.

Printed in Gatineau at
Imprimerie Gauvin
Depuis 1892
gauvin.ca

Renaissance gratefully acknowledges the support of the Canada Council for the Arts

For all the trans folks out there who considered all the obstacles, considered all the dangers, and all society that wants them to be someone else, and declared quietly: I'm going to be me.

NOTE TO READER

While this is a YA novel, it's on the older side of YA and there are some heavy themes inside. Please review this list and be careful of your mental health while reading. If you would like a more detailed description of any warning, please feel free to contact the author.

- Explicit violence, killing and death
- Drugging an unsuspecting person
- Implications of sexual violence
- Confinement / Kidnapping
- Forced evacuation
- Panic attack
- Mentions of transphobia
- Brief sexual activity
- Mentions of involuntary medical confinement
- Mentions of torture
- Mentions of conversion 'therapy' (magical)
- Cursing

CHAPTER 1

Fuck. I'm a girl again.

I ducked back into the locker room with an arm across my chest. Luckily, there was only one guy left from the crowd of a few minutes ago, and he was focused on retying his shoelaces.

I'd been female only a couple of days ago. To switch again so soon, and with no warning… My hands shook as I dialed the combination lock.

Finally teasing the lock open, I turned my back to him, quickly shucked off the stupid mesh phys ed jersey, and yanked my T-shirt over my head. I had just pulled it down when the locker room door burst open.

"Mike?" Ian called, his slim but well-muscled frame poised in the doorway, holding the door open with one hand. "Coach is waiting for you."

I hunched over, keeping myself half turned, tenting my shirt over my chest. Making my voice as hoarse and deep as possible, I replied, "Tell him I'm going to see the nurse. I'm cramping up again."

Bowel problems were something no one wanted to challenge, but I hated using it as an excuse in front of Ian. He was already way too popular to be hanging around me like he'd been doing all year, and I didn't know what might jinx it. His friendliness meant a lot to me. Especially with Angela avoiding me over the past few weeks.

"Sure, man." He flashed me one of those bright smiles that always made my fickle heart speed up, then took a step into the room. What if he offered to walk there with me? The little tingle in my stomach had nothing to do with cramping, but was equally disturbing.

I slammed the locker, abandoning my jeans. "Later!" I gave him a half wave that hopefully looked casual and fled.

~*~

The halls were quiet during classes, but not deserted. I headed for my locker, where I kept an emergency kit hidden with some girl gear: tape for binding my chest, a poofy jacket to conceal my shape, a pair of old shoes that fit my smaller feet, and pads for when the timing was particularly bad.

Thankfully, at least so far, my face had an androgynous look in both genders, so I'd generally been able to get away with a sex-switch without anyone noticing, as long as I took some pains to mask my body and voice. Gym shorts and a T-shirt were not going to cut it.

I peered around the last corner and saw my English teacher, the vice principal, and another teacher having a little confab about ten feet from my locker. *Double fuck.* There was no way to get into it without some serious explaining. The downside of having essentially the same face: it made it hard to pretend to be someone else.

I edged away and double-timed it to a little-used exit. It was pouring rain outside. Huge cold drops bounced as they hit, making a continuous spray across the asphalt. Walking home in my shorts and guy-sized shoes was going to suck.

Good thing I never wear white tees, I thought as I stepped out.

~*~

The rain was relentless, plastering my shirt to my body. The skin on my bare arms and legs quickly numbed, but power walking kept the chill from my core. If I hurried, I might be able to change into something concealing and get back to school for my last-period chemistry class.

I turned onto my street, hoping like hell my parents hadn't come home early. A grocery delivery van idled in front of a run-down house on the block before mine, and the unmistakable sounds of an argument drifted through the storm.

"There's no way I'm carrying boxes up that thing," the delivery guy yelled up to the house. "Not even if it was dry."

"That's all right with me, like I said." The woman standing in the doorway of the house yelled back. She had an English accent, or maybe Australian. I could never tell. "Just leave and I'll get them."

The guy was standing by a pile of boxes at the bottom of a makeshift wooden ramp leading to the front door. The front porch had completely collapsed last winter. She must've been hard up to have rented this place.

He shook his head. "I can't leave them on the sidewalk. You could make a complaint and get me fired!"

"You don't understand ... I ... can't." Her voice cracked.

The last thing I wanted to do was talk to people. I wanted to slip by 100% unnoticed by anyone I might meet later when back in male form, but she was shaking, with a faint sheen of sweat at the hairline of her tightly curled mass of black hair. The guy, in his mid-twenties, was looking belligerently stubborn. A simple argument I could have left behind, but I couldn't see that kind of fear and not help.

I walked past the grocery store-branded delivery van to where the irate driver stood a few feet past the front bumper. I called up to the woman. "Can I help?"

She smiled welcomingly and nodded.

The driver turned to me, surprised. His eyes tracked up and down my body, pausing noticeably at chest height where my soaked shirt was plastered to my skin. My breasts weren't large, but it was definitely not a male chest. What a day to be girl-shaped.

"Up to you." He waved at the boxes. "Company rules. I can't cart boxes up that thing. Anything happened, I'd be off work with no comp."

I studied the ramp. There were wooden cleats nailed in every couple of feet, but the wet wood in between looked slippery, and who knew how stable the whole thing was.

"Okay. No problem." I crouched and hefted one of the boxes off the pile, then climbed the ramp slowly and easily. The woman took the box from me as I reached the top, lifting it with no apparent strain.

I picked my way back down the ramp. The delivery guy was holding up a box for me to take. All working together, we finished quickly. He stalked back to his van, slammed the door, and took off with a roar of the engine, leaving behind a cloud of acrid exhaust fumes that was quickly consumed by the downpour.

"You're a life-saver, you are," said the woman from the doorway. "Please, let me make you a cuppa and get you out of the rain. You must be freezing."

I hesitated. She was right, and I was tempted, but I kept to myself while in female shape for good reasons. Then, with a shock of fear up my spine, I saw Ian crossing the street a couple of blocks away. He was looking in the other direction, but he'd spot me the instant he glanced this way. I leapt up the ramp.

The woman jerked back, raising a hand, but relaxed when I stopped right inside the door.

"Sorry," I said. "I ah ... just don't want to talk to that guy right now."

Ian topped the list of people I did not want to see while in girl shape. Even above my parents.

"Of course," she said as she leaned past me to close and lock the door. The way she said it suggested a world of implications about Ian and my relationship to him. I immediately wished I'd thought of any other excuse, especially when she moved to peer through the gap at one side of the dirty white metal-slat blinds covering the front windows.

Was Ian coming to visit me? If so, how had he known where I lived? I didn't remember telling him my address. Had he been worried enough about my sudden departure from school to ask someone?

"Ex-boyfriend?" she asked with a knowing look.

My mind stalled, lost in the utterly improbable idea of asking Ian on a date. As a guy or a girl. I would combust and melt into a puddle first. Also, my current relationship situation with Angela was complicated enough without adding another point of chaos.

"Current boyfriend?" she asked, looking more concerned now. Was she worried Ian was dangerous? Crap, I had to tell her something.

"Not a boyfriend," I blurted out. "He's a good guy. I'd just be, uh, embarrassed to see him right now."

"Oh, of course," she said, glancing back at me for a second, before her attention was captured outside again. She'd said it like that was obvious, which confused me for a second, then I remembered my wet and clinging T-shirt, and my current shape, and felt embarrassed all over again, though not nearly as keenly as when the delivery guy had been ogling me.

She gasped and stepped away from the window. I caught a strange expression on her face that I couldn't quite decipher. Surprise? Fear? Anger? It was gone before I could decide which, replaced with a bland smile.

"I'm so sorry. You're still standing there, soaked. I don't have a lot of warm jackets but ..." She opened a closet, which had three jackets hanging in it. Only one was suitable for this weather: a bright pink raincoat.

Of course.

I put it on as a cover for my chest and a little extra warmth. I was still shivering.

"I'll bring you some nice hot tea," she said, heading for the back of the house. "Take anything in it?"

"No, black is good," I said.

To the left of where I stood at the door was a large front room that was empty except for a loose coil of coaxial cable at the base of one wall. The closet in front of me and a wall to the right blocked my view any further into the house. I was curious, but also reluctant to take my shoes off or intrude on her privacy. It seemed she really was new here.

She brought me a mug with a radio station logo on it that I was pretty sure had changed formats a couple of years ago. I took an experimental sip. It was strong enough to be slightly bitter but flavourful, and I gratefully wrapped my chilled fingers around the mug.

She had her own fresh cup of tea and leaned her shoulder against the closet wall in a relaxed pose. "I'm Sarah, by the way." I took my first really good look at her. She was wearing tan leggings and a white top with pink flowers embroidered around the neckline. She looked younger now than I'd guessed at first glance from the street. Late-twenties? Her dark brown skin was smooth and wrinkle-free.

Belatedly, I realized she was waiting for some kind of response to her introduction. I opened my mouth, then closed it again. I couldn't say I was Michael. Michelle was stupidly close. I hadn't dared speak my original girl name in ten years, even with my family. I certainly wasn't giving it out to a stranger.

Michaela? Still too close. "Kayla! That's my name," I finally blurted out.

There was another awkward silence.

"I'm so glad you came along," she filled in after a while. "That guy was ser'ously creeping me out. And he was there with a van …" She shook her head. "No way I was leaving the house."

Her concern seemed a little on the extreme side, but she'd really been scared. Though a Black woman alone in a new place probably had every right to be extra cautious.

"I can see that," I said. "He really should have backed off."

She nodded.

"Did you just move here from … England?" I asked, hazarding a guess.

"No, lived in America for a while first, and I was bouncing around the continent for a while before that. But yeah, grew up in the UK. Birmingh'm," she said, with a funny twist to her lips.

I nodded stupidly. I would have to search that up when I got home. My knowledge of the UK pretty much began and ended with London.

"I used to live in the US too, but we moved here when I was eight," I told her. I'd repeated it often enough over the years that it had become a bland statement. The residue of horror from that time was completely scraped off with use. I had been feeling a strange kinship with this woman since I stepped in, and it finally clicked. I'd spent my time in a mostly empty house, too, after we fled from our old lives.

"Do you live nearby?" she asked, taking a sip of her tea after.

"Ah, a few blocks over." I waved a hand, indicating a vague direction. No way did I want her coming around asking for 'that nice girl I had a chat with the other day.' "I was on my way home from school." I groped for a distracting topic. "When do you think you'll have a porch again?" Mom and Dad had been certain this place would sell as a tear-down. It shouldn't have been rented in this condition.

"Not sure really." She frowned and shook her head. "Guess I'll need to do something about that."

"Yeah, there's no way your landlord should get away with leaving it in this condition," I said.

"Yeah, I guess she shouldn't," Sarah said, eyes twinkling. "It's me. I bought the place."

"Oh," I said, feeling adrift in the conversation again. "Yeah, that's a different problem." It occurred to me that enough time had likely passed for it to be safe for me to walk home. I could exit this conversational minefield before I gave myself away as knowing very little about how to exist as a girl.

She let me go as soon as I suggested it. "Just bring my jacket back to me when it's sunny again, a'ight?" She smiled.

"I'll return it. Thank you," I said quietly. I wondered briefly if we should hug. Girls seemed to do that a lot, even with people they'd just met. It didn't feel right, though, and the moment fortunately passed without awkwardness.

I hopped down the slick ramp, from cleat to cleat, rain pattering on the vibrant jacket. I could mail it back to her. I didn't intend to be caught out as a girl this way again. I fled down the street at a quick walk—walking only because running could draw too much attention.

CHAPTER 2

Mom was off work today, so I needed to kill some time. Getting home too early would mean stiff questions. And worse, I might run into Ian if he had made it all the way to my house. Best to head in the opposite direction. That would help in case Sarah was watching, too.

I ambled back toward school, planning to go a few blocks then circle back through the alleys. As I neared the last corner, two guys with book bags appeared ahead. I thought I was safe from the school crowd for a little while yet, but some people had a last-period spare or were ditching.

My knees weakened when I realized it was my friend Ravi with the guy who'd been retying his shoes in the locker room when I was exposed in girl form. We'd been in the same school for two years, but I blanked on his name.

I silently apologized to the pink raincoat, my saviour. I hugged it around me and kept my head down, hoping the hood and my strangely lengthened hair would shield my features. We passed each other without incident, but as I started to relax, I heard Ravi laugh. I shivered in fear and tried not to let it show.

"Donny! Are you checking her out?" Ravi asked, surprised.

"No!" Donny sounded embarrassed and defensive. "I just thought..."

"You were *so* checking her out."

"Shut up," hissed Donny, still clearly audible. "She can totally hear us!"

A laugh bubbled up inside me, and I had a sudden ridiculous urge to moon them to see the looks on their faces, but that would've been stupid on so many levels. I kept walking as normally as possible until I turned the corner. I had no idea if they continued to watch or not.

When did Ravi start hanging out with Donny? That was weird.

The gravelled back alley was a field of puddles, as usual. I picked my way toward the garage behind my house, trying not to get my oversized shoes stuck in the mud. About a year ago, I realized that my days of switching seamlessly between boy and girl were over, so I hid some bulky clothes there in case I needed a disguise for exactly this situation.

I pulled the box down, then dug out a sweater, jeans, runners, and an old ball cap. I kicked off my shoes, wrapped them in paper, and put them in the box. I was about to ball up the pink raincoat and toss it in the box when I reconsidered. I dried it off as much as I could first, using paper towels from the roll Dad kept out here.

It was actually kind of cute, with a nice pattern of roses on the lining. I folded it loosely and laid it carefully inside before replacing the box on the shelf. I'd work out how to mail it later. In the back of my mind, I was freaking out about being identified as female in my own neighbourhood. I needed to avoid Sarah at all costs.

I pulled the gym shorts off and put the jeans on as quickly as possible. Standing half-naked in my garage made me feel vulnerable; my parents walking in would be uncomfortable at any time, and catastrophic with the wrong genitals. I pulled the sweater over my head and stuffed my feet in the shoes, lacing them loosely. They were starting to get too small. I'd need to find the money to buy another pair soon.

I dithered with the gym shorts, then realized I could say I was bringing them home for a wash. Mom might faint in shock, but she'd be happy enough not to question it. Finally, I thoroughly ruffled my hair and plopped the ball cap on.

I wandered as naturally as possible out through the side door, skirted the edge of the garden, and walked through the side gate to the front of the house. If Ian or Ravi hadn't already talked to my mom, maybe I could head them off.

No one was out front, though. I sat on the front porch steps for a few minutes to make sure, but no one came by. I gave up and went inside.

A laundry basket sat beside the basement door with a pile of darks waiting to be washed. A lucky break. I hurriedly stuffed my gym clothes into the middle.

"Oh, don't take that down yet." Mom came down the stairs with a bundle of towels. Maybe not the best luck. Another thirty seconds and I could have snuck up to my room while she was in the basement. I waved and quickly buried my head in the refrigerator.

"Honestly," she exclaimed fondly, "do boys think about anything other than food?" She dropped the towels into the basket.

'Girls' was the first thing that came to mind, but that was not a topic I wanted to bring up at the moment. I grunted. Thankfully, grunts were relatively unisex. I had spent a fair amount of time practicing lowering my tone by recording my voice and listening back until I could reproduce a fairly good rendition of my guy voice while in female form. But my voice kept changing, so my best bet was to stick with monosyllabic responses.

"So, how was school?"

"All right," I mumbled. I grabbed a jug from the fridge without looking and went to the cupboard to get a glass, keeping my body turned away. Maybe Ian hadn't knocked? Maybe his route had been pure coincidence?

She gently tugged the back of my hair. "I'm beginning to think all this food is going straight to your hair. Didn't you get a haircut last week?"

I shrugged, inwardly cringing. What was up with my hair? I couldn't remember anyone ever mentioning my hair length before, or seeing it change like this after a switch.

There was an awkward pause. "Well, I can see I'm not going to get much out of you until you've unwound from school. Too much like your father." She headed for the basement stairs. "I'm about to put supper on. You get started on your homework."

I made another non-committal noise and finished pouring my … apple juice. *Damn. I hate apple juice.* With a sigh I put the jug back in the fridge and escaped upstairs to my room before Mom returned.

Once I reached my room, I took my concealing sweater off and gladly shucked the still-damp T-shirt. As much as I tried to avoid it, I caught sight of myself in my dresser mirror while I was getting another one.

The rain had turned my dark brown, normally wavy hair into a tangly mess. It did look longer. I picked up my comb and confirmed it. That had never happened before. I tried to focus only on my hair, but it was hard not to see the rest of me.

My girl face wasn't all that different from my boy face, but it looked subtly wrong to me, with the smaller jaw and nose. I grimaced when I hit tangles, and the altered face replicated the expression.

I rarely looked at myself as a girl. I dealt with whatever part needed attention and ignored the whole, but I couldn't pretend like I was watching someone else now. I turned away from the lying mirror, fighting back tears. Unsuccessfully.

I'd been working at hiding these switches from my parents, from everyone, for as long as I could remember. The fear and shame never changed. Against my will, I was once again back inside my earliest clear memory.

~*~

Even back then, I knew it was dangerous. I had been lying to my parents for years, hiding my switches into boy form. In second grade, I just wanted to be a normal girl and be invited to the most prized, long-awaited outing—a sleepover! And then, I finally was.

Of course, my body decided to be boy-shaped that night. But Marnie Crawford was the star of our class, and I knew I was incredibly lucky to get an invite. If I turned it down, I could kiss any chance of being a part of the cool crowd goodbye forever.

Only … Marnie was suspicious. Or maybe it was just the worst timing in the history of the world, because I had to go pee in the middle of the night, and she barged into the bathroom just as I was standing up and saw … everything.

Boy, did Marnie raise hell. She brought her parents in, and they called my parents. I sat sobbing at their kitchen table, repeatedly snotting into the one tissue I'd been given. I could still recall the pastoral farm scene on their placemats. It was a common one, and it still gave me a shiver of dread every time I saw it in a store.

They yelled at my parents on the phone for 'endangering' their daughter and the 'other' girls. They threatened to call the school. They said they'd post on the neighbourhood chat, and a bunch of other stuff about God and biology and women's sports. I don't know, I tuned it out.

The other kids were supposed to have gone back to bed, but I could see them peeking down from the top of the stairs, witnessing my complete humiliation.

My parents picked me up at three in the morning. They were both fully dressed and hard-eyed. Dad's were rimmed in red, and Mom dabbed hers with a tissue. I was still in my pyjamas with my purple Rapunzel hoodie overtop, clutching my overnight bag and the doll I'd meticulously dressed and styled for the special night. They silently hugged me before settling me in the car and giving me a tissue box.

We didn't head home. I remembered thinking, as they drove through town, that maybe this could turn out okay after all. Maybe we were going for ice cream and a long talk about how to deal with my switches.

But we didn't stop. They drove through town to the interstate and just kept on driving.

Mom and Dad didn't talk.

They didn't turn on the radio.

I clung to fragile silence as hard as they did. I knew everything had changed, but as long as we didn't talk about it, I didn't have to face it yet. Then my exhaustion won out over my emotional turmoil, and I fell asleep.

I woke again with the sun peeking over the horizon and illuminating the rolling hills ahead of us. Dad was turning off the highway at some random town. He parked at the far end of the lot of a shopping centre and we opened all the car doors. The air was fresh, woodsy, and I could hear birds chirping over the hiss of cars and trucks passing on the interstate.

"How long have you been switching to a boy?" Mom asked as she came to sit beside me in the back seat.

I tried not to panic. What answer did she want? What answer did I want to give? How could I tell them I'd been switching back and forth all the time? And not just fully boy or girl shapes. Sometimes a little of both, or neither.

"Uh, a while," I admitted. "Are you angry?"

"No, no," she said. "If that's who you are, then we'll support that." She looked away, across the parking lot, but I think she was seeing farther than that. "You don't have to decide about the rest of your life, but we do need to know how you want to present for the next few weeks. It's important."

I'd never minded being a girl before, but in that moment, still dealing with Marnie's betrayal, thinking of how happy I'd been lately, running around with the boys when they let me, I said I wanted to be a boy.

My dad went off and came back with kids' jeans and a blue T-shirt with a superhero on it. I changed in the back seat, trying to ignore a growing ache in my stomach. We went to a pancake place and had breakfast. Everything tasted like cardboard, and no matter how much syrup I put on it, every mouthful stuck in my throat. While we ate, Mom disappeared with the bundle of my pyjamas, doll, and overnight bag, all wrapped up in my beautiful Rapunzel hoodie. She came back empty-handed. It hurt, but I guessed it was the price I had to pay.

It wasn't until we were back on the interstate that I summoned the courage to ask. "When are we going home?"

"We're not," Mom replied firmly. "We're never going back."

"But, why?" I cried, half strangling myself with the seatbelt as I craned around to look out the back window. I don't know what I was hoping to see. Maybe a last glimpse of anything familiar to hold onto. But my home and friends were already too far away. There was nothing but a generic highway, strangers in cars, and dead, brown fields.

"There are people who will hurt you, hurt all of us, if they find out what you are," she said levelly, bluntly. "We can't fight them. We can only hide."

And that's how I started my new life. A new city, in a new country, with a new name, and a new gender to learn. My parents got new jobs, eventually, though not nearly as well-paying as the ones before. We got a house, though not nearly as nice as the one before, and we tried hard to put it all behind us and be happy as a family.

And we were, for a while.

~*~

I never stopped switching, but I got really good at hiding it. Whenever I'd wake up to find I'd gone girl-shaped again, I'd rush to wash and dress before Mom or Dad saw me. That just meant I was a good kid who could look after myself. They had enough other worries keeping us housed and fed. But I got older, and it was becoming harder to disguise the changes as my body developed.

I thought about telling them a few times. Especially those odd times when my mom would give me that look. Like, she knew I was in female form, and she was disappointed, but she wasn't going to embarrass either of us by bringing it up.

I desperately wanted to get it all out in the open, but I remembered the one time I brought it up, just a few months after we settled in Calgary. Dad was out working a night shift, and I found the courage to tackle Mom while we were doing the dishes.

"You want to go back to being a girl?" she asked. She didn't sound entirely happy about it, but she wasn't dismissive or angry. She was just tired. "It's okay, we can make it work."

But the thing was, I also didn't want to leave the boy version of me behind. There were things I missed about being a girl, but certainly not everything. I tried to express this in a clumsy way, without the right words that I would only learn later. She told me something I never forgot.

"Michael," she said. "There are others in this world who can dangle between boy and girl, who don't need to decide firmly on one gender, but that's not a safe path for you. If you ever want to live a normal life, you need to pick one. Boy or girl, it's all the same to us, but for our safety and yours, you must pick one. Do you understand?"

I could still remember the fear in her eyes that night, while she repeatedly wrung the dishcloth. I hated being the cause of that fear. I vowed to focus on being a boy and hoped that one day my body would get the message and cooperate.

Over the years that followed, I would ask Mom or Dad about the enemies we had run from, but they always blew me off, saying I was too young. When that excuse wore thin, they switched to saying it was so long ago it didn't matter now.

The last time I had asked was a couple of years ago, when I was fifteen. I challenged them both at the dinner table. I started out calm and reasonable, like I'd practiced, but that fell apart in the face of their resistance.

"How can you say I don't need to know? How can I prepare if I don't know what I'm fighting?" I asked heatedly.

"That's the problem," Dad said stridently. "What we know is all hints and guesses. It's just enough to send you off chasing shadows but not enough to actually help you."

"And we don't want you to grow up with the same fears we did," Mom added. "You're better off if we don't fill your head with that noise. There's nothing to be done about it anyway, other than keeping your switching under control like you're doing."

I had a choice then: to let them know I was still switching sex all the time and leave them worrying when I would be discovered, or to let them live in peace. I chose peace, vowing to never force them to give up their lives because of me again.

It went well for a while, but for the past year, there had been some new horror every month as my male and female forms diverged. The random hair length change was just the latest indignity. I couldn't handle much more of this. Something had to break, and I was terrified of making my parents pack up and run again. They'd lost so much in our last flight. I couldn't do that to them a second time.

I put my concealing sweater back on and dropped into my desk chair, scrubbing the tears off my face with both sleeves. I had developed a few methods over the past couple of years that worked reasonably well to get me back into boy shape. Activities I strongly associated with hanging out with the guys seemed to work best, and the easiest were certain video games. I started up the old DOOM demo I kept for this purpose and hacked, shot, and blasted hapless computer-generated monsters, reminiscing about good times with Ravi until something inside me shifted and I felt male again.

Just in time for Mom to call me for supper.

"Michael, you're supposed to be doing homework, not playing that awful game," she grumped at me from the doorway.

"Sorry." I gratefully shut down the game. "Lost track of time." Honestly, these shoot-em-up games were more Ravi's thing than mine.

"Well, we're sitting down to supper," she yelled as she went downstairs. "You can finish your homework later."

"Okay. Okay. Geez. I'm coming already." I secretly smiled to myself. It was silly, but this was the normal I craved. If only things could stay this way.

The mouth-watering aroma of honey-glazed ham wafted up as I followed her downstairs. Tears pricked my eyes again as I wondered how much longer I could stay here.

CHAPTER 3

Schlepping back to school to retrieve my bike, after finishing my homework, wasn't fun, but I had made the right decision to walk home from school earlier. If Ravi had seen me in girl form on my bike, it would have been game over.

I wore my full 'switch day' kit to school the next morning, even though I felt solidly male-shaped today. The baggy jeans and added sweatshirt left me extra sweaty by the time I glided to a stop at the bike racks, but after the shock of yesterday's sudden switch, the added protection was the only way I'd been able to force myself to leave the house.

I made it through the morning without any switches, even though the chem teacher made me balance a reaction on the board. She had a process that was almost like math but seemed to involve pulling bits of information out of thin air to add to the equation. Good thing my switches weren't triggered by that kind of stress, or I'd never have made it out of junior high.

Ravi and his girlfriend Debbie were camped out at our usual table in the cafeteria with, I was both happy and horrified to see, Ian. They were discussing something intently.

Ian didn't normally sit with us, but he'd been dropping by our little spot in the corner to say hi more often lately. It made me suspicious for other reasons, but now, I was trying not to think about the last time I'd seen them both, in my girl form. My paranoia took free rein. Were they comparing notes?

I'd been friends with Ravi nearly as long as I'd known Angela. We had all been outsiders to the class when I joined after first moving to Canada, and we bonded. Their acceptance of me had played a big part in my deciding to stay male-presenting.

They had been around me in girl form many times over the years, but I'd had the chance to firmly establish a male identity while I was young. I had hung on to an androgynous look well past puberty, but in the last year, my body had been looking more male and more female. No one had leapt to 'my friend is changing sex!' yet, but what if they were starting to put the pieces together?

"Hey," I said with forced casualness as I slid my tray onto the table and dropped into the remaining open seat. Their conversation broke off as both Ian and Ravi looked over, Ravi with a faintly guilty look. Debbie barely glanced up. We'd never really clicked, but she'd been extra cutting since my break with Angela. They were friends. Angela and I had drawn Ravi and Debbie together originally.

"Hey, Mikey!" Ravi seemed genuinely happy to see me, at least. "You in better shape today?"

"Huh?" *What did he mean by that?* My brain shrieked, then the more obvious meaning occurred to me. "Oh, yeah. Feeling better." My throat was a little sore after getting soaked, but I wasn't going to mention that. I looked at Ian. "I hope Coach wasn't too mad?"

"Not really." He delayed biting into a crispy onion ring to reply: "Though you'd better find a way to make the last class next Monday, or he'll have trouble assigning you a final grade. His words, not mine."

"Good to know," I said, busying myself by squeezing a sriracha packet into my instant noodles. I'd forgotten we had one last class stuck in an unusual Monday slot. I was counting on my PE mark to keep my average up. One more stress I didn't need.

"And we were supposed to go for a run," Ravi said.

"Oh, yeah. Sorry." I forced my brain into turbo mode. I was pretty sure I heard gears grinding. "You free today after school?"

This level of interest made me feel naked. I liked to be forgettable. There were real perks to being a wallflower. I desperately wanted to know what Donny and Ravi might have been discussing on the way to my house. I had escaped discovery once more, but I couldn't bring myself to be happy about it. I was exhausted with the whole game and didn't know how many extra lives I had left.

Suddenly, Ravi looked up and winced. Debbie smirked, and Ian showed a bright smile, giving me a clue as to who it might be. I regretted taking a chair that put my back to most of the room.

I turned too quickly and just about knocked over my instant noodles. I caught the bowl, but a wave of soup splashed out, and only Ian's quick action with a clump of paper napkins stopped the flood before it dripped all over my pants. I stuck a couple more napkins over the mess, smiling at him in thanks for the rescue, but most of my attention was taken by my ex, Angela, standing a few feet away from the table.

"Mike," she said, after giving us a moment for cleanup. "Walk with me." Her expression was very neutral today, which was actually an improvement from the hostile looks I'd been getting for the last few weeks.

"Sure." I tried to calm down. At least she wasn't here to see Ian. Yet. I followed her halfway across the room to stand in front of the mostly glass doors to the inner courtyard. They were rarely open but had to be kept clear of tables in case of fire; it made this a convenient idling spot in the busy cafeteria. Her scent, sandalwood and flowers, drifted in her wake. I tried to ignore it and the uncomfortable feelings it raised.

"I wanted to make sure you remembered our date this weekend," she said, as soon as she stopped. "I'm not sure you're even reading my texts."

"Oh, come on, yes, I still read your texts!" I said, feeling stung. I didn't want to admit that reading her words made me feel so sad and lonely that I could only handle doing it every few days. "I even replied to that one about The Witchery shutting down. Which really sucks."

Angela worked part-time at a local pagan and occult store, but they'd recently had so many complaints under the new Misinformation Act that they'd decided to close their physical storefront and go exclusively online. Which meant she was going to be out of a job soon.

She opened her mouth to reply, but then the rest of her words caught up with me, and I blurted: "Wait, date?" The world briefly tilted sideways. How did we jump from the Cold War of these past three weeks back to dating?

"Yeah. My cousin's wedding, remember?" Some anger crept into her tone. I knew her well enough to hear the edge of fear underneath. "I get it, you need space, but this is important."

Comprehension dawned, and my stomach started to hurt. "Oh, yeah, right. The wedding." Some cousin was getting married this weekend, and Angela's parents had insisted she come, and she'd only agreed to go if I came for moral support. She hated crowds, especially crowds of her family. Some very bad experiences there. "I'm sorry, I wasn't thinking. Of course I'll be there. If you still want me to be?"

"We'll pick you up Saturday at one," she said, in somewhat less stressed tones. "You don't need to wear your suit. There'll be a place to change once we get there."

"Sure. Sure. No problem."

"Don't flake out on me." Her tone was low and serious as she looked directly into my eyes. "As a friend, if nothing else. This is important."

"I promise, Ange." I tried to look as trustworthy as possible, but the fact that I couldn't honestly add 'I won't leave you hanging' hung in the air between us.

"Hmm," she said, and walked away into the milling crowd of students.

Holy crap! I was sweatier than I'd been after my ride this morning. Like an asshole, I'd forgotten about the wedding, which also meant I had forgotten to rent a suit. The reception was going to be in a fancy hotel, so I couldn't wear casual clothes. Angela's immediate family was rich, but from what I'd heard, the branch of the family hosting this thing made them look poor.

I was so screwed. I shambled back to our lunch table, looking up suit rental places on my phone to see if there were any within biking distance. Normally, Angela would have given me a ride, but I couldn't let her know how much of a flake I'd been.

"So, if it's not just the graduating class," Debbie was saying as I slowly approached the table, "how do you decide?"

I groaned. I'd asked them not to bring up the stupid after-grad. Everyone in school wanted to get into the most exclusive party of the year. Did they think Ian was going to spill the details to them just because he and I hung out at school sometimes?

"It's really not up to me," Ian said, exasperated. "I keep telling people. My family's been hosting an after-grad for decades. Just because I'm graduating this year doesn't mean I'm involved in making the guest list. I don't have any special power to invite friends. And I wouldn't want it!"

From what I'd heard, it was mainly the rich and well-connected kids who managed to cadge invites—or their parents did it for them. Random students were sometimes invited, though, and that kept everyone hoping there was a secret trick.

"Stop it," I said, slapping my phone down on the table. "Didn't I tell you, no after-grad talk? Nada. Zip. No way." If they kept pestering Ian, he wasn't going to want to sit here.

Debbie blinked at me like I'd burst into her living room. Ravi had the grace to look embarrassed. They must have been talking about this before, too.

"I should go, anyway." Ian stood up, pushing his plastic chair back. "Is Angela okay?" He looked over at me.

"Yeah, she's fine," I said, still distracted by the looming wedding. I understood the look of concern on his face, but it wasn't anything that I wanted to deal with here and now. And the idea of super-hot, popular Ian taking a personal interest in Angela made my gut clench.

I gave him a half wave as I sat down to my rapidly cooling soup. He smiled and nodded before returning his attention to deftly navigating the lunchtime chaos of the cafeteria.

"She is so, *so* not okay, dude," Debbie scoffed, pulling my attention away from Ian's back.

I waved my spoon at her in acknowledgement. My head hurt trying to figure out how I was going to not only find a suit, but the money to rent it, and the time to pick it up before the end of the day tomorrow. And maybe get a chance to start patching my friendship with Angela.

My phone beeped.

Ian >> Sorry, saw you looking at suits on your phone ... Need one in a hurry?

I jumped to reply.

<< Omg yes. Can you help?

Ian always had the best clothes. Hadn't he mentioned something about his family owning a clothing store, or maybe a chain of them?

Ian >> For sure. Meet after school today?

<< Absolutely!

<< Just ... remember my budget is limited. Really limited.

Gods, I hated typing that. Having richer friends was a bonus in many ways, but it could suck when they forgot I couldn't afford the same things they did.

Ian >> Don't worry. I can get you a great deal.

<< Thanks!!

I breathed a sigh of relief in one sense, but another worry was waiting to take its place. I'd never quite understood why Ian had been so nice to me this year. It had likely started because I was one of the few who offered him a decent challenge in gym class, but he kept up the interest outside of class, too.

For a senior like him to befriend someone in the grade below was unusual, even if he was younger than most of them, and doubly unusual since I didn't run with the popular crowd even in my own grade. Then, I noticed him starting to ask more questions about Angela, in an extra casual way, and seeming to have a sixth sense that let him show up when she might be around.

This left me deeply conflicted. Ian would be an awesome boyfriend for Angela. For anyone, really. I didn't have any right to stand in the way, not since I'd effectively dumped her with my 'let's take a break' move.

But it hurt. It really hurt.

I returned to my soup with little appetite, but I needed to eat or I'd be starving later.

~*~

I zoned out during my afternoon classes. When they finally ended, I hurried for the main doors, eager to meet up with Ian to get the whole suit issue resolved so it wasn't preying on my mind. However, I stepped out of the main doors and into a protest.

A dark-haired girl, Dana, I thought her name was, stood on the shoulder-height concrete base of the flagpole, holding a wireless mic. Speakers were set on all four corners of the plinth, blasting out her words. She was in grade 12 and I'd seen her advocating for marginalized people and the environment since my first day of high school.

"The government wants us to believe the Misinformation Act is for our protection! But who is it protecting? Aaron Menendez? Mary Topolski? They went to our school! Did it protect them?"

A general cry of "No!" echoed back from many voices in the crowd. Most people knew about Aaron, a trans guy in my grade. He'd been very active in protesting the new 'protection from misinformation' law and earlier anti-trans laws. He'd been arrested at a protest at the legislature in Edmonton a couple of weeks ago and committed to a mental health facility under the rules of this new law. His parents had sprung him after three days, but he was still recovering from the experience.

I hadn't heard much about Mary's case yet, but Dana was blasting it to the crowd.

"… She was turned in by her own parents. Because she insisted on, and persisted in, declaring herself female. She's been committed under this law and sent to a private psychiatric facility that many have said practices conversion therapy."

I sent Ian a quick text saying I was at the protest for a minute. I couldn't afford to stay long, but I hated to leave. This law was horrific. Anyone falling into one of the very narrowly defined 'misinformation' categories, like 'misrepresenting your gender' or 'promoting occult practices,' could be sent for psychiatric evaluation. An evaluation that conveniently had no defined time limit. If you didn't have anyone going to bat for you to get you out, you could linger there for a long time. Maybe even get lost in the system.

I noticed Jenn Chaika, now our school's only out trans student, passing through the crowd, handing out leaflets. I moved to meet up with her path. I'd always looked up to her, ever since she came out when I was in grade 10. I didn't think I could quite claim to be trans, since I generally found myself switching, physically, to whatever gender I was most aligned with at the time. But, since I had to maintain my male presentation all the time, even when I was feeling female, I empathized with trans women the most.

"Hi Mike," Jenn said as she walked up, handing me a leaflet. I envied her blue-and-white-striped sundress, not because I was feeling particularly feminine today, but because it looked cool and refreshing with her arms and shoulders bare.

"Hey Jenn. Thanks," I said, gratified—and a little unnerved—that she knew me on sight. The infographic on the paper linked the upcoming referendum about allowing provincial sherifs to arrest people in cities to the misinformation law, warning that more people would be impacted. "This is so true. The only thing keeping a lot of people from forced psych evaluations is the city police in a pissing match with the province, unwilling to take on the extra policing work without more funding."

"Yeah." She looked angry. "It's absolutely shocking that language made it into a law, and with no media coverage. I'm sure the Supreme Court will get around to nullifying it at some point, but that's not going to help anyone who gets put away in the meantime." She shook her head. "It's so dangerous, not just for trans people, but Wiccans and Pagans and really anyone whose beliefs aren't covered under the 'organized religion' exemptions. I've heard that some intersex people have been targeted too."

"And even if they're not directly charged, it's got a lot of people running scared. Like …" I was about to mention The Witchery closing when suddenly Jenn grabbed my arm.

"Shit!" she hissed.

I looked in the direction of her gaze and saw a cop moving through the crowd towards us. He was plainclothes, but the aggressive way he moved, combined with his archaic wired earbud, gave him away.

"I can't be caught with these papers." She looked at me in mute appeal.

I opened my mouth to reply, but I couldn't quite get the words out. Or reach my hands out to take the pamphlets. A hot flush passed down through my body. All I could envision was switching gender in jail. Caged and monitored. I would be trapped.

And worse, I could see Jenn's face fall. Her realization that I wasn't going to help her.

Why did I keep having to fail people?

The cop was almost on us. Jenn turned in the opposite direction. I stepped between her and the cop. Maybe I could at least delay the guy.

"Thanks for holding those for me, Jenn," I heard Ian say behind me. I turned in surprise.

The cop barrelled around me but pulled up short when he saw Ian. Jenn stood partially behind his tall, lanky frame.

"Hi Officer," Ian said cheerfully. "Enjoying this lively summer day among students exercising their freedom of expression?"

"That doesn't give them the right to spread misinformation," the cop replied sternly, holding out his hand. Ian handed over the pamphlets. Of course, anything the government didn't like was considered misinformation too. It wasn't worth arguing with the cops about it. Pamphlets could be reprinted easily enough. I had already stuffed my copy deep in my pocket, as, I was sure, had most of the crowd.

The cop glared at Jenn, but took another look at Ian, sighed, and stalked back the way he'd come.

"Oh. My. God." Jenn hung on to Ian's arm, breathing hard. "I may pass out."

"Oh! Can you swoon dramatically into my arms?" Ian said, striking a comical pose. Jenn laughed. It was hilarious. I wished I could dislodge the huge lump of shame from my throat so I could join in. I wanted to hit myself.

Dana, facing both the cops and the administration, had turned off her mic and jumped down from the flagpole base. The demonstration was breaking up. It hadn't been intended to last very long, just to take advantage of the end-of-school rush to educate as many people as possible.

Jenn said goodbye to Ian, with a laugh, and waved to me. I did my best to act cheerful. She didn't show any outward sign of her disdain, but I'd seen the look on her face as the cop bore down on us. It had to be there.

"You ready to go?" Ian asked, looking a little concerned. My face must have been echoing my feelings.

"Yeah, let's ride." Exercise and motion had always helped me deal with my feelings.

~*~

Ian and I rode our bikes north up 5th Street, straight into the heart of downtown. He always biked, like me, even in winter, though his bike and gear were top-of-the-line, not scrounged together like mine.

We zipped through and past the packs of commuters trying to make it out of downtown before rush hour fully took hold. That nearly-flying feeling on a bike was exhilarating, with an added spice of danger as we made dozens of split-second decisions to find the best path through all the moving cars, pedestrians, and other cyclists.

For as much as we'd clicked in class and chatted at lunch, I had never hung out with Ian outside of school. I figured my lowly eleventh-grader status would hurt his senior cred. His going out of his way to help me now made me wonder what was up.

It wasn't until he swerved into the underground garage of a condo building that I picked up on the fact that we weren't headed to a store. The massive doors opened obediently as he flashed his key card. He unlocked what looked to be a private storage space with the same card and rolled his bike in. It was half-full of boxes and miscellaneous household items.

"Not that I object to seeing your place, Ian," I challenged him as we entered a spacious elevator, "but how is this getting me a suit?"

Ian stabbed the twenty-second-floor button with a finger. "I thought it was obvious." He looked me up and down. "We're about the same size. I'll lend you one of mine."

"Ah, I see. That's cool." Duh, with his family in the biz, he probably got suits for birthdays like other kids got socks.

"If nothing fits, we can visit the store." He shrugged. "I'd hate to bother them if there's a simple fix."

The elevator was quick. I noticed the buttons started at fifteen, so this was an express to the top floors only. The doors opened onto a short hallway. Ian turned left and led us to 22C. The key-card reader was low enough that he didn't even take his wallet out of his back pocket. He just hitched one hip up and brushed the sensor.

"That's a talented ass you've got," I blurted, immediately wishing I hadn't, as a whole host of alternate and entirely pornographic interpretations sprang to mind.

Ian laughed. "You have no idea."

My cheeks heated. Fortunately, his back was turned as I followed him through the door. I kept my head down as I dropped my backpack on a bench and removed my shoes, taking longer than expected to get my blush under control.

When he'd mentioned living in a condo, I had assumed something like a regular apartment, but this place was huge. To our left, a set of open-riser stairs ascended to an upper level. From this foyer, I could see a full kitchen and a living room that together, were larger than my house.

Ian bounded up the stairs as soon as he slipped off his shoes.

I slowly backed my way up the stairs so I could take in the room. Half of it was open plan with a double-height ceiling. A bank of huge windows displayed a panoramic view of the Lion's Gate Bridge and hills across the river.

Following the click and scrape of hangers, I found Ian's room, where he was hunting through a massive closet covering all of one wall. It was filled with an abundance of casual clothes and suits in an array of earth tones. No wonder he always seemed to have the right shirt for every occasion at school. My much smaller collection was generally plain, or last year's style if I was lucky.

"Your family's not home?"

"I live with my uncle," he said. "And he's away in Texas on a business trip."

"Ah, cool." I winced internally. Not the suavest response. I realized I'd never heard him talk about his parents or his home life and had never questioned it. Were they still alive? Would it be insensitive to ask?

Ian's room was no bigger than mine, but his had high-end furniture that all matched, as well as those built-in storage cupboards and drawers that could hide a huge amount of mess behind a smooth surface.

A jumble of posters on the walls depicted a mishmash of music and movies from across the past forty years. A well-used acoustic guitar on its stand occupied one corner. One poster in particular caught my eye.

"Uh, Ian … why do you have a poster of a guy in a skirt?"

"It's a kilt, Mike, not a skirt," Ian said in a patient tone, rifling through the clothes hanging in the closet.

"Right." I cringed at my blunder. "But I thought kilts were supposed to be red. That one's mostly green."

"They come in all sorts of colours and patterns," Ian explained. "It's generally called a tartan, and is specific to each clan, or in this case, a scotch label."

"Ah, cool." I noticed now, the outsized bottle of alcohol Photoshopped in beside the kilt guy. "But why the poster?"

"Oh, Laphroaig is the best!" Ian beamed. "It's like drinking the distilled heart of a peat fire. Pure blazing smoky goodness. It's sharp as a blade and smooth as silk all at once."

That … did not sound particularly appetizing, but I could see he wasn't joking, and he seemed to know a lot about drinking for someone who wasn't quite eighteen yet. He probably could have gone on longer, but he clamped his mouth shut and pulled his gaze from the poster back to the closet. Had I touched on something painful there?

"Is your family Scottish?" He could be, with his dark hair and pale skin, but obviously, there was a lot I didn't know.

"Maybe a little. Mostly English and French, though we've been in Canada for a long time."

"My family is more of a French, Italian, and Spanish mix," I said. "From a couple of generations back on both sides. A bit of south-European stew, really."

"A paella?" Ian joked with a grin, taking some hangers off the rod. "Here's a couple of pairs of pants I think might fit."

Laughing, I barely grabbed the mass of black fabric he thrust in my direction before he turned back to the closet. I wrestled with it for a while to get hold of the hangers and started backing out of the room.

"Where are you going?" Ian peered around the closet doorframe.

"Um." I pointed at the hall. "To a bathroom, to change."

He gave me a long-suffering look. "Dude, we change in front of each other all the time."

"Because we don't have a choice." A lot more general frustration escaped into that statement than intended. Ian's eyebrows rose. There was an incredibly awkward pause. He raised a hand and lazily gestured to the door behind me with two fingers, and I fled to the bathroom.

~*~

Both the pants fit well enough at the waist. They were slightly too long, but one was good enough. Ian was broader than I, but if there was an ounce of fat on his body, I hadn't seen it. I headed back to his room wearing the pants.

He examined me critically. I bunched my sweatshirt above my waist so he could see the fit of the pants and obediently turned in place when he gestured.

"Very good," he commented when I completed my revolution. He handed me a creamy white shirt and a heavy suit jacket. "You might as well borrow a shirt, too. What kind of ties do you have? Pretty much anything should go with this combo."

"Ties?" I felt numb. "I think I might have one, somewhere."

Ian rolled his eyes. "Never mind. I'll pick one out for you."

I returned to the bathroom, feeling scruffy and uncultured.

The shirt was beautiful—thick cotton which still managed to be soft against my skin. The little mother-of-pearl cuff buttons were a real pain, but I eventually got them fastened.

Ian was pleased when I returned.

"Wow. That's even better than I expected." He had me raise my arms. "The sleeves might be a little short, but not enough to notice."

"And for the final piece …" He looked into my eyes and held a strip of silky fabric to my cheek, his fingers brushing my skin. I felt a sudden flip in my belly, and prickles of cold sweat blossomed all over my body. Had I switched? I oh-so-casually felt around my hip. No. Still male-shaped.

I was starting to feel that coming here had been a mistake. I'd been able to keep my growing feelings for Ian under control within the confines of school, but if we started hanging out together outside of that, I was going to slip up.

Ian's eyes narrowed, and he grinned. "It's just a tie. Nothing to be afraid of." He held a different one up to my face.

"You think so?" I tried to manufacture a grin. "Ties symbolize the brain-numbing, soul-crushing corporate hive-mind existence. What's scarier than that?"

"Huh. I guess you've got a point. Prepare to be shackled with social convention." He looped his current choice around my neck and then closed the bedroom door, revealing a full-length mirror. He'd picked a rich emerald green with a subtle sparkle that would definitely elevate the outfit from corporate drab.

Ian circled behind me. He started looping the strip of fabric around and pulling it through, and somehow, I ended up with something that looked like a tie. Had I tried it myself, I would have ended up with a knotted mess a sailor couldn't have unraveled. I should have paid more attention, but I was distracted by his earthy scent … and the tantalizing implications of a closed bedroom door.

He patted me on the shoulder. "You're going to kill at this wedding." He chuckled. "I'd make sure to bring a condom or two, if I were you."

"You know Angela and I are just friends," I said hotly to cover a rush of feelings entirely unrelated to her. That was the usual line we'd held for so long, even when we started dating. I could only hope it was true again.

I saw my blush in the mirror and cringed inwardly. He was obviously assuming it was for Angela. *Why am I like this*, I wailed inside my head. Only a few weeks out from critically wounding my relationship with Angela, and here I was lusting after Ian?

"You never know. Play the consummate gentleman through the wedding, and with all that romance in the air, she might get inspired."

"I'm not trying …" I looked at his grinning face in the mirror and realized he was teasing. "Oh, never mind." I stalked to the bathroom to change back into my civvies.

~*~

I bundled the clothes into my backpack as carefully as I could, ready for travel. Ian hovered at the foot of the stairs, looking uncertain and vulnerable in a way I'd never seen before.

"Hey, did you want to stay and …" Ian's voice trailed off, and his face shuttered shut as an interior door off the living room opened, revealing a hefty man in a very nice suit with a home office setup behind him.

The guy stopped abruptly on seeing me, and his expression made my stomach knot. He had that dead-eyed look, like the one cops got when you'd been demoted from 'citizen' to 'problem.'

Then, he saw Ian behind me, and a mask of human feelings returned. "My boy!" He boomed. "I managed to catch an earlier flight," he said, laced with an odd humour that I didn't understand.

"Yes, Uncle, sir. I was just lending my buddy an old suit. For a date. With his girlfriend." His whole demeanour had changed. Cocky, confident Ian had folded into a walled-off, obedient package.

There was serious undertow here, so I decided to roll with his lead. "Thanks, man. She's going to love it."

I fled after some polite goodbyes. I didn't even get any more alone time with Ian in the elevator, since he simply handed me an access card from a stack in a box beside the door that he said was single-use, for guests. Fancy. And infuriating.

Even if Ian hadn't been hurrying me out the door, I wouldn't have wanted to stay around his uncle for longer than absolutely necessary. I'd never seen Ian afraid before, and I hated seeing it now. There was something very wrong with his uncle.

I hoped it was just a really bad mood coming home from a business trip, and Ian didn't have to live with that every day, but the way he'd made himself smaller suggested otherwise. A knot of sadness built in my chest.

And adding to that sadness, at a purely selfish and personal level, was wondering what opportunity we'd missed out on, to perhaps become closer friends. Would he have shared some of the messiness he kept tucked away behind his smooth surface? It killed me that I might never know.

CHAPTER 4

Angela's parents showed up a few minutes early to pick me up for the wedding, much to my relief, as it interrupted my parents' photo-fest. My mom, in particular, was overjoyed to see me dressed up. She insisted on taking picture after picture: of me, of me and my dad, and then my dad had to take pictures of me and her.

At least I was solidly in male shape, so I didn't have to hide from the camera.

It was a good thing Angela was wearing jeans and a T-shirt, or the picture frenzy would have doubled. Only her hair was done—carefully arranged in an updo pinned with little gold clasps. She shot me a quizzical look, likely wondering about the suit.

The only way we could break away with any speed was to say that Angela's parents were waiting in the car. My parents had long been fond of Angela, the first friend I made after our move here, once they got over worrying that she was going to tempt me back into girl shape.

Thankfully, she had been a raging tomboy in those days, and most of her friends were guys, making it easier for me to transition from girl social life to boy social life. Over the last few years, my parents had bugged me, lightly, about when Ange and I were going to admit we were dating.

I had pushed back so strongly that, for years, I never quite told my parents about our shift to official dating, and so I hadn't, yet, had to talk about our current problems.

"Didn't I mention you could change there?" Angela asked, heading around the back of the car.

"You did. I decided not to." I swung into the curbside back seat beside her. My parents waved madly from the door, so Angela's mom and I both obliged them with a few waves out the open windows as we drove away. The wedding was in Banff, about a ninety-minute drive away.

"Ah…" She sounded contrite, leaning toward me to talk low and close. "I forgot you hate changing anywhere public." She gave me some side-eye. "You must have hated gym this semester."

"It had its awful moments." I let loose a very real shudder. "Which was a nice break from the general horror of high school." The sheer terror of my sudden switch this past week was still hovering.

"Now we just have to make it through finals." Her voice held an entirely appropriate mix of fear and longing. "Personally, I'd rather strip in public than take my math exam."

I laughed a little too loud. It felt good to banter with her again. I knew this outing wasn't supposed to mean anything in terms of our relationship, but it was hard not to be cheered by any time we got to spend together, not arguing.

~*~

The wedding was pretty much as expected: lots of people in formal wear, jabbering away. The most interesting thing about it was the Banff Springs Hotel itself. The building was a fantastic pile of carved and ornamented stone. It had at least three wings and hundreds of rooms.

For the party, we were herded from the entrance into one of the ballrooms and to our assigned seats. Once we'd put in some time here, I planned to skip out and explore as much of the hotel as I could. I wondered if I could entice Angela to come with me.

"I'm going to go make the rounds, say hi to the cousins," Angela said while we were still finishing the main course. I thought her parents might object, but they just nodded stiffly. The whole family had seemed on edge since we'd arrived in Banff, and I wasn't sure why. I hoped it wasn't related to Angela and me. She was very open with her parents sometimes, so I couldn't guess what she may have told them about us.

Angela's absence lingered through dessert, and I felt more and more trapped. The other two couples at our table of eight were older and without kids. They kept up a lively chatter about dividends and market growth in the hospitality sector, but conversation on my side of the table was sparse and stilted. I reached a point, after dessert had been cleared away and we were midway through what appeared to be an endless series of speeches, where I couldn't stand it.

"Um, Angela seems to be taking a long time. If it's okay with you, I'll go to see if I can find her?" Both her parents were relieved that I wanted to search. Sometimes I got the vibe that they felt I wasn't quite good enough for their daughter to be hanging out with, but tonight at least, they seemed happy I was here.

Filtering through the tables, I was struck by how white and hetero this crowd was. The whole wedding process had me depressed. The row of bridesmaids and groomsmen all dressed the same, the unsubtle displays of the bride's purity (but not the groom's, of course), and the giving away of the bride were designed to affirm the gendered roles in all of society. It really rubbed me the wrong way today.

I tried to imagine my hypothetical future wedding, where the guests wouldn't know whether I'd be waiting at the altar in a tux or going down the aisle in a dress until the day of. For some reason, my mind found that idea hilarious. I had to disguise my laughter as a coughing fit so people didn't think I was commenting on the current speech.

A buzz from my phone distracted me. I had turned off most of the notifications for tonight, so this message might be important. I retrieved my phone from the inside jacket pocket to take a look.

Ravi >> Dude, rescue me. Dad needs a car picked up, and I'm supposed to be with Deb.

Sweet! Ravi sometimes sent work my way. I'd finish longer car pickups or deliveries when he was busy. I got the cash he would have been paid, and he got the free time. It was a win-win.

<< When & where?

Ravi >> Tonight! And it's in Banff. Natch I thought of you. Can you get out of the wedding?

<< Probably. Maybe. Gotta find Ange and see if she's willing.

Ravi >> Also, the car. It's a Porsche. Just sayin

<< Ooooo

Ravi wouldn't normally pass up a Porsche. Either Debbie was annoyed, or he had high hopes for this date. Lucky bastard. I scanned the room for Angela's red hair, though that was less unique in this gathering than usual. I had to stroll the room looking for her. My phone buzzed again on the way.

Ravi >> I'll pay double man. I need this.

Then, maybe to spur me on, he sent me the pickup address too.

I intensified my search. The curve-hugging green dress Angela wore tonight, along with the copper of her hair, should be pretty visible, but after two circuits of the room, checking outside, and even asking her mom to check the bathroom, I still hadn't found any trace of her. She wasn't answering her phone. Sweat trickled between my shoulder blades.

My phone buzzed again.

Ravi >> I gotta be on the road in 5 man. No $$$ for you.

"Fuck!" I said sharply to myself, jamming my phone back into the jacket pocket. An old woman scowled and humphed at me, edging away.

I started exploring some of the side halls leading away from the long main lobby of the hotel, in case she'd been wandering down there for some reason. I was just crossing the lobby once again, wondering if I should check back at the table, when I saw her.

She was slowly descending the grand staircase, one hand trailing on the banister like she didn't have a care in the world. Her rich green dress and copper red hair blazed against grey steps. Annoyance boiled up in me. I'd been freaking out, and she had decided to take a leisurely stroll through the hotel without me?

I hurried over to make some sarcastic comments, but the closer I got, the more worried I became. Her glassy eyes stared straight ahead. Her gaze was fixed on the far wall, ignoring the steps under her feet. As I hurried toward her, one foot came down half over the edge of a step, and she swayed drunkenly. I burst into a sprint up the steps, putting every ounce of energy into it with my tendons at the edge of tolerance, and I got my shoulder under her just as she collapsed forward. I barely managed to keep my footing, so neither of us went head-first down the cut stone stairs.

If it were anyone else, I'd say she'd been drugged, but I'd seen Angela go unresponsive like this a few times when we were younger. Plan A was to get her away from the area where she'd been affected. She'd always recovered after some distance, before.

I guided her shuffling steps down the stairs and across the thankfully short distance to the coat check, retrieved her coat using the ticket from her purse, and shuffled her outside, trying to make our walk look natural.

I'd just finished settling her coat over her shoulders and putting up the hood to help conceal her slackened face when I saw him.

Ian's uncle.

He strode out of an elevator wearing, of course, a well-tailored dark blue suit and tie. A step behind him was a hard-faced guy who wore a dark grey suit and looked like security. They both scanned the lobby like they were searching for someone. After a brief discussion, they strode briskly in opposite directions.

Searching for Angela?

Probably not, but I didn't care to stick around and find out.

Thankfully, the cabbies were eagerly awaiting anyone exiting the hotel, so we were on our way without having to loiter. I took a few seconds during the short ride to text Ravi that I was picking up the car. Then I took a deep breath and texted Angela's mom that I'd found her and that I could take her back to Calgary unless they wanted to meet up. Angela had always seemed as shy of bringing her parents into her struggles as I was.

I expected a major reaction, but her mom just texted:

Ange's Mom >> Thanks. Sounds good. We'll get on our way home too.

Parents. Who could understand them?

I was on-site and halfway through the paperwork for the car pickup before Ravi managed to text me back.

Ravi >> WTF! I already cancelled with Debbie.

Ravi >> I'm at the fucking bus station.

Ravi >> I already bought a ticket!!!

<< Sorry. I need this ride. I'll explain later.

Ravi >> Whatevs. Don't expect to get paid dude.

<< We'll talk about it.

I sighed. I really could have used that double money. I wouldn't feel right about taking that now, but I could probably still get what he would have been paid if I guilted him a little.

I flew through the inspection, taking a bunch of pics that I hoped would pick up any existing damage clearly enough to protect Ravi's parents' company from lawsuits. Just my luck—this guy was one of the chattier customers. He'd gotten some promotion at his tech job and had to move closer to Toronto, but there was no way he was leaving his baby behind.

I promised I would personally escort it to the CN railyard, where we chained the cars securely on the covered railcars and shipped them to our office in Scarborough. There, another employee would lovingly unchain it and drive it to his new house near—I checked the file Ravi had emailed me—some place called Peterborough. It didn't occur to me until the end that he probably thought I'd worn this suit to impress him!

Finally, I got his signature, emailed him his copy, and quickly drove around the corner where I had stashed Angela on a park bench. Seeing her still there unwound the knot of fear in my gut. She was in the same condition, but at least she hadn't wandered off.

I shuffled her over and helped her collapse into the low passenger seat of the Porsche. I got us out of there fast, in case the owner happened to go for a walk. The only passengers allowed during a transport were supposed to be named in the paperwork, and only in the case of shared driving responsibilities.

I kept to the speed limit in town and to the park boundary, but then let the speed creep up to 120 kph. I racked my brain trying to come up with a plan in case she didn't snap out of this before we got back to Calgary. She'd always been afraid of going anywhere near a hospital with her mysterious condition, and doubly so now, with that new misinformation law. Sometimes she talked about nonsensical things while she was out of it.

I hadn't spent much time wondering about her strange seizure-like episodes for several years, since she said they didn't happen anymore. Now, I wondered: had they ever really gone away? Or had she learned to hide them like I did my switches?

I remembered the first time. We'd been maybe nine years old. There was an adult party at Angela's big fancy house, and I was over for a playdate. I'd found her stuck, hugging the wall in a room, staring at nothing I could see, even paler from shock, and trembling.

The adults had been ignoring her. I'd taken her hand and pulled her away to the front hall closet where we nestled behind the coats until her fearful shaking slowly bent to the shudders of sobbing, our hands locked together.

She hadn't explained, and I hadn't pushed her for answers. I had my own secrets. It had brought us closer together, though. Before that, she'd always seemed so in control. I was relieved there was something I could offer her.

She had a few more episodes. Sometimes inside, sometimes when we were out. I never figured out any common factor, and Angela refused to talk about it. Around thirteen, they trailed off and seemed to stop, much to my relief, and a little jealousy—my switches were still going.

Fortunately, shortly before I could have a complete mental breakdown due to worry, she shuddered, groaned, and then screamed in terror, clutching at anything she could get her hands on. She found the Porsche's 'oh shit' handle and my arm. Her fingers felt like steel claws digging in, even through the sleeve of my suit jacket.

I fought the car back under control from my shock-induced swerve— these Porsches were a little too maneuverable sometimes—and slowed down, looking for a spot to pull over in case we needed to. Angela didn't scream again, though she panted hoarsely for a while, head bowed over her knees. I sped up again, but only to just under the 110 kph speed limit.

"Where the hell are we?" Angela looked around in surprise at the inside of the car and the scenery flashing past in the evening light.

"Just past Exshaw," I said. "Heading back to Calgary."

"And my parents? Whose car is this?" She ran her hand over the expensive leather seat.

"It's a pickup for Ravi. I volunteered at the last minute since we needed a ride in a hurry."

"Oh. Okay. Did I faint?" she asked, her voice clotted with confusion. "I thought …" She stopped talking abruptly.

I sighed inwardly. She never opened up to me about what happened when she got like this.

"I didn't see. I found you sleepwalking in the hotel lobby," I said as gently as I could manage. Now that the immediate emergency was past, it was sending chills down my spine. "You remember plan A?"

The second time I'd been there for one of her episodes, we were playing in the woods when Angela fell over and did nothing but babble strange words. I eventually did the right thing, helping her stumble away until she recovered, but I had been panicky, and very close to shouting for someone to take us to the hospital. After that, she'd come up with The Plans. A was to get her out of the area and hope she improved (DO NOT involve her parents). Involving them was Plan B. Plan C involved running away together, which had sounded great as a kid.

There was actually a glimmer of humour in her voice when she responded, "Yes, I remember The Plans." The capitalization was clear in the way we'd always said it. With a note of sadness creeping in, she asked, "It's been a long time, hasn't it?"

"Yeah." She seemed as horrified as I was that the mystery that had shadowed her childhood had suddenly returned.

I hoped it really had been five years.

Half an hour had passed and over fifty kilometers had rolled under us before I spoke again. She wasn't sleeping, but seemed deep in thought.

"Where do you want to go?" I asked. "I mean, once we get back to Calgary."

"Home," she said with conviction.

I wanted to argue, but she knew what she needed better than I did. It frustrated me when people pressured me when they couldn't understand what I was dealing with. I wouldn't do that to her. I just hoped she'd reach out to me.

Three weeks ago, she might have. We'd been getting closer, but I screwed that up. Self-destructive guilt flared inside me, and I bit hard into the side of my cheek to prevent any kind of outburst that might be misinterpreted.

"You were looking very handsome tonight," she said, suddenly. "I'm sorry I didn't mention it earlier."

"You looked very beautiful tonight," I replied. "I'm sorry we didn't get to have even one dance."

"Me too," she said softly.

My heart hurt for what could have been.

~*~

A month ago, I'd been on top of the world.

After an entire year of thinking about it, Angela finally confessed that she was attracted to me. I admitted that I'd been doing my best to hide an attraction toward her for about a year, too, afraid of what it might do to our friendship. We had a good laugh about that. Those happy memories were a cut to the heart now.

We ended up in her bed a week later. Her parents had a far more liberal view of teen sex than mine and, even better, they were out of the house. We'd both stripped down to underwear, happily running hands over all the skin we could reach, and tentatively stroking the areas still concealed.

It had all been fantastic until she ducked into the bathroom. Alone in her bed, I started to have second thoughts. Was I really ready for this? What if I fumbled it? What if she was bored?

Then I realized I'd made one of the rare switches where I ended up not quite male or female but a unique mix of both. I'd always heard that losing your erection was a real worry for guys, but yeeting the entire penis? That was a little extra! And in this case, I hadn't even replaced it with a vagina. I knew someday I would have to reveal my switches to Angela, but not like this. I felt like a freak.

I somehow made it out of the house and onto my bike. I was almost home before I realized that even though I'd grabbed my shirt on the way out, I hadn't put it on. Thankfully, my chest had been pretty flat.

We only had one short conversation after that. Angela was willing to see the funny side, up to the point where I said I wasn't willing to try again. And my refusal to come out with any reasonable explanation as to why didn't help. I knew her anger flowed from hurt. I just didn't know how to fix anything.

I'd proved to myself that there was no safe way to be in a physical relationship. I could only hope there was some path back to friendship for us.

And now this?

Just when our shared trust needed to be at its strongest, my fucking sex-switches had taken a wrecking ball to it.

CHAPTER 5

I pounded along the top of the concrete retaining wall, building up speed. The long drop on one side of the narrow ledge had freaked me out the first time. Thanks to it being a regular part of my runs for almost a year, it was now as easy as walking down the sidewalk—except this sidewalk ended abruptly. I'd better get my head in the now before I hurt myself.

I hurtled into space at the end of the wall, jumping up to catch hold of the metal railing on the parking garage's second story. My feet slapped securely against the wall below. I pushed off again with my legs, transferring my grip to the upper bar, and then slotted my body through the railing with a practiced twist of my torso. Once more, I was off and running. Ravi had grabbed an early lead and was already halfway across the second level.

My breath rasped in my chest, but my adrenaline was pumping. I felt truly alive. This parking lot was mostly empty on Sunday mornings, but I noticed an old pickup parked in a convenient spot today and diverted from the usual path. A quick hop up on the rusty, work-scared tailgate. Then, a short leap to grab the thick metal standpipe. I scaled the wall, using the pipe for leverage, and pulled myself up and through the railing on the third level.

From there, it was a short sprint to the stairwell enclosure. The walls were set up perfectly for the trick we had mastered over the past few months. I tic-tac-ed off an adjoining wall, giving me enough height to grab the roofline. Then, some lateral hand-over-hand across the wall brought me to convenient footholds that were enough to propel me up and over the edge onto the flat, gravelled roof.

I lay there panting until Ravi joined me, also puffing away. This was where we usually took a break before heading back down. It was an incredible feeling to know you'd made it up here with just your own power. Also, whoever arrived last had to buy the Slurpees after, which explained Ravi's exclamation on arrival.

"Shit." He rolled onto his back beside me. "Thought I had a chance today."

"I got a lucky break with that truck."

"Smooth move." Ravi was a great training partner. He liked the workout but wasn't obsessed with winning the way some of the more hardcore parkour guys at the club were.

"Yeah." I smiled. "Ian keeps harping on my situational awareness in gym. *Eyes up, Mike!* Maybe I'm learning something."

"Ian seems to drop by a lot these days," Ravi said in an overly neutral tone. "That was the third time in two weeks, I think."

"Yeah," I said, attempting, less successfully, a neutral tone.

He gave me a sharp, confused look. "What, you're not happy? He seems like a cool guy."

"A little too cool," I said. "And a little too interested in Angela."

"Oh really? Is Mr. 'We're Just Friends' a little widdle bit jealous?"

"Oh, fuck off," I said good-naturedly, but he'd definitely hit a sore spot. Angela and I had been friends for years. A few months longer than I'd known Ravi, actually. As we had drifted closer to becoming a couple, we agreed to keep it on the down-low. We'd dealt with so much 'oh, sure, you aren't dating nudge, wink' bullshit over the years that we wanted to avoid the smug 'I told you so' looks as long as possible.

That turned out to be a shit strategy. When we broke up, or whatever it was we were doing now, I couldn't talk to anyone about it since we were never officially dating in the first place.

It suddenly struck me that Angela might be having the same problem. I was such an idiot!

"What makes you think he's not interested in you, my friend?" Ravi broke into my downward thought spiral, sounding amused now.

"Huh." That was a thought. "I haven't heard anything about him being gay."

"Really?" Ravi said. "According to Debbie, it's what all the girls think since none of them have managed to get him into bed."

"Debbie spend a lot of time speculating about Ian?" I asked, probably a little too pointedly.

I got a sharp, verging-on-angry look in response. Oops. I hadn't meant anything more by it than my usual dislike of the gossip mill.

Had Ravi caught the sultry looks Debbie cast Ian's way every so often? I wanted to tell him not to worry, since Ian hadn't once asked me about Debbie, only Angela, but that could be considered a diss toward Debbie, and perhaps violate the bro code by suggesting he might have reason to worry. Maybe? It was exhausting trying to remember all the rules.

"I think he would have said something by now if he were into me," I said, hoping to shut down that gossip. Dear gods, my life was already complicated enough without gaining the hatred of nearly the entire het-female population of the school. However, I noticed my heart was thumping a little harder at the thought.

"Then what is up with you and Angela?" Ravi asked, concerned. "I thought she was mad because you were making time with Ian."

"Not even close." I shook my head. There was no way I could talk about this without also getting into Angela's private life, which I knew would make it back to Debbie, which would get back to Angela for sure. "I can't really talk about it. It's just an argument. We'll be okay in a little while."

Ravi was willing to accept that. He'd seen Angela and me fight before and knew better than to get in the middle, no matter how good his intentions.

I wished I could tell him the truth. When I dropped Ange at her house last night, she'd walked in with barely a backward glance, after summarily dismissing my offer to keep her company until her parents came home.

"Are you still planning to try out for Devon's summer parkour camp jobs?" I found myself asking. Also not a safe topic, but I wanted to talk about anything other than Angela at the moment. Devon worked at a parkour studio downtown and ran a summer program for kids every year, and he always needed junior instructors. It was my dream summer job.

"Yeah." He looked over to me, obviously not buying my excuse about Angela, but willing to let it go. "You worried?" He grinned evilly. "How about this: I drop out of the competition if you help us crash the after-grad."

"Ravi," I said in a near growl, then sighed. "Why is Debbie so fired up to get into this party anyway? Neither of you is even in grade twelve!"

He stayed silent for long enough that I started to get up, but his hand shot out and he held his palm against my bicep.

"Wait, I'll tell you."

He took a deep breath.

What was he finding so hard to say? It worried me.

"You know the rumour, that there's a secret ritual at the after-grad that makes people successful?" Ravi said.

'Oh, come on, you can't believe that crap!"

"Debbie and I crunched the numbers. We found a list of all the attendees at the after-grads for the last thirty years, up to three years ago. Probably a leak from the school records. We cross-referenced that with a list of all the notable graduates and found that the people most likely to succeed in life, by a huge margin, all went to that party."

I raised a hand and opened my mouth to reply.

"And that's not all," he ignored me and kept going. "Students who attended during grade 11 were even more likely to succeed!"

"Ravi!" I couldn't contain myself. "That's not a random group. They mostly pick out all the people who have well-off families and are already on their way to success. That's kind of the point. It's a 'good-ole-boys' club. Sneaking in is not like being selected!"

"I know there's no magic success pixie dust," he argued. "But the same pattern applies to the few regular kids they select every year, too. Scholarships. Internships. Invites to prestigious clubs. Once we're there, people will think we've been selected, so then it's all about networking. Maybe pick up a few hints about how the inner circle works?"

"Do you really believe it?" I asked. "That there's some kind of club you can join? That you can get on the right server, learn the secret handshake, and have success handed to you?"

"There are always secret and not-so-secret societies, Mike," Ravi said. "It's worked for white guys for years and years, hasn't it?" His tone held no heat. He was confident of my position on that point.

I nodded. "I have to give you that one."

"It's not just about success. It's about finding ways to get close to the centres of power, to maybe change some things one day."

"I don't know about that." I shook my head, thinking about the protest at school. About Aaron and Mary. "It's feeling like we're going to need something more radical to actually change anything."

"Great, so you're on board with our crashing plan then," Ravi said with forced enthusiasm. "It's a radical plan!"

"Don't even think about it," I said in a warning tone. "I've heard people try to sneak in every year. They always end up wandering around lost in the woods until morning." Then, allowing the underlying amusement back into my voice. "Besides, I'm better than you at parkour, and with the kids, so I'm not worried in the slightest!"

I arched my back and flipped to my feet before Ravi could stop me again, took a couple of running strides to the edge of the stairwell enclosure roof, and jumped down.

Only once I was in the air did it occur to me there might have been someone heading in or out of the door below, but thankfully it was clear. I let the balls of my feet slap briefly, then rolled out, the pavement harsh against my shoulder, then I was up and ready to run.

"Mike!" Ravi landed with a thud beside me. "I'm sorry, hold up."

I turned.

He looked contrite. "I know you're Devon's favourite. I was just being an ass earlier. There's no way I could take your spot if I tried. I'm only competing so I can show my dad there are other jobs out there for me!"

I was achingly jealous of his guaranteed income, but I also saw how much it hurt him when his parents assumed they owned all his time. It bit hard when he had to cancel plans at the last minute because a car needed to be picked up or delivered, or any of the other myriad tasks of the family business. Most of his friends were pretty understanding, but Debbie used it as a wedge issue whenever they were arguing about something else.

"I know," I said. "And if there was a way to sneak you into that party, I probably would just because the elitism sets my teeth on edge. But I can't ask Ian. Whether he said yes or no, I'd feel like the biggest asshole. You know?" To be honest with myself, I was scared to ask. And I didn't know if I was more scared of a no, or of finding out I meant enough to Ian that he'd say yes.

"Yeah, I guess I do." There were no jokes in Ravi's eyes now, just understanding. "Come on." He slapped my shoulder. "Race you to 7-11!" He took off and I followed, laughing hard enough at his pettiness that he picked up a substantial lead and kept it all the way there. I didn't mind. The thrill of running was enough for me. We parted after hitting up the convenience store for our drinks.

Play time was over. I had two papers due and needed to study more for finals. I walked the rest of the way home as slowly as I could bear.

CHAPTER 6

woke up on Monday excited to start the day, yet dreading it at the same time. One final day of classes before I was free from the vicious fishbowl that was high school for the summer. It was going to be a hell of a day. Everyone would be running around with yearbooks looking to 'connect' one last time. And I'd woken up still in male form.

Normally, I'd be happy about that, but I knew deep in my bones that a switch was coming. I hated the days when I switched in the middle. It was so much easier to plan my day and clothes when I could feel my shape was going to be consistent for at least the next twelve hours.

A glance at the coded doodles on my desk calendar confirmed I might be starting my period. Perfect. Dread curdled in my stomach thinking about the final PE class today that I absolutely had to show up for. At least it was in the morning, so there was a chance I could stay male-shaped for it.

I tucked a couple of pads from my secret stash at the top of my closet into a pouch in my bag. I wished I could carry them more openly, now that it was cool for guys to do that in a supportive way, but I couldn't afford that kind of attention, and they weren't cheap enough that I could afford to give them away. I already had trouble buying enough for myself since I couldn't explain to my parents why I needed the extra money. Ravi's cash side-jobs were a lifesaver for many reasons.

Guilt swept over me as I wondered if the woman I'd met, Sarah, was able to get the supplies she needed. I remembered how much my family had depended on kind neighbours to help us when we'd first arrived here. A kind person would at least make sure she had been able to get enough food and that all the utilities were still turned on. Could I afford to be kind? I still hadn't returned her rain jacket. That was a dick move.

Maybe combining the tasks would work. One more quick foray as a girl in public should be safe enough.

Was the racing of my heart fear? Or anticipation?

Some crazy part of me wanted to be seen as a girl when I was in girl shape.

Okay, I had to admit that wasn't crazy. I was a girl when in girl shape. It made sense that I'd want people to see me that way, the same way I wanted to be seen as a guy when in guy-shape, or a gender that society didn't want to acknowledge when my shape was mixed.

I abruptly shoved all those thoughts out of my mind. I had to stay in guy shape for gym. After that, my body could go wild if it wanted. Though when I combed my hair, I was reminded of how it had lengthened with my last switch, then gone back to normal after. I had no idea how that happened, and I really hoped it wouldn't happen again.

I made sure to put an extra, heavier shirt and binding bandages in my backpack. Binding with tape or bandage had become more uncomfortable this past year after my breasts had grown, and today was likely to be even worse with my period coming. I fantasized about getting one of those binders designed specifically for trans guys. They were supposed to be more comfortable and definitely safer, but would also be very hard to explain away if my parents found them.

~*~

The yearbooks were distributed after class. Ian and I braved the crush around the tables. My extreme relief from surviving gym, in male shape, left me feeling euphoric, like I could do anything!

I slid in between two other students like a striking snake, grabbed a couple of books, and passed one to Ian on the way out of the crowd.

"Can we sign?" Ian asked.

"Sure!" I said, happy to be able to chat freely. We retreated to a dead-end side hall together while I searched for a pen in my bag.

"Oh, I was going to ask, when can I return your suit? I wasn't sure if I should bring it to school." The truth was, I hadn't managed to get it dry-cleaned yet.

"Oh no. Don't worry about it." He waved my concerns away, handing back my book, and in a lower voice said, "It looks great on you. It would make me very happy if you could wear it."

The warm and inviting look in his eyes made my heart beat so loudly it drowned out the sound of passing classmates. His warm hands brushing mine sparked a tingling trail that continued up my arm and to my core, then began to expand in a wave of change.

The intoxicating moment of closeness hardened into dread. I snatched my yearbook from his hands and spun away.

"Ian! My dude!" Three guys, yearbooks out, clustered around us. I dodged around one of them just as my switch completed. I stumbled one step in the off-balance moment while my hips adjusted, and my height dropped an inch as my body settled into its new shape.

"I forgot, I have to run!" I called back gruffly.

"Let's meet up after school! I'll message you," Ian called out.

"Sounds great!" I replied in a strangled attempt at my male voice and fled, shoulders hunched, for the bathroom. To bind, and weep for yet another missed chance.

On the third floor of the school, one of the hallways ended in a narrow little corner created when they'd renovated to pack a couple of extra classrooms into this old concrete-and-brick pile. Few people came this way, since the stairwell at this end was steep with narrow steps that only accessed the first and third floors.

Sometimes people used it as a shortcut at peak volume. Rarely, someone used it as a quiet spot to chat, but since the hallway didn't leave enough room for more than one person to pass, it didn't encourage lingering.

And I wouldn't have any use for it either, except for one key element: there was a window with the excessively deep sill common to most in this school. It had spanned the entire width of the original hallway about six feet up, but now it was half-blocked off by the new classroom wall.

Everyone thought it was out of reach, since the steep stairs started right at the end of the hall, putting the window eight feet up from the nearest step. But with a little effort, I could tic-tac off the wall and onto the heavy stone banister before pulling myself up onto the ledge. Of course, a slip would mean a painful tumble down the stairs, and likely broken bones, but the risk just made it more satisfying.

I kept it secret from everyone, only going in or out when no one was watching. I didn't even tell my friends it existed. It was my own personal, private spot with a beautiful view. The window faced away from the bustling commercial strip that was 17th Avenue, showing instead the tree-lined streets of an older residential neighbourhood. Today, the leaves on the upper branches fluttered in the sunshine, and birds flitted from tree to tree.

A perfect metaphor for my life: Hiding in a cement box, watching everyone else enjoy their freedom. The hormones were hopping today. Much period, so angst. Still, I was thankful for my secret spot. It worked for days like this when I ended up girl-shaped, but prepared, so I didn't need to flee the building. It kept me from having to mingle any more than necessary.

It also meant I wasn't tempted to spend money on food at the caf. I morosely chewed through the dry sandwich and carrots of my bagged lunch from home while taking one last read of my final essay for English class on my phone before submitting it.

It was amazing how many typos slipped through, even with my careful edits. Mr. James was an absolute tyrant about spelling, formatting, citations, everything. I wanted it to be perfect.

My concentration shattered on hearing Ian's voice call out: "Angela!" Curious, I leaned forward and peered around the partition wall. Ian was standing with his back to me, on the threshold of the main hallway. I ducked back into concealment quickly, guessing he would move on soon.

He didn't, and within a few moments, Angela joined him.

I stayed as still as I could. They might not be able to see me, but any sound would echo in this space.

"Yeah?" Angela said.

"I have some news." Ian's tone was serious. "You've been selected for the after-grad at my family's cabin."

What? I felt anger build. I'd been so worried about not putting him in an uncomfortable spot, and yet here he was, handing out invites to impress girls he liked?

It didn't seem like Ange was impressed, though. She snorted in derision. I knew that sound. I could imagine clearly the look on her face. There was a rustle of paper, and she asked, "What's this?"

"It's a radio. Don't show it off, just make sure it's on when you're driving out. There are more instructions, but right now, I'd suggest reading … this one."

"Huh." Angela's expulsion of air sounded like she'd been gut-punched, but like she'd expected the blow. It was an unsettling combo. "You?" she said, accusingly.

"Believe it or not, I'm in a similar position. I don't want to see you get hurt," Ian said.

"This is supposed to help me?" She sounded incredulous.

"I think perhaps we could help each other."

Silence.

"Or we could talk now," Angela said. "Assuming we actually have any-thing in common." Her words were reaching for nonchalance, but the burr of fear underneath wouldn't quite let her get there.

"That won't help me," he said. "For a few reasons that I can't get into here."

"And if I just leave?" she said quietly.

"You're willing to drag your whole family through that?"

Another pause.

"Why should I trust you?" The words seemed dredged up from a well of pain I hadn't expected existed in her. Shivers danced up my spine. How had this already terrible conversation veered into officially scary?

"Well, let me show you something. I think you'll find it convincing."

Ange gasped.

I leaned further forward without thinking, and the slight scrape of my shoe in the grit on the window ledge sounded far too loud to my ears. I froze again. Fortunately, they'd been too involved to notice.

"All right, fine," I heard Ange say in a shaky voice. "But I have some conditions ..." Their footsteps retreated down the stairs while talking. I thought I heard my name mentioned, but the words were drowned in echoes.

Holding myself still took every bit of willpower. I wasn't even sure that had been the right choice. Should I have interrupted to make sure Ange was okay? But I didn't know what I'd just heard. And if I revealed myself now, they'd know I was creepily listening in on their whole private con-versation. I was certain Angela would see that as a betrayal of trust.

As soon as their footsteps faded, I crammed all my stuff into my back-pack. So many conflicting emotions were churning in me, I couldn't tell what I felt. I slid over and dropped, with familiarity of long practice, onto the railing with one foot and one hand still on the window ledge just for a split-second to break my momentum, then pushed off to clear the top of the steps and land in a deep crouch on the tile floor.

Two guys just rounding the corner from the third-floor hallway recoiled hard enough at my sudden appearance that one of them fell on his butt. I just waved and launched myself down the stairs. If Angela and Ian reached the first floor hall too far ahead of me, I'd have no chance at all of catching up.

If those guys happened to mention the encounter to staff, I could probably kiss my refuge goodbye next year. I consoled myself with the thought that I likely wouldn't be in this school next year anyway, unless I managed to figure out how to lock down my sex.

I ran down the stairs, no longer concerned about being heard. I sped past the library's emergency exit door on the second floor and only checked my speed at the bottom, both from not wanting to look silly cannonballing out of the narrow doorway and not wanting to accidentally slam into anyone.

Since I'd already started to slow down when Jenn Chaika stepped into the doorway, I managed to come almost to a complete stop before running into her. We ended up in a slightly awkward, unintentional embrace in the doorway, instead of the hideously public display of me knocking her on her ass then landing on top of her in the middle of the school's main hallway.

"Cool your jets, Orea, you just about flattened me," she said, but she was grinning mischievously as we separated. "But actually, I'm glad I ran into you. Can I have a minute?"

"Sure, just two seconds, okay?" I edged around her and out the doorway, looking all around for Ian's height or Angela's telltale coppery hair.

Nothing.

Fuck.

I turned back to Jenn. "Hi. Sorry about that." I had trouble looking her in the eye after nearly letting her get taken in by the cop at the protest. I'd been avoiding her all day. I couldn't brush her off now.

"I wanted to apologize," she said, which grabbed my attention.

"What? No. I need to apologize!"

"No. I put you on the spot. That wasn't cool. I'm not asking any questions, but ..." She handed me a card. "It's getting dangerous to talk in a lot of online spaces. If you need someone to talk to, this is our Discord. Invite only. We're here for each other."

"Oh. Thanks." I took the card, still processing the abrupt reversal. "I'm still sorry I froze on you. I should have helped." I shook my head. "We're just both lucky Ian was there."

"Yeah, he's been a huge support," she said. "I would have taken twice the crap I have here, if he hadn't made it clear to everyone, from day one, that he accepted me."

The end-of-lunch bell reminded us we had places to be. Jenn hurried up the stairs with a wave, and I headed to class.

Of the people who would probably be cool with my switches, a trans group would be a good bet. We'd have so much to talk about. But I couldn't risk anyone knowing; what if someone couldn't keep the secret? After all, I was something even more secret than trans, wasn't I? I couldn't do that to my parents, or myself. Not again.

~*~

I messaged Angela during the breaks between afternoon classes, but I didn't get any reply. Then Ian cancelled our planned after-school meetup via text.

What the hell? A wave of disappointment hit. This was probably the last time Ian and I would get to hang out together, with school ending. Maybe it was for the best since I was in female shape now, but I'd really been looking forward to it.

At the end of the last class, I rushed to Angela's locker, hoping to catch her there, but she didn't show. I knew she didn't have anything after school today and would almost certainly hit her locker on this, the last day of class. The halls were full of people clearing out the stuff they'd accumulated over the year.

While waiting, I realized with a rush of cold sweat that I'd been so worried about the whole Ian/Angela thing that I hadn't actually finished my read-through of my English essay, and I hadn't submitted it!

I hurriedly pulled up the courseware site, waded through the crappy interface until I could select my latest doc, and hammered the submit button with only a couple of minutes to spare before the deadline.

I double-checked that it was marked as received and for the correct class, section, and teacher. *Phew*! I leaned back against the lockers, wrung out. That mistake could very well have tanked my English mark, and getting good grades this year was a big part of proving to my parents I could look after myself.

With Angela a no-show after half an hour, I had to admit she wasn't coming. After what I'd overheard, I needed to see her, in person, to be sure she was okay. I ran to my bike and rode all the way to her house in the afternoon heat, arriving dripping with sweat. Her conversation with Ian kept repeating in my head, taking on more sinister overtones each time.

Ringing the doorbell, I waited through agonizing minutes. What was I going to do if she wasn't home and still wasn't answering texts? Wait for her parents to get home and see if they were worried or not? And if they were worried? My stomach churned.

I was about to voice-call her after ten minutes and two doorbell rings, when the door finally opened. She was fresh from the shower with her hair wrapped in a towel and wearing her oversized fuzzy green robe.

"Really, Mike?" she said, exasperated. "This couldn't have waited a few hours?"

My worries suddenly felt silly as I stared down the barrels of those narrowed grey-green eyes.

"Ah, yeah, well, you weren't answering texts, and I didn't see you at school. I just … wanted to see how you're doing."

"You wanted to see how I'm doing."

"Yeah."

"Now. Not for the past few weeks. But now?"

Crap, I wished I could bring up Ian. That would have made this so much easier. But there was also the other recent weirdness.

"After what happened at the wedding. I'm worried."

"Well, it's fine. You don't need to worry," she said, anger sharpening her voice.

"Okay. I just want you to know I'm here for you, to talk, or hang out. Like we used to."

"Mike …" Her lips tightened into a thin line. "You're the one who said you needed space. Well, I need some too. The best thing you can do is leave me alone for a while. I've always appreciated how you've supported me without trying to force me to explain, and without making a big deal out of it. I'll let you know when I'm ready to get back to how we used to be. Okay? I need time." Anger slowly drained from her voice as she spoke, and by the end, she sounded more pleading.

"I get that, Angela. I'm sorry. You're right. That's what I asked for, and you should get the same." I backed away, down the porch steps. "Just … know I'm here for you. Any time. Okay?"

"You'd be my first call," she said softly.

She watched from the door as I picked up my bike and rode away. Fuck my sex switches. They were such fucking bullshit. I'd never wanted any space from Angela. I still didn't. My chest hurt. A lot. My face felt hot, and tears began to trace across my cheeks, blown by the wind. I rode as hard as I could, driving my body to exhaustion while I sobbed. Maybe I could get it all out of my system before I had to go home and pretend everything was awesome.

CHAPTER 7

I was naked, female, and standing in the school gym locker room. I ran around trying to open the lockers to get some clothes, but the locks all had dials with multiple concentric rings covered in arcane symbols. Suddenly, everyone I'd ever met, starting with my parents, began to flood into the room. I fled to the communal shower, which was warm and billowing with steam. A familiar musky, earthy scent tickled my senses.

I felt safer in the steam. It concealed and caressed my body. I slowly relaxed and began to enjoy my naked state. Here, in this space, I wasn't just female-shaped. I was a woman.

A figure resolved in the steam. It was a naked man, tilted back as if leaning against the wall, with his arms raised above his head. His face was shrouded in the fog, but the details of his well-muscled chest and abs and everything else were perfectly clear.

I walked up to him and ran my hands across his chest and down his sides. I swayed my hips to the beat of the music echoing in my head. The feel of his slick flesh under my hands and the spicy scent of him started a slow heat building in the pit of my belly. Then, I was kneeling in front of him. I could feel a tingle of pleasure as my stomach muscles tensed.

I woke up, still tingling, my nipples rubbing almost painfully against my sheets. I had never been this turned on as a girl. At least not enough to feel the need for an orgasm, which I was craving now. My hand was sliding down my stomach to maybe do something about that, even with the wrong anatomy, but images from the dream floated back into my memory, hard abs and caressing … *Aaah!*

I forced myself out of bed and into a shower several degrees colder than normal. I knew that being attracted to guys wasn't wrong in any way, but those kinds of thoughts were so strongly associated with my female form that I hated to encourage them. I desperately needed to get back to my male form for a while to clear my head.

The first week I spent studying for exams had passed smoothly. I'd been able to push worries about Angela, as well as questions about Ian and everything else, to the back of my mind and focus on studying. Mostly. My dreams were not under my control.

They alternated between sex dreams and nightmares of Angela, catatonic, like she'd been at the wedding. Though half the time, Angela looked like Sarah, which was weird.

Sometimes Ian kissed her, woke her up, and they ran off together so fast that I couldn't catch up. Other times, he drove a knife into her chest, saying it was for the best. In one, I thrust the knife in. I'd woken up sweating and shaking from that dream.

Monday again, and I was ready for a rest day. I found it helpful to goof off the day before an exam. The accumulated studying stress would kill my concentration during the test if I didn't release it.

At least my parents were at work today, so I could hang around the house without fear of discovery. I grabbed a big bowl of cereal and sat at the kitchen table, munching and thinking. None of my usual remedies for switching back to male form had worked, and I had to admit to myself that the reason for my unexpected switches to female-form was most likely my strong attraction to Ian.

And there was nothing I could do about that. People thought guys were the extra-lusty ones, unable to control themselves, but I'd never felt anything in guy form as strong as the whole-body waves of lust that rolled over me in girl form.

Fortunately, the physical impacts were less visible in girl form. Though I still sometimes needed to sit down. Weak in the knees from desire was, apparently, not just something old-time writers made up as a euphemism.

Being stuck solidly in girl form reminded me of something else, outside of Ian and Angela, that had been disturbing me. The more I thought about it, the more I worried about Sarah alone in that house. What if she had no one to help her get the next food delivery or medication? Her house was only a few blocks away, and I had the time.

Now that I'd come to a decision, I knew what I had to do to take at least one worry off my plate. My mind raced ahead to the preparations I would need to take, but I forced myself to finish my cereal. My parents bought it especially for me. I wasn't going to waste it.

Clothing would be a problem. A real girl could get away with wearing boy clothes, but I needed to draw a sharp line between my boy self and girl self in public. Having Sarah recognize me on the street when I was supposed to be a boy could very well be the crack in the dam that busted my secret wide open, forcing another move away from everything and everyone I knew. I shuddered to think where we'd end up this time, and what more my parents would have to endure because of me.

Mom's clothes wouldn't be much help. She was several sizes larger than my girl form and liked things loose-fitting. As much trouble as my hips and breasts caused, I was still quite slender and small-chested. *Maybe I could find some of her older clothes?*

That thought dredged up an old memory. She kept some clothes from when she was younger on the top shelf of her closet. 'Sentimental reasons' was all she said, but I couldn't help but wonder if they were things she'd planned to give to me, back when she thought she had a daughter.

Well, in any case, some of them probably fit. Fear rippled through me. I would have to be very careful to put everything back the way I found it. If I were caught…

I checked my social media notifications before heading up. *Blah, blah, blah* … I saw that Angela and Ian both had recent activity, but I kept my interactions minimal, just a few 'likes' here and there. Ian hadn't contacted me directly all week, nor had Angela, which was pretty much what I had expected, even if it hurt like hell.

I pulled the old suitcase down, trying to minimize the disturbance of the other bric-a-brac. A slightly spicy scent wafted out when I popped the old-fashioned catches and lifted the lid. I smiled and breathed deeply. Little sachets of dried lavender and orange were tucked in with the clothes. I might've been a guy most of the time, but I still appreciated Mom's little touches.

I had no idea what I was looking for, maybe some tighter-fitting jeans and a girly top?

I found some old suit pants and one pair of jeans, but they were pink denim with flowers embroidered all over them and obviously for a younger girl. Too small for me. Oddly, they also had big raw cuts all over them. One of the legs was almost completely severed. Seemed like an odd thing for Mom to keep.

There were a couple of tops, but they looked more like pyjama tops, excessively long with a neck hole pretty much wide enough to fit my entire body through. *Ugh*. Finally, at the bottom, I found a light-blue strapless dress with a built-in corset and heavily ruffled skirt. It looked like it might fit.

Under the dress was a small bundle wrapped in old brown paper. It was far too small to contain anything wearable, but I couldn't resist taking a look anyway. Carefully opening the crinkly shroud, I revealed a little boy's acid-washed jeans and a brightly coloured shirt with random geometric shapes. Totally 80's style. Running my fingers down the shirt fabric, I felt something hard underneath.

Unfolding it, I saw an old Polaroid of a baby wearing the same outfit, sitting on a couch I didn't recognize. Why would Mom have a picture of a random kid, from back when she was a kid? Did she have a brother I'd never heard of? She didn't talk to her family, and they didn't talk to us, so it was possible.

I was curious about the rest of our family, but it was a forbidden topic in our house. Fleeing our old lives had meant cutting ties with family, too. My dad, particularly, still carried a lot of pain over that. And the kinds of research I might do on my own to find out more about family—genealogy, genetics—would be criminally stupid in our current situation.

I carefully tucked the picture back into the clothes with a sigh, rewrapped them, and put the bundle back in the suitcase the same way it had come out.

~*~

It felt weird to strip down in my parents' bedroom, particularly as a girl. I had made sure the curtains were closed before starting my pilferage, but I still felt exposed.

The dress was oddly constructed. It flopped open all up the back with hooks up one side and rows and rows of eyelets on the other. I stepped into it and tried hooking it up behind my back for a few minutes with little success. In desperation, I turned it around on my body so I could at least see what I was doing, and then spun it back around once it was done up.

That worked, although my breasts were not very happy with the spinning process. I wondered how girls with larger chests managed this as I massaged an abraded nipple through the heavy fabric.

When I was done, I checked myself out in the full-length mirror. The skirt covered a lot less leg than I liked. I tried tugging it down, but that exposed too much breast. It was essentially a tube of slightly reinforced fabric wrapped around my body. It wasn't so bad, from what I remembered of the girls I'd seen in dresses. It just felt drafty, like my lower half was still naked, even though I was covered down to mid-thigh by the skirt ruffles. The top felt cumbersome, but also snug and secure. It pressed my breasts up and together to create the first cleavage I had ever displayed.

I stopped focusing on minutia and took in my entire image. My chest clenched tight with panic. A girl was looking back at me. This wasn't a hint of femininity in the angle of my face or the length of my hair that I could pretend wasn't the 'real' me. The tight top accentuated my breasts, and the short skirt showed off my bare legs. I turned away from the mirror before my dizziness got any worse.

The dress fit so well, it could have been made for me. I had a brief *Twilight Zone* moment before I realized it was simple genetics. Even as a boy, people always said I looked like my mom. In girl form, it wouldn't surprise me if I were sized and shaped like she'd been at this age. I plucked at the dress. Did Mom wear this when she was seventeen? Well, why not? As much as it pained me to think of my mom as a teenager and why she'd wear a sexy dress, I couldn't deny that it must have happened.

I realized my hands were pressed together on my stomach. It was so weird to think there was a uterus in there, and ovaries, and all that crap they'd showed us in health class. I knew there must be because I had a period, but I'd never thought about what that implied. Theoretically, I could get pregnant.

Even if I were willing to contemplate the actions it would take to become pregnant in the first place, I couldn't imagine it would be good for a baby to be flipping in and out of existence whenever I switched. I shuddered. *Best not to experiment.*

I packed up the suitcase again, re-folding the discards and replacing the sachets, also keeping out a plain white denim jacket. It was a little short, but fit well enough and had pockets, which the dress certainly did not. I closed the suitcase and snugged it back up at the top of the closet where it would likely stay undisturbed for several more years.

My girl-sized running shoes didn't even remotely match the dress, but they were all I had. People could deal. They at least fit the bill for not looking male. I snorted. No one was going to mistake me for a guy today. Unless I shifted back suddenly. Fear twisted my insides, but I pushed it down. I wasn't going far. Worst case, I could cut and run for home.

I snuck cautiously out the rear door of the garage. I didn't see anyone in the back lane, so I hurried away from my house before anyone could associate me with it.

I took the same circuitous route back to Sarah's that I had before, carrying the pink raincoat bundled up in one hand. A breeze constantly ruffled the skirt around my legs, making me feel naked. I kept double-checking that my ass was still covered, and I had to remind myself not to tug the dress down every ten seconds.

~*~

Sarah's front porch was still missing, though the ramp looked far less treacherous when dry. I felt lousy for not checking up on her. What if she was holed up in there, surviving on crumbs? I really wished I'd thought to get her phone number or email address last time, so I wasn't arriving out of the blue.

It seemed my worst fears were realized when she very hesitantly opened the door, nervously glancing around. But then her face lit up with a huge smile, and she practically dragged me through the doorway. She definitely wasn't weak from hunger.

"Kayla! So great to see you!" She quickly shut and locked the door behind me.

I suppressed a surge of claustrophobia. She was dressed in jeans and a flowery top with a deep V-neck. Her hair was braided now, flat cornrows across most of her head falling to short, above-the-shoulder braids at the back.

"I wanted to return this and, you know, say thanks." I awkwardly recited my pre-planned phrase, holding the raincoat up in front of me like a shield. I was relieved she remembered the name I had invented because I'd forgotten it minutes after leaving last time.

"Oh, sure." She looked slightly less animated. "Stay for a cuppa?"

"Uh …" I didn't want to stay too long and risk a switch, but her eagerness for company tugged at my heart. "Sure. Sounds good." I remembered from before that 'a cuppa' meant strong tea, which actually did sound good.

"Brilliant!" She smiled widely, took the coat from me, and then held out her hand for mine. I briefly considered resisting, but that might have seemed rude, so I shrugged my jean jacket off and handed it to her. She hung them in the closet, which boasted two more coats now, as well as a collection of boots and shoes. She chatted as she went.

"What a cheery dress." She glanced back at me. "Vintage?"

"I guess," I said. It was true enough, in a way. It felt safer to stick with short sentences. I usually lowered my voice in girl form to sound more like my male voice. I was trying to find a more natural female register now, but it all sounded wrong to my ears.

"Ooh, yes. I used to adore hitting the shops at Brick Lane. Always found the most amazing clothes." She turned back to me, lifting her arm to make a little motion with one finger. I looked at her blankly until she lost patience. "Well, turn 'round, you ninny.'"

I flushed and complied. How could I forget the obligatory 'spin'? I'd seen girls do it often enough.

"Smashing. You need some knee-high boots to go with it, though," she said, heading for the kitchen and motioning me to follow. She chattered about jewellery while putting the kettle on.

I hadn't considered accessorizing. Just as well. I probably would have messed it up. I wasn't even entirely sure what most of the terms she used meant. Who knew being a girl was so complicated? This was where Angela would have been a huge help. If only I could talk to her about any of it.

I stumbled to a halt upon seeing the living room. It had been bare before. Now it sported a shelving unit that doubled as a stand for a sleek widescreen TV. The rusty, half-broken metal blinds had been replaced by stylish wooden ones. Still firmly closed. A sectional wrap-around couch and a solid-looking coffee table sat on a large blue-and-red area rug that blended bold geometric sections with a profusion of flowery detail. I liked it.

"Sit anywhere you can find space." Sarah waved to the couch and ducked into the kitchen. "Won't be a moment."

I jerked out of my daze. Perhaps she wasn't as helpless as I'd thought.

The couch and coffee table were covered with magazines. Most of them were glossy, bright, and very girly, but I noticed a couple had guns and people in camouflage on the covers. I lifted one of the trashy magazines to see the title of the one underneath, upon which a scantily clad blonde girl brandished a machine gun of some kind. The title read *Soldier of Fort—*

"Ooh, are you a *HELLO!* girl too?" Sarah materialized out of thin air at my elbow. I panicked and spent a couple of seconds trying to figure out if 'hello girl' was British slang or some girl-specific term that I ought to know. Then, I noticed the title of the magazine in my hand: *HELLO!* in big red block letters.

"Ha! Ah, no." Better to go with the truth than try to pretend I knew the first thing about—I glanced at the cover again—'how to disguise bulging eyes.' *Really?* There were so many, many things I didn't want to know about being a girl.

"Oh, well," Sarah gestured across the littered table and couch. "I've got lots to choose from." She put a steaming mug down on top of a gun magazine. "I hope you're okay with coffee. I just made a pot."

"I am more than okay with coffee. Studying for exams is killing me!" I picked it up and took a large, grateful slurp. "Yeah. That's the sh—stuff," I said, adjusting my language, with a quick glance at her reaction.

Sarah laughed, a happy, unrestrained laugh. "You're priceless, you are!" She patted me on the shoulder.

I shrugged, bemused and embarrassed. The skin-to-skin contact felt intimate. I wasn't used to having my shoulders bare, and I wasn't at all sure what I'd done that was so funny.

She grilled me for a while about what I had been doing lately. I related some recent events. The wedding, minus Angela's seizure. Delivering the Porsche. Parkour training. She was less impressed than I thought she'd be about the luxury sports car. She seemed more curious about where I'd driven and the whole car delivery process.

"Weren't you nervous?" she asked.

"A little, I guess." I would have been scared, but my terror over whatever was happening with Angela had swamped all of that. "I think that's the most expensive car I've ever been in, and the owner was pretty uptight—"

"As a Black woman, of course, I'd hate to be driving a posh car I didn't own here." She shook her head and rolled her eyes briefly upward. "But I meant meeting with a strange guy in the middle of nowhere, with his car as the only exit," she said flatly, giving me an odd look.

"Oh, uh …" I tried to think of something sensible. How could I say, 'I'm not used to the idea of men trying to attack me'? I couldn't see a girl ever saying that. "I'm used to it. I do this a lot," I finished lamely.

"Hmm. That would have made me very nervous, even before. Now …" She shuddered and quickly switched to some questions about parkour.

I described the training club and some highlights from my usual run.

"I heard there weren't a lot of women involved in that," she said. "It's nice to see."

"Yeah, it's definitely a bro crowd," I said it lightly, but I cringed inside. Presenting as male allowed me to avoid the sexism she was likely imagining. I couldn't help it, but I still felt like I was lying to her. "The skill and danger really get me out of my head when it's too full of other crap," I shrugged. "And it's a hell of a lot cheaper than downhill skiing, or even proper mountain biking."

"Is the unshaven look just an exam time thing, or are you making a statement?" she asked in a friendly way.

"What do you mean?" I rubbed my girl-smooth chin in sudden fear before realizing that wasn't where she was looking. My shins, and more sparsely right up past my knees, were covered with short dark hairs. Legs! Girls shaved their legs! Shit.

"Sorry. I didn't mean to embarrass you," she said quickly. "I think it's fine, either way."

"Naw. It's cool." I tried to calm down and lighten my voice. I'd been frightened at the thought of telltale male facial hair, not embarrassed. "It wasn't an intentional statement. I'll blame exam time. Things tend to get a little hairy." I grinned weakly. I was starting to feel embarrassed now.

"Can't say I ever let school distract me from maintaining my appearance," she chuckled. "But I make a terrible example."

I wasn't sure what I should say to that. Agree? Disagree?

This was only my second time presenting as a woman in public. I felt like I was walking a tightrope. However, scanning the covers of the women's magazines covering the table, I got the impression that being a woman wasn't exactly a walk in the park, even for those who'd been at it since birth.

"Can I offer you a refill?" Sarah asked, gesturing to my nearly empty cup, and absolving me of making a response.

"Oh, no. I don't think so," I stammered out. "Actually, I should get home. So much studying to do." I had already stayed longer than intended. Then I remembered part of my mission here: to be a good neighbour. I didn't want to walk away with the same worries I came with.

"Is there anything I can help you with?" I waved an arm around to encompass the whole living room. "This looks awesome. I guess you're not having as much trouble with deliveries?"

"It's better. I've found that individual sellers are more willing to accept my conditions, and I can pre-screen them to some degree so I know who I'm going to be talking to. I found a smaller company that will pick up my groceries and is more flexible about delivery." She paused, looking thoughtful.

"There's one thing you could do for me. I need to get a builder 'round to replace that porch and some other things. I would appreciate some company. I should be okay, but …" She looked up at me hopefully.

"Yeah. Sure," I said, then remembered I had to make sure I was girl-shaped. "I mean, if I'm free that day. You know, exams and stuff." I trailed off.

"Brilliant. I'll check with you first, of course."

"I'll do my best!" I said, and I actually meant it, even knowing it significantly increased my danger of discovery. I enjoyed talking to Sarah, and she seemed happy to talk with me. She had an energy about her that made me want to laugh, even as I tiptoed around the conversational minefield.

"How should I contact you? About the builder?"

"Oh, right," I remembered my earlier angst at not having a way to contact her, but I didn't want to give her my number. It was probably listed somewhere under my family name. "Can I get your phone number?" I reached for my pocket where I usually kept my phone and hit the warmth of my thinly covered hip.

"Oh, my phone is in my jacket," I said, embarrassed. I hopped up to retrieve it from the closet. Had she seen me go for my pocket? Was that a slip?

She stood too and followed. I brought up my contacts and reflexively held the phone out to her. Then, I thought about the amount of personal data potentially on display and wanted to jerk it back, but fought the urge since that would look even more suspicious.

"I don't have a phone number," she said, while poking rapidly at the phone. "But this should do well enough." She peered over the phone at me. "You use Discord?"

"Ah, yeah, a little." Prickles of fear went up my backbone. What if she asked me for my account name? I'd originally used it to cautiously see if anyone else switched sex like I did, or knew of anyone who did. Over the last couple of years, though, I hadn't used it for anything but occasional gaming with Ravi. It didn't have my real name on it, but it was a distinctly male identity. Which I guess wasn't uncommon for girls gaming online, so maybe it would be fine?

No awkward questions came up, though. She handed back my phone.

She'd entered a Discord server address in my notes app. I started breathing again, heart pounding.

We said our goodbyes, and I waved as I hopped down the ramp. I was relieved to see her doing well. I owed her one more visit to help with the builder, but that was all I could afford. Every time I left and returned to my house in girl clothes, I risked questions being asked, and possibly even being stopped by someone I knew.

It would also be much, much better if I had some less memorable clothes; my parents would recognize Mom's old dress instantly. Also, Sarah would likely find it weird if I showed up in the exact same clothes again.

Damn. I would have to find time to go shopping for some different, girl-style clothes before I came back. I felt myself being pulled farther and farther into this girl identity. I knew how dangerous it was, but I couldn't seem to stop.

CHAPTER 8

ate afternoon the next Tuesday, I got a Discord message from Sarah saying the builder would be coming tomorrow around 3 p.m. From our earlier discussion, I knew she meant a contractor. British English was very similar to Canadian English, but with a few deep potholes.

I had set up a new Discord profile last week, soon after our meeting. First, I set up a new email account as kayla.torean (I'd needed a last name that wasn't 'Orea,' so just added a couple of letters). Then I set up a Discord account as 'Kayla'.

I hadn't realized it would be so easy to establish an alternate online identity. It had taken me less than five minutes. I joined Sarah's channel. She had responded with a quick acknowledgement of my message, but I hadn't received anything else from her until this afternoon.

It was the day after my last exam, and I had been taking a much-needed break from everything. Ravi was done too, and wanted me to come for a run in the afternoon. But as the day wore on, that edgy feeling that I was going to switch grew, so I had to cancel.

If I were lucky, it would hold off until after supper. Then, I could pretend to have a headache and go to bed to avoid my parents. What an exciting life I led.

The people I really wanted to talk to were Angela and Ian, but they had gone silent on social media, and I didn't have the courage to directly contact either of them right now.

~*~

I woke up on Wednesday, Sarah's appointment day, happy about being solidly female-shaped for the first time in many years. I felt very little pre-switch enervation, so I could expect to stay in girl shape until late evening, or maybe longer.

This meant I was free to show up at Sarah's. But more importantly, it meant I could go out and find some more sensible girl clothes for my visit.

I needed a recognizably girl outfit, nothing like what guy Michael would wear. The clothes needed to make a hard line in Sarah's mind, or anyone else who happened to see me outside, that Michael and Kayla were two distinct people with no relation to one another.

I cleaned up my dishes and trudged back upstairs for a shower. I had time to skim through a few YouTube videos about leg shaving while finishing up breakfast. It didn't look too hard. I didn't want to be memorable on this trip, and even though my legs didn't seem overly hairy, I could see they might draw attention when presenting as a girl.

~*~

Twenty minutes later, I would've quite happily put those trash-fire internet video creators on trial for crimes against humanity. Shaving your legs was hard. Much harder than those scammers made it appear. There was … a lot more hair to remove than I'd expected.

My legs felt like they'd been skinned. I guess it could have been worse. Only one of the cuts was still bleeding after I finished my shower. I fished an old box of transparent band-aids out of the cupboard and covered it. Sadly, it was right near my knee, so it was very noticeable. Oh well. Hopefully, it would stop bleeding by the time I reached the mall.

I pulled the dress I'd worn before from the bottom of my drawer and shrugged it on. It was rumpled, but not too badly. It wasn't like I could hang it up in my closet. This time, I remembered jewellery. I didn't want to go too wild, but Angela always seemed to be wearing something these days unless we were hiking or swimming.

My mom had an assortment of necklaces and bracelets in all sorts of colours. Unfortunately, I had no idea what would look reasonable, so I went with a little silver rose on a chain and a silver bracelet that had some kind of flower-and-leaf pattern.

I felt bad touching her jewellery without asking, but she'd likely be more upset over the dress, in a general sense. I felt nauseous thinking about how she, or my dad, would react to the sight of me like this. I pushed it to the back of my mind.

My hair was longer again. Even longer than last time. It nearly came down to the top of my shoulders when combed out, lying in fairly neat waves. I wasn't sure I liked it, but I wasn't about to try any styling. Not yet.

Another snag presented itself as I was about to leave. After slipping on a pair of my mom's sandals, I went to put my house keys in my pocket and remembered the dress had none. I'd used the jacket pockets last time. It was already hot and sunny enough that I didn't relish the idea of wearing a jacket. What did real women do in this situation? Then it dawned on me—I needed a purse.

Eventually, I found an old dark-blue purse in Mom's closet. Good enough. Her alternate purse was there too, but I didn't want to take one that she was currently using. I was already trespassing far too much on her private life. I transferred the usual contents of my pockets—wallet, phone, money, keys—to the purse and tried to balance the strap on my shoulder.

Sneaking out through the garage, I walked down the alley and a few blocks to the bus stop. Hopefully, no one would see or mention the strange girl coming out of our garage to my parents. I really needed a better place to change clothes. The sandals were a pain, flopping on my feet. I had to step carefully. I added shoes to my shopping list. Surely, it wouldn't cost too much to get a basic pair of shoes in my size.

I was so caught up in planning that I didn't notice the bus until it groaned to a halt in front of me. I jumped up, remembering to grab my purse at the last second, and carefully negotiated the steps in my unfamiliar footwear. It wasn't until I reached the top of the steps and slapped my hip that I remembered my money was somewhere in the depths of my purse.

Then, I forgot to adjust my dress before sitting, and it rode up high enough that the backs of my thighs touched the hot seat. I quickly reached between my legs and tugged it forward under my thighs, but the sensation shocked me into acknowledging the reality of what I was about to do.

This wasn't a game of dress-up. This was real life. I was going to be a girl. No, scratch that. I was currently a girl, out in front of everyone. What had seemed a simple task—going to the mall to buy some clothes—was starting to feel like a major expedition into uncharted territory.

~*~

Arriving at the mall, I hopped off the bus and nearly landed flat on my face as I caught the toe of my sandal on an uneven piece of pavement.

I snatched at my purse strap as it dropped off my shoulder for the ump-
teenth time and limped onward. New shoes moved up in priority on my
list, along with figuring out how women kept purse straps on their shoulders. I was starting to suspect glue was involved. Some secret formula
passed from mother to daughter.

With school out, the mall was a zoo, or maybe an overpopulated jungle. Between the people, advertising, and merchandise, it was a riot of
clashing colour and sound. The chaos soothed my nerves, though. With
so many people, dressed in so many styles, one more face wasn't memorable. I passed a few people I knew from school, and while a couple of the
guys looked my way, I didn't see any spark of recognition.

I wandered randomly for a while, not sure what I wanted to look at
first. I spotted a store with pictures of teen girls on the posters and went
in. The jeans and top from the picture were displayed on a mannequin
beside the front rack. I had to admit, they looked pretty sweet.

I checked through for my size, and a price tag caught my eye. I jerked
back involuntarily, drawing a dirty look from the girl beside me. I backed
away and let the flow in the mall carry me along, slightly numb. $120 for
a pair of jeans? Seriously?

A shoe store came into view, and I ducked inside. I needed to get rid of
these flip-flops before I broke my neck. A bewildering array of shoe-lined
shelves wrapped around the store from floor to ceiling. Rows and rows
of shelves.

I walked up and down the aisles for a few minutes. There were flip-flop
sandals, strappy sandals, running shoes, shoes with no heels, shoes with
heels, strappy shoes with heels, high-heeled running shoes with open toes
(*WTF?*), high boots, short boots, some kind of open-toed high-heel ankle
boot/shoe thing. Hundreds of different styles and colours. I hit sensory
overload, unable to focus on anything, stuffed myself into an unoccupied
corner, and closed my eyes.

On one hand, I adored the kind of colours and patterns I could wear
as a girl that I'd never get away with as a guy. I wanted to bring a dozen
pairs home with me already, but the number of choices melted my brain.
I could dimly recall automatically seeking out my favourite shade of purple when I was eight, but I'd missed out on all the practice in between
that would help me make sense of this chaos. I didn't have time to reflect
on my lost teen years now, no matter how much I wanted to. I had to
simplify.

Okay. What kind of shoe did I actually want? Something that would go reasonably well with various styles of clothing, was comfortable, and wasn't too ugly. *I should probably get something without a heel, at least for now*, I thought. I mentally reviewed the options. There were some fairly simple shoes: a cloth upper, no heels. Easy to slip on and off. I could get them in basic black. Black went with everything.

It still took longer than I'd expected, but I eventually strutted out in my new shoes, with my mom's sandals in a bag, feeling far more secure now that I had stable footing. The shoes, called 'flats' apparently, were light and comfortable, almost like wearing slippers.

While waiting in line to buy them, I'd spotted an advert across the mall that gave me an idea. It showed a girl in jeans that had been rolled up to form a broad cuff above the knee. I had an old pair of jeans at home. The cuffs were frayed, and the knees were worn out, so I wouldn't feel bad cutting them up. I could trim them off, and they'd make passable shorts.

The pre-worn look seemed to be in, anyway. Even new jeans came pre-ripped and fake-worn. *Just the latest way for rich kids who could afford new wardrobes every year to make sure there was no social space for the kids who were actually poor and had to buy clothes that would last more than one season.* I shook my head to get my mind back on track.

Now I only had to find a shirt. I headed back to the first store and gathered up a few that looked like they'd fit. They all had numbered sizes, but I had no idea what they represented. Probably not neck size. I didn't know my measurements anyway, so it didn't really matter. Trying them on was my only option.

It felt odd going into a women's change room for the first time since I was a little kid, like I was trespassing. No one gave me a second look. Although it would've been odd if they did. I looked down for a quick double-check. Yup, still girl-shaped.

I had thought about how to best try on the shirts and came to the conclusion that I'd have to take the whole dress off. It was too bulky to try things on over top, and I couldn't undo the top and expect the skirt to hang on my hips. It was such a pain to unlace and lace up, too.

Some of the shirts were way too large, and some were sized for what I can only imagine were starving Grey aliens, but there were a couple that fit. I tried on one, and then the other, and then the first again. They looked okay, though the sleeves felt too tight around my biceps on one and the other one bunched up oddly at the front.

I wasn't sure how much of my dissatisfaction lay with the clothes themselves and how much was due to my expectations not matching what I saw in the mirror. It still felt like there was a stranger looking back at me. Did that shirt hang oddly, or was I just not used to the shape of my breasts showing through the clothes?

What I needed was a second opinion. The women working the change room looked a few years older than me. They'd probably have some good advice. I was about to throw back the curtain when I remembered I wasn't wearing any pants. I picked up my dress, then realized I'd have to take the shirt off to wear the dress.

Crap! How was I supposed to do this? Stupid dress. Was it permissible to wander out of the cubicle in your underwear? Even if it was, I bet boys' gonch would be beyond the norm. That was another thing I needed to add to my list: girl undies. If only I had some shorts, or pants ....

I groaned at my own stupidity. I was in a clothing store with entire racks of pants. Shopping was so much easier as a guy. I took the shirt off again and pulled my dress back on. On the good side, I found an easier way to do the back-to-front spin. I pushed the whole dress down, so it didn't cover my breasts while spinning, then pulled it into place after.

I stalked out of the cubicle with the rejected shirts. Then I stalked back in, picked up my purse, and stalked back out again. That was it. I was never leaving the house without pants again.

Out of pure spite, I picked up a pair of the $120 jeans to try on. I also grabbed a couple more of the shirts I liked, but in the right size this time.

The jeans fit perfectly. I twisted and turned in the cubicle trying to get a look at my ass. They felt good, probably looked great too. *Dammit.* I put on my favourite shirt of the bunch and headed out to get some second opinions.

I approached a girl who was organizing a rack of discarded clothing at the entrance to the dressing rooms and tentatively asked what she thought of my outfit. She happily ditched her task and looked me up and down. Her scrutiny was uncomfortable, and I had to quash my first instinct, which was telling me to run and hide.

"The jeans are hot and the top is nice, but a bit short on you. Raise your arms."

I complied and felt cool air on my stomach.

"Yeah. Hold on." She checked the tag at the back of the shirt and tsked. "It's a petite, and you're definitely a regular. Let me go check the racks." She disappeared and came back empty-handed. "Looks like we're sold out of that shirt in regular. I could phone another store and see if they have it in stock."

"That's okay. There are a few more I'm considering. I could use your help, if you don't mind?"

"No problem." She grinned. "This is way more interesting than what I was doing."

I went back to the changeroom and came out wearing my second choice, a fitted light blue T-shirt with a black tattoo-like design of a butterfly on the chest. The girls had multiplied, and there were now two waiting for me.

The new girl frowned as I spun for them. The original girl's nose wrinkled, and she bit her lip. She came closer and whispered, "Um. If you're planning on going braless, this is not the top for you."

I looked in the mirror and grimaced. The darker circles of my nipples were clearly visible under the thin fabric in the dressing room's bright spotlights. I crossed my arms over my chest. "Uh. Yeah. I guess a bra would be a good idea. How does it look otherwise?"

She looked confused. "But … we can't tell if you aren't in the bra you plan on wearing with it. It'll totally change the fit around the chest and neckline."

It took me a moment to parse through what she said, and I still didn't fully understand. I felt lost and alone, but I had to power through this. "Right. Uh. I've got one more shirt to try."

I went back to the changeroom, decided against another shirt I could tell would be nipple-rific, and came back wearing the last shirt. It was a loose, lemon-yellow, cotton, sleeveless blouse. Nice and cool for the hottest part of the summer, which was just around the corner.

Another girl had joined the first two. She was older, and from how the others deferred to her, I guessed she was the manager. She smiled broadly at me and gushed about how beautiful the colour was with my dark hair. I looked at myself in the mirror again. The colour was nice and the shirt fit okay; no parts pulled uncomfortably when I moved. I thanked everyone for their help and changed back into my dress.

When I handed the two rejected shirts to the girl at the counter, she leaned forward and whispered. "Don't get the yellow one. The empire seam is way too high. It cuts across your chest and looks bad. Trust me. No bra could raise your boobs that much. It's just badly made. Come back with your bra and try the butterfly T-shirt again. I think it'll look great. Barb just wants you to buy the more expensive one."

I nodded and handed over the yellow shirt. This whole shopping thing was a field of landmines. I was barely making it through with help from kind strangers. I had been teetering on the edge of a deep sorrow, wondering if I'd ever really fit in as a girl, but her conspiratorial help was a lifeline to solid ground. She didn't offer it because I was a guy, but because other girls needed this kind of help too.

I reluctantly put the jeans on the counter, sad to disappoint her after all her help.

"These looked great on you. I'd kill for your legs."

"I'm thinking about them," I lied. "I'll have to check my budget." I thanked her again for her advice and escaped.

I would have felt worse about giving up the fabulously comfortable and expensive jeans if I hadn't realized they had no damn pockets. They had fake seams that *looked* like pockets. I was beginning to think there was something fundamentally wrong with women's fashion.

CHAPTER 9

Well, I still didn't have a shirt, and now I needed a bra. I headed to a store I'd seen by the food court. As I got within range and smelled food, my stomach rumbled. I fished my phone out of my purse to check the time and saw it was almost noon already.

Crap on a stick! I fired a quick Discord chat message to Sarah:

<< Still running errands right now, but I should still be good for 3.

Then I grabbed a cheap slice of pizza and bolted it down while checking for updates and messages. There was nothing urgent.

My phone pinged.

Sarah >> Thanks. Just let me know if it changes.

To cover my activities on the Michael side of my life, I updated my social media status, making sure location tagging was off, to: "Heading to the pool." That ought to have explained my absence from home in a plausibly deniable way. I locked my phone, stuffed the last half of the crust in my mouth, and disentangled my purse strap from the chair. Now to brave the women's underwear department.

Hustling over to the department store, I wasn't paying attention to my surroundings and almost bumped into a red-haired girl leaving a shoe store.

She was turned away from me, talking on her phone, juggling a purse and a bulky bag. She reflexively avoided me, not even looking up. *Crap!* It was Angela. Random people from school might not recognize me in these clothes, but Angela would. I was sure of that.

I ducked into the nearest store and pretended to browse the cheesy T-shirts with funny memes on them, while covertly watching Angela. She continued walking without looking back. I enjoyed a second of relief until I saw the guy following her. It was the same security guy who'd been talking to Ian's uncle at the Banff Springs Hotel. He sure wasn't mall security, though.

The way he was walking, pausing when she stopped to look at something, and even idling when she went into a store, made it clear who he was focused on. I let them both get well ahead of me and used cover when I could. He never looked back in my direction, and, checking back down the hallway, there didn't appear to be anyone following me either.

I took in the strangeness of his behaviour for a while, until I realized why it seemed so odd. He didn't try to hide at all, but he wasn't acting casual either. He was always shifting to make sure he wasn't in anyone's way, sometimes having to flatten himself against the wall quickly. It seemed, as ridiculous as this was to contemplate, that the other shoppers couldn't see him.

I was able to snap a couple of pics and even take a short video. Just in case. I wasn't sure what I would do if he got too close to Angela. Break my cover? Could I help without her recognizing me? Doubtful. But for her to be in any danger, he would have to follow her somewhere less busy and crowded than this mall, so she was safe for now.

Only when she ran into a group from school did he seem to have had enough. He abruptly turned back in my direction. I turned too and feigned great interest in the … jewellery on display. Fortunately for my heart, this gave me access to several mirrors that I could use to catch glimpses of the guy. He definitely had that cop look. Private security?

He turned into a small service hallway for a second, and then turned and stepped out again. Now, he walked normally through the mall, and the other shoppers treated him like they could see him.

The school crowd was too much for me as well. Several of them knew me well enough to recognize me if they got more than a glance. I waited for the stalker guy to be out of sight, then retreated. The parallel between our behaviours wasn't comforting, but I would have to find some way to bring it up with Angela. It was too creepy.

I stayed hypervigilant all the way through the mall. I really didn't want to run into either of them. For very different reasons. No messages from Sarah yet, but I'd burned over thirty minutes following them. I needed to get back to my original mission.

~*~

Bras proved far more complicated than I could ever have imagined. I'd seen bra sections in department stores, so I knew they were huge, but I had assumed it was more about fashion than utility. It was actually fairly technical. There were two measurements: the infamous letter and the number of inches, which I assumed was chest size of some description. I was pretty sure I was an A, but I had no real idea as to chest size. When I asked one of the saleswomen, hoping for some quick assistance, she insisted on taking me back to the fitting room for a bra sizing.

I stumbled through answers to a flood of questions, like where and when I'd wear the bra, what level of support I needed, as well as under-wires, fabric, colour, and cost. Eventually, we made it through, and I started pulling up my dress with relief when she put the tape away. But she told me to stop.

"Hold on there. I'll be right back with some bras for you to try on."

Holy crap, we still weren't done? She was gone before I could stop her, and then I felt stuck.

After trying on three different bras, she determined I was either an A or B cup, depending on the bra style, which left me confused as to whether I was midway between the two sizes or if bras were just as screwed up as the rest of women's clothing.

I'd been hoping to wear the selected bra out, but she tactfully reminded me it would look odd with my strapless dress. I smiled to cover my embarrassment and thanked her for her help. I was happy to have a proper bra, even if it had taken longer than expected.

I changed in the stall, alone this time. Getting the clasp undone behind my back was a struggle, so I tried pulling my arms out of the straps, which allowed me to spin it around and undo it in front.

With the bra off, I pulled my dress back up and awkwardly adjusted my underwear, which had been tugged down. At least I wouldn't need to also adjust my non-existent penis.

I carefully peered out of the door to the change rooms. No Angela. No creepy security dude. I dashed to the tills, snagging a package of basic white panties on the way by. They were a minor cost compared to the shockingly expensive bra.

I headed toward the nearest washroom after leaving the store. My bladder had woken up midway through the bra sizing and was now screaming at me.

I was paying too much attention to scanning the mall and nearly walked into the men's washroom. I was saved only because I met a guy coming out. He looked more embarrassed than I, and I was blushing hard.

I needed to pay more attention, or else I was going to do something really stupid. A vision of me walking up to the urinal and standing there trying to find the zipper on the front of my dress popped into my head. I held it there long enough to burn it into my memory. May it serve as a warning.

The sad part was, I felt just as embarrassed walking into the women's. It was no different from the men's, except for being busier, particularly since it seemed like half the women had kids with them, and there were no urinals to take quick pit stops at.

The bathroom was even busier when I came out. Pretty much everyone was washing their hands, too, which made the sinks crowded. I would have been relieved to leave if it hadn't meant a return to scanning every face in the mall.

~*~

Shortly past 1 p.m., I made it back to the shirt store and checked my messages again. No updates from Sarah. I strode in with a purpose: to get at least one decent shirt and get out as quickly as I could.

The girl had kept the shirt and ridiculous jeans under the change-room counter. I took them back, along with the shirt I hadn't tried on for nipple reasons. I stripped my dress off and changed into the new panties. They were quite comfortable. Much less bulky at the crotch than guy underwear. Then I hooked my new bra on, pulled on the jeans, and shrugged into the butterfly T-shirt. Looking at myself in the mirror was hard. In these clothes, with my hair brushing my shoulders, I looked like a normal girl. Even the dress hadn't been this disturbing, since I could pretend it was only costuming. Make believe. The girl in the mirror now could be any number of girls from school. She could be me in school, if I dared.

I flinched away from the mirror and went to get the salesgirl's opinion.

~*~

A few shirt changes later, I had confirmed the butterfly shirt and also found an orange one with a stylized fox face across the chest that everyone liked. Thankfully, the manager had stepped out, so the girls were free to give honest feedback. I reluctantly changed back into my corset dress and brought the shirts up to the cashier. I wished I had the money to buy a pair of pants so I didn't have to rush back to my house and change before going to Sarah's.

I was only going to buy one shirt, since the bra had been so expensive, but they were fairly cheap and I liked them both. I decided to splurge.

Having more than one shirt would come in handy. I also found some plain tank tops; perfect for working in the yard.

When I approached the cashier, I realized the manager had come back and was manning a till. She took my tops, rang the foxy one through, and said in an overly excited voice, "Lucky you! There's a two-for-one deal on these."

"That's nice," I said, trying to smile.

She looked at me as if I'd reverted to a five-year-old. "Would you like to pick out another one?"

"What about that one?" I pointed to the butterfly T-shirt.

"No. This one," she held up the first one. "Is from that table over there, part of the two-for-$12 special." She picked up the butterfly shirt and passed the scanner over it. "This one is from that rack over there, part of the fifty-percent-off sale."

"Wouldn't it be easier to put all the shirts on the same sale at the same time?" I asked innocently. She gave me a look I reserved for people who asked me why I didn't just go to the gym instead of climbing on buildings for exercise.

"Never mind." I gathered up my shirts. "I'll be back."

I returned to the pile on the table and noticed the little sign now. It was one for $10 or two for $12. A shirt for two bucks. I was down for that. I looked for one in the same style, so I didn't need to try it on again. I eventually found one in pink, with a pattern of hearts traced out in silver. It was way girly, but good enough.

I returned to the counter with all three shirts.

"Don't you want a second one?" she asked as I separated out the butter-fly T-shirt and pushed it off to the side.

"Nope." I enjoyed wiping the smug look off her face. I held up the two for $12 shirts. "I only wanted two shirts, so I'm done."

Her expression turned sour. "Okay." She tucked the butterfly T-shirt behind the counter. "We also have a two-for-one deal on accessories." She waved to a set of displays holding a bewildering array of necklaces, earrings, and bracelets.

I shuddered. "Oh, hell no." I coughed and adjusted my tone to be more congenial. "Just the shirts, please."

She scanned them while I took enough money out of my purse and wallet to pay, double-checking that I still had enough coin for the bus ride back.

"Would you like to sign up for our customer loyalty card?" Her too-cheery voice broke my concentration.

"No," I said flatly. Receiving adverts from teen girls' clothing stores at my house would not be a happy thing.

She carried on unaffected. "E-mail address?"

"Why?"

"So we can let you know about sales and send you promotional gift cards."

"Oh, sure." I gave her my new 'Kayla' address. I wasn't sure why. I didn't plan to spend any more time than I had to presenting as a girl, and even the limited clothes I'd bought so far would be an unexploded bomb as long as I lived with my parents.

After that last hurdle, I was finally able to hand over my money, get a receipt, and escape.

~*~

I left the mall a lot closer to 3 p.m. than I'd wanted, exhausted and bewildered. Mostly from navigating the shopping, but my side-trip following Angela's stalker hadn't helped. I messaged Sarah that I was on my way, and got a terse 'ok' back from her. For my pains, I had a pair of shoes, three pairs of panties, a bra, and two shirts.

I spent twice as much as I intended, but I'd also bought twice as much. I hoped it was simply due to my inexperience and not a problem endemic to clothes shopping as a girl, but I had a sinking feeling my clothing costs would skyrocket if I planned on spending more time as a girl in public. Particularly because I wouldn't be able to hit up Mom and Dad to buy any of it for me. A hysterical laugh threatened to bubble up at the idea of asking my dad for money for a new bra.

CHAPTER 10

Reviewing the pictures and short video I'd taken on my phone, I grew increasingly unsure of myself. I wondered how Angela would react if I showed them to her.

Even the videos didn't seem to capture the creepy feeling I had had while watching the guy follow her through the mall, and the way people seemed to ignore him. It felt really strange at the time, but maybe he'd just been playing around? Why would people move if he were already out of their way? Besides, everyone was ready and willing to avoid eye contact with anyone acting strangely in public.

Had I wanted to see Angela so bad, even in this shape, that I'd subconsciously tried to invent an excuse?

That. Was. Creepy.

I could only imagine Angela's glare as I laid out my pitiful story about invisible men following her. 'I told you I needed space, Mike,' she'd say. 'What's with this bullshit?'

I sighed. The bus was nearing my stop on 17th Avenue. I needed to clear my head to go help Sarah.

My phone pinged.

Sarah >> He's here.

I hammered out a quick response.

<< Almost there!

Holy crap. I rushed off the bus as soon as the doors opened and jogged all the way home, grateful for my new shoes and underwear, even if it did feel uncomfortably like my butt was bare to the world.

At home, I hurriedly stripped off the corset dress and shoved it to the bottom of my drawer, dumping the purse on top. I would have to pack it all back into Mom's closet tomorrow.

My old jeans were right there. They had some worn patches, but I had really stopped wearing them because they showed off the shape of my hips in girl form. That was a bonus today. No one was going to mistake me for Michael.

I hooked up the bra with minimal fumbling, using the handy back-to-front method again, and slipped on the orange fox shirt. I stuffed the pink one and the rest of my purchases in my bottom drawer, bags and all. I could get rid of those tomorrow, too. I was getting increasingly nervous about keeping all this girly stuff in the house.

Halfway downstairs, I realized my wallet and everything else were still in the purse and had to run back up. I grabbed the whole purse, figuring I could transfer stuff to my pockets later.

With great relief, I saw the contractor's van was still parked outside Sarah's place as I ran up, purse clutched to my side and my new shoes slapping on the sidewalk. Runners, they were not.

My panic fully abated when I saw Sarah standing calmly in her front doorway, talking with an older South Asian guy. She smiled when I ran up, puffing.

"Sorry!" I said, with my remaining breath.

"It's okay. Mr. Khawaja and I were just done discussing the porch. Could you take him around to see the garden?"

"There's a garden?" I asked. The weed-choked state of the front yard hadn't given me hope that the back had been cared for.

"Ah, I think you'd call it the back yard." Sarah smiled, pronouncing the word distinctly.

"Oh, yeah. That makes sense."

I led the contractor around the side of the house. The shaded area between the houses was gravelled, so it was less overgrown than the front. There likely should have been a gate where the wood fence started, but there was just a gap. The neighbour must have replaced their fence at some point, because it was in fairly good condition. Unlike the rear fence that backed on the alleyway, which was half-fallen down. Some posts leaned at an angle.

The backyard had been left to run wild. Now that we were near the height of summer, some patches were thick and overgrown while others were bare dirt. An overgrown tree dominated one side of the yard. Bushes grew in a couple of spots in the middle of the lawn. We found out that one tall patch of grass concealed an old, rusted engine block when I nearly tripped over it.

I heard noise from the house and turned to see Sarah open the back door and step out onto the small concrete pad. The ground level was higher at the back.

"That looks bloody terrible, all right," she said, looking around the yard. "Can you check out the gar'ge too?"

We forged through the lawn to the man door at the side of the detached garage. The overhead door faced the back alley. Other than needing paint, the structure seemed solid, though when we opened it up, we found it stuffed with old furniture and car parts.

Mr. Khawaja looked very pleased with the amount of work this was likely to take, and was even more pleased when Sarah promptly signed the initial estimate, conveyed back and forth to her post at the door by me, and provided the initial deposit in cash.

~*~

"Thank you for your help today," Sarah said, as we sat for what had become our customary cuppa. Strong tea again this time. With sugar. Which wasn't my norm, but I'd had a hard day, and I was craving sweet.

"I'm so sorry I was late," I said sincerely. I felt terrible. She'd been counting on me, and it could have been a huge issue. I wanted to tell her all about Angela and the creepy invisible security guy, but I couldn't think of any way that it didn't sound completely nuts, so I settled for over-simplification. "My friend Angela needed my help."

"It's okay." She sat on the other section of the couch, her knees drawn up in front of her. She cradled her tea in her hands as if to absorb its warmth, but hadn't even sipped it yet. She continued after a pause. "I'm realizing that there are things I'm going to need to do, and I'm not sure I'm ..." She looked as if she considered and discarded a few words before settling. "... well enough to do them right now." She looked directly at me for the first time in this conversation. "What would you say to helping me out, on a paid basis?"

"Ah ... I'd say I'm not even remotely trained to be a ..." I paused. "What exactly would you want me to do?"

"Just ... be here, like tonight, when I need someone." She took a deep breath and let it out slowly. "I'm being very careful not to push myself over into a panic attack. Having someone I can lean on, as needed, will help me expand my comfort zone without relapsing."

"I think I could do that, but ... you know, I have that parkour camp position lined up this summer, and I won't always be free."

"That's all right," she said, smiling. "I can work around your schedule. I'll put off anything challenging until you're free."

That sounded a little dubious to me, but I wasn't going to disagree with her. I could really use an extra side gig, and Sarah needed the help. It would mean inventing an entire girl identity, but as a part-time thing. It could work. Maybe?

"What kind of pay are you thinking?" I tried to look confident, and not like someone who'd barely managed the logistics involved in buying a shirt at the mall.

"That's the rub, isn't it?" she said, looking up at the ceiling. "How about twenty US dollars an hour? With a two-hour minimum any time I call on you?"

"US dollars?" That seemed odd.

"I have some US money hanging around, and I've had trouble getting to the bank. I can pass it on to you." She grinned.

I smiled back. It was hard to resist her cheer, even when I knew I shouldn't let it distract me. "That seems okay. How do we keep track of hours?" I racked my brain trying to think of loopholes. She hadn't made any mention of a SIN or contracts. Under the table was very all right with me, though.

"How about you keep track and submit a timesheet to me at the end of each week. It'll be good career practice for you." She grinned again, with a sharper edge.

"I'll go for that," I said.

"Please include all your time today on it and ..." She hesitated briefly, "If I can have some more of your time, could we take a short walk around the neighbourhood?"

After an initial spike of fear, which must have shown as hesitation because Sarah's expression shifted toward disappointment, I realized it was unlikely anyone would connect Mike-me with Kayla-me, especially if I was out with Sarah, someone unconnected with my 'Mike' life.

"Sure!" I said, and Sarah looked energized again. She was ready quickly, putting on a pair of white-and-pink running shoes, sunglasses, and a droopy-brimmed white hat. To my relief, I noticed at least two other hats in the closet. One of them was a pink woven hat with a stiffer brim, which Sarah was happy to lend me. That would one hundred percent complete my disguise.

"Anywhere you'd like to go?" I asked as we set out, though I fully intended to lead her away from my house and school.

"Not really. I might have some trouble with the busier streets, but I'd like to try them out."

That worked for me. I led her through the residential streets to the commercial strip of 17th Avenue. There was a cross street every block leading back to quieter streets, so we always had an easy out if she needed it.

She seemed fine as we strolled. She did some window shopping, but went inside one small store to pick up some scented soaps. There, Sarah had a lively, meandering conversation with the woman at the till in French. I only understood the edges of what they said. It sounded like they were talking about some towns in France where the owner had lived. I smiled and nodded a few times to be sociable and was able to say "merci" and "au revoir."

There was only one issue: when a woman screamed.

Sarah whipped around so hard that the little plastic bag of soaps hit my arm and then dropped into a crouch. I turned too. Some guy had grabbed a girl from behind. Her initial scream shifted to laughter as he loosely draped his arms over her shoulders. She tilted her head back and to the side, going up on her tiptoes for a kiss.

Sarah reached her hand back toward me, eyes still focused on the couple who were walking off together with no sign of coercion. I took her hand and she squeezed mine. Hard. I winced, but didn't pull away.

"Let's get back," she said, keeping hold of my hand while I headed to her house, cutting down the nearest cross street. Her grip relaxed slightly once we were off 17th Avenue, but she kept hold of my hand.

My phone pinged when we were halfway back. I fished it out of my right pocket with my left hand, so as not to disturb Sarah's grip.

Chills went down my back when I saw the time. It was well after five. My parents would be home soon. I really didn't want to have to change in the garage again, and I needed to replace Mom's necklace before she noticed it was gone.

Then I read the text.

Mom >> At Superstore. Please check TP and paper towel.

I breathed a large sigh of relief. I texted left-handed.

<< Ok. Riding. Check in 10 mins?

Mom responded quickly

Mom >> Sure ♡

I had probably an hour until they got home. My whole body relaxed.

"Are you all right?" Sarah asked. "Did I scare you back there?"

"No, it's fine," I said. "I just realized I need to get home soon, but it's not super urgent."

"Oh, good," she said, giving my hand a gentle squeeze. "You're a massive comfort, you know."

By the time we reached her door, she was nearly back to her usual self. I returned her hat and said goodbye without going inside.

"I'll ping you on Discord to schedule some time," Sarah said. "Having you with me when the builders start clearing up the yard and re-building the porch would be helpful. And don't forget to write down your hours."

"I won't!" I said, stepping down the ramp.

Calgary summer afternoons were bright and warm, and today was no exception. As usual, the height of the sun belied how late it really was. I walked home, enjoying the feel of the wind toying with my hair. It was the first time I could remember being out in public in girl form without feeling like a complete imposter since I was eight. A good pain rushed through my chest, like that first careful stretch of a healing muscle.

"What's wrong with being a girl, anyway?" I grumbled to myself.

The world was set up to be explicitly gendered: Pick a colour, pick a side, pick a bathroom!

What if, by nature, you were both? Or neither? Where could you fit in?

That I didn't actually hate this body came to me in a rush. I'd been hating how hard it was to be female, while still being expected to live in the male box. I had mixed that up with hating my switches for so many years, but I was starting to let go.

What I really hated was the idea that everyone would look at me differently, treat me differently, because I'd changed a few bits of flesh. That was not a problem I could fix on my own. People like Aaron, Jenn, and so many others were working on it, but the people who ran things just wanted us to disappear.

Or die. Whichever came first.

I sighed and scrubbed the wetness off my cheeks as my house came into view. Surely not everyone would treat me so differently, or report me to the cops, but the hell was that I couldn't know who would be cool with it and who would freak. And it would only take one loose-lipped person to force my entire family to lose everything, again, and have to restart somewhere else.

The only other solution I could think of was to get away. Set up by myself somewhere else where no one knew me, and no one could trace me back to my parents. Then, whatever happened, they would be safe.

I had been hoping I could hold out until I finished grade 12 and graduated, but I wasn't sure I could wait that long.

CHAPTER 11

There was a big crowd at the Glenmore Athletic Park on Saturday morning. At 9 a.m., the slight chill that was common after a clear night, even at the tail end of June, was being swiftly replaced by what promised to be a clear, hot summer day.

It was a beautiful location. Nestled alongside a cluster of public parks and golf courses that edged the Elbow River at the foot of the Glenmore reservoir, it was an easy sell to get families out for a morning of demos and summer program signups, followed by some biking, boating, or picnicking. Our parkour club was one small fish in the collection. With what seemed like every program in the city set up here, followed by the food trucks and local artists, it had turned into a small fair.

This was good news for Devon and his programs, but I would have been a lot happier with a lower turnout. As we hauled out the mats and arranged the equipment, I kept hoping I'd feel the telltale internal shifts that indicated a switch back to male. They never came.

It wasn't like I had to be in male shape to do parkour, though I had to admit those extra little bits of height and arm length did help. Mostly, I was just uncomfortable being the focus of any attention in female shape, and here I was about to go on display for everyone.

I lagged behind for as long as I could while the rest of the group started running through exercises. When I saw Devon's eyes on me and his questioning frown, I knew I couldn't stall any longer and threw myself into the melee.

Warmup went well, but it was only some hurdles and tumbling. I needed to show far more action to stay at the top of Devon's hiring list. I decided to show off on the hurdles with a handstand, but once I was up, holding the handstand, I felt my shirt falling to expose my stomach and possibly my chest. I freaked out, lost my balance, and fell off the beam.

I hit hard, mostly on the mat. The blow to my confidence was far worse than the physical shock. I rolled and tried to get back in quickly, hoping no one had noticed. I hit the vertical pegboard. That was generally a good way to show that I was as good as anybody on the crew, even guys several years older than me.

In my rush to make up for the botched handstand, I forgot to compensate for the slightly shorter reach I had in female form. Or maybe my loss of focus would have had the same result in male form. I would never know for sure.

Normally, I hit the eighth hole solid. This time I missed it by a hair. The jolt caused me to lose my grip. I dropped, had a bare moment of weightlessness to contemplate my mistake, then hit the mat. My left foot hit an edge between two mats that wouldn't have been there in our usual practice space and folded sideways. I dove into a roll, but not quite quickly enough. I could tell I'd done some damage.

The worst thing I could do would be to put pressure on my ankle before knowing how badly it was hurt. I forced myself to sit still, ignoring my adrenaline, which screamed at me to run, or at least crawl away. Devon was already jogging over.

"That's right Mike, take it easy." From the relief in Devon's voice, he'd obviously expected me to jump up and tough it out. He gently prodded my ankle, which was already starting to swell. I hissed as he wrapped a Quick-Ice around it.

He helped me hobble to the staging area where we'd left our bags and miscellaneous gear. I tried not to cringe away from his arm, way too close to bumping up against my taped boob.

"Keep this on for a while and don't put too much weight on it for a couple of days. If you're still in pain at that point, get to your doctor or a medical clinic." He patted my shoulder, and I knew what was coming. "I'm sure you know to avoid any training for a couple of weeks. It's too easy to reinjure a joint and end up with a chronic problem."

"I know," I choked out. It wasn't only the ankle. Even with my sucky showing today, I might still have swung a paid position based on past performance, but both of us knew that the summer schedule started next week. There was no way he could justify hiring someone with an injury, for my own sake, or for the program's.

I sat, resolutely facing away from the demonstration. I should've been a good sport and cheered on my fellow club members. I knew turning away like this looked petty, but I couldn't stand to watch.

I was positioning the Quick-Ice for another round of cooling when Ravi came over, wiping sweat off his forehead and the back of his neck with a towel.

"This blows, man." He dropped down on the grass and took a long pull from his water bottle. "You barely got into your set."

"Yup," I said gruffly, both to help disguise my female voice and because I was doing my very best to hold back tears. I'd had plenty of time to catalogue the list of bad decisions that led to this point. Right back to where I was thinking it would have been better to have skipped the demo entirely. Perhaps I should've tried convincing Devon to let me do a private demo at the club when I was back in male shape.

Or, maybe I'd been fooling myself that I could hold down an actual, scheduled job.

"Want a ride home?" Ravi asked. "I can help you to my car."

"No. I'll wait for my dad."

I so desperately wanted to ride home with Ravi, but I would have to get way too up close and personal—he'd have to support me so as to not put any weight on my bad ankle. It was too risky in girl shape.

Ravi shrugged. He sat with me, chatting randomly about video game stuff until my dad came. That almost made me cry again. He was a good friend.

~*~

From the minute I saw Dad's face, I knew I was in trouble. The only question was which failure I was about to get hammered for. The slow trip home in our creaky old car was agonizing in its heavy silence.

Dad glanced over at me.

"Can I assume you won't be getting that summer job?" he half asked, half stated.

"Yeah. That's toast," I said bitterly, anticipating some angry responses. "With my ankle messed up, Devon has to offer the job to someone else."

"That sucks," Dad said. "You were really counting on that job." Then, a few seconds later, he added, "Is there a backup plan?"

"Uh …" There wasn't one, but Dad was going to hate that. Then, I remembered Sarah and her offer. "I have a temp job I've been setting up.

I don't know how many hours I can get, but the pay is okay. Maybe I can ask for some more hours."

I didn't think Sarah would need me for enough hours to matter, but it was something to tell Dad to keep him from freaking.

"That's good." Then, just as I relaxed a little, he said. "Your mom's been noticing some things."

"Things?" My heart was pounding, echoed by little shocks of pain from my ankle at each beat.

"Your voice. The way your hair's been changing lengths. The way you've been avoiding us." He said softly. "You do a pretty good job of disguising it, but we can tell."

Despair flooded my body. I'd been hoping I could skate through this. Like I'd hoped that I could get through the parkour demo. Of course not.

"Yeah," I admitted. My throat as dry as dust. "It happens. Sometimes."

"Happening kind of often, lately."

I tried to sink lower in my seat. *For fuck's sake.* What else had she noticed? Had they found my clothing stash? How dead was I?

The car went over a bump, jolting on its worn-out shocks. I gasped as it jostled my ankle.

"Oh, I'm sorry!" Dad slowed the car further, even though there were already people angrily passing us. "That one snuck up on me."

"Yeah, I know what that's like," I said, deadpan.

"Hmm?" He replied, momentarily distracted, navigating the least-bumpy route around a pothole.

"Nothing."

We rode in silence for the rest of the trip. It wasn't a terrible silence. Dad wasn't like that. He might get angry sometimes, but he never stayed angry. Not like Mom.

When we arrived home, he helped me into the house and let me sit in his recliner while Mom placed a bag of frozen corn wrapped in a towel on my ankle. It would have been awesome, except for the disappointment I saw in their eyes and the unspoken words behind their silence. What could any of us do?

Mom brought me a grilled cheese sandwich and a glass of milk. Comfort food. It was sweet, but you could have cut the tension with a knife. I could tell they were holding it all in.

Until when? I could only guess. Would they give me a full day to recover, or start in on me as soon as I finished lunch?

Shortly after Dad took my dishes away, Mom approached with her laptop in hand. Dad followed close behind as soon as he was done in the kitchen. They both looked very serious.

I guess 'as soon as I finished lunch' was the answer. The cheese lay heavy in my belly, and now I wished I'd eaten more slowly. Anxiety roiled in my gut. I'd been out in feminine clothes. Had someone taken a video? Had they posted it somewhere? I broke out in a cold sweat.

Mom opened the laptop and set it in my lap. Instead of Instagram or YouTube, I saw the school's website. Mom pointed an accusing finger at a specific mark.

A B- in English. That's what the stern faces were about? I laughed, high-pitched, in a mix of relief and stunned disbelief at the mark. If my parents hadn't already known I was in girl form, I would have given it away with that laugh.

"How?" I asked. I'd forgotten that grades would be released this week. It hadn't been on my list of things to worry about. A- in Chemistry. That was expected, as was the A in Social Studies, but the B- in English Language Arts floored me.

"That's what we'd like to know," Mom said, arms crossed.

I tried to think back to my exam. It was the first one out of the gate after classes ended. That whole week was a blur. Only the Ian/Angela conversation I'd overheard and my first return to Sarah's house really stood out. I always did well in English classes, but Mr. James had been tough this year, always ready to pounce on the smallest issue.

"They didn't offer any breakdown of exam marks versus course marks?" I asked. I scanned the screen quickly, hoping to answer my own question. "Ah, in the fine print here, it says we can call the school to set up an appointment to discuss," I offered in a hopeful tone.

We all understood why top grades were important. Scholarships were my only hope of attending university, and I was going to need to start applying soon. I couldn't tell them that university was an unattainable dream for me. With my constant switches, I didn't think I was going to make it through grade 12.

"That sounds like a good idea," Dad rumbled. Satisfied that I would deal with it, for now, he went back to preparing to mow the lawn. Mom stayed standing beside the table, looking down at me. Ignoring her earlier canning bubbling on the stove.

"Why now?" she asked.

I knew she wasn't talking about grades.

She didn't wait for an answer before continuing, "Could it have anything to do with that handsome boy who came to the door looking for you that day that you came home, switched to girl?"

"Mom!" I objected. "Why didn't you tell me Ian came by?" Inside, I wailed, '*Why didn't you tell me you noticed my switch?*'

"You know it's perfectly okay to have a boyfriend, as a boy," she continued, almost smugly. I heard Dad coughing at the back door.

"Mom! I know." I curled forward in the recliner and handed her the bag of corn from my ankle. I wanted to leap up and storm out, but I had to force myself to move carefully. "It's not about Ian." *Really?* My inner voice supplied. "I don't know, okay? It just happens sometimes." *All the time.* "If I could fix it, I would." *Would I?* "But I can't." I pushed the footrest down with my legs. It jarred my ankle a little, but the ice had helped bring the pain down.

"Dad!" I called. "Can you help me to the garden? I'll do some weeding." My most-hated chore, but anything was better than talking to my mom right now.

Dad supported me all the way to the back door, where he plopped a sun hat on my head, then helped me to the edge of the garden plot that took up nearly half the backyard. He brought the tools over and left me to work out my frustrations.

Hacking at weeds lessened some of my angst, but working in the summer heat with a sweatshirt on was slowly roasting me. I caught Dad's looks by accident a couple of times as I wiped the sweat from my forehead. Each time, he decided not to say anything.

It was silly to keep up my disguise since everyone in the house knew I was in girl form, but I had already loosened my tight binding. I couldn't make myself work out here in just a T-shirt in front of my dad like that. What if my bindings fell off?

I would be happier to go upstairs and put a bra on, as well as one of the lighter-weight girl shirts, but my parents would flip out if they thought I was actually dressing as a girl in public.

I tried to focus on weeding and exclude everything else—summer jobs, school grades, and Ian. Especially Ian. It worked for a while. I was able to access a zen-like state of calmness, my thoughts focused on nothing but distinguishing weed from non-weed as I worked my way down the rows on hands and knees. The throbbing of my ankle ceased to be a distraction, but rather a kind of meditative focus in its own right.

The absence of pain was the first thing I noticed when I switched back. Then I noticed the other physical changes. Finally, I felt that deep-down sense of calm that meant I was going to be in this form for at least a day, if not more.

I rose up into a kneeling position and bent backwards to stretch my back, a big relief. Then, I carefully took my sweatshirt off for an even bigger relief. The coolness of the wind drying the sweat-soaked back of my shirt was nice. I wanted to take it off, too, but I didn't want to reveal my binding.

Eventually, I finished weeding all of the garden I could reach without putting stress on my ankle. Dad helped me inside again for another round of icing, though my ankle didn't really need it now.

I thought about telling my parents how, sometimes, injuries I had in one shape didn't transfer to the other. It was frustratingly inconsistent, as was everything to do with my switches. Sometimes a cut would disappear, only to reappear later with the next switch. Sometimes it would stay gone. But, bringing any of that up could lead to a discussion about how often I was actually switching. Continuing to treat my now-significantly-less-sprained ankle wouldn't hurt, and might help.

My phone dinged.

Ravi >> Don't hate me

I stared at his message, newly alarmed. What now?

<< Um …

I waited.

<< Okay. I won't hate you

His response arrived quickly.

Ravi >> Devon offered me one of the parkour camp spots … And I took it *ducks and runs*

I sighed. That was a perfect cap on the day, but I couldn't complain. I'd put myself out of the running. I answered honestly.

<< It's okay. It sucks, but I'd rather you get that slot than anybody else

<< Wait. Don't you already have a job?

Ravi >> Sort of. This is me. Striking out for independence.

<< Rock on, man!

Ravi >> Thanks, Mike. I knew you'd understand.

We exchanged a few more messages, discussing his dad's probable reaction to Ravi taking another job, and my, only mostly in jest, offering him a place to crash. He sent me a couple of jobs he knew of that were still hiring at decent pay. They were both short-term gigs, but I was open to anything at the moment.

I locked my phone and put it face down in my lap. Yeah. I was very understanding. Angela had been swept off by Ian. Neither of them needed me around anymore. Ravi got the sweet summer job I'd been working toward for months. And I was a screwup who couldn't manage to stay in one sex.

My parents must've seen how depressed I was. After supper, Dad brought out some of our old favourite movies. They reminded me of the first couple of years after we'd moved to Canada. We had family movie night every weekend. A lot was hard during those years. Mom and Dad were stressed from their new jobs. I was stressed from navigating new friends, a new school, and a new gender. However, there were also so many happy memories laced through like veins of shining gold through dull rock.

I went up to bed after the movie, accepting help from Dad out of an abundance of caution, but it was a long time before I fell asleep.

Even if my ankle stayed healed, it wouldn't help with the parkour job. There was no way Devon would believe I'd healed up enough to work in just a few days, regardless of the state of my body. Even when my switches were helpful, I still got screwed over by being different.

Without the steady money from the summer parks program, I wouldn't have enough in my getaway fund. Messing up my grades would make it harder to convince my parents I could look after myself. I felt trapped again, doomed to uproot my whole family if I couldn't pull my life together.

CHAPTER 12

I woke up on Tuesday with my next switch feeling very close. I was still in guy form, but I could tell I wouldn't be for long. Catching a look at myself in the bathroom mirror while starting the shower, I was surprised to see a male shape. My mind already expected something more feminine. A major sign that I was in the last few hours.

Checking my phone over breakfast, I peeked at Sarah's Discord as usual, and there was a message from her. Nervous excitement butterflied through me as I opened it.

She wanted me to come by today! That would be tough. I had a long list of chores, and I wasn't sure exactly when I would switch. Then, I read that she most critically wanted my time tomorrow and tried to calm my heart rate.

I replied that today wasn't good, but that I could be there early tomorrow. That would be much easier. I expected to be female-shaped for most of the day tomorrow if I switched today. I could normally count on at least twenty-four hours in one shape before my body moved on.

I posted about not getting the parkour day camp job, mainly to stop awkward questions from anyone who wasn't in the loop. In the same post, I added that I would be working at a summer camp just outside the city some days, when they needed help. That was the excuse I'd given my parents, which would hopefully cover the days I was at Sarah's.

I hadn't heard back from any of my job applications. I hadn't heard back from the school about the meeting to discuss my English mark. Angela hadn't contacted me. I was stuck in limbo, specifically in the sense that this felt like the gateway to hell.

I threw myself into house chores, mostly as a distraction from my worries. I thoroughly cleaned the bathroom, vacuumed the whole house, and cleaned my room. I made sure the kitchen was tidied, but I left the deep clean for Mom because she hated it when I moved things. Said I never got them back in quite the right spots.

By the time I finished my chores, I had switched. More or less. I was mostly feminine, but my crotch remained more or less male-shaped. Emphasis on the less. I could work with that. It wasn't like I was going to be trying to have sex with anyone in the near term. Or possibly long term. I sighed.

At least my ankle felt better with the switch and not worse again. I wiggled it and tested it with some deep stretches. It had still been a little tender while I was doing chores, but it felt fully healed now. Yay me.

Surveying our small but hyper-organized kitchen, I wondered what kind of relationship I would have had with my parents if I'd kept trying to make a go at being a girl when we arrived here. Would I be closer to my mom? Personality-wise, I was more like my dad, but maybe Mom and I would have had more shared interests. Maybe I would be helping her with the canning, instead of helping Dad keep our car running. Probably not. I liked working on the car, no matter what form I was in.

I shook myself out of daydreaming. Thinking about Mom reminded me that she'd wanted the meat taken out of the freezer for dinner. I hurried to do that before I forgot again.

With my house chores done, I could focus on my own work. I cut the legs off the old jeans I wore on my last Sarah visit, rolled them up to make a cuff like I'd seen on the billboard, and tacked them up with some clumsy stitches. Hopefully, they would hold up well enough for a while.

With some time left in the afternoon, but not quite enough time to be worth going to Sarah's and back before I'd need to be home and male-presenting, I decided to test out an idea I'd had about a safer, or at least more anonymous, place to swap my gender presentation. I bound and dressed in guy clothes, put my girl clothes in a backpack, and jogged down to a local coffee shop, named rather plainly 'Bistro.' It would've been great if I could avoid coming in and out of my own house in girl clothes. A neighbour was bound to notice at some point and mention something off-hand to my parents.

Jogging was painfully slow compared to biking, but I obviously couldn't use my regular bike, my pride and joy, with the decals and custom gear I'd tricked it out with this past spring. I pondered picking up a cheap second-hand bike, but then, where would I store it? I resigned myself to getting even more exercise this summer.

It wasn't just that this coffee shop was close—there was another reason it stood out as the best choice. The men's and women's bathroom doors were conveniently located next to each other at the end of a short hallway, so it would be easy to slip out unremarked. Even better, it had old-school stalls in a shared room rather than single-user rooms, giving some plausible deniability that the boy who came out was a different person from the girl who'd gone in, even if either he or she were entering/leaving the 'wrong' bathroom. If anyone was paying that close of attention, which I devoutly hoped they were not!

I picked the smallest stall and did a complete clothes change, right down to skin, which was refreshing after my jog. I dressed in my new girl clothes, bra included.

The bra and shirt didn't fit like I remembered at the mall. My breasts were about the same size, but my chest was a little larger, closer to my male shape. The bra was tight, even on the last set of hooks of the strap. Thankfully, I was still able to hook it properly. I didn't want to have to buy even more clothes, especially not a bra!

During a real swap, I'd have to wait for the bathroom to be empty, or at least until no one was outside of a stall, and dash for the exit. I peered through the crack in the door and listened, heart hammering, as if I was actually going to do it.

And what if I did?

I stood shocked at my thought. It was one thing to dress up like this for Sarah, but the strength of the urge I felt to walk out into the coffee shop scared me. I hurriedly stripped off all the women's clothing and replaced them with my safe, familiar guy's clothes and binding.

My phone's message notification tone echoed unnaturally loudly as I stood naked from the waist down. I just about crapped myself. I'd left it on the toilet paper dispenser while changing pants.

As I went to check it, I thought I heard a thud from out in the main area of the washroom, which was weird, as I hadn't heard or seen anyone come in.

I glanced at the screen, hoping for Angela, or even Ian, but it was just my mom asking if I'd taken the ground beef out of the freezer yet. I made a quick reply, saying yes, then hurried to get my underwear and pants on and return all the girl clothes to my backpack.

When my phone went off again, I picked it up casually, thinking it was still my mom. I just about fumbled it when I saw it was Angela.

Angela >> Sorry to hear about the parkour 🙁 I hope your ankle is feeling better!

I thought about what to reply while I finished packing my clothes.

Back in the coffee shop, I ordered one of their cheapest coffees and sat in a quiet-ish corner. With a lot of emotions bundled up in my belly, I took out my phone and texted Angela.

<< Thanks. Ankle isn't too bad. How are you? Any lingering effects from the wedding?

I stared at it for a while, but I couldn't think of a better way to phrase it. I worried that in the worst case, a police officer or some unfriendly psychiatrist might be able to read her messages. I wished again that I had interrupted her chat with Ian that day at school. If we were in-person, maybe I could gently introduce the idea that I'd accidentally overheard, but not like this. I pressed send with jitters in my stomach.

She replied quickly.

Angela >> I'm OK. Still on plan A. Thanks for being there for me. I know you always will be.

Then she sent a bunch of texts, as quickly as she could type, it looked like:

Angela >> Remember when we used to go horseback riding in the summers?

Angela >> Wish I could go back there. Even Friday. But I have plans.

Angela >> Remember how we used to stay in touch, if we got separated?

Angela >> Remember it was 24, not 23. You got it wrong one day, and then I was just calling and calling.

I stared at the texts, chills chasing up and down my spine. This Friday was the after-grad party. Angela was in some kind of trouble. I knew it. She wouldn't be calling out like this if everything were fine. And it had to be related to Ian and his family. That security guy who had been tailing Ange at the mall. Maybe even as far back as whatever she'd run into at the wedding.

I managed to answer shortly after her last text arrived.

<< I won't make that mistake again. I'd like to go riding, or whatever, with you on Friday. Sounds more fun than your other thing.

Angela >> Yeah. No doubt. Can't be helped. I know you're a good fiend, but this is something I have to do myself.

I clocked the misspelling of 'friend' in the text she'd just sent me. It was an old joke between us. We'd spent most of—what was it, grade 5 maybe—calling each other 'best fiends.' And her other reference to the

CB radio channels. It had been channels 3 and 4 when I got lost that time. Her message was loud and clear to me, though.

She was going to be out in the Waiparous area on Friday night, where we used to go riding together. She couldn't say exactly where, but she would be on CB channel 24 with added info.

I got another coffee and nursed it for a while, hoping she might text again. I resisted texting her back. I was certain it wouldn't do anything but annoy her, as well as increase the risk to both of us.

While waiting, I glanced around and realized Donny was there. He was sitting alone, across the room at a table with a laptop. He was facing his screen, not looking at me, but something about seeing him here made my skin itch.

Maybe it was just seeing someone from school? Another reason I'd picked this little place was because it wasn't a popular hangout with the high school crowd, especially over the summer. It was in the heart of the Gay Village, and most of the customers either lived or worked nearby.

Maybe it was because he hadn't been sitting there when I came in?

I left eventually, avoiding looking in his direction. If he'd really seen something the day I switched in the locker room, surely, he would have spread it around before this. Stalking me didn't make sense, so I was almost certainly being over-anxious.

Almost certainly.

~*~

I was still solidly female-shaped on Wednesday, the day I'd set aside for Sarah. I told my parents that I was catching a charter bus to the summer camp out of town and left the house in the early morning before they got up to get ready for work, so they couldn't see my shape or ask any awkward questions.

Bistro had great early and late hours, and it was always busy with the morning coffee crowd during the week, so changing was suitably anonymous. The bathroom was busier, but people were focused on getting in and out and didn't comment on my appearance.

When I arrived at Sarah's house, markers had already been laid out for the porch, and two guys were hauling junk out of the backyard and garage. They were both bare-chested and nicely tanned, one browner by nature. It wasn't hot yet—Calgary had notoriously cool mornings even during the summer—but they were glistening with sweat already.

I was not glistening, I was just sweaty from my jog. Having to keep both my bra and shirt on would make working outside later suck, but not quite so bad as the heavy shirts I had to wear when pretending to be a guy. At least the cut-offs I'd made kept my legs cool.

"Hey guys," I called out as I came out from between the houses. They were struggling to lift the old engine block out of the grass. "Oh, let me give you a hand." I set my backpack down and jogged over, slipping on my work gloves. They seemed taken aback. I made a mental note to introduce myself properly once we got this moved. They probably thought I was some random neighbour.

I squatted and shoved my hands under the block, finding a firm grip. "Okay, on three?" I remembered to keep my voice light and high, since I was actually presenting female.

I looked them in the eyes, trying not to feel too self-conscious. They nodded, still looking stunned. "Right. One…Two…Threeeee!"

With all three of us pulling, we ripped the engine block off the ground and carried it over to the pickup truck parked in the back alley that they were filling. Thankfully, it proved easier to carry than to lift, and we half-tossed it into the truck bed. The mass of broken roots trailing from the now-exposed bottom of the engine gave a clue as to why it had seemed stuck to the ground.

I dusted off my gloves and the front of my shirt. Part of the engine had dug into my right arm, leaving a red welt and some small scratches.

"Uh, who are you?" one of the guys asked.

"Sorry." I pulled off my glove, offered a hand, and opened my mouth to say Michael. I managed not to voice the 'M', but it was close. "Kayla," I finally blurted out, my face heating. "I'm with the house." I jerked a thumb over my shoulder.

"Ah. That makes more sense." The lighter-skinned guy grinned and clasped my hand in a firm shake. "I'm Alex, and this is Ramiro." The darker-skinned guy smiled broadly and gave me a much looser shake. I was sure he'd try to test my grip, so I squeezed harder than intended. His smile dimmed. Oops.

"I wanted to ask if you thought you'd get to the lawn today?" I gestured to the scraggly wasteland of grass and weeds the size of small trees choking more than half the backyard. It completely hid the bottom half of the old fence.

"Yeah. I think so," Ramiro replied. "That cocksucker …" He gave me a quick, embarrassed glance. I resisted rolling my eyes. "Uh, that engine was the last big piece. We're going to fire up the trimmers and hack that jungle down before trying to pick up the small stuff."

"Awesome. Let me know when you're done. I want to take a closer look at the fence. From the way it's leaning, I'm worried most of the posts are rotten."

"Sure." Ramiro shrugged. "We'll be done by this afternoon, anyway."

"I'll pop out once in a while in case you have questions." I smiled, trying to keep the next bit friendly. "It would be best if you don't knock on the door. My friend is … sensitive to loud noises."

They agreed to that condition, not seeming particularly curious about Sarah, which was all good. When I approached the back door, Sarah opened it to let me in, then, perhaps because I was there, left only the screen door closed. Though I did notice she locked the screen door.

She put the kettle on while I washed my hands in the kitchen sink, bumping her hip into mine to nudge me aside as she stole water for the tea.

Sitting with tea led to chatting. Sarah had a talent for moving a conversation along and pulling stories out of me, though not in an aggressive way. Still, I had to do a lot of quick thinking to stick to the parts where I'd been in girl form and gloss over the fact that I was presenting as male all the time.

I wasn't sure what she picked up from that patchwork of impressions, but she didn't seem concerned. Sarah didn't ask any particularly probing questions, even when I'd obviously skipped over some parts of a story, or suddenly stopped in the middle.

We went out to chat with the guys every hour or so. Checking up on them, really. 'Showing the Flag,' as Sarah called it. Near lunchtime, Sarah made them sandwiches and drinks. They were very grateful for the free food. I noticed that, while Sarah actually came out into the yard today, she kept her distance from the guys, but also never let me get directly between her and them.

I understood my job here was to keep Sarah distracted while the guys were cleaning up the yard, to keep her anxiety in check. I could see her keeping a very close eye on their movements when we were outside, and she flinched a couple of times when they moved too fast near her. But still, I felt like I was taking advantage of her if she considered just sitting here talking to be 'work.'

After lunch, though, she opened up about her own life, and I was so fascinated that I forgot about my qualms.

"I was a huge geek when I was in my early teens," she said. "That was around 2006. Social media was a big deal. I got curious about poking around in the corners. Met a bunch of people online. People who were too old for me, to be honest." She chuckled ruefully. "I ended up learning a lot about cybersecurity and hacking from some real experts, but as well-meaning as they were, they got me into a lifestyle that wasn't very good for me."

"Is that why …" I started to ask, then I wasn't sure how to end the question without being offensive. Thankfully, Sarah picked it up like it was no big deal.

"Oh no. That crew was really good to an impressionable kid, looking back. They took good care of me in their own way. It's only been about … seven months since the attack." Her mouth pressed into a hard, thin line. "I didn't realize it had been that long." She shook her head. "You want to watch some TV?"

"Sure!" I said. I was horribly curious, but her vibe shouted 'leave it alone.' "Distractor number one, ready for duty!"

The intro to the show she put on was a bit of a shock.

"What language is that?" I asked. "Japanese?" That was my best guess, but it didn't seem quite right.

"Korean," she said, pausing the show. "This is one of my favourite K-Dramas, so far. A comfort watch."

"I've heard a fair bit about K-pop online." The fans (stans?) were hard to miss. "I don't know much about the TV shows."

"I started watching in my teens. One of my friends had moved from Japan and we used to watch Japanese dramas together, but lately I've been bingeing the Korean ones. The romance dramas, mostly," she said. "Though I'll warn you, even those can sometimes drop you right into some really hard topics without warning. I recommend reading reviews for trigger warnings." She paused. "Do you have any concerns? There are some parents who die in this one, and references to the death of a child."

"I'm good," I said. "The only thing I really don't like watching is anything where people are confined. Like prison, or in a hospital." Even thinking about it made me shiver.

"I think we're safe there. Though there's definitely some others you should avoid." She restarted the show, and I stayed quiet to give it my full appreciation. There was a lot that didn't quite make sense or wasn't fully explained, even with the English subtitles, but I figured it would come clear as I watched more. If not, I could ask Sarah later.

I was surprised when she first mentioned romance. To the extent I'd thought about it, I'd figured she'd be into angsty British detective shows or deep slice-of-life dramas. Romance seemed too frivolous. But seeing her relax as she watched, I had to admit it was doing something for her.

The show was good. The production was slick, and the actors were hot. Sarah liked the older guy, a reporter played by Yoo Ji-Tae, while I liked the younger, more action-star type guy who she said was played by an actor named Ji Chang-Wook.

The first episode was a little slow, though the snark between Chang-Wook's character and his handler, the IT expert, was pretty funny. And the ex-cons teaching little Young-Shin how to crack safes—I laughed out loud, revelling in being able to do that, in female form, without worrying about exposing my voice.

It was the first time I'd truly laughed in my girl voice since I was eight years old.

Sarah said she must be getting old. The first time she'd watched this K-drama, she'd identified more with the action guy. This time, she felt a lot more empathy for the IT Expert, who appeared to never leave her office, and not just because her own job had a lot of computer work.

"You have a job?" I asked, shocked into showing more surprise than was perhaps polite. I felt like biting my tongue afterward, but Sarah just laughed.

"Where did you think my money came from?" she asked with a slight chuckle.

"Uh, the government? Savings? Sorry. I guess I just assumed, since you seem to be free all the time."

"I admit, I have been on something of a sabbatical, only taking care of urgent business, working more on therapy, but I do have a job."

"It's cool that you can take the time off," I ventured.

"It can be a very demanding job." She stared at the floor, lost in some unpleasant memory from the look on her face. "But it has its perks too."

~*~

When Alex and Ramiro left, a little after four, Sarah brought up another task for me.

"I'd like to go for a drive."

"For real?" I said, surprised. That was the last thing I expected. "Um, I don't have a car handy."

"Oh, I have the car," she said smoothly. "I just haven't driven for a while, and I'm worried I'll get myself into some situation I can't drive out of, which would be … awkward." She smiled grimly.

I'd passed by the white BMW parked out front a few times today, but people often had several cars and parked them wherever they could find space, so I hadn't connected it with Sarah.

She pulled out slowly and continued slowly down the street, but with none of the hesitation I had seen from nervous, inexperienced drivers. She was driving slowly because she wanted to.

"So, where should I go?" She asked at the first stop sign. Put on the spot, I tried to remember the whole road layout. There was a map on the console screen—this was a fancy car, but that wasn't half the story.

"You want calm and quiet like this, before you face traffic?"

"Yeah, that would be brilliant," she sighed.

"Okay!" I gave her directions to circle around and head back toward Mount Royal. There was some traffic, which she seemed to deal with well. Then we threaded through the back streets of one of the wealthiest neighbourhoods in the city.

"Ah, this kind of reminds me of home," she said, driving down the tree-lined streets. "Some of the nicer spots. Not nearly big enough hedge-rows though." Given the size of the old, well-established trees and hedges through here, it made me curious to see England.

When she was done, I guided her back home, this time relying on the GPS map to find the best route. I was looking at the next turn when there was a loud bang beside us. The car suddenly accelerated, shoving me back into my seat. I wasn't enough of a car nerd to know the BMW's 0-60, but I was willing to bet it was a small number of seconds because we were suddenly moving awfully fast for this little street.

Sarah yanked her foot off the gas pedal almost as soon as she'd applied it. Glancing over, I saw her white-knuckling the steering wheel, face grimly determined.

That's how I missed the kid running into the road, but Sarah didn't. She slammed on the brakes hard enough that they went into the rattle of anti-lock. My shoulder belt bit into my collarbone. I had a brief glimpse of the bright red ball as it went under the bumper and exploded with a *pop!*

We stopped an inch from the parked car on my side, thanks to Sarah's very precise swerve, so close that the kid, who must have been about five, could lean on the side of the car to look down at the remains of his ball. Sarah stared at the kid. She reached down, slammed the gearshift into park and started to say, "I think—"

Suddenly, there was an angry white guy at Sarah's window, waving his arms and yelling. She jumped. Her leg worked, and I'm sure if the car was in drive, she'd have taken off. Then, she reached for her door handle, but the guy started banging on the window, and she just huddled down with a terrified look on her face.

There was no room to open my door. I rolled down my window and snaked out until I was sitting on the window ledge. "Hey!" I said, as soon as my head was above roof-level. "Back off, dude!"

That stopped the banging anyway.

With one hand on the roof of Sarah's car and the other on the car beside us, I lifted my body until I could get a foot on the window ledge, then walked down the edges of the hoods on both cars. It wasn't the best thing to do to a car's paint, but it wouldn't dent it.

"She just about hit my kid!"

"Tell your kid not to run out into the road!" I shot back while I walked around the front of the BMW.

"I saw you stop. How fast were you going?"

He had a point. I was sure we'd exceeded the speed limit for a second there, but I wasn't going to debate it with him.

"Dude," I said again, sliding between him and Sarah's window, "Maybe if you're concerned about your kid's safety, you should take him off the street." The kid was now tugging futilely at the corpse of his ball, wedged under the car's front tire.

"I want to see her driver's license. Does she even have one? These people come to our country and think they can do whatever they want …" He put his hand on my shoulder and tried to shove me out of the way, but I just slid one foot out to the side and bent my knees a little, and I was already leaning back against the car. He was ineffectual. But from the rage building on his face, I was going to have to decide soon how to handle this.

"David? David! Why is Rylan playing in the middle of the street? Get him back here!" A woman stood at the front door of the house directly across the street. The kid had tired of the ball and was now investigating a row of anthills occupying a crack in the pavement. Another car was coming down the street, the opposite way. It was slowing, no threat, but between that and his wife, he took the kid off the road.

Roughly. In his anger, he grabbed the kid's arm and jerked him forward. Startled, the kid started to cry. The wife was yelling something else, but I didn't pause to listen. As soon as he'd walked away, Sarah unlocked the doors, opened the driver's door, and scooted over the center console. I opened the door and dropped into the driver's seat, closed the door, and gently but firmly accelerated away from the racist guy and his neighbourhood.

I breathed a sigh of relief until I remembered that I didn't have a license. At least, not one I could use in this form. And even if I did, it showed a completely different identity than what Sarah knew. And a male identity. I drove even more cautiously.

Sarah's breathing had mostly recovered by the time we reached our neighbourhood again, and she was sitting up straighter.

"I'm sorry," she said. "I saw something moving in my peripheral vision, then the bang." She shook her head.

"Yeah. Roofers throwing shingles down into a metal bin, I think," I said.

She nodded. "That would do it. Sorry to put you through that. I should know it's too late already when you hear the bang, but …" She trailed off.

"It was pretty intense. We're fine, though. Nobody got hurt."

"Only because you put yourself between us," she said quietly, but firmly. "That was a huge help. Thanks."

I shrugged. Mostly I was focused on getting this damn car back to Sarah's house. I was convinced police were hiding behind every bush, waiting to pop out and haul me off for driving without a license, and then worse when they found the gaps in my identity. I was sweating by the time I parked the car near Sarah's house. Someone had taken the spot right in front while we were away, of course.

"Would you like to stay for some supper?" she asked, looking suddenly more vulnerable. "I would rather not be alone with my thoughts right now."

"I'm okay with that." I had warned my parents that the camp hours could extend into the evening, or even overnight, just to cover all my bases.

Sarah's brilliant smile broke out again. Energy regained, she hopped out of the car, and I followed her to the house, locking the car behind me.

~*~

It was past nine before I even started for home. Luckily, I had packed a sweatshirt, as I always did, even though I hadn't expected to need it. I did a partial change at Bistro, leaving my underwear on since I had gotten all sweaty and gross, and the boy ones I'd worn this morning were practically clean.

Sarah and I had made supper together, which was fun. Mom rarely let Dad and me cook. Something about paying too much for food to see it go to waste. Then we watched more of our K-drama, which I was really getting into.

I never did ask her where the car had come from. Maybe she'd had it all along, and it had been parked down the street? She was in such a good mood after supper that I hadn't wanted to bring up something that would remind her of the recent scare.

On the way home, it occurred to me that I hadn't thought about how my voice sounded since the argument on the road. Somewhere in there, I had forgotten to be self-conscious about the pitch and had just let the natural voice of my female form come out. It wasn't as high-pitched as I had tried to force it before, overcompensating. It was mellow and warm, and felt right. I was sure, now, that I could reproduce it whenever I needed.

Mom and Dad were in the middle of a TV show when I came in, so I didn't have any trouble slipping up to my room. Which made me very glad since I was exhausted—or knackered, as Sarah liked to say. Entirely appropriate, since I felt as lively as a dead horse by the time I made it up the stairs.

They knew I still switched sometimes, but I needed to keep them thinking it was a once-in-a-while thing. And I definitely needed to hide that I was presenting as female out in the world. They would flip out, and maybe even start packing.

Half-conscious, I stripped off my clothes and fell into bed. Then I had to get back up and hide my dirty underwear. My parents bugged me in the morning sometimes, and a pair of panties on the floor would be a real conversation starter.

CHAPTER 13

"I still can't believe you're doing this, man!" Ravi enthused from the driver's seat. "You're the best!"

I was having trouble believing it, too. The last thing I'd expected to be doing this Friday night was guiding Ravi and Debbie out to the super-secret after-grad party in Ravi's beat-up old Hyundai.

"This car smells like oil," Debbie grumped. "Couldn't you have at least borrowed your mom's Mercedes? I'll feel like a loser getting out of this car."

"I'm supposed to be over at Mike's, Deb," Ravi explained for the second time. "Why would I drive Mom's car to Mike's? Plus, we're literally sneaking in. No one's going to see you."

"That's not the point," she said with a heavy sigh. Thankfully, they didn't continue the argument. For now.

Debbie should've been glad she wasn't in the back seat. The smell of oil was even worse back here. I really hoped I had interpreted Angela's cryptic text messages correctly, because this whole situation had snowballed. I needed a car to get out to Waiparous. I couldn't take my parents' car overnight since Mom might get called into work early the next day. I had to hit up Ravi, but Ravi wouldn't go without Debbie, since she'd never speak to him again if he did. So here we were.

I'd used the camp job I'd made up as an excuse to be out here until early tomorrow morning. Ravi had lied to his parents, saying he would be over at my house. I had no idea whether Debbie had done something similar or if she had actually secured her parents' permission.

At least I could relax more with Ravi driving. Sarah and I had done two more drives since the first one. Both of us were nervous after that first unlucky experience, but they had been far less eventful. Sarah was a good driver from a pure reflex standpoint, but at times it felt like she'd learned to drive in a war zone.

Her quips left me wondering, but she hadn't elaborated on that part of her life, for all my gentle prying. Her stories got up to the point when she'd left England about ten years ago, when she was nineteen, then stopped.

I felt bad because I had to cut my last drive with Sarah this morning short, since the nagging feeling that I was about to switch had peaked in the middle of the drive. I mumbled some excuse about an appointment and bailed out of the car as soon as she got it parked. We exchanged a couple of Discord messages later, so I was pretty sure she was okay, but she liked to hang out and destress after.

It wasn't until this drive with Ravi that I realized I felt extra bad because I also missed our hanging out time. I'd only known Sarah for a few weeks, but she felt like a friend already. I had to be wary of that feeling. She was a job to me. A way to save up so I could prove to my parents that, if I had to run, they didn't need to uproot themselves again and come with me. I knew getting too attached would make me more likely to blow my cover, but I couldn't help it.

With Ravi and Debbie doing most of the talking, and me wrapped in my own thoughts, I didn't notice the kilometres going by until we passed Ghost Lake Dam. I pointed out the turn to the forestry trunk road, and we headed up into the hills. The road was in good shape right up to Waiparous Village. I had Ravi pull off at an old, overgrown drive where we were not likely to be disturbed.

We had a half hour before 9 p.m., when the chosen seniors would be leaving grad and heading to the after party, joined by a few other special invitees like Angela. Ravi stopped on the empty drive, reversed into a spot on a small dirt side road, and killed the engine.

I had let Ravi know that Ian and crew would be using radios to keep the party goers on track, though I'd let Ravi believe it had come from a detail Ian let slip to me, not from Angela's messages. I didn't think they knew Angela would be there, and I hoped they didn't run into each other—unless Angela really did need help, then they would be added allies.

Ravi unexpectedly got out of the car, opened the hatchback, and crouched, fiddling with something.

"What are you doing?" I called back.

"Swapping the plate. I drive this car to school sometimes. Don't want anyone recognizing it."

I turned sharply in my seat to look back. "Isn't that illegal?"

"Well, yeah, I guess." He didn't sound overly concerned. "But out here, a cop would have to run the plate to notice it's bogus, and that's unlikely."

I sighed. I didn't like it, but I wasn't driving, and maybe it was a good idea. Ravi finished and got back into the driver's seat. I opened a bag of chips and a bottle of pop from the stash we'd bought. "Want a drink?" I asked. Debbie accepted, but Ravi waved me off, focusing on the CB radio we'd tuned to band 24 and left on, sitting on the console.

"Staring at it isn't going to make it work any better," I chided.

"You're sure that's the right frequency?" he asked, once again.

"Yes," I said, somewhat forcefully. And if it wasn't, if I'd misinterpreted Angela's texts, perhaps it was better that we just sat out here all night.

Eventually, Ravi relaxed or got exhausted maintaining the intensity of waiting. He slumped back into the driver's seat and accepted a drink and a bag of Cheezies.

"How's the parkour camp going?" I asked. Ravi hadn't been talking about it, probably out of sensitivity to me.

"Good!" he said. "It's more fun than I thought it would be, dealing with the rugrats. And it's got very consistent hours." He grinned at Debbie, who smiled. "Dad complains that I don't get paid enough, but I'm actually getting the same hourly, I'm just working fewer hours, so he can stuff it."

"That's cool. I'm glad," I said. There was no way I could have lived Ravi's life, with my switches. His parents were way too up in his business. My parents were generally too busy keeping a roof over our heads to worry, unless, like lately with the parkour camp, my English mark, and my noticeable switches, I gave them reason to worry.

I hoped my fictional sleepaway camp work would cover me for tonight's outing. My dad had been looking a little skeptical. I had better collect some money from Sarah and deposit it this weekend. That would go a long way to easing his concerns.

"Sorry, Mike," Ravi said.

I guess I had been silent a little too long.

"No, I really am glad." I gripped his shoulder. "Your dad should back off. I'm happy you've found a solid way to push back at him."

A subtle orange tint crept into the sky from the setting sun. It was just past 9 p.m.

We waited through another ten tense minutes before picking up our first broadcast.

"…ohnson's hair? WTF, it's like she got wild lemurs to style it."

Ravi tossed me his phone and started the engine. We both knew that voice. Vicky. A senior and head mean girl of the school.

A large black SUV blew past on the trunk road, coinciding with a sudden jump in the volume and clarity of the ongoing chatter. The voices dissected the clothes and hairstyle choices of other graduates and provided opinions about the moral choices that could have led them to that state.

"Yeah!" Ravi yelled. He gunned out onto the road right on the tail of a second black SUV. They were not easy to follow. The aged Hyundai was shaking and rattling like it was about to come apart. Debbie hung grimly onto the 'oh-shit' handle. I hung onto the front seats, peering out the front window.

We were tearing down the loose-gravelled road, bumping up and down hills and skidding around the corners. The headlights in front of us kept appearing and disappearing as hills and trees obscured our view.

Fortunately for us, as the number of tiny, winding backroads proliferated, the girls switched from critiquing fashion to complaining about the roads.

"… Oh my god, what's with this bridge? It's barely wider than the truck! Scott, Scott, I don't think … eeeeee …"

"Vicky!"

"Oh shit, we made it! Close your eyes now, Sam, you don't want to see this …"

And more like that.

A few minutes later, Ian's smooth voice came on. *"Please, don't use the radios for random conversation. They need to be free to help anyone who's lost!"*

Even after everything, my heart thumped just hearing him.

And then the radio went silent.

Ahead of us, the road split, heading in different directions.

"Which way?" Ravi cried.

The taillights hadn't reappeared, but I knew that bridge. "Left! Left!" I yelled over the road noise. Ravi slewed to that side, hit the corner faster than he should have, and we panicked as tree trunks flashed by way, way too close in the headlights.

Debbie shrieked.

We made it out of the corner intact, then flew across a single-lane wooden bridge. Not a big challenge for this little car, though hitting the sharp uphill on the other side sounded, and felt, like it was close to taking out the suspension.

"Shit!" Ravi said and gunned it again. At least this part of the road was fairly flat.

Then, I saw something go by on the left. A couple of tall stone pillars? At the same time, the car shuddered and shimmied on the loose, top layer of gravel.

"Whoa! Slow up!" I tapped Ravi's shoulder.

"What? Why?" he asked, but did it anyway.

"That gate we just passed. And the road. Nobody's been driving on this section lately."

Ravi turned the car around in a three-point turn, making me grateful we didn't have a massive SUV like the people we were following, and nearly drove past the gate again.

"Turn! Right turn!" I pointed frantically as he skidded to a stop.

"But … there's no road there!"

"I don't see it either," Debbie said.

"Okay, fine. Follow me." I opened the door and hopped out. How could he miss the pillars and big iron gates standing open? I walked up the lane between them, beckoning him forward like I was part of an airport ground crew. It was paved in individual blocks like a backyard patio. Solid and smooth underfoot. Even without my dad's experienced eye here to tutor me, I could tell it was impeccable work.

Ravi followed, maddeningly slowly at first, in jerky steps, hitting the brakes hard every few seconds until he managed to find the gas pedal and drove up beside me so I could get back in.

He was shaking his head. "I swear, man, there was nothing but trees, then suddenly …" he waved toward the view in front of us. Debbie nodded vigorously, looking weirded out.

"Maybe it's some kind of light projection?" she ventured, but none of us were convinced.

Past the gate, the single-track lane wound deeper into the forest. I resolved to drive on the way back. Ravi and Debbie were obviously suffering from some kind of eye strain.

We were distracted from further contemplation by a flash of painfully bright lights behind us and a blaring horn. Ravi gunned it, and we drove as fast as we dared, which wasn't nearly fast enough for the belligerent truck. We white-knuckled it all the way.

My stomach churned as I wondered what kind of reception we'd get. The lane ended in a flat space among the trees, stuffed with vehicles—trucks,

SUVs, and even a couple of sports cars. Amber-hued lights in trees at each corner lit the clearing comfortably, if not brightly.

Ravi turned off as early as possible to tuck our little Hyundai under the trees near the lane. The truck bypassed us to take a spot closer to the rest of the group. Two couples piled out, whooping in excitement. The guys wore tuxes, and the girls wore fancy dresses and sneakers, carrying high-heeled shoes. The guys pulled two bags each out of the back, pretending the girl's bags were nearly too heavy to lift. They ignored us completely and soon vanished down a footpath edged with rows of small, ground-level lights.

"Whew!" I let out my breath. "Let's not do that again."

"Wimp," Ravi chided, but his voice was weaker than usual.

He and Debbie got out of the car into the humid night and straightened their outfits. Ravi in a tux and Debbie in a cool-blue dress with long, simple lines that looked great on her. Both of their outfits were a little creased, but I'd bet everyone here's would be after the trip.

"Good luck!" I said. I was comfortably wearing jeans and a T-shirt, with no intention of getting anywhere near the main party.

"You sure? Could be the chance of a lifetime!"

"All the nopes, my friend." I pointedly picked up a chip bag and put a few in my mouth, waving them off.

"You've still got the spare key?" Ravi asked. I checked my pocket and gave him a thumbs-up. Debbie was already walking in the direction we'd seen the other partiers go, also wearing flats and carrying her heels. Ravi waved and followed her.

I watched them walk to the path and disappear at the first turn. After the several rushes of adrenaline I'd had, the chips tasted like cardboard. I turned all the car's interior lights off to avoid attracting bugs or any other unwanted attention.

I kept the CB radio on. If Angela needed help, she might call on it. There was no cell service out here. There were a couple of Wi-Fi access points, but I didn't think it would be smart to try to connect to them. I turned my phone off entirely so it wasn't draining power.

Two trucks came in shortly after, to disgorge more brightly-plumaged partygoers. I leaned the seat all the way back. It was more comfortable and also kept my face from accidental exposure by way of headlight glare. Then, it was quiet. It looked like we'd arrived near the tail end of the crowd.

~*~

I jolted awake at the sound of another SUV entering the lot. There wasn't much room left now, so they stopped close to me. I kept my head down until I heard men's voices. They were loud enough that I could hear them through the closed windows.

"Of all the nights," one of them grumbled. "Look at this mess." A truck door closed.

"Exactly this night, I think," another one said. "Maybe she thought we'd have our guard down." There was the sound of a back hatch opening.

I lifted my head over the lower edge of the side window. Craning my head around, I could see the two guys, lit up brightly by the interior lights of their truck.

One of them was Angela's stalker from the mall. The guy who'd been working with Ian's uncle at the Banff Springs Hotel.

"Let's go get her then," Stalker Guy said to his companion. They were both wearing suits like a uniform.

Cold sweat instantly coated my body. I debated with myself as the sounds of them walking off across the gravelled parking area faded. They were going after Angela. They had to be.

I double-checked that the Hyundai's interior lights were off, then slipped out of the car and closed the door without fully latching it. I headed in the same direction as the stalker and his buddy. I knew what I was doing was crazy, but I couldn't stop myself.

I hadn't told Angela about the guy following her at the mall, not wanting to sound any crazier than I already did. Now he was after her again, on what had to be his home ground. I wanted to believe, with everything I'd seen from him, that Ian would protect her if he were around. But I couldn't be sure of that.

When they were almost at the mouth of the tree-lined path, two girls walked out into the parking area. I tensed. Neither of the girls was Angela, but that didn't preclude some kind of harassment.

Both girls walked by the goons without even a glance. They didn't act like girls who'd just met two strange guys in the woods at night. They didn't step closer to each other or stop chatting with each other; they simply blithely walked on by, one of them telling a story about being accidentally pantsed at soccer practice, and the other laughing loudly.

It was just like at the mall. They couldn't see the goons. He truly was an invisible stalker. My stomach hurt as my worry for Angela redoubled.

CHAPTER 14

All my nerves jangled as I followed the two goons further. I was making far too much noise. My only consolation was that they were probably making just as much. And I was sure I wasn't invisible to them. The only thing I could do was to let them get farther ahead so I wouldn't be in direct sight if they looked back.

Then, I reached the end of the path through the woods where it opened into a wide expanse of manicured lawn. Ian's 'cabin,' a massive three-story edifice, stood higher on the hill to my right. Its brightly lit windows overlooked the lawn, which swept down to the flat darkness of a small lake.

I saw teens in a mix of formal wear, bathing suits, and regular clothes scattered around.

I saw no goons.

Unless they had somehow expanded their invisibility to include me, I had missed them somehow. I spun, terrified they might be right behind me. The deep darkness of the forest path, lit only by tiny solar lights, wasn't reassuring at first, but my eyes readjusted quickly to show it was still empty.

Pushing down my panic, I realized I didn't need to find the security guards; I needed to find Angela. But where to look? I didn't want to wander out on that broad lawn, well-lit by the blazing lights from the cabin. Seriously, they were bright. Were they using 300-Watt bulbs in there or something? I also didn't see much point in going up to the cabin. If she were there, she was likely as safe as she could be, surrounded by lots of people.

I turned left toward the lake and skirted the shadowed edge of the forest. The underbrush was trimmed under the first few ranks of trees.

These were high-branched deciduous trees, not the usual pines of the area. A little strip of forest as manicured as the lawn.

There were gazebos scattered along the edge of the trees. The first two I passed were occupied by couples who were definitely … occupied with each other. I slipped by as quietly as I could in the deepest shadow, steadfastly not looking, though I was strongly tempted by the noises being made.

Then, I ran into something.

It wasn't physical. It felt like someone had thrown an itchy wool blanket over my soul. I wanted to scratch all over, but my bigger concern was the sound of a deep voice calling, "Got one! This way." Two people ran toward me: one from uphill near the cabin, and another from deeper in the forest.

I bolted downhill. Maybe that was in the opposite direction of safety, but I didn't like my chances with either of the two guards, nor with running out into full view on the lawn. Maybe if I got enough of a lead, I could hide in the forest, then creep back to the car.

I ran freely. The colours of the forest around me were washed out into shades of grey, like the haze of twilight, but lighter than before. I didn't have time to question it. I could hear the guards crashing behind me. They were struggling through the forest, falling behind, but they were still headed directly for me.

I saw a possible trail and quietly cut deeper into the forest. I sped down the trail until it ended in some heavier brush and stopped up against the bole of a pine. I hoped and prayed for the crunching sounds of the guards to pass by, but I heard a voice call out again, "She's turned back into the forest. Bear left! This way."

Oh hell. They were tracking me somehow. Sickening fear pooled in my belly, and my legs suddenly weakened.

No! I wasn't going to just sit here and let them get me.

I bolted. Directly through the forest, not caring how much sound I made now. Just before I turned onto the forest trail, I saw one. A gazebo. I didn't care who I interrupted now. Witnesses might not help me, but they couldn't hurt.

I burst out of the brush, still in the shadowed, manicured border to the wild forest. The gazebo was off to my right. Fairy lights twined in the rafters lit up what was going on there as if it were in daylight.

I was starting to wonder if this was all a nightmare.

A very, very realistic feeling nightmare, because what was laid out in front of me was ripped directly from my worst fears—Ian and Angela, locked in a tight embrace, kissing. He was shirtless. She was half in his lap, one strap of her dress off, and that side pulled down far enough that I could see side-boob where she was pressed against Ian's bare chest.

A wave of heat snapped through my body. How dare he …

I fell to my knees on the grass as the most extreme balance shift from a sex-switch I'd ever felt hit me. At the same time, the scratchy wool blanket feeling evaporated.

With safety in sight, now that I'd switched, it was impossible for me to run out to Ian and Angela.

Neither of them was looking in my direction, but I knew that could change in an instant. I retreated carefully back to the deeper shadows. A loud noise now might draw the eye …

Just as I was about to sneak behind a bush, I stepped too heavily on a branch hidden under leaves. At its crack, Ian's head turned, and he stared directly at me. I didn't think he could see much other than a dark form in the darkness, but he definitely realized someone was out here. I slid behind the bush.

"Where now?" A voice called out.

"I … don't know!" the tracker said. "She's … gone."

"What? Let me see that thing." There was a pause. I decided to huddle where I was, for now. The voices were farther uphill from the gazebo where Ian and Angela were still clutched together, not too close to me.

While I peered out between the branches, Angela separated from Ian and tugged up her dress. Ian left his shirt off.

Three guards, all in identical dark grey suits, strode out from the trees. Stalker Guy, who was leading them, walked into the lit area of the gazebo holding a tablet in a rough-use case. The others stayed in the shadows.

"Sorry to bother you, young sir." His words were formal, but he spoke like Ian was definitely beneath his level. "Have you seen anything suspicious in the last few minutes?"

"No, Brent, I haven't seen anything." He slid an arm around Angela, who was sitting cuddled up to his side, eyes down, pretending to ignore the guards. "I've been busy."

"I see," Brent said stiffly. "Call it in immediately if you do." He turned away, directing his guards to follow him with a jerk of his arm. They moved twenty feet away to confer in low voices, with a lot of angry pointing at the tablet.

Ian and Angela returned to their embrace.

I'd seen enough. Security obviously wasn't looking for Angela. I felt like an idiot now, barging in. But this certainly raised new questions. What was that 'wool blanket' thing, and how had it let them track me? Was it some kind of electric charge? A super security system only known to a few really rich people?

I slipped through the forest, favouring stealth over speed for now. If I ran into another one of those tracking-traps, I would have to run for it again.

My weird night vision had stayed with me through the switch, so moving through the woods wasn't too hard. I listened keenly for any sound of pursuit, expecting to feel that scratchy wool envelop me again with every step.

As the immediate terror faded, I realized my jeans were way too tight around my hips. I paused to undo the top button and unzip the fly to relieve some pressure. Patting myself down, I could tell my hips and breasts were bigger than usual, and, as I jerked back from motion at the corner of my eye, I realized my hair now fell past my shoulders. Well, fuck. There was no way I could pass for Michael like this. I was going to have to wait to switch back or find my own way home.

I could be in for a long walk. When I saw a dead branch of a convenient length and size for a walking stick, I picked it up. It was handy for intercepting spider webs strung between branches before my face did, and sometimes for keeping my balance on abrupt down-slopes. The forest allowed me only brief glimpses of the sky. Thankfully, my sight was good enough that I could use landmarks, mostly odd-looking trees, to stay walking in a straight line. Otherwise, I would have been going in circles until security found me.

I was in a box, though. I would either hit the lake, the river, the road, or the path from the parking area to the house. From any of those, I could work my way back around to the parking lot. I tried to veer more toward the lake, the widest and wildest part of the search area. I would rather hike all night than run into those private security goons again.

That would hopefully give me more time to get back into male shape, if possible. If not … I hated to steal Ravi's car, but it might be the only option. There were enough people here that I knew he and Debbie would find a way home. Or, if I managed to return to male shape by morning, I could come back for them.

Noise erupted in the woods ahead of me—grunts, crackling of brush, thuds. A woman cried out in pain. Then I was in motion, running as quietly as I could, before thinking about it.

A guard in the standard suit had her face down on the ground, her arm held up and backwards in what looked like a very painful position, his knee on her back. He was groping at her body while she bucked and kicked, trying to dislodge him. They were both breathing like steam engines.

"The more you struggle, the more this is going to hurt," he growled at her.

The solid dead branch I'd been using as a walking stick made an effective club across the back of the guard's head. Maybe too effective. I'd meant to stop him, but I was alarmed at how he keeled over sideways and how fast the woman was up and on top of him.

She made a few quick motions, then looked up and over at me, still standing holding the stick, wondering what the hell to do next.

"Kayla?" Her eyes were wide, even with the lines of exhaustion in her face. "What are you doing here?"

"Sarah?" I replied in a strangled shout. "What the fuck?" I gestured toward the guard. "Uh, is he ok?"

"Shouldn't you be asking me that?" she said harshly.

"Well, yeah, but ..." I held out the branch helplessly.

"He's good," she said flatly, then crawled over and patted around for a few seconds. The guard lay limp, not moving at all, and Sarah seemed entirely unconcerned about him. She scooped something off the ground and tucked it into a pocket on her vest as she stood, then wavered back and forth, and would have fallen if I didn't grab her arm.

She released a strangled cry of pain and grabbed hold of me with the other hand.

"Not that arm," she gasped. "Shoulder."

"Ah, right. I'm so sorry." I cringed. I'd seen the way the guy was pushing her arm up.

"We have to get out of here. Now." She pinned me with a fierce gaze. "You coming with me, or doing this on your own?"

I blinked at her, brain racing. We'd be safer together, maybe, unless being with her put me at more risk. But, if I let her go like this, would I ever find out what she'd been doing here, and how Angela might be in danger?

"Fine." She turned and stumbled away, holding her right arm tight to her body with her left.

"No, wait. I'll come with you," I said, hurrying to her side.

Sarah accepted my help, me steadying her as we walked. She seemed to know what direction she wanted to go, but I soon realized that she couldn't see in the darkness the way I could. I subtly guided us to the more open paths and around the biggest roots, but I didn't explain. I wished I had an explanation for my sudden night vision, but I veered away from questioning it. It might go away if I did, and it was too useful right now.

"Stop!" she commanded, at one unremarkable portion of the forest.

I froze. "What?"

She extracted a black plastic folder from her jacket's inside pocket and took out a slip of yellow paper covered in characters that looked vaguely Chinese. She looked sidelong at me.

"You're about to see something that will change your understanding of the world. Please don't freak out or ask me any questions right now. I'll explain when, and if, we make it to a safer place."

"Ah, sure." I'd already experienced plenty of weirdness tonight. Sarah being here must mean she was in the thick of all this too, somehow. It reaffirmed my need to stick with her. To get some answers.

She held the long paper up in front of her, and, to my surprise, tacked it in the air like she was putting a sticky note on an invisible wall. The paper immediately charred from the center out, a round wave of embers that didn't stop at the edges of the paper, but burnt an expanding ring through the air until it was a portal large enough for us to step through, though the view of the forest on the other side hadn't changed.

"Go!" Sarah said as she stepped over the glowing edge of the ring. After reaching its maximum extent, the portal immediately started to contract again. I hopped over behind her and watched the ring collapse to a bright spark, which faded out.

"Was that …" I started, but her glare silenced me, and we continued our hike.

There was no change in the landscape. We hadn't jumped anywhere else. It looked a lot like she'd just carved a hole in some kind of invisible fence to get us through. I thought back to the guards obviously tracking me. Had I been blundering into these magic fences? I was even more convinced now that she knew what she was doing, and my best bet for survival was to follow her lead.

I tried not to think about the guard we'd left unmoving on the ground.

Was he dead? Had my blow to the head killed him? Or had it been Sarah? I wasn't sure which scared me more.

My dark thoughts were interrupted as we reached the lakeshore.

Sarah waded into the marshy edge of the small lake, ducking down to stay low in the thin margin between forest and water. At this end near the river, cattail reeds stood at least four feet above the surface, gently waving in the breeze coming off the lake. She was well-concealed in the water and waved me over.

I took my phone and wallet out of my pockets and left them on a convenient rock on the beach, making a mental note to come back for them before we totally vacated. Nothing like leaving a calling card! Then, I sighed and squelched in, ducking like she had. As I neared her, I ran into something sitting on the bottom. With her one good hand, she guided me to several head-sized rocks sitting on it, and motioned for me to take them off, which I did. With every rock removed, it rose higher until it revealed a matte-black single-person-sized double-pontoon float.

There was a waterproof bag attached, where Sarah stowed some of her gear, including the black plastic folder she'd taken the yellow paper—*spell?* —from and a phone. I retrieved my phone and wallet and added them to the bag. Sarah grimaced when she saw my phone.

"That thing off?"

"Yeah," I reassured her. I didn't want anyone tracking my phone out here. A vision of the guard's still body jumped into my head, and I ruthlessly shoved it back out. I refused to feel guilty for defending Sarah.

She responded with a somewhat approving-sounding grunt.

It was a good thing Sarah and I were both slender. We lay side-by-side on the float and took turns pushing the foot-pedals that propelled it, while the other shoved at reeds when they were too thick for the boat to push aside. The pedals moved smoothly and silently; this boat was top of the line.

Again, Sarah directed us. I noticed now that she had a wristband with a display screen that was constantly flipping between different displays. One of them was a compass. That made sense. I wondered what some of the other functions were, but didn't have the time or energy to ask.

Soon, we landed on the other shore. It wasn't a very large lake at this end, and the little pontoon boat was efficient. I got another surprise when I stood up and my pants fell down. I grabbed them before they fell fully into the water, in full panic mode as Sarah looked questioningly at me. Had I shifted to male form?

Sarah chuckled briefly. "Boxers?"

While pulling my pants up and fastening them, I shook my shoulders and did a quick inventory. My hips and breasts had returned to their usual size for my girl shape at some point, but I was still in girl form. Relief briefly replaced overwhelming fear and confusion.

"They're more comfortable with guys' jeans," I replied, remembering Angela saying that once.

"Hmm," was her only response.

After taking all our stuff out of the dry bag, Sarah got me to weigh the boat down with rocks again.

"This location is probably burnt anyway after this job, but no sense in making it easy for them."

She guided, while I supported her, through a mix of forest and small clearings. We emerged onto the lawn of another stately cabin, though not quite as stately as Ian's. We skirted around the building, so as not to trigger any of the motion-sensitive floodlights she silently pointed out.

Approaching buildings spiked my anxiety that had been dulled by the feeling of isolation on the lake. Buildings meant people, and people might be enemies we would need to hurt, or be hurt by ourselves, and the thought of either scenario made me ill.

On the opposite side of the house was a parking area similar to the one at Ian's cabin, though this one was much smaller and emptier. Stuck in a far corner of the lot was a familiar white BMW.

"You'd better drive," Sarah said, still holding her arm.

I helped her into the passenger seat. She handed me the keys once I was in the driver's seat. I had a strange kind of déjà vu moment—memories of us doing this previously, but I no longer recognized the people we'd been before … all this.

"I don't know how this is going to turn out, for either of us, but I'm bloody glad I ran into you tonight, Kayla," she said, leaning back in her seat and closing her eyes. Her fingers traced a complex repeating design on her thigh in time to her deliberate, regular breathing. "Thank you for saving my life."

"Did I really?" I asked in a rush of almost panic, remembering those chaotic and confusing seconds. My hands trembled now, even though I didn't remember having any reaction then.

"For certain." She sighed. "More details will have to wait, I'm afraid. Just get us back to Calgary. And stick near the speed limit. We do not want to be noticed tonight."

~*~

After driving through the forest, with my eyes still doing that weird grayscale night vision thing, the lights of civilization and passing cars were excruciatingly bright. I had to veer to the side of the highway and sit for a few minutes until my eyes recovered.

Sarah's hand gripped vice-like around my upper arm while I still had my eyes closed.

"What's going on?" she asked urgently, her words slightly slurred. She'd mentioned one of her medications might do that.

"It's okay." I tried to reassure her. "I'm … my eyes are just tired. I need a few minutes."

"Oh." Her hand relaxed, and she dropped it to her lap again. "Okay." She didn't say anything more.

Cautiously opening my eyes just a crack every ten or fifteen seconds, I found the blinding brightness of reflected light from passing cars dimming and colour seeping back into the world. That was a huge relief. Brightness could be handled with sunglasses, but I would hate to lose colours permanently.

Twenty minutes later, we were just passing Cochrane in its river valley when Sarah opened her eyes and asked me to pull over in a pained voice.

"If they haven't caught up with us yet, a few minutes' break isn't going to make any difference," she said.

I turned off at the next crossroad and parked out of the way, not that I expected any traffic at two in the morning.

Sarah took several pill bottles from the glove box, one at a time. I had to help her open them and then fill the little cup from her thermos so she could take them. I recognized the ibuprofen, but not the others. Last, she pulled out a couple of instant cold packs, and I helped her position them behind and in front of her left shoulder.

She hissed as they touched, but seemed more relieved than pained.

"Head for the Sheraton in Eau Claire," she said. Her eyes closed again, but she held the cold pack steady on her shoulder with her good hand, protected from the cold by the sleeve of her coat.

"I was thinking something more like a hospital?" I countered.

"The shoulder's not dislocated, just sprained. I'll be fine."

Her shoulder wasn't the only thing I was worried about, but I couldn't see forcing her to go somewhere she didn't want to. And, I had to admit that, based on what I'd seen tonight, she was working on a whole other level than I was used to, so I'd better follow her lead.

The GPS on the car came in handy, taking me right there. I turned into the drop-off lane, but Sarah told me to park because we were both going in. Fair enough. She was pretty fragile right now. Needing company after everything we'd just been through was understandable. I needed it too.

When she put on a cloth mask and motioned for me to wear one too, I asked, "Are you worried we caught something tonight?"

"Not any more than usual. It's mostly to make facial recognition harder."

That made sense, but also increased my tension. Every precaution she was taking underscored the level of danger she thought she was in, and how much I might be facing along with her.

She checked in under the name Sarah Forbes and ushered me into the elevator. I went along, figuring I could give her some moral support for a while, then go back down and figure out the bus schedule to get back home. I was longing for my bed so hard right now.

The elevator doors opened onto a generic hotel corridor, and I walked beside Sarah, wheeling a small suitcase that she had pulled out of the trunk, until she found the right room. I stared at the door as she swiped the card, trying to figure out how to politely say what I needed to. "It's after 3 a.m. I can stay for a bit, but I really need to get home soon. I don't want my parents waking up in the morning and realizing I never came home."

"Kayla." She sighed, closing her eyes for a moment. "You can't go home yet, for reasons I think are better explained in private. But, I can say you could be putting your family and friends in deadly danger if you go home now."

"What?"

"The people we got away from. They have ways of tracking that are hard to detect and impossible to counter. The only thing we can do is wait it out."

"How long?"

"Three days."

"What?" She expected me to disappear for three days? How?

Her haggard face reminded me that she really was at the end of her strength, and I was keeping her standing in the hallway. I silently followed her into the room.

CHAPTER 15

I realized it wasn't a standard hotel room when I walked in. It was a suite with a large main room and smaller separate bedroom. Being stuck here for three days was starting to look a little less dire. The main room had a small kitchen and eating area. A sectional couch over by the windows would either give a view of downtown skyscrapers or the Bow River. I couldn't tell from where I was standing.

I remembered the view from Ian's apartment and was uncomfortably reminded that he and his uncle lived not too far from here. I hoped that, however Sarah had set this up, we could successfully hide in the masses of people occupying and travelling through the city core. She seemed to know what she was doing, but I couldn't relax.

"Can you take off my boots?" Sarah sat on one of the couches and held a foot out for me. "I'm going to have the longest, hottest shower I can stand. And can you call the desk and ask for the strongest painkiller tablets they can send up?"

"Will do," I said as I ditched my own gross shoes and socks at the door. Then, I set to work on her boots, prying the waterlogged and since-dried knots open. They smelled like swamp. But then so did I, so I couldn't complain. I'd seen what that security guy did to her arm and winced just remembering it. There was no way she could have gotten these off without assistance, at least not without some really sharp scissors and a lot of pain.

Eventually, I got both her boots off, and she shuffled off to the bedroom. I was tempted to ask if she needed help out of genuine concern, but we really weren't that close. She solved some of that quandary when she reached the doorway. She leaned on the side and looked back at me.

"I'm going to leave the bathroom door partway open. If you hear a thud, or it sounds like I need help, come check on me, all right?"

"I will," I promised.

She smiled briefly and disappeared into the room, presumably to an ensuite bath.

I found the hotel directory and made some calls. Yes, they would send up two ice packs and some Aleve for that muscle pain. And yes, while the kitchens were still closed, I could order some pre-packaged foods— sandwiches, yogurt, fruit, and a selection of chocolate bars. I asked for the works, not knowing what Sarah might like, and hoped her account could handle it.

I felt like a billionaire in this room.

Bringing myself back down to reality, I started the kettle for tea, then thought about my pants. They were itchy where they'd picked up swamp water and dried, but I didn't have any spare clothes. And, even disregarding switches, I didn't want to parade around in my underwear.

I explored the closets, wondering if they might have a robe or something I could use and was rewarded with one of the fluffiest robes I'd ever seen in the bedroom closet. I felt guilty taking it for a minute, but I noticed a similar hanger and plastic wrapping discarded on the bed, so I guessed Sarah had brought one into the bathroom with her.

Thinking of Sarah, I stood close to the partially opened bathroom door.

"Are you all right?" I called loudly to be heard over the running water.

"Yeah," she replied after a pause. Her voice sounded a little choked up, but I didn't press.

I pondered the bedroom. One thing that was definitely lacking in this suite was a second bedroom. And this bedroom only had one bed. Admittedly, it was a bed so wide it was a square, which I'd only seen on TV, but I resolved to check if the couch in the main room folded out once I had more energy.

There was a knock at the door and I rushed over, opening it without even checking which, I realized when the door was half open, was possibly a fatal mistake. I slammed the door shut again and checked through the peephole to see what appeared to be a confused and slightly offended woman in a hotel uniform. I opened the door again, blushing.

"Sorry. I, ah, slipped."

She nodded and fake-smiled. I took the three trays of random food she handed me, including the bottle of Aleve, and she left. I locked the door and made sure the weird hotel door-lock thing was engaged.

My stomach growled, but I also desperately wanted to get my itchy pants off. Sarah solved my dilemma by coming out of the shower wrapped in her fluffy robe. She had a Band-Aid on one hand, one on her neck, and one on her cheek. They were tinted dark enough to do a credible attempt at matching her skin tone. I bet the hotel didn't stock those. She must have brought her own supply.

The bandages made me realize that most of the scratches and bruises I'd accumulated over the course of the night had healed during my switch from overly curvy to regular girl form. That was normal to me, but I hoped Sarah hadn't noticed the disappearing injuries.

"Your turn!" she said, looking and sounding a little better. "The bonus of hotels. Endless hot water!" Then, she pounced on the Aleve. "Ah, that's brilliant, thanks!" She took one pill with some water from the kitchen. "And tea too," she noted with excitement. "Oh, and you got snacks. You're a treasure, you are. I should eat something, I guess." She sighed.

I left her pondering the snacks and went into the bathroom, which was nicely misty and warm. It was a hot July night, but the hotel's air condi-tioning kept the rooms on the cool side, and the muscles I'd abused were all stiffening up. It was a huge relief to skin out of my clothes, with the bathroom door firmly closed and locked, and step into the hot shower.

Washing my hair, I realized it was still long from my previous shift, coming down past my shoulders. Why had I shifted to that overly curvy form? I had a sinking feeling I knew exactly what it was. *How dare he?* My thoughts at the time echoed in my memory. When I looked back at all my unexpected switches to girl form, it was all Ian. And especially shifting with, ahem, enhancements. That had to be the result of my deep desire to attract Ian, combined with jealousy at Angela's gorgeous curves pressed up against him.

I laid my forehead against the relatively cool tiled wall, tears welling up as a hot mix of frustration and despair caught in my throat. I resisted banging my head against the wall, since I wasn't sure I'd be able to stop if I started, and it might alarm Sarah, who didn't need any more shocks tonight.

I dragged my mind away from that well of self-pity. I had so many other questions buzzing in my head. Was it really safer to stay here? With what I'd seen tonight, what did I really know about Sarah? And how long could I avoid switching in front of her?

On the other hand, it sure seemed like Sarah might have answers to some of the unbelievable stuff I'd been seeing lately, and maybe even some old questions about Angela's troubles, and my own switches. I wasn't going to switch soon, but I would probably switch sometime tomorrow. I had some time to think. Some time to maybe get a few answers before I had to decide.

Assuming the private security goons didn't find us here. I was going to have to trust Sarah on that. And, if they showed up here, at least we would be together. I had to admit, as much as she had been keeping secrets from me, I felt safer with her.

When I came out of the bathroom, wrapped securely in my fluffy robe, Sarah was already in the gigantic bed with the covers pulled up to her neck. She wore a purple sleeping cap. The lights were off in the bedroom, but still on in the main room. I quickly turned the bathroom light off, with only a little fumbling. For a second, I thought I might get away with leaving her sleeping, but her eyes opened.

"Come and lie down for a couple of hours. We'll get up at seven-ish and I'll help you contact the people you need to before they get too worried."

"I, ah, I was thinking I'd just sleep on the couch," I said, haltingly. Smooth, I was not.

"Bollocks," she said. "There's two beds' worth of space I'm not using. Come lie down. We can get housekeeping to make up a bed in the main room for tomorrow night if you want."

"But I don't have …" I waved a hand at my body.

"I laid a pair of shorts and a T-shirt at the bottom of the bed there, along with a toothbrush and toothpaste from the hotel. Go get ready and come to bed, Kayla. We're both exhausted."

I went back to the bathroom, brushed my teeth, and put on Sarah's clothes. The shorts were well-worn and had 'Juicy' written across the butt. They were loose on me. The T-shirt had a faded movie poster from that '80s movie *Labyrinth* with that guy, David Bowie? It was an interesting combo.

I lay down in the bed as carefully as I could, staying right at the edge, and I was asleep before I could worry about anything more.

~*~

"Well, what do we have here?" The cop shoved my license back to me.

I stared at it in horror. It was mine, but it read 'Kayla Torean' and showed an obviously female headshot with long hair and a V-neck shirt. I glanced down. I was in male form, wearing male clothes.

The cop leaned in the window, putting his face close to mine. I wanted to run but felt like I couldn't move, not even to take my hands off the steering wheel.

"Yeah, let's see what you've really got under those clothes," a new voice said in quietly menacing tones from inside the car. I realized it was Ian, lounging in the passenger seat, dressed in the same charcoal-grey suit as the private security guys. There was an angry twist to his mouth.

In that second, I knew it was a nightmare and clawed my way into wakefulness, shaking off the feeling of impending doom.

I had these stress dreams once in a while. I would suddenly realize I was female-shaped and either naked or in a skimpy swimsuit, so there was no way I could hide. Everyone was taking pictures and videos while I begged them to keep it quiet.

Sounds of whimpering came from Sarah's side. She had thrown off half her blankets and was huddled, curled up on her side, turned away from me.

She wore similar sleeping gear to what she had provided me—pale green shorts and a deep green tee. What caught my attention, though, were the lines of ridged scars on her lower back. Angular lines that at first glance seemed random, but I quickly realized they could make up three arms of a swastika. Where the fourth arm would have been was smooth, unblemished skin. Like someone had been roughly carving that into her back but hadn't finished. The wounds were fully healed, but not old. They definitely fit the seven-month timeframe she'd mentioned before when referring to the assault she was recovering from.

I tried pulling the sheet up to re-cover her, but that change to warmth didn't seem to ease her struggles. Maybe I could wake her a little? It was fully light out now, and the archaic clock/radio on the bedside showed just past eight. If I could trust it, we were supposed to be up already. I deeply missed my phone.

When I carefully nudged her hip, it didn't help. I jogged her hip back and forth a little more, calling her name. She rolled slightly onto her back. Then, her eyes shot open, and there was a fist heading for my face. No, my throat! I threw myself backward. Her knuckles grazed my throat and connected slightly more solidly with the side of my jaw. I rolled off the bed onto the floor, landing in an awkward pile, but not hurt.

I wiggled my jaw. It hurt, but far less than the sore muscles and remaining scratches from yesterday that I'd jostled in the fall.

Sarah's face appeared over the edge of the bed with a horrified expression.

"Kayla! Are you all right? I'm so, so sorry! I've never done that to a friend before."

"I'm okay." I sat up, internally cataloguing my body, now that I remembered. I seemed to have everything in the same places as when I'd gone to sleep. I would have to judge my switch stability later when I had time to concentrate. Sarah still looked highly concerned and upset. I stood up.

"See, I'm fine." I smiled. "It's not the first time someone's thrown a punch at me. Besides, I figure after the day you had yesterday, you deserve some latitude."

She scooted her bum up, then rose so she was sitting on her heels, legs folded. She still held her injured arm close to her chest, using only her other arm. She didn't really need more than one, I could attest. I resisted rubbing my jaw where she'd clipped me.

"Thank you. I appreciate it," she said, looking relieved. "I probably should have warned you not to touch me when I'm sleeping, or especially when I'm having a nightmare."

"I'll remember!" I said, with a grin. "I'm thinking it wasn't you getting hurt that you were worried about when you thanked me for preventing anyone getting hurt after that dad came to yell at us in the car."

"Ha! You're not entirely wrong," she said with a feral grin, then looked around. "Oi. It's getting late."

"Yeah, I want to make sure Ravi got home okay," I said worriedly.

"Give me a minute in the loo, then I'll set up a safe way to call." She held out her good arm. "Help me off the bed?"

"Are you okay if I order breakfast?" I asked as I steadied her.

"Of course! Order me up a big stack of pancakes. And whatever you want for yourself."

She went into the bathroom and fully closed the door this time, though she didn't lock it.

I put on my robe. I had to pee, but that was never as big an issue in girl form. I could hold it.

~*~

As soon as she was done, Sarah opened an app on one of her laptops that let me make voice calls securely. She was adamant that it was too dangerous to use my phone. She wouldn't even let me take it out of the special signal-blocking bag we'd put it in last night. I realized I remembered precisely four useful phone numbers without my contacts app: Mom, Dad, Ravi, and Angela. Fortunately, they were the key people I needed to contact.

She left me as alone as she could to make the calls by going into the bedroom with her other laptop. Of course, the app might be secretly recording, so I tried to keep my conversations short.

When I tried Ravi's phone, I got barely two seconds of Ravi's very relieved-sounding voice before his dad took the phone and started grilling me.

"Where were you two last night? When I couldn't reach Ravi this morning, I called your parents, and guess what? They had no idea Ravi was supposed to be with you."

I faintly heard Ravi in the background yelling, "You don't have to say anything!" and, muffled, but louder, his dad telling him to be quiet.

"I'm sure it's a misunderstanding Mr. Patel," I said.

He grilled me again about where Ravi had been and if Debbie was there. Mr. Patel really didn't like Debbie. I probably shouldn't have done it, but I didn't want to talk too much in my lowered, male-passing voice near Sarah, and I was running on just a few hours of sleep.

"Mr. Patel," I broke into a pause in his tirade. "If you want to know what Ravi's been doing, you should talk to Ravi. I have to go now." I clicked the 'end call' button on the screen.

I leaned back in the hotel's uncomfortable chair and sighed. I felt bad for Ravi, but, given everything else that had happened, I was just happy to hear his voice and know he was safe. From private security goons, anyway. I wasn't so sure about his father.

The call to my parents was easy due to my pre-existing arrangement of the fictional sleepaway camp. I tried Mom first and, as I'd hoped, they were still on their way to work. Dad was driving. She appreciated my checking in with them like they'd asked me to and told me to call later if I wasn't going to be home tonight.

I debated calling Angela, but it was too early in the morning for that call, for both of us. Also, I figured I should probably talk with Sarah before contacting Angela. There could be extra security concerns.

Room service came to the door with breakfast, and I put aside my worries about Angela to fill my stomach. Sarah popped out of the bedroom and was also eager to eat. Our conversation was sparse for a while, mainly centred around Sarah's browsing of the hotel's catalogue of services, which included in-room massages, pedicures, a pool, and a hot tub. She said we both needed to relax, and I couldn't argue that point. Sarah was still alternately heating and icing her shoulder, very carefully testing its movement between cycles.

Even with everything else going on, I felt oddly relaxed. Maybe it was just knowing there wasn't anything I could do at the moment, like when a vacation takes you away from all your chores at home. Then, I realized a big part of it was that I didn't feel a switch coming on at all. Not even a little bit, which was weird for my female shape. I had only felt this before in male shape, when I expected to be stable for several days. I sagged in relief. Nothing was certain, ever, for my body, but this was as certain as I got.

Perfect timing. Suspiciously perfect timing.

Maybe my body was actually starting to listen to me?

Or maybe it had always been listening, and I'd just been giving it mixed messages?

"What are you thinking about?" Sarah asked, and I realized I had let loose a heavy sigh.

"Angela," I said. Which was true enough, since she was always in the back of my mind. "I'm worried about her."

"You've mentioned Angela before. Your best friend, right? What about her?

"Ian specially invited her to that after-grad party."

"Oh, the recruitment party." She nodded, looking serious. "Angela's white, right? And rich?"

"Uh, yeah, more or less, on the rich part. Very pale. Redhead."

She nodded. "Do you have any reason to believe she might have some mage talent?"

"… Mage? What would that look like?" I asked with a stir of dread that I knew exactly the kind of things she was going to say.

"It often looks like symptoms of mental illness that come and go, randomly. Reacting to things that no one else can see, feel, or hear. Sudden terror or anxiety for no known reason."

I think Sarah picked up everything she needed to know from my look of dismay. I didn't mean to give away Angela's secrets, but it seemed Sarah could have some highly relevant information.

"Ah. Well. If she might be a mage, that puts a different light on it," she said. "Every year, they scan the current crop of graduates to see who might be most useful. They choose either potential minions or people they think may have mage potential. Mages are brought into the Clan over the next few months, or they die in some convenient way."

"Hold on. When you say 'they scan,' who are 'they?'" I had a sinking feeling I knew already, but I needed it confirmed.

"A group of powerful mages. They call themselves wizards, and they're organized into what they call 'clans' which hold certain rights or territory, or both." She looked at me directly. "Ian's uncle is a high-ranking member of a wizard clan. A leader of the local chapter, and he's been training Ian to join."

My mouth went dry as new terror bubbled up. Just when I thought I'd reached my limit.

"I wish we'd had this talk a couple of days ago, before Angela went to that fucking party."

"I expect they've had their eyes on her for quite a while. Likely from before we met," she said. "Don't beat yourself up over the past. Let's focus on the future."

"So, if the people they recruit can't or won't do what the Clan wants, the Clan kills them?"

"Yes." Sarah nodded solemnly. "They've been doing it for hundreds of years. Seeking out anyone with significant mage talent and either assimilating them or killing them. Real-life Borg, basically"

"I need to get Angela away from them!" I'd seen enough Star Trek memes to understand the Borg reference.

"If she was at that party, then she's already been marked." Sarah shook her head sadly. "She would need a full extraction."

"Okay, let's do that," I said breathlessly.

"Kayla." She sighed. "I'm on my own out here and injured. In several ways." She wiggled the cold pack she was holding to her shoulder. "I don't have the resources or authorization to call in an extraction for your friend. I'm sorry."

"Can't we call the police?"

"And tell them what? My friend went to a party at a rich white guy's cabin with a bunch of other teens, and she's still there? What are they supposed to investigate?"

"Do you have any proof about the murders?" I challenged.

"Yes." She said firmly. "But nothing local and recent enough to be interesting to the cops. And also," she took a breath, "It's likely any questions we ask will be reported back to the Clan. The police are usually lousy with Clan agents. They make an effort to get loads of their people on police forces at all levels."

"Um … Yeah, I can see your point," I admitted, looking down and collecting my thoughts. This conversation had detoured from the original point, which was getting Angela away from the Clan. "Wait, you said 'authorization?'" I looked straight at her. "Who exactly do you work for?"

"That's well above your pay grade." She gave me a stern look. "We're structured into independent cells, but I have some channels to call for help … if I think the gain is worth the cost. How far are you willing to go to get her out?"

What would I do to keep Angela from getting hurt? Was that why Angela had called me to the party? Was she looking for an escape at a time when the private security following her around—possibly invisibly—would be distracted? Had I blown my chance with a sex switch due to my own insecurities?

"I'm in, whatever it takes."

"I just want you to know that it could take a lot," she said intently. "These people will not hesitate to kill. If we get into this, you're going to need to do exactly what I say, or you could get both of us killed."

"I will," I said solemnly.

Sarah nodded. "All right. I'm willing to consider an extraction. If we can come up with a viable plan, I'll consider taking this forward to my people."

CHAPTER 16

The first thing we did was go back to bed. We were both running on a couple of hours of sleep. With my next switch postponed, it seemed into the indefinite future, I let Sarah convince me to share the giant bed again.

I didn't wake up until the early afternoon. Sarah was still sleeping, lying on her back at the moment. She seemed peaceful now, though she'd shoved her blankets off again at some point. Looking at her, I had a strange double vision, knowing that in my male form, I would find this rumpled scene erotic, but in this form, it barely registered.

I gently laid the blankets a little higher on her and slid quietly out of bed. Unlike my situation with Ian, I didn't feel any indication that I was going to switch to male shape due to potential desire. That might become an issue later, though. I didn't have any trouble with Ian for most of the year until my feelings grew to the point where I couldn't deny them. I really hoped I didn't develop some half-baked crush on Sarah in male shape. That would be awkward.

I carefully swung the bedroom door mostly-closed and, heart pounding, hurried across the bristly hotel carpet to Sarah's bags. I might only have a few minutes to check this out. I ignored the two laptops on the desk. There was no way I could break into them, and she could check for any attempts.

My first target was her large laptop bag, but I didn't find anything weird other than a couple of oddly-shaped devices with network cable ports. Frustrated, I moved on to her suitcase but a quick search, trying not to disturb the folded clothes too much, didn't turn up anything more alarming than a sex toy. I hurriedly tucked everything back and zipped it closed.

I sat back on my heels, scanning the room. What was I even looking for? Something that would give me a clear sign that I either could or could not trust her? What would that even look like? Perhaps I'd just know it when I saw it.

The jacket she'd worn last night caught my eye, where it was hung on the back of a chair. Excitement uncurled in me. Maybe …?

It had a lot of pockets, and every pocket had something interesting—a folding utility knife, an old-school analog compass, and the spell papers in an inner pocket, which were protected inside a plastic envelope. They didn't feel like anything more than ink on paper to me, but I'd seen what one of them could do with my own eyes.

She had two different wallets, each one stuffed with at least two thousand dollars in cash, along with a driver's license and other miscellaneous cards. One licence was Canadian, under the name Sarah Bonet, and one American under the name Sarah Forbes, that she'd checked in with. I tucked them back in their pockets.

One remaining, heavy bulk in a pocket turned out to be a sleek, lethal-looking taser. I tucked that carefully back where I found it.

I stepped away from the jacket, leaving it hung as best as I could manage in the exact same way it had been before, then went to the fridge and took out leftovers to snack on while my heart settled and I could think about all of this. I had stepped off the edge of the world that made sense to me. Now I had one foot descending into empty space, not sure where the next step down would be. Or if there was a step at all.

Who was Sarah, really? Her real name probably wasn't even Sarah, but that didn't matter to me. All I could do was choose to trust her or not based on what I'd seen so far. The contents of her pockets matched her story. Maybe I should have tried searching around her house before, but how could I know I was going to be thrown into the deep end with her?

Of course, her story was terrifying. Wizard clans in control of the world? I could see why she'd told me, back in the woods, that this was going to change everything. It was the kind of story I would have dismissed as a crackpot conspiracy theory if I hadn't seen her carve a hole in thin air with a piece of magic paper, or Angela go catatonic in a hotel with the wizards hunting her, or my sudden ability to see in the dark.

It was a lot, but I had always known something terrible was out there, a looming shadow my parents saw no way to fight and could only run away from. Shining a bright light on at least one part of it was good, even if what I saw was horrible.

But which part of the shadows were hunting people like me? Was it the wizards? Or Sarah's anti-wizard organization? Both? The enemy of my enemy could just as easily also be an enemy. Maybe it was some other group entirely? Sarah probably knew, but could I take the chance of asking her?

Maybe after we rescued Angela, I might feel secure enough to ask.

Noises from the bathroom reminded me to finish warming up and setting out the leftovers. I managed to finish just before Sarah came out in the hotel robe. She sat at the table and tucked into the snacks with no apparent suspicion.

"Shall we book a massage today?" she asked. "I could really use one. How about you?"

"Ah, sure?" I said. "I've never had one."

"What?" Her eyes widened, and she gripped the table in obviously fake alarm, then grinned. "I'll definitely book them. It's past time you experienced a good massage." She sighed and looked around the room.

"I'm going to be quite busy for the rest of the day. I've got a meeting with my therapist, then I have to spend some quality time deciphering the data dump I grabbed from the wizards' compound."

"Therapist?" I asked, curious.

"Yeah. I've been going for a while, remote visits, since my last job ended very … badly." A haunted look clouded her eyes.

"Is it helping?" I asked quietly. If the end of her last job had something to do with the incomplete swastika, I could see the need for therapy.

"It does help," she said firmly, then qualified, "some days more than others. It's a long process, they tell me." She looked down, making designs in a small puddle of condensation on the table. "And stuff like last night doesn't help. Hence, the session today."

"I can see that. Maybe, I could help you with the deciphering?"

"Maybe," she said, a hint of skepticism escaping. "I need to do some specialized work first, but I'll let you know. The most important thing you can do for me right now is provide a picture of Angela and another of yourself, so I can get some alternate identification for you both."

"Fake ID?" I asked, surprised. "You can do that?"

"It's a big part of our organization, keeping agents secure and anonymous as we move from job to job."

"Huh, well, I have a bunch of pictures of Angela on my phone," I suggested dubiously. I would have to turn it on to access them.

"Brilliant." She grinned. "I can connect to your phone without taking it out of the RF bag, then you can help me select a picture of her. I'll take one of you now to send in. We should be able to get some IDs by Monday or Tuesday."

~*~

Once she had her pictures, Sarah asked me to help tie her left arm in a sling so she wouldn't be jolting it all the time. Then, she gave me some cash and told me to go for a walk, as long as I stayed inside the hotel. I got that she wanted privacy for her therapy, and probably her technical work would go better without me hovering. I had to admit, I was eager to get out and walk around. Sitting around doing nothing while battling anxiety about everything was not a good time. My body needed to move.

The first issue I had to deal with to leave the room was my clothing. Sarah said she would have the laundry service pick up our dirty clothes, but that didn't help me right now. There was supposed to be a boutique just off the lobby where you could buy clothes, so I took myself down there wrapped in my hotel robe, hoping people would just assume I was on my way to the pool.

I bought shorts, a T-shirt, and a hoodie—all emblazoned with a maple-leaf-and-mountain motif. Very touristy. Certainly not something I would ever ordinarily wear, which felt good on the disguise front, if nothing else.

I even found some underwear in my size tucked in the back of the store. I also bought a two-piece bathing suit for a shocking amount of money, added to the room tab, more so to have some kind of bra than to have for swimming. If my shape stayed as stable as it was feeling today, I might be tempted by the hot tub later. I had learned to swim well enough when I was young, but post-puberty, I stayed away from pools and the body-revealing swimwear they required.

Wandering the hotel was only interesting for a couple of hours. I loved searching through buildings to find their little architectural quirks. Dead spaces, liminal spaces, spots where a little climbing and jumping could get you into places you weren't supposed to be able to access … but even though I found a couple of promising sites, I had to ignore them. The last thing I wanted to do right now was to draw attention to myself.

My most interesting find was a bookshelf the hotel kept as a little free library. Without my phone, I was locked out of all my e-books. I enjoyed scanning the titles until I came across the second book in the *Wheel of*

Time series. I ran my finger down the spine, an unexpected spike of sorrow putting a hitch in my breath.

Ian had convinced me to watch the series with him. Not directly together, but to watch the episodes so we could talk about them. He had read all the books and was a real geek about it, but he seemed to love hearing my newbie impressions.

Knowing what I knew now, I wondered how much of his friendship this past year had actually been designed to win Angela's trust so he could trick her into his family's cult. I hated the idea that, in falling for Ian's charming surface, I'd played a part in trapping her.

I picked it up anyway. What my head knew and my heart felt were distinctly different. Even with everything I knew now, my heart was still reaching for a connection to him.

~*~

"You want room service again?" I complained to Sarah when we started discussing plans for a late dinner—words I never thought I'd hear myself say. While spending the evening working my way through the thick book had been relaxing, I was not looking forward to spending more time in this room.

"Bored with the hotel menu already?" she asked with a raised eyebrow. "We could order in. Calgary has a surprising array of diverse restaurants for such a small city."

"No, just wanting to get out among people."

"Can't risk it, especially now." She shook her head. "Too many cameras everywhere—the official ones and social media videos. It's all monitored for familiar faces. And that monitoring is available to the wizards."

"Oh. Yeah." I grimaced. On some level, I knew that, but I'd never thought it would apply to my life. Then, my brain made connections, reevaluating some of my memories. "You haven't been house-bound, really. You're just afraid of going anywhere with a camera?"

"Mostly." She nodded. "When we first met, I wasn't sure whether the grocery guy was trying to lure me out to attack me or not. Either as an agent of the wizards, or just as a man, you know. But yes, the truck likely had a dashcam and could have identified where I was living."

"Scary, living like that." I shook my head.

"What, on the run from the wizards?" she said and then, with a glint in her eye, "Or as a girl?"

I felt my eyes go wide as a shock of fear ran up my backbone. "I …

what?" I stammered, and knew I'd blown my cover as soon as the words were out.

"You're living as a bloke, right?" she asked.

"I … How?" I stammered, blowing another opportunity to break out of this death spiral. Sweat slicked my body, and my stomach turned sour. How much had she figured out? Did she know about my switches?

"How could I tell? Oh, many little things. Existing as a woman in this world leaves its marks, and you're missing a bunch."

She seemed a little too calm to be talking about sex-switching. I focused on slowing my breathing to calm my racing heart. The more I freaked out, the more suspicious she would be. It was time for a little truth, but not too much.

"You're right," I said softly. "I've been living as a guy since I was eight years old. I missed a lot of the girl stuff, growing up and …" I took a deep breath, and let loose something I had barely admitted to myself. "When I met you that first time, and you assumed I was a girl … I didn't want to correct you. I don't want to stop being a guy, but I also want to be a girl sometimes. Does that make sense?" I was still sweating, but this felt good to get out. Forcing myself into the 'male' box had left its own marks, but forcing myself into the 'female' box would have left just as many. There hadn't been any good options for me.

"Completely!" She smiled. "Sounds like you may be nonbinary, maybe gender-fluid?"

Most of the tension that her revelations had ramped up drained from me in relief. I didn't try to hide it. She would see it as my relief that she accepted me as trans. That was still too close to the reality of my switches for me to be comfortable, but it was far better than the real truth. Though there was one more thorny issue I had to bring up.

"Are you sure you're okay? I know you had some issues with guys, and we've been sleeping …" I gestured vaguely to the bedroom.

"I'm entirely okay with you, in any gender. I don't expect you'll trip any of my triggers, but …" Her face shifted from her smile to a concerned look. "Have I been making you uncomfortable? I kind of forced you to share a bed."

"No," I said. "Not really, it's okay. I'm just not used to sleeping with anyone," I said, and only when I saw the corner of her mouth quirk did the other meaning of my words occur to me. I felt my face heating. She moved on quickly, though.

"I'm pretty sure Kayla isn't the name you normally use. Would you like me to call you by another name? And change pronouns?"

That put me on the spot. If she didn't already know, I didn't want to give out my usual name. But I also didn't want to look like I was hiding it.

"Can we stick with Kayla?" I asked. "It's probably good for security if I use a different name, right?"

"That's very true." She nodded. "And you're okay if I keep using she/her pronouns, for now, to fit the cover identity?"

"I'm good with that." It was a huge relief that her suspicions had been diverted, for now. That wouldn't hold through an actual switch at these close quarters, but I was still feeling no urge to switch, so I was likely safe there. For the next day or so, anyway.

"Sorry to scare you," Sarah said, a little contritely. "I've been seeing that edge of discomfort, and I wanted to make it easier for you."

"Ha!" I let out a short, sharp laugh. "It's okay, I'm relieved." And I was able to give her a genuine smile, which she returned, with a gentle clasp over my hand on the table.

"Now," She returned to her more businesslike attitude. "I think it's time you made some calls to family and friends again, so no one freaks out and stirs up a mess trying to find you."

"I agree," I said vehemently, then, more tentatively, "And, you're okay if I call Angela, right?"

"That would be a good idea. If you're ready to handle that? I would keep it short. You can't let on that you're concerned about her." She finished in serious tones.

"I know. I can do it." I assured her.

Sarah set up the app and sent me to the bedroom with the laptop so I wouldn't disturb her work, but I still felt easier at the thought of using my lowered, boy voice in calls, knowing I had an iron-clad excuse now.

I psyched myself up for the call to Angela, but her number quickly went to voicemail. Disappointment weighed me down. I desperately wanted to confirm she was okay.

Next, I called my dad and reassured him I was still busy with work. He told me he hoped I was making some good money with all the time I was spending there. I assured him I was. And I hoped Sarah would back me up on it. I would be in for a lot of questions if I had nothing to show for this time.

I managed to talk to Ravi too. He said his dad had calmed down after a while, but the whole debacle made him miss a shift at parkour camp and Devon was pissed. Everything was good, otherwise. Best of all, he passed on that Debbie had seen Angela at the after-grad and that Angela had asked them to make sure I was okay, which warmed my heart a little. I asked Ravi to check up on Angela and make sure she was okay, too, or to see if Debbie could do it.

Ravi assured me they would and wanted to talk longer, but I cut the call short with an excuse that a camper needed me.

~*~

"This first thing you need to know about magic is that everyone has to find their own path to using it," Sarah said from where she sat at one end the suite's couch, both legs curled up under her. I sat on the other end. We were drinking freshly-brewed tea, and while we waited for our room-service supper to arrive, we were finally diving into the discussion about magic that Sarah had been promising me since our unexpected meeting in the woods.

"The world has capitalized on technical processes that make people replaceable. The same actions on the same inputs always produce the same results. That's really handy, to a point." She sighed. "The energies we collectively call 'magic' are less predictable. What you can do with them depends heavily on who you are. Most people have very little connection to them, some have a little more, and very few people are immersed in the energies, whether they like it or not."

"You're one of the connected people?" I asked. Or maybe it was more of a statement, given what I'd seen her do.

"In a way. I'm in the 'a little more connected' group. Just enough to have some sensitivity to magic, but not enough to do much with it."

"But yesterday you—"

"Magic can be bound in writing, and sometimes other mediums like metal or stone, though they are extremely hard to work with. A mage I work with gave me those spells for interrupting wizard wards."

"And wards are?" I was fascinated. If I hadn't seen and felt what I did last night, I might not have believed it.

"A lot of things … I'm not going to be able to fit an entire magical education into a few hours, but in short it's a name for a kind of spell that can be applied to an area, sometimes a large area if you have enough power available, to detect specific things moving through it, like say a human. When that happens, some other spells are invoked."

"But the canned spells you carried were like keys?"

"Canned, I like that." She chuckled. "More like lock-picks, designed to make a temporary hole in the ward so you can pass through without it invoking the linked spells."

"And one of the linked spells could be that tracking spell that we might have on us?"

"Correct. The tag binds down close to the core of your being, your unique life energy. They are really hard to dislodge without killing the person. The only good news is that since life is always changing, it's practically impossible to make one last longer than three days."

It sounded a lot like the spell I shrugged off yesterday with my switch. I must have run into a ward which had lost its lock on my 'core' when I'd switched. That was a little disturbing. I'd always thought of my switches as a very superficial thing that didn't really change who I was, but maybe it went deeper than that.

"If making magic is very personal, how about the impacts of magic? Is everyone affected by spells the same way?" I asked, carefully nonchalant.

"It depends on the magic." Sarah looked thoughtful. "If a mage creates fire, it's going to burn everyone equally, but magic that specifically affects the mind or body can be tricky. There's a specific type of mage who is not affected by tracking tags, or even most wards. Even mind-clouding doesn't work very well on them, which limits one of the best tools in the mage's toolbox—a kind of practical invisibility. They can also walk straight through most magic protections." She shook her head. "They're scary! Everybody wants to get their hands on them."

My brief moment of elation, hearing Sarah describe something very close to what I had experienced with the security goon at the mall and the weird, itchy blanket feeling at the party, crashed into fear and disappointment. I took a lingering drink of my tea to disguise my expression. It shattered my hope that perhaps, if there were two or more sides in conflict, one could offer a safe haven. It seemed there might really be no safe place for me.

Fortunately for me, our dinner arrived at that very minute, interrupting our conversation. By the time we got over the initial rush of setting up and eating, we'd moved on to areas of discussion safer for me, though just as disturbing.

"You have to understand that while Angela, on some level, knows she's in danger, she will likely fight any attempt to remove her from the wizard clan's influence. It's one of the first types of mental conditioning they slip in," Sarah said as gently as possible.

"I'll have to convince her to come with me?" I asked dubiously. Even without magic, Angela was hard to budge. I tried to think of some things that had worked for us in the past. "Is there some kind of range to the conditioning? Like, if I got her some distance away, she'd come to her senses?"

Sarah shook her head. "Sadly, with Angela starting at some level of trust for Ian, they'll almost certainly use a type of conditioning that stays in her head until it's removed."

"Forcing her isn't going to work. Even if we were alone, I'm not sure I could do it. Plus, I expect Ian or some other Clan members would be around?"

She nodded. "There's likely to be at least one invisible guard too. I can deal with the guards, I have some tools to track them, if you focus on Angela."

I would have to be careful not to let on to Sarah that the invisible guards were visible to me. That could be tough, unless, like Angela's stalker at the mall, they were outed as being invisible to everyone else through the surrounding people's reactions.

"Getting her drunk is out. She's way better at holding her alcohol than me." I sighed. "Hey, what about some other kind of drug? I've heard of people being roofied."

"That's a possibility." Sarah brightened. "There are drugs like a roofie, but without the disturbing memory loss, that you can slip in a drink."

That painted a much nicer picture. I vastly preferred half-carrying a seemingly drunk Angela to trying to wrestle her out the door and likely failing. She fought dirty when she had to fight. I could only hope she'd forgive me later, once we were able to deprogram her.

"There is a way to uncondition her, right?"

"Yes," Sarah said. "I can't do it here, but as soon as we get her out, we're going to need to move anyway. We can take her to a group in …" She paused to think. "Vancouver, probably. We could drive there and wouldn't have to cross a border."

"This is all feeling very real," I said as my stomach churned.

"As real as it gets." Sarah's face was set, hard, but her eyes were understanding. "I won't lie to you. This is very dangerous for everyone. But it's the only way to keep Angela from being sealed to the wizard clan. Once that's done," she shook her head, "her mind won't really be her own anymore, not when it comes to any major decisions."

I must have looked slightly dubious. I was trying to keep it off my face, but I had to wonder. So far, Sarah was the only source of information I had about the wizards, and about her side—the anti-wizards? —All the evidence I'd seen, from the private security goon's behaviour to Sarah's obvious wounds, including the recently healed partial swastika, was strongly supportive of her position. Even Angela's behaviour pushed me toward Sarah's side. Why would Angela call for help in such a coded way if she wasn't worried?

"I'll let you read a case file," she said and then added, firmly, "Tomorrow. This isn't something you want to read and then try to sleep right after." She looked bleak. "It will give you a better idea of the kind of people we're dealing with and whether you want to be involved in this at all. At the end of the day, this is your call. I'm not going to push you into anything."

She held her right hand out across the table, her left still bound up in its improvised sling. "Let's eat dessert, watch some more K-drama, and forget about wizards and danger for the rest of the evening, okay?"

It could have come across as patronizing, but there was real pain in her voice. She was asking for herself, as much as she was trying to protect my mental state.

"Of course!" I enthused. It was hard to believe that at this time last night, I'd been naively on my way to crash the after-grad. So much had changed in the last twenty-four hours. I didn't have the capacity to absorb any more. It was time for a break.

CHAPTER 17

We both managed to get a good sleep, and after a quick breakfast the next morning, we got back to work. Sarah had been very right to tell me not to read the case file before bed. The details were nightmare fuel.

She'd set me up on one of her laptops so I could read the file while sitting on the couch as she worked at the desk. She had her chrono device plugged into one of the weird adaptors I'd seen while snooping, and the other adaptor plugged into her laptop. I wasn't sure what they were for, and when I tried to ask, she diverted my attention, saying she was busy.

Judging by her hunched posture and the number of curse words in several languages she was muttering under her breath, I believed her.

The case file she'd given me listed in brutally clear terms the setup at a private prison in the US where prisoners were tortured by agents of the wizards, who were on the payroll as prison guards. Because, of course, the private prison was owned by an agent of the Clan.

The torture wasn't just for fun. They singled out people who, like Sarah, had some small amount of magical talent and used the torture as a way to siphon magic from them into a kind of storage that could be used by other mages. Like the canned spells Sarah had, but more general.

After an operation lasting several months, one agent managed to gain access to the Clan's most secure network and copy the details of all prisoners who were singled out for the torture program, the identities of the fake guards who were doing the torturing, and videos of the actual torture. Another agent had gone undercover inside the prison and managed to break out with two of the prisoners who were being tortured. The hacker agent was discovered shortly after sending the files and tortured for nearly three hours before a backup team could arrive and free them.

Afterwards, the duplicate prisoner files were sent to state and federal authorities and to the media. Most importantly, summaries were spread widely on the internet. The prisoners' wounds had been examined and documented at a hospital before the hospital management knew what a hot potato they had on their hands. State authorities had no choice but to investigate, and the public attention limited their scope to whitewash it.

Afterward, the prison company simply folded. A few mid-level admin staff were in custody awaiting trial, but all the top people conveniently disappeared. A short paragraph at the end of the conclusion detailed the fate of the agents. The undercover agent was listed as uninjured, reassigned. The hacker agent was listed as injured and on medical leave.

I double-checked the dates on the file.

Last December. A little over seven months ago.

I browsed through the appendices while I waited for Sarah to take another break. They included some raw videos of the prisoners' torture. I watched the first two minutes of one, but had to close it, nauseated.

Sarah got up to refresh her drink.

"Sarah," I called out softly, still using my 'girl' voice. "Can I ask you about this case?"

"Sure. What would you like to know?"

"That agent, the hacker. Was that you?"

She took a deep breath, let it out, and nodded.

Even though I'd expected it, the confirmation hit hard.

"I … don't know what to say," I admitted, ashamed. For all the challenges I'd seen, nothing in my life had prepared me to have the right words for this situation.

"It's okay," she said quietly. "That's a better response than any empty platitudes. There really aren't any words. You can't know, until you've been through a situation like that, where you're staring down your own death." Her voice grew huskier, and she took a moment to clear her throat. "And when you have been through it, you don't need any words."

"I'm sorry to bring that up."

"Don't worry." She gave a ghost of a smile. "I knew what I was getting into when I got you to read that file. But let's drop it for now."

"For sure," I said. "Thanks."

I returned her computer to her, and I went back to my *Wheel of Time* book to try to clear my head. It was a little confusing since I hadn't read the first book, and I vastly preferred the female characters in the show, but I could still let its fictional troubles distract and calm my mind.

Sarah was forced to take a break again when our in-room masseuse showed up mid-afternoon. My first real massage was fantastic. I felt like a warm puddle afterward, curled up on the couch while Sarah had her massage on the mobile table in the bedroom.

It felt weird to get mostly naked for a stranger, but Sarah had warned me about that part in advance, so I knew what to do with the towels for cover. She dressed in a halter-top and said she was going to limit the massage to some therapeutic loosening of her shoulders and neck, so that was also an option for me.

Sarah's massage must have been good too because she emerged with her arm out of the sling, saying it was still tender but felt good enough that she could move it around. A great relief to her, since she'd really been missing the use of her other hand while working on the decoding.

With the bedroom free, I thought it might be a good time to try calling Angela again. When I raised that question with Sarah, she agreed with me and set up the secure calling app for me.

This time, Angela answered.

We got through the initial greetings. She sounded … not bad. Not overjoyed. Maybe a mix of relieved and apprehensive, with a slight tinge of buried annoyance?

"Thanks for being there last week," she said. "It turned out okay, but I felt better knowing you were around if I needed you."

"I'm glad you were okay." I winced. She had needed me, but she'd already been too far under to know it. I hadn't been much help since I was busy being chased around by the guards.

Angela let out a slow breath. "I'm glad you were okay too, because I'm afraid I'm going to need you again."

Part of me jumped for joy, but a bigger part said 'whoa!' I hadn't had fun last time, and reading Sarah's case report had given me whole new definitions of how bad things could go. It might blow my chance for a rescue, but I had to be true to my gut feel of what I would say if I didn't have ulterior motives.

"Ange," I said. "As much as I want to be here for you, always, I can't do this again without knowing what's really going on. All of it."

There was a deep pause on the line. I waited anxiously. In the end, I would probably go anyway, but how she responded might give me some clues as to whether this was a real call for help or the wizards trying to lure me into a trap.

"Okay, you're right," she said, sounding tired. "We … I owe you some kind of explanation. That's part of what I would like to talk to you about. If you come."

Her response sounded genuine. Too eager to tell me everything, or refusing to do so, would both be worrying.

She gave me the details. It sounded wild. A costume party at a bar? An event open to people aged sixteen and up, she said, so it was plausible. It was also where Ian was holding his birthday celebration. I'd vaguely known his birthday was coming up, but I'd forgotten about it.

"I'll be there," I promised.

~*~

I worried Sarah would need a lot of convincing, but she turned out to be more excited about the event than I was.

"It's perfect," she said. "A very public place. Chaotic. In and out with Angela, and we can be on our way out of the city."

"Ian's not going to just let her go," I said dubiously. "Along with whatever other security is there."

"Let me worry about the security," she said. "Your job is to spike both their drinks, then get Angela out while they're under the influence."

"I'm not sure it's such a good idea for you to go. Your shoulder …"

"I'm good enough to be a distraction," she said, waving my concerns away. "I know how to stay safe."

I let her have that point. I wasn't in any position to determine what she could and could not do.

"We'll have to put together costumes quickly. The party's on Thursday. That's only four days. From the reviews I read, they're strict on costume and will turn people away if they half-ass it."

"Don't sweat it." Sarah grinned. "I'm aces at costumes. But, know that I'm going to be sending you all over the city to get what we need." She sobered. "One very important question I need answered first, though …" She paused, leaving me hanging for a second. "Are you going as a guy? Or a girl?"

~*~

I got some freedom from the hotel on Monday as Sarah's errand girl. She located stores where we could purchase the necessary supplies while

I went and bought them with the cash she provided. And I got my phone back! On a very limited basis. She said it should be safe enough now to use while I was away from the hotel, but to turn it off and put it in its radio-frequency-blocking bag unless I was actively using it to contact her.

My first stop was Walmart to pick up shoes, stockings, and a selection of makeup for our costumes. I also acquired a new bra for myself, which I wore immediately. The bathing suit top helped prevent my T-shirt from being too nippley, but it didn't offer much support for running. After that, Sarah sent me back and forth across downtown, and to a couple of points on the C-Train outside of it, seeking costume pieces—a cheesy wig of curly red hair and fishnet stockings for me, black nylons and black boots for Sarah. The boots were the hardest to find in the right size. I visited two separate stores that swore they had them, only for them to be out of stock or try to sell me something very different.

Walking the streets of downtown and taking the train were very different experiences while presenting as female. Lots of leering looks from random men, especially the business suit types. Guys sitting or standing way too close to me, whenever they could find an excuse. And, of course, trying to talk to me. I wasn't ready to talk to anyone, let alone guys ten years older than me.

I didn't get done with the last store until shortly past three, three train stops out of the city centre on the west leg of the blue line. I gratefully collapsed onto a bench seat inside with all my purchases. They weren't heavy individually but carrying them all at once made me wish I'd brought a backpack.

The train car was fairly empty when it stopped at Sunalta, heading back towards downtown for the afternoon rush. A girl about my age hurried through the doors, looking nervous, and started up the length of the car. A guy in his mid-twenties with a weighty backpack and a shirt with an anime girl on it barged in just as the doors closed, jolting them to a stop with his arm to make room.

The girl suddenly plopped down beside me and said in a loud voice, "Hey, good to see you!" And then, much more quietly, leaning toward me with her face turned away from the guy. "That guy was creeping on me at the store and followed me here."

I had heard about this type of thing from Angela, but I never expected it to happen to me. In a similarly loud voice, I said, "Girl! Glad you made it. I was worried you were going to be late for jujitsu class."

I'd thrown her a curveball, but she caught it with panache.

"Miss class?" She scoffed. "And miss my chance to make grown men cry when I pin them to the mat?"

"You're right. I should have known you'd never skip that."

With our seats facing toward the back of the train, we could keep an eye on the guy without appearing to look his way. I saw her relax when he took an empty seat a few rows from us.

"How far are you riding?" she asked.

"3rd Street." I still had a several-block walk to get back to the hotel that I wasn't looking forward to.

"Oh, that's too bad," she said, downcast. "But the train should fill up going through downtown. It'll be hard for him to reach me after that, let alone make a scene."

"If it's not full enough, I can ride to City Hall," I offered. "I'm not in a rush." It would make my walk a couple of blocks longer, but I would survive.

"Thanks!" She smiled. "I'll text my brother to come and meet me on the way home, just in case he tries to follow me again."

We chatted about nothing much for the rest of the ride. I related some of my struggles finding a pair of stockings in just the right colour and size. She responded with a shopping horror story of her own, and then we went deep into complaining about the entire experience of trying to find women's clothing at a reasonable price, in a reasonable timeframe.

We got so engaged that I blew right by 3rd Street and nearly missed the City Hall stop. I jumped up with my bag of bags and said a hasty good-bye as I slid past her. I fought my way to the mid-carriage door, catching it just before it locked, and escaped onto the platform. The train was certainly full enough. Hopefully, it would not thin out too much before she had to get off.

The whole experience left a warm spot in my chest. I was glad to help, and also happy to connect with another woman on a level that was out of reach when I was male-presenting. It made me realize how lonely I'd been, all these years, during the times I'd been female-shaped, cut off from the kind of connections I craved. I didn't want to give this up again.

~*~

"I don't know how I let you talk me into this." I sighed. However, I had to admit the hot water felt great, soaking all the stress from several days out of my muscles.

"I offered to buy you a different swimsuit," Sarah said contritely, soaking alongside me in the hotel's hot tub. "Sorry if this is really triggering your dysphoria."

Sarah was wearing a one-piece, probably because it covered her lower back. From the look of her figure, she'd rock a bikini like the one I was very self-consciously wearing.

I reflexively said no to her offer because my frugal upbringing balked at buying a whole other swimsuit at the horrific prices of the hotel shop. I didn't feel anywhere near a switch, and on this Monday evening, the whole pool area was nearly deserted, so it was silly to feel so exposed. Still, I was having trouble letting myself relax and enjoy it.

"Don't feel bad. It's not a dysphoria thing. Like I mentioned before, I find myself feeling more like a girl some days, and more like a guy on others. And sometimes not really like a guy or a girl."

"And right now you're feeling?" she asked.

"More like a girl," I admitted. "I'm just not used to wearing this little fabric in public."

"Of course. I remember having to get used to that." She looked down and shook her head, then looked back at me. "How long has it been since you've really dressed up as a girl?"

"Ah, since I was like, seven?"

"Right." She nodded. "You've missed out on a lot! Let's have a girls' night tonight. We can do our nails, at least, and see if we can finish our drama?"

"That sounds fantastic," I said, starting to feel a little more relaxed. It was so liberating to be around someone I could talk about gender stuff. Even if she'd come at it from a wrong assumption, it was exactly the support I needed right now. Of course, a wriggle of fear in my gut reminded me this was temporary. What would happen when I inevitably switched back to guy shape?

"I think I'm actually going to miss being stuck in this hotel," I said, a sentiment I never thought I'd express after initially feeling so trapped here.

"Me too," Sarah agreed. "But I'm looking forward to seeing the house tomorrow."

"You think they're still working on it?" I asked, sitting up more.

"Oh, yes. I've had a couple of chats with the builder. They don't need access to the house. He says the front porch is done, and they're working on the fence. They won't be able to finish the garage clear-out until I let them know if there's anything I want to keep." She sounded satisfied, even happy. It seemed an odd thing to worry about, considering.

"Ah. Sarah, I've been wondering," I started, not sure how to say this without being rude, but she returned an open and accepting look, so I continued, "I get the impression you're going to move on from here? Once this part of your job is done?"

She nodded. "I never stay too long in one place."

"So … why do you care so much about a house you're going to abandon soon? Maybe never see again?"

She was silent and thoughtful long enough that I started to worry, but her answer wasn't forced.

"You're right, maybe it's silly. The organization doesn't really care if I improve the property or not." She cupped her hands in the water, lifting them out and letting the water drip through her fingers. "I think it's because I do … what I do. I clean up a little mess here, and another mess there, and it's hard to see whether the outcome makes the world better or not. A little landscaping? It's immediate gratification!" She grinned broadly.

"I get it," I said. "Like weeding the garden when my problems all gang up on me. It helps."

"Something like that."

We sat in silence for a while. The hum of the hot tub and the rush of jets provided a white-noise background that cancelled any awkwardness.

"Do you think we can really rescue Angela?" I asked, finally voicing the worry that was really on my mind.

"I think we've got a good shot," she said. "That was a lucky break, her wanting to see you … like she's reaching out for help." She reached out and clasped my shoulder. "Don't worry, we've got this one."

CHAPTER 18

woke up to blood.

I'd completely forgotten about my period, and now I'd stained Sarah's shorts, as well as bled through to the bedsheet.

"I'm so sorry!" I said, mortified, calling from the bathroom as I rinsed the shorts in cold water in the sink.

"Eh, it happens," Sarah replied from the bedroom, entirely unconcerned. 'You can borrow a pad. They're in the blue case, on the counter."

"Thanks," I called back. "But the bed!"

"I'll add extra to the housekeeping tip."

And that was that.

At the end of a lazy breakfast, Sarah turned serious again. She took out a bundle of cash, mostly US bills, but also some Canadian, and handed it to me. It looked like most of what I'd seen in the wallets in her jacket.

"Should anything happen, don't worry about me. If you have a chance to get away clear, just run."

"Okay," I reluctantly agreed. "I'll hate it, but okay."

"Getting Angela free of the wizards has to be your top goal," she said, sliding the sleek taser I'd seen while snooping across the table. "Do you know how to use one of these?"

"Stick pointy end at bad guy and squeeze the trigger?" I suggested.

"Basically, yeah. Try to get a good, solid connection to flesh. The prongs will go through most fabrics, but heavy leather can defeat them."

With that stark warning of the dangers we faced fresh in my mind, I felt a spike of fear when I saw a silver Acura in the spot where we'd left the white BMW. I grabbed at Sarah's arm in warning, but she intercepted my hand before it could connect.

"It's okay. I'll explain in a minute."

She visibly relaxed once we were out of the dim, echoing parking garage and filtering through the streets of downtown. It was well after rush hour, and downtown traffic was manageable, so Sarah had some concentration free to alleviate my confusion.

"Ghosts brought the car."

"Um …" I stared at her. A week ago, I would have laughed and waited for the real explanation, but now I had no idea if she was being literal or not, and that left me feeling deeply unsettled. She relented quickly with a chuckle.

"We have people who help us out. Anonymously," she explained. "They run their own cells separate from the main org for their safety. We call it the ghost network, or ghosts, for short."

"Phew! You had me wondering if you were going to drop a whole new paranormal revelation on me."

"No, sadly. Ghosts, as the common imagination paints them, aren't real."

"Sadly?"

"There are some people I'd really like to see again," she said wistfully. "Even as ghosts."

It was a quiet trip after that. Sarah didn't speak again, and I didn't want to disturb her thoughts. We arrived at the house with no surprises, thankfully.

Though I was surprised to still be solidly in female form, with no switch expected. I was starting to wonder … was this the form I was supposed to be in? The more I relaxed into interacting in feminine mode, the happier and more solidly female-shaped I felt. Had I been fighting against myself all these years, trying to stay in a male shape, when I was supposed to be female?

It was an uncomfortable thought that I buried, for now. There were times before where I'd stayed in male form long enough that I wondered if my switches had finally stopped, so there was no point in worrying … or celebrating anything.

Sarah parked around the block and had us walk through the back alley to the house. Even then, she went ahead of me.

"If it's clear, I'll give you a thumbs-up. If I make an 'OK' sign." Her voice turned grim. "Run, and don't come back."

The back yard was completely clean now, having been thoroughly raked and mowed, with grass seed planted in brighter green splotches.

Most of the fence posts had been replaced. Alex and Ramiro were cutting and installing new fence boards between them. I waited, as asked, while Sarah exchanged greetings with the guys, and then unlocked the back door and entered the house.

I spent a very tense five minutes pacing outside until she opened the back door again and gave me a wave and a thumbs-up.

Freed from that concern, I turned to something else that had been nagging me while I waited. A couple of posts at the back hadn't been replaced. I walked past the work truck parked beside the garage and knelt at the first post. I probably would have replaced it, but the wood at the bottom was still acceptable. I moved on to the second. Alex had followed me and loomed as I dug a fingernail into the spongy wood. It definitely looked rotten.

"Yeah," he said, thumping the post. "This one feels pretty solid, so we left it in. Saved you some in cement, labour, and disposal."

"I appreciate the thought, but it's got to go." I pointed down. "It's rotting at the bottom."

"Ah, it's fine. Don't worry about it." He pointed to the two posts on either side that had been replaced. "Even if it's loose, the other posts will reinforce it once the fence is in."

"I don't think you're getting what I'm saying." Anger bubbled up at being ignored. What was this guy's problem? "It needs to be replaced, so replace it."

"Why are you making such a big deal out of this?" he huffed. "That'll add at least an extra day now that we've packed away the mixer and cement tools …"

He was still talking, but I didn't feel like arguing. Sarah hastily exited the zone and disappeared into the house. I went to the garage and yes, it was still there—a large sledgehammer with a tracery of rust. I crouched and grasped the handle near the head to lift it.

Walking back, I kept the sledgehammer close to my body until I was at the post. Alex gave me an odd look. He didn't seem to notice the hammer at first. His eyes widened, and he took a quick step forward, but I'd already brought the hammer up and was spinning around. He prudently hopped away from the post.

The head of the hammer hit the post with an echoing crack, followed closely by a soggy splintering sound. I loosened my grip as it struck, but it still stung my unprotected hands. I let the hammer head fall to the grass with a dull thud and rubbed each tingling palm on my hip in turn.

"Holy shit!" Alex cursed. The fence post was leaning at a steep angle now, almost completely separated at the bottom where the wood met the cement footing.

"Yup," I said. "I'd say that post needs replacing."

"You are seriously off your meds!" Alex shouted at me. "What the hell?"

I started back to the garage carrying the hammer.

He stomped back to their work truck, taking out his phone and voice-dialling the boss before getting in and slamming the door.

"You got a boyfriend?" Ramiro called from where he was standing by the table saw. I was relieved to see he was grinning.

"No," I called back, giddy from the rush of emotion. "But I am in a complicated situation with my ex-girlfriend."

"Fair enough." He touched two fingers to his forehead and made a casual salute.

I stayed in the garage for a few extra minutes to get my head back down to earth. What had I been thinking? This was not the time to cause trouble. And what did I care if a post on a house Sarah would never live in fell down a few years early?

Once my shakes subsided, I ambled out of the garage. To my relief, the guys and the truck were gone, though they hadn't packed up all their tools, so it was likely they'd be back soon.

In the house, Sarah was on the phone. This was the first time I'd seen her using a mobile phone. It was curiously small and skinny with only a tiny screen. "Yes, Mr. Khawaja. One hit. Knocked the post right off, or near enough."

"I understand completely."

"Thank you. You have a good day too."

She ended the call and closed the phone. I realized she'd been talking on an old-style flip phone.

"Sorry." I approached nervously. "He was being an ass about that post. It pissed me off."

"No problem at all, Kayla. The builder said any post that can be one-shotted by a teen girl doesn't meet his idea of quality." She paused thoughtfully. "Also, remember why I'm doing this work? We're pressured to accept these 'rotten posts' all the time. I don't want any of that in my landscaping!"

"Oh. Good." I reevaluated my emotions. "I hope I didn't startle you too much?"

"I'm fine!" She smiled broadly enough to put a slight wrinkle at the corners of her eyes. "The look on Alex's face was priceless. I wish I had a video of that moment. You'd go viral."

Seeing the look of horror on my face, she added. "Of course, I don't post anything to social media."

"Right, of course not."

"Oh," Sarah said, picking up an envelope from the counter. "We got ghost mail." The envelope wasn't addressed and had no stamp. It must have been hand-delivered. She opened it and slid out two Alberta driver's licences, then handed them to me. One had Angela's picture, with the name Annie Thomas, and the other had my picture, very much in girl form with my longer hair, labelled Meghan Alonso.

"Hmm. It could be worse," I said.

"Sorry. We don't get much choice for names on the driving licenses, especially on a rush order."

I noticed we were both listed with birthdates one year earlier. "You made us eighteen?"

"It will come in handy if you need to access some places or even book a hotel room." She said.

"Well, at least I'll feel better about driving in girl mode." I waved my license. I tried to hand the other one back to Sarah, but she declined.

"Keep it on you, in case you get an unexpected chance at Angela."

I nodded. The closer we got to the meeting at the bar, the more real this was becoming. I was really going to do it—get Angela away from the wizards and hopefully help keep my family, and her family, safe from them by taking us both out of reach.

~*~

I spent the next day driving across half the city. Sarah had found a very specific red minidress for her costume and a classic maid's outfit for mine from private sellers. They were the crowning pieces for our costumes, and I could free up Sarah to work on more decoding while I picked them up.

She gave me enough in US dollars to pay for the costume pieces in one envelope, and a second, thicker envelope containing my pay for the hours I'd submitted from our previous hanging out, as well as pay for our entire quarantine time at the hotel. I'd objected to being paid for the time I'd been sleeping, but she'd insisted.

My first stop had to be a bank to exchange the US dollars for Canadian dollars, then I had to get to the sellers who lived at opposite ends of the city, so I spent a couple of hours driving back and forth. I found driving soothing, though, regardless of traffic. It was something I always enjoyed about doing pickups and deliveries for Ravi. Cars always felt like my own personal bubble where no one could bother me.

The costume collection went smoothly, and the long drive on Stoney Trail gave me time to continue the thoughts I'd started after Sarah's revelations. It was easy to sit behind someone going 105 kph in the centre lane and turn my mind to other worries.

With what I knew now, I might be able to shake more information loose from my parents. Though I would have to be very careful in what I revealed. They would run again if they knew what I planned with Sarah, probably tying me up and putting me in the trunk if they had to. But the information I gained from them might help me figure out if telling Sarah would be worth the risk.

I also knew I couldn't just disappear with Angela without first hearing their side of what they knew about my switches. And, if the worst happened and we didn't make it, there were some things I wanted to tell them. I looked down at my emerald-green nails. There was a lot I'd been hiding from them. I didn't want to leave with that hanging over us.

I also realized that most of the fear I'd felt before, when I thought about opening this conversation with my parents, had vanished. Whether it paled in the face of my pure visceral terror running from the wizard guards, or my deep concern for Angela, or simply that I'd decided I really did want to live as a girl part of the time, I wasn't sure, and that was okay.

I stopped at the mall to pick up some supplies for my plan, which I had more than enough money for now, thanks to Sarah. I made it home a good ninety minutes before I expected Mom and Dad to return from work, even after dropping off the costume purchases to Sarah, who was deep in her decoding work again and barely acknowledged my coming and going.

Back at my house, I put away a few extra peace offerings I'd bought: my mom's favourite cereal and the more expensive brands of tea and coffee they sometimes got. Then, I ran upstairs for a quick shower. I'd only been away for four days, but home felt strange to me. A lot had happened since I'd last been here.

Feeling refreshed, I got started on the main offering. Treat foods that we didn't eat very often, but that I knew I could cook: wild salmon, fresh asparagus, mushrooms, and a store-bought chocolate raspberry cheesecake for dessert. This was going to be a tough discussion, and I hoped a good meal would help smooth over any wounds.

After swapping the salmon to the stovetop to cool and the grilled asparagus and mushrooms into the warming drawer, I ran upstairs to dress. My parents would be home from work any minute.

I changed into the new green dress I had chosen at the mall to match my nails. I thoroughly brushed my hair, still a few inches below my shoulder from my last switch. I slid in a couple of barrettes to keep it out of my face and accent my whole look.

Considering my face, I followed what Sarah had shown me last night. I brushed on a very restrained amount of light green eyeshadow, then applied some lipstick. It was a traditional red shade, not too bright against my skin. The change to my face still amazed me. How could a couple of little accents of colour make such a huge difference?

The unmistakable creak of the worn-out suspension of my parents' car hitting the lip of the driveway yanked me back to my plan.

I hurried downstairs and started shifting food to the table. I made sure to be standing idly at the edge of the counter when my parents came down the hall.

I had kept myself busy enough that I'd managed not to think too much about what this moment would be like. But, in those last ten seconds, listening to the rustling of shoes and jackets, I had to force myself not to flee back upstairs and change into boy clothes. My stomach felt like a lead brick sitting in my gut.

Mom saw me first. Her pleased smile, which had blossomed at the smell of the salmon, disappeared. Her lips thinned, and the skin around her eyes tightened.

"Stephen ..." The warning in her voice cut short my dad's rambling story about some work conflict.

His face held a great deal more surprise when he saw me.

"Mom. Dad. I think it's time we had a talk."

"Oh, baby, no." Mom rushed over, but stopped short of touching me. "Don't do this to yourself."

"What do you think I'm doing?" I was surprised at the intensity of her reaction.

She gave me a hard look. "You know very well, young ... man." She stumbled on the last word and waved a hand violently up and down. "You shouldn't be playing around with this. It's dangerous."

"I'm not playing." I tried to contain my anger and keep it from my voice. I hadn't expected a lecture. Did she think she actually had the moral high ground here? "This is part of who I am."

"It's part of you, yes," she said sadly. "But you mustn't let it take over. You have to stay disciplined or you'll never stabilize as a man."

"Why would I want to?" I asked in honest curiosity, forgetting for the moment that it had been my most fervent wish only two months ago.

"You know the world won't accept you like this." Her expression hardened into stubborn lines. "How do you expect to live, hold down a job, get married, if you keep flitting between male and female?"

"I'm starting to understand why I keep shifting," I said excitedly, but from the way Mom's face congealed, it wasn't something she was ready to hear. I snuck in one last comment before she went off. "For sure, I know that denying all the non-male parts of me is not helping!"

"You'll never be in control," she spat out. "Once you let the curse get the upper hand, it will ride you forever." She was shaking, tears gathering in her eyes. "I saw it. My uncle—or what should have been my uncle. He couldn't keep the same form for more than a few days. It broke him. No one could trust him to show up for a job. Eventually, he … he killed himself."

"He disappeared, anyway," my dad rumbled. "They never found a body, did they?"

Mom glared at him. "Don't confuse the issue. The important thing is—"

Her words grew distant as I descended into thought. Had my great-uncle really killed himself? Or did a wizard get him? Was that why my parents had been so terrified of my sex switching being found out?

Or, did he find help like I did, and say 'screw this unsupportive family?' Did I have an extra bunch of relatives wandering around somewhere?

For the first time in my life, I purposefully interrupted my mother in the middle of her sentence. "All of this is bullshit! I don't want to hear about what you think might be dangerous if other people know. I want to hear why you both left me to struggle with this my entire life!" Tears gathered in my eyes, and I let them. "Couldn't you see how much it was hurting me?"

"But that's exactly what we were trying to protect you from!" she half-yelled, tears openly running down her cheeks. "We had a rough start, with that awful Marnie girl." She scowled. "But we knew once you settled into being a boy, things would get better. And they did." Her voice was full of abrasive compassion.

"Right, well, it didn't work out that way, did it?" I was full-on angry now. "I never stopped switching, not even for a single week."

"Impossible!" She looked truly shocked.

"Maybe for you," I said bitterly. "I learned very young to hide the switches so I wouldn't be punished."

"We never punished you, son," Dad weighed in, his voice calm and sad.

"I don't mean you took me out behind the barn with a strap, but not being allowed to go outside or play with your friends sure feels like punishment to a kid."

Silence. Dad looked thoughtful, but Mom's anger and, I think, most of all, fear, were still in control.

"From the way you're talking, I get that this is a family thing? Did you go through it?" I asked, pulling back from re-hashing my childhood. I had promised myself I wouldn't go there in this talk. Maybe there would be time for that later.

"Yes," my mom admitted, staring at the floor. "I … I was beaten when I couldn't stay in boy form. My girl clothes were destroyed."

"Huh?" My mental gears clashed to a halt, and I recalled the cut-up girl's jeans from my mom's bin of keepsakes.

"My parents expected me to be a boy, but I was always a girl inside," she said in a quiet voice. Then, she grasped my hands between hers. "But you always wanted to be a boy. Don't give up on that!" It was clear none of this was news to Dad, thankfully.

"What made you think I wanted to be a boy?" I tried for an even, light tone, but I think she and I both felt it land like a slap across the face. For the first time, she was on the defensive.

"Because … that's what you said. And you were always out running around with your friends, riding your bike, climbing on *everything*." She had a faraway look in her eyes for a moment. "You never wanted to wear a dress or cook with me …" She eyed the full supper spread with some consternation.

"Mom, really?" I prevented myself from rolling my eyes. "I made one pronouncement when I was eight years old, and that was supposed to fit for my entire life?" I sighed. "You realize my friend Angela liked, and still likes, exactly the same things?" At least up until we grew up and other interests intervened, but she was still horseback riding and target shooting.

"But … I don't …" Her former certainty was gone.

I looked between her and Dad. They *knew*, they had *always* known, and they still didn't understand. But the little glimmers of uncertainty in their eyes gave me some hope. This conversation was far from over, but at least I had started it.

I strode to the table, the fabric of my dress rustling around my legs. "Can we finish this after supper?"

They both nodded, eyes widening at the laden table. They went upstairs together to wash up and change out of work clothes—and most certainly to talk privately.

Once they returned to the table, the rituals of serving and eating eased some of our tensions. No one was allowed to argue until we finished our first platefuls. I treasured this last interlude of family life, knowing how soon I would need to leave it.

"So, you're going to be a girl now? Is that what you want?" My mom fired the first salvo, continuing the argument. At least she was asking now, not telling.

"No," I said softly, but very firmly. "I'm going to be me."

CHAPTER 19

The next couple of days at my house were uncomfortable. My parents and I tiptoed around each other. My mom was touchy enough that my dad was getting splash damage, and both were giving me the silent treatment.

Three days later, I drove with Sarah downtown to a parking lot near the bar where Ian was hosting his eighteenth birthday party. Angela was one of the guests.

It was only eight o'clock now. An early start for a bar event, but the 'all ages' entry only lasted until ten. Angela *might* be able to flout the rules, as Ian's … date, but I couldn't count on that.

Sarah had helped me put the final touches on my costume. We'd dressed me up as Magenta from *Rocky Horror Picture Show*. Sarah suggested that theme when we first started planning, and I agreed it was perfect. It worked whether I was expected to be presenting as a girl or a guy.

Good thing too, because although I'd switched back to male shape the day after the big talk with my parents (the only upside was skipping the last two days of my period), I had switched back to girl form this morning. While this made getting dressed at Sarah's easier—I was almost, sort of, starting to trust that my body and my switches might be on my side for a change—it meant I had my breasts bound for a more androgynous look, since I still needed to pass as a guy for Angela and Ian.

It struck me, then, that I was a girl, needing to pass as a guy, cosplaying a girl.

The absurdity of it brought bubbles of laughter to my chest, which I worked hard to suppress. There was no way I could explain the joke to Sarah. Thankfully, we reached the parking garage at that moment and having to navigate its twists and turns gave me plenty of distraction.

Sarah's costume was not even slightly androgynous. I had to admire her as we got out of the car: the classic red minidress uniform, gold hoop earrings, and black nylons and boots. She wore her own braided hairstyle instead of the '60s hair, but I had to call that an improvement. The final touch was the black-box-like thing with its strap slung over her shoulder. It actually had blinking lights on it.

"You make an absolutely fantastic Uhura," I said. "But where did you get that prop?"

"This Tricorder?" She held it up with a grin and triggered a whirring sound. I immediately recognized it, even though I'd never really watched *Star Trek*. "I've had this for years. And don't give me that look. How can you have known me for this long without realizing I'm a complete geek?"

"Fair point," I said, and sighed. This was the part of the plan I liked the least, since it required that we not be seen together. "Well, good luck and all."

"Good luck to you, too," she said gently, with a wistful look that I found hard to decipher. I hoped she would be okay in the packed bar, but I wasn't going to bring that up again at the risk of sounding like I didn't have any confidence in her. I waved and headed on my planned route while she went on hers.

Shuffling past the bouncers with contraband strapped to my thighs was nerve-wracking. On one side, I had a slim flask with Ian's favourite Laphroaig scotch. On the other side, I had Sarah's taser. I was a physical manifestation of the carrot-or-stick metaphor.

Except the carrot was drugged, so, psych?

Thinking about the drugged scotch returned me to the sweet memory of Ian going out of his way to ensure I had a nice suit for Angela's cousin's wedding. It left a bitter taste now, because, of course, he'd just been making sure I stayed tight with Angela so he would have easier access.

People in line ahead of me casually flipped out their licenses for the bouncers, paired with a twenty for the cover. Those under eighteen held out their right hand for a bright green, fluorescent all-ages stamp.

Waiting in line gave me too much time with my thoughts. Worrying about what I would find in here tonight. Worrying about how I'd left things with my parents. They'd been about the same this morning as they left for work. I had taken the cowardly route by leaving them a note explaining that I needed to leave for a while, but that I would post updates at a specific Discord address.

I had no idea what I would write in my updates, but that was a future problem. I had to make it through the next few days first.

I didn't feel smooth or nonchalant at all, but I made it through the door. The bouncers only quickly glanced at my driver's license and didn't search me like they did some of the underagers. That was the main reason I had decided to use my fake ID: someone who could legit buy alcohol didn't have a need to sneak it in. Usually.

Quite a few people had gone all-out with their costumes. I guessed this event must've been a draw for the serious cosplayers. I saw a fair bit of *Star Trek*, *Buffy*, and *Battlestar Galactica*, including some guy in a fantastic full-body original series *Cylon* costume complete with voice modulator.

I also saw some *Potter*-esque costumes, which made me wonder if people understood the 'cult classic' concept. Though anybody making a big show for Potterverse stuff these days was either living under a rock or essentially signalling their alignment with the Gender Conservative Cult, so I guess that fit.

My costume came in as solidly middle-of-the-pack, which was fine with me. I didn't want to be memorable. While searching, I tried to simply experience the party. The smell of alcohol was thick in the air, laced with a hint of weed carried over from the smoking rooms. Sarah had done my makeup and helped with my hair. The looks I was getting suggested I looked pretty hot.

I appreciated the thought, but kept moving and tried not to make eye contact with anyone.

I could have texted Angela and asked where she and Ian were, but I preferred to run across them without a trace, if possible. Ian might not have any idea I was coming, and if that was the case, the less warning he had, the better.

If I was lucky, I wouldn't need to use the drugged scotch at all.

I left my phone where it was, stashed in the front pocket of my fancy maid dress, along with a small vial of the same drug that was in the scotch. My phone was turned off and in an anti-RF bag, on the chance someone was tracking it. I could use it if needed, but it couldn't be used to find me.

The bar was in the centre of the main room … go figure. Having a drink in my hand seemed like it would be excellent cover. Plus, I had never ordered anything at an actual bar before. I couldn't let this moment pass.

However, I didn't want to order anything that I'd be tempted to drink too much of. I wasn't here to party. "Gin and Sprite," I called out once I managed to get the bartender's attention. That got me a funny look, understandably. It was something my mom drank, and the only thing my overloaded brain could come up with in the moment. The bartender handed it over in a red plastic cup, without comment, in return for cash. Way too much cash. That was one expensive drink!

Wandering through the party felt similar to what I'd experienced in girl form while walking in the mall or down the street. The personal space I was allowed dropped to zero, and too many eyes tracked my movements. Another time, I might have enjoyed the extra attention, but here, tonight, it made my skin itch knowing there were potential enemies in the crowd. I'd have no idea who harboured dangerous intent and who was just horny until after they struck.

Huh. Welcome to womanhood, I guess.

Eventually, I spotted Angela and Ian at the far end of the games room. They were sitting alone, close together on a couch, not embracing this time, but deep in conversation. The room boasted a pool table with red felt and a couple of card tables, each of them supporting active games. A collection of red solo cups at Ian's elbow suggested he'd been drinking a lot.

Angela was dressed as the Dread Pirate Roberts from *The Princess Bride*—a character she adored, and an economical reuse of last year's pirate costume, with the addition of a black mask over the top half of her face.

Ian was wearing a black T-shirt with the sleeves cut off, a bad, shaggy brown wig, and dark sunglasses. Maybe he was trying for a disguise, but I'd spent far too long ogling the lines of his smoothly-muscular arms and the fine bones of his hands to fool me.

The icing on the cake was Brent: the chief goon from the after-grad party; the one I had seen working with Ian's uncle at the Banff Springs, and again following Angela at the mall. The way he stood stiffly in a corner in that charcoal suit that just screamed 'private security.' It also suggested he was likely invisible to everyone else. Again.

I forced my head and eyes to keep moving, scanning the room, not stopping on the goon. I suppressed an urgent desire to back away before Ian and Angela saw me, but that would also look odd to the guard, and wouldn't help free Angela. I took a deep breath and continued forward.

Ian and Angela were fully focused on their conversation. His arm stretched across the top of the couch behind her. Her hand rested casually on his thigh. The knowledge of Ian's motives and Angela's vulnerability wasn't enough to smother the coal of jealousy I was desperately trying to ignore. Instead, it fanned into a live flame.

A couple of steps closer, and Angela's head came up, looking at me. For a moment, her eyes were shuttered like there was no recognition. Then a grin blossomed.

"Mike!" she said in a surprised, yet pleased, tone. "I didn't expect to see you here!"

Ian's head snapped in my direction. For the briefest instant, I swore I saw an expression of relief on his face before it dropped back into a controlled, bland look. But that couldn't be right.

"I was just thinking the same thing, Ange." I had guessed right. This was supposed to be a random encounter. How much did she know about the hovering, invisible guard? "Hey Ian. How's your summer going?"

"Surviving," he said, scanning my appearance. "What the hell are you wearing, man?"

"Uh, a costume? For the party." I went for a 'puzzled' look. *Bluff it out*, I told myself. I felt more uncomfortable in my costume than before, hyper-aware of every feminine curve, despite knowing I'd hit more of an androgynous look.

"A surpassingly good costume," Ian said with a genuine note of appreciation. "*Rocky Horror*, if I'm not mistaken … Columbia?"

"Magenta," I said. A short while ago, my insides would have been glowing warmly at his approval, but I was mostly numb to it now, knowing what he was pulling Angela into.

"Aaah, of course!" Ian chided himself. "I'm always mixing those two up."

Now that he'd turned toward me, I saw that the front of his sleeveless black tee was emblazoned with a white skull and crossbones and the word poison below it.

"Oh! Oh! *Spinal Tap*!" I exclaimed as the band name jumped into my head. I remembered Ian talking about them in one of our rambling chats at school. About the whole weird fan lore around 'the curse.' He'd sent me some articles. "The doomed drummer guy? Or one of them, anyway?"

"Right in one!" Ian said, smiling, but with a cutting edge. Or was I just projecting?

For a moment, it felt like we were back in school, just friends chatting. But I wasn't the same person as I'd been, and Ian had never been who I'd thought. I mourned the passing of our friendship while forcing myself to stay light and friendly on the outside. I had a job to do, even if I wasn't sure how to do it under the eyes of that goon. I kept flashing back to the goon attacking Sarah. What would Ian do if Brent set into me? Join in? I shivered.

"Come sit!" Angela said, patting the couch beside her. I took the invite. It was much better than standing and dithering. I tried one of my planned conversation openers.

"Yeesh. I haven't seen either of you since the marks dropped. How was it?"

That got some good conversation rolling. I was so keyed up, I processed just enough to make appropriate happy and sad noises, but I couldn't have remembered any details if my life depended on it. It did seem like all of us had at least one grade lower than expected, though they were both oddly fatalistic about it.

Even Ian, whose grades would be heading off to university admissions, seemed remarkably unconcerned. I suspected the drinks played a role in his attitude. I'd never seen cool, collected Ian drunk before, so I wasn't sure if the tension that was underlying his relaxed pose signalled suspicion, or if it was just his usual reaction to alcohol.

I had been checking on the goon/bodyguard regularly out of the corner of my eye, so I managed to catch the moment he sauntered out of the room. Ian had obviously also been keeping a lookout, too. The next time he oh-so-casually turned his head, noticing the goon was gone, his whole body relaxed.

He lay his head back, staring at the ceiling for a minute while I caught Angela up on Ravi's side of the Debbie drama and his taking on the parkour job.

Abruptly, Ian sat up and his body language changed. He didn't seem nearly as drunk as before. Angela's look turned serious, too, when she saw the change in Ian.

"I have to come clean. I didn't invite you here just to catch up." Angela smiled. "Though it's been great. I missed you, but we need your help." She sounded genuine, but this was all taking a very weird turn.

"Heh. Okay," I said, faking a stretch and using the opportunity to look around and make sure none of the goons had snuck up behind me. When I was done, I looked at both their serious faces. "Lay it on me."

They looked at each other, then Angela focused on me.

"I didn't want to bring you into this, Mike, but I …" She glanced back at Ian. "We have a problem."

"Okay." I nodded for her to continue, but this was obviously Ian's plan. *So cringe.*

"I'm not going to tell you why, so don't even ask." She had her 'don't push me' face on. "I have some firmware I need to hack, or at least figure out what inputs to tweak so I can disable them. I have the make and models of the devices, and some schematics, but it's not enough."

"And you expect me to understand it?" I felt my eyebrows raise. This was worse than I'd thought. Was Ian getting her into some kind of criminal hacking, too?

"No, not necessary." Angela waved both hands. "I have a program I'm pretty sure can generate the response code I need, but someone else will have to run it and feed me the response. I can't sneak the kind of computing power required into the room where I'll need it. Ian is going to be distracting the … people … while I'm doing it."

"Ah, so you need me somewhere else with a high-powered computer?" I ignored her pause, but I desperately wanted to know what she'd held back. Was this why so many of the new converts died by suicide? The Clan used them as cat's paws for illegal shit and some got caught?

"Somewhere nearby," Ian said. "We can handle communications, but only short-distance."

"I have the code here, and some money to get any hardware you need," Angela said. "As well as the location, which I don't want to say out loud, but it's within a two-hour drive."

I looked between the two of them. Their faces were expectant, though Ian's was a little more guarded. They both seemed to genuinely need me, but all I could think of was that this sounded like a trick to get me to a remote location. Maybe the cult had decided I was valuable after all?

"I don't know what you're involved in," I said, "And maybe you've got some good reasons to keep me in the dark. I just want to know one thing. Is this going to make Angela *more* or *less* safe?"

I searched their faces. In truth, I didn't care about their answers, since I didn't plan on leaving Angela here to be roped into any of Ian's schemes, but I had to make it look like I was concerned.

"More safe!" they both responded immediately, sharing equally grim looks.

"And thank you for not prying," Angela said. "You're right, it's important to keep you out of this, but I can't explain why …"

"Because that would be bringing me into it!" I finished for her.

"Yup," she said, frowning.

"Sure. I'll do it," I said, after enough of a pause to show I had thought it through carefully. "I don't know what you're involved in, but I swear I'll do everything I can to get you to safety." That, at least, I could swear with perfect honesty. Besides, the more details I could gather, the better. Maybe those details would help prosecute Ian and his uncle.

My lie worked. The two of them relaxed, looking at me happily.

A lifetime of fooling people had some uses. I felt ill.

I shoved my anxiety and discomfort down and smiled. This was as good a time as any. I needed to end this charade before I puked.

"Oh, I almost forgot your birthday present, Ian!" I lay on the fake cheer. I scanned the room and didn't see anyone who looked like bar staff or goons, so I started pulling up my skirt.

Angela chuckled low in her throat. I glanced up to see her eyes dancing in merriment, and Ian's wide in concern.

"Relax, guys. What dirty minds." I stuck my hand under my skirt, unhooked the strap on the flask, and pulled it out. I held it low where it stayed hidden from the rest of the room, but they could both see it clearly. "The woman I'm doing some work for had an almost full bottle of that 'la-frog' scotch you like sitting on her shelf, so I asked if I could have a taste, and she said to just take the whole bottle!"

I was really getting into my story. I saw Ian's face do something part-way between a wince and excitement as I mispronounced Laphroaig.

"What did you think of it?" he asked.

"Tasted a lot like pickled smoke, and not in a good way." I made a disgusted face. "But I pretended to like it, so I could snag the bottle for you." I chuckled. "Hope my parents don't find it!"

They both laughed, but I realized my mouth was starting to run away with me. No more. Now.

I waggled the flask at Ian. "Want some?"

"Sure! Let's see what you've scored here." Ian held out his hand and I passed it over. He poured some of the golden liquid into a couple of red plastic cups from his collection on the table, kept one, and handed one to Angela.

Well, that was a relief. I hadn't even needed to convince her to try it. Sarah said the drug would take a minute to kick in, then hit hard. No one would question helping a drunk friend leave the bar. That was one benefit of appearing mostly female tonight.

Ian sniffed the drink, made appreciative noises, then took a sip. "Ahhh, that's got to be at least an eighteen-year," he said.

"Pretty sure the bottle had a twenty on it," I said, still not having a clear idea what that meant, other than higher numbers were considered better. Ian looked even more impressed.

"You mind if I have more?" Ian asked. "I'm guessing you're not interested given your 'pickled smoke' comment." He chuckled and shook his head, like he couldn't quite believe it.

"Not at all. Drink up!" I said cheerfully. Perhaps a bit too much fake cheer, but he didn't appear to notice. He poured the rest into his cup and handed the flask back. I tucked it back under my skirt.

Angela took a sip, and to my surprise, looked cautiously appreciative.

"Hmm … might take some getting used to, but not bad."

Ian sighed deeply and took another swig from his cup.

Angela took another, larger mouthful, swallowed, then rubbed her neck. "Is it supposed to make your throat kind of numb and tingly?"

Ian looked confused, rubbed his own throat and swallowed like he was noticing a similar effect for the first time.

Oh shit.

His face went utterly blank, and he reached a trembling hand up to place it over his plastic cup. A blueish glow flickered under his hand. Once, twice, and on the third time, the contents of the cup glowed briefly through the plastic, a distinct olive-green shade, before the cup crinkled, smoked, and little red flames flickered into life.

I jumped up and backed away toward Angela. I bet plastic cups weren't all he could burn. I groped for Angela's hand to draw her away with me.

Ian clenched his fist over the mouth of the cup sharply. It crumpled into a red, white, and sooty-black ball, flames and smoke instantly snuffed cold. He dropped it on the ground and lashed out, slapping Angela's cup from her hand. Liquid splattered across my dress. Angela jerked back, reacting a split second late. Ian turned to me, eyes blazing with fury.

He didn't seem the least bit sleepy.

"Who are you?" he yelled, also getting up. "How long have you been working with them?" His eyes pleaded for an answer I was not about to give.

I found Angela's hand, but she pushed me away.

Ian lunged for me, hand outstretched, and for the first time ever, I saw danger in his broad athletic frame instead of envy or attraction.

Then, he dropped to the hardwood floor, clutching his stomach and groaning.

Angela knelt beside him and put a cautious hand on his arm. She pulled it back quickly when he flinched and curled up more tightly. Our eyes met as she looked up to where I hovered. I was caught between equal desires to comfort and flee.

"Go," she said, holding a pleasant smile on her face with grim determination. "We'll talk tomorrow." To the encroaching crowd, drawn by the eruption of drama, she raised a hand and called out, "It's all right. He's all right. Just had a little too much tonight."

"No! Now's your chance. Come with me!" I pleaded. A long shot, but I had to try.

Her smile slipped, revealing a glimpse of the fury behind it. She didn't seem drowsy either!

"GO!" she yelled. Then more quietly, pitched just so I could hear it, "You don't have a clue what you're fucking with and you're going to get us all killed. Get out of here!"

I fled.

CHAPTER 20

stumbled through the bar, bouncing off people who refused to get out of my way, my mind whirling. I shoulder-checked a couple of guys who were taking up too much space, leaving angry grumbles in my wake.

How?

What?

Something was very, very wrong. Everyone was lying to me, and I wasn't sure who was good or bad anymore. Maybe there wasn't a good side.

I could only keep one thought in my head: *find Sarah.*

I didn't know what I'd do once I did, but I knew I had to find her.

The pounding music, laughter, and shouting of excited partiers felt like spikes being driven into my skull. I actually had to pay attention to people as more than just obstacles if I wanted to find Sarah, but they had all started to look alien to me.

I spotted the goon first—Ian's bodyguard. The way he casually slipped through the crowd, avoiding people who clearly couldn't see him, marked him like a spotlight. But what really caught my eye was the slim steel knife in his hand, glinting in a rainbow of reflected colours.

I was halfway across the room to him when I noticed his target.

Sarah was standing at the far corner of the bar, near the bathroom sign. She was staring down at her prop Tricorder, not watching the room. Not that watching would have done her much good. He was angling in, invisibly, from the side. There were dozens of people between them, but I knew it was her he was after.

I ducked and weaved through the crowd. I needed to get to her, but I couldn't afford to make a disturbance that would get me noticed. The look of that long, narrow knife made my stomach turn.

Heart racing, I edged the stun gun out of its sheath as I walked, pressing it against my side, covering it with my hand. It was a macabre race. I was moving faster than him, but I had farther to go. It would be close, one way or the other.

Suddenly, he rushed across the last gap at a fast walk, dodging between two people who were entering and exiting the bathroom door respectively. I was almost there, but had been caught off guard. I sprinted to catch up, but I could tell I wasn't going to make it!

I tried to shout, to warn Sarah, but I didn't have enough breath in me to make my voice loud enough to penetrate the clouds of sound blanketing the room.

The knife flashed forward …

… and Sarah was spinning out of the way, heading for the door to the bathrooms.

I sprinted the last three steps, dove forward, and shoved the sharp end of the stun gun into the back of the goon's thigh.

He dropped with gratifying speed, and we landed on the floor together. A few laughs burst out behind me as I scrambled onto my hands and knees to deliver a couple more good jolts to his back and side. I struck out and swept the knife away from his hand.

Sarah stopped it with her foot and bent quickly to pick it up. She looked at me, not with the relief I'd imagined, but with a kind of resigned anger.

My 'rescuing damsels in distress' career was getting off to a real rocky start.

The goon aggressively twitched and moaned. Even with his nerves jangling, he was managing some vaguely coordinated motion, able to slide his hand inside his jacket. His back arched and his hand spasmed in an electro-after-shock, flipping his jacket back to reveal a shoulder-holstered handgun.

Sarah strode over. I thrust my hand out before my brain fully comprehended the downward arc of her knife toward his throat. I blocked her arm and not the knife blade, luckily.

"No!" she yelled, furious, but I couldn't let her kill someone right in front of me.

The guard got his hand around the gun's grip and started drawing it from the holster. I kicked it, and the weapon slid across the floor. He rolled away and started army-crawling after it.

Sarah glared at me again and dropped the knife with a look of disgust.

"Time to go," she said. She grabbed my hand and dragged me away. I kept the taser in my front pocket but gripped it tightly in case we ran into more guards. My mind was a whirl of confusion.

People were starting to react, but no one tried to stop us as we left the bar and jogged back to the car. Sarah seemed to be dealing better with the attempted murder than I was, but then she had seemed to expect the guard's attack. Like she'd just been waiting for him to get close.

So she could kill him?

I had really stepped off into the deep end here, hadn't I?

I got the car out of the parking lot with record speed, and we were soon zipping along the downtown streets, as fast as the speed limit and traffic lights allowed. I drove for distance's sake at first, making right turns at red lights and missing turns back toward our neighbourhood in favour of constant movement.

Sarah huddled in the passenger seat, typing on her phone. She hadn't said anything on the way back to the car and was still silent. In a low-voiced, monotone command, she told me to keep an eye out for anyone following us.

I was familiar with how to shake someone trying to follow you. Mostly from being on the follower side, trying to convoy to Ravi's car deliveries. I slowed to scrape through orange lights and made random turns onto small side streets, all the while keeping a close eye on the rearview mirror. We had no obvious followers.

I couldn't seem to get quite enough oxygen. I put it down to fear for a while, but then realized it was my binder constricting my chest. Then I realized it was extra tight because I'd shifted to male shape at some point.

Oh, great. As if things with Sarah weren't already complicated enough tonight. I couldn't struggle out of the binder in the car. I'd have to put up with it until we stopped. It was okay as long as I focused on breathing extra deeply, more so with my stomach than with my chest.

Once I felt safe enough to head back toward Sarah's, we found ourselves waiting at the first red light. It offered enough of a pause to pull my attention away from driving and ask the first question on the top of my list.

"What did you give me to drug Angela and Ian with? It made Ian sick, and neither of them sleepy!" My voice went up at the end, though I'd tried to stop it. My heart started hammering again. I felt like such a fool to have trusted Sarah.

"Did they both drink it?" she asked, her expression blank and voice flat. Maybe she didn't care and never had, maybe she was still epically pissed at me, or maybe it was just from emotional exhaustion.

"Yeah. Ange said it tingled and made her throat numb, but Ian fell over holding his stomach in pain."

"Ah, good." She sighed. Some of the tension left her pose.

"Good!?" I nearly yelled, but remembered at the last second to keep my voice lighter, and more in the female range, so it came out kind of strangled. "What did you give them? Are they going to be okay?"

"They'll be fine," she said in a clipped tone. "Ian must have a sensitivity to that particular drug, and I guess Angela didn't get enough to knock her out. You said her alcohol tolerance was high."

"I guess. At least it used to be. Oh!" A honk behind me reminded me that the light was green. I hit the gas harder than intended, and the Acura really took off. Sarah grabbed the door handle in a brief panic. "Sorry!" I said quickly, lifting my foot to keep us under the speed limit.

"Now that we've tried once, they'll be more wary of a second attempt," I said bitterly. All I could see was Ange's furious face, telling me off, but it also seemed weird for Ian and Angela to be reaching outside the rich-and-powerful Clan for help. Unless the whole thing was a smokescreen to lure me into the Clan's clutches?

"Yeah," Sarah said tiredly.

Though my trust in everything had been severely shaken tonight, I needed Sarah's knowledge now more than ever. Maybe she would have some insight into what Angela and Ian were planning?

I described Angela and Ian's strange request to her, as well as my concerns about what Ian might be trying to lure me into.

Sarah paused in thought before speaking. "I agree, there's no way they would pull in an outsider for any Clan-sanctioned job. I expect Ian's got some side scheme and figures he can use you and Angela to get it done. I don't know." She sounded defeated, which scared me. She was Angela's only hope.

I reminded myself that we were both tired and not anywhere near our best. We were nearing her house, and with any luck, things would look better in the morning.

Could I risk staying here, in male shape, tonight? Heading home in this costume would be awkward. It was too late to change at Bistro, and my parents would really wonder at my coming home after eleven. I felt trapped by my sex. Again.

"We can come up with a new plan tomorrow," I said, trying for a more hopeful tone.

"No. We won't," I heard her say in a hard tone from the passenger seat. It sent a shiver down my spine.

"Ah, what?"

"There's no 'second try,' Kayla," Sarah grated. "We're done. That was our shot."

I slammed on the brakes. Sarah threw her hands up as she jolted forward in her seat.

"Kayla! Please!" The sudden edge of tears in her voice tugged at my heart, but not enough to calm my anger. My emotions were a whirlwind. With the car stopped, I turned to glare at her directly.

"Did you even have a plan to rescue Angela? Or were we just dupes acting out your plan?" I was starting to consider how vague she'd been about her part in the plan. How had she lured the guard away? And why did she seem so determined to kill him?

"There was a chance." She sighed with a bitter edge. "Not a good chance, but if everything went perfectly, you might have gotten her out."

She edged away in her seat, hand on the door handle.

"My friend's life is on the line here! Is this a game to you?"

I regretted the words as soon as I said them. I'd seen her scars, inside and out. She surely wasn't taking this lightly. Her expression turned to stone. She unbuckled her seatbelt and got out of the car. In a clipped tone, she said: "Park the car here and leave it unlocked with the keys in it, then … go home, Kayla, or whatever your name is. Don't come back to this house. I won't be here."

She slammed the door and walked toward her house. It was close, just on the next block. I wanted to go to Sarah and apologize, but that would likely just continue to traumatize her. In my own anger, I could see an echo of the guy pounding on the car window. If only I had managed to stay in female shape. I would have been just as angry, but I would have given off different vibes, and maybe Sarah wouldn't have been so freaked.

And I still desperately needed to get this binder off.

I laid my head on the steering wheel for a moment, willing tears to come, to help ease this ache deep in my chest, but my eyes stayed frustratingly dry.

I backed into a clear spot at the curb and reluctantly followed her instructions, leaving the keys in the console. I stayed standing by the car until I saw Sarah go into her house, close the door behind her, and turn on a light.

Reassured she was safe, as safe as any of us could be, I left.

~*~

By habit, I walked directly away from my house after leaving Sarah's. I took a minute to pull out my phone and turn it on. I was relieved to see some messages from Angela.

From an hour ago:

Angela >> Good to see you tonight. Just want to make sure you got in OK?

And from 33 minutes ago:

Angela >> ??

I wrote a quick reply. If it was truly Angela, I didn't want to leave her hanging. If not, it couldn't hurt. It was the expected thing to do.

<< All good. Just got home.

Angela's and Sarah's parting words still stung deeply. Ian's as well, even though he might still be trying to hurt Angela. I wasn't as sure now. My purpose had seemed so clear earlier today: I would sweep in, rescue Ange from the traitorous Ian, and everything would be good between us again.

I should have spent way more effort wondering about Sarah's motives. She put a lot of effort and money into this rescue. *Of course* she had her own agenda. I was an idiot. A deep well of anger stirred in me, but I didn't know who I should be most angry at—Sara or myself—so the feeling just sat there in an unformed lump.

Going home tonight didn't seem like the best idea, and not only because of the time and the way I was dressed. While Sarah hadn't mentioned it, the thought that someone may be tracking me and that this could all be brought down on my unsuspecting parents was too much. It sucked, since I could really do with a wardrobe change using the backup box in my garage.

Good thing it was warm out, or as warm as Calgary nights ever got at our elevation, which meant the wind was still cold on my bare legs, but not too uncomfortable. I didn't relish the idea of sitting out in it all night.

I walked toward 17th Avenue. There were a few twenty-four-hour places along that strip. I ended up at the Micky-D's. It was nearly, but not quite, empty of customers. A lone staff member appeared at the counter a few minutes after I walked in. I ordered a coffee to gain access to the bathroom, both of which I desperately needed.

The women's and men's symbols on the doors gave me pause. I normally used the men's, unless I was both female and presenting as a woman. This was new for me. I was dressed as a woman, but was male-shaped. The only other option was the single-occupancy disabled washroom, and I never liked stealing that space from someone who might need it. I sighed and entered the men's. I might be wearing a dress, but I wasn't feeling particularly womanly at the moment. If I were forced to use binary gendered washrooms, I would prefer to use the one for the gender I was feeling. It was weird otherwise. If people didn't like how I was dressed, I'd have to deal with it.

I went into the single stall, pulled down my dress, and took off the now far-too-tight binding. Being able to breathe freely was invigorating. Then I did my business and washed up at the sink, both my hands and my face, scrubbing the makeup off as best I could with a dampened paper towel and hand soap.

Fortunately, only one other guy came in and he ignored me, either on purpose or out of pure obliviousness. Men were well-trained in the 'never make eye contact' rule.

Back in the restaurant, I picked up my coffee and ordered a midnight snack of chicken nuggets and fries. Getting some food in my belly might ease the chilled exhaustion I felt. Checking my phone, I noticed a new text from Ange.

Angela >> Good to hear. I'm home too.

My finger hovered over the keyboard, but I still didn't know what to say to her. Anything honest wouldn't be safe, given that someone else might be reading her messages, and I couldn't stomach sending anything dishonest.

I checked Discord in case Sarah had contacted me, but there was nothing.

I had never felt so lonely and broken before.

When I was uprooted from my life at eight years old, I had at least had my parents for emotional stability. I was practically an adult now. Even if they wanted to, and I was willing to put them at risk, they couldn't help me with this tangled mess. Angela's face intruded into my thoughts again. Her features twisted in a level of anger I'd never seen from her before. And all of it directed at me. I didn't have the strength to endure that again. As far as Sarah was concerned, it was a done deal anyway. I had failed my best friend, and she was lost. My eyes burned with unshed tears as I stared down at the dull, scratched tabletop, stuffing food into my mouth without tasting it.

Maybe it was time.

This past year, my pressure release had been imagining running away, going somewhere no one knew me. Then I would no longer be in any position to hurt my friends or family. The biggest flaw in the plan, as usual, was only having a few thousand saved up in my bank account. The pay from Sarah had allowed me to add nearly another thousand, but it still wasn't enough. Helping my parents out had given me a keen eye for how much things cost.

Then, I remembered the money Sarah had given me for my envisioned getaway with Angela. I delved my hand into my purse and felt the reassuringly thick bundle of cash. Whether she'd meant to leave that with me or not, I felt justified in taking it now.

Ten thousand.

If I rented a room, or a small apartment somewhere, it would be enough to keep me for a while. Long enough to figure something else out.

After eating, I felt a little warmer in body, if not in soul. With vague plans of making my way to the bus station, I lay my head in my arms. I swore it was only for a second, but I woke up to someone kicking my foot under the table.

CHAPTER 21

"Look alive, hun. We got bacon coming," a deep-timbered, yet feminine voice said from across the table.

I opened my eyes to see a middle-aged woman dressed in a low-cut top that showed a lot of cleavage.

I glanced around and saw what she meant. A couple of cops had come in. After a moment of panic, I could see that although one of them was looking over at us, they appeared to be buying food and had not been specifically called here to deal with me.

Sure, I'd seen that guy about to knife Sarah, but it didn't seem like anyone else was paying any attention until I dropped him. To the casual observer, it would've looked like I'd attacked him out of nowhere. Then Sarah had tried to slash his throat. I was extremely conscious of the highly illegal stun gun in my purse.

"Thanks," I muttered.

She nodded and smiled. "You doing okay?"

"Yeah," I said without thinking, then, "I guess so. Sorry, it's been a long day and a longer night."

"You have somewhere to go?" she asked in a friendly tone.

"Oh, yeah," I said, then had to recant. "Well, not specifically tonight. But in general, yeah. I'm just avoiding my parents' place right now."

She nodded as if this made all the sense in the world.

"Um … how's your night going?" I asked, feeling socially awkward. I noticed she didn't have anything in front of her. "Hey, can I buy you a coffee or something? I owe you one."

She laughed. "Oh, no, hun. I've got food over there. I left it to save your ass. I'll go get it when …" She made a tiny head jerk toward the front where the cops were leaving with their orders.

A couple of minutes later, the cop car pulled out of the parking lot, and my saviour went to collect her things from a nearby table. I took the opportunity for a quick check in my purse. Falling asleep in a public place had been a terrible call. I could easily have woken up without my phone or any money, except for the few bills I'd secreted in this dress's front pocket.

My new friend came back with her tray as I gingerly dabbed at the tears in my eyes, forgetting for a moment that I had already scrubbed my makeup off.

"I had a tough session with a client tonight and can't quite face home yet either. This is a good distraction." She gestured at the room in general. "Why don't you tell me about your day, take my mind off it."

"Crap, where do I start?" I tried to remember everything that had gone down, but it was like remembering a previous lifetime. "So, this guy tried to knife a friend of mine. I managed to take him down before she got hurt." The terror of those moments came flooding back, and I noticed my hands were shaking.

"It's okay," she said softly and took my hands in hers. They were warm and solid. Then in a firmer voice, she said, "It is okay, right? Are you, or your friend, in any danger now?"

"No. Well, maybe. I don't know. She's home and I think I'm good," I said, forcing a weak smile. "She wasn't entirely happy with my rescue. She had a different plan."

"Does she know the guy?"

"Yeah. I think so. It's complicated."

"Hmm."

"I think she wanted to beat him up herself." I wasn't going to go into the whole cold-blooded murder thing, but I also didn't want her thinking Sarah had been planning to go easy on the guy.

"I see." The corner of her mouth twitched up in a slight smile. "There's always a risk when you intervene, even with the best of intentions."

"Yeah, but the really terrible part is that the woman I saved hurt some other friends of mine tonight. And she used me to do it. I don't know if they'll ever talk to me again." My tears overflowed, and I didn't brush them away. "I still would have tried to save her, for sure. I'm not going to let anyone get murdered in front of me, but … now I really don't know if I've been playing on the right side, or even how many sides there are, and I've probably lost my best friend, and maybe even put my family in danger by doing it." I shut my mouth. There were a lot of parts to this that I couldn't talk about, and I was treading dangerously close to them, driven by my emotions.

"That's some shit." She shook her head.

"Don't I know it. Yesterday, I felt like a million bucks, and now I feel like trash."

"Hey kid, speaking from lots of experience with both, you'll feel like a million again soon enough. Don't let one bad night take you down."

"Yeah," I said shakily. I gently drew my hands back, took a few paper napkins, wiped my eyes, and blew my nose. I looked up at her again. "Thanks."

"Don't mention it. I think all you can do is try to make amends with your friends … the ones that were hurt."

"I think in this case, the best thing I can do is not bother them anymore," I said dully.

"Oh, sweetie," she said, her voice full of compassion. "That's the second-worst thing you can do. When you've hurt someone, and you leave that wound to fester, there's no going back and healing it. You have a limited window of time to sincerely make it right."

"How can I face her, though?" My voice came out plaintively. "I don't think I can handle another realization that I messed everything up, having her look at me that way …"

After a few seconds, the woman spoke in my pause.

"That's the kicker, isn't it? If you truly want to make amends, you've got to let them express their hurt, if there's a safe space to do that. Avoiding them is still something you're doing for you, not them."

"I … think I can see that," I said. Truthfully. She was making sense. I wanted to run from Angela's anger because I knew, on so many levels, I had failed her. It didn't matter what I'd been trying to achieve. We had been friends for close to a decade. I knew her, and my trust should be with her, regardless of Ian or the Clan's supposed influence. She was too savvy and stubborn to be taken in without a fight. And she would never help Ian with something that didn't align with her ethics. Running away now wouldn't help her. The festering analogy was right. It would hurt more over time than it would re-opening that fresh wound and cleaning it out right now.

I could leave afterwards, if it still felt like the right thing to do.

But something my unorthodox, early, early breakfast companion had mentioned before nagged me. *Something about mistakes? Oh, yeah.*

"You said leaving was the second-worst mistake?" I asked. "Just curious, what's the first-worst mistake?"

"Getting defensive while trying to apologize, and turning the whole exercise into another fight about who was more right, or more wrong," she said bluntly.

"Oh, yeah." I nodded, then scrubbed my hands through my hair and over my face to peer at her concerned look over the top of my fingers. "Sorry, it's been a really long day, and night, and, quite a few weeks before this to be honest. I really appreciate you looking out for me. I'm guessing you're a therapist or something?"

"Sex worker, actually," she said with a broad smile that crinkled the corners of her eyes. "But I've taken some courses. It's really helpful in my work."

"Oh, yeah, that makes sense." I probably should have been shocked, but this was the most normal thing I had encountered all night. "I think you're right that I need to talk to my friends and own up to my own shit, before dealing with the other shit."

"Yup. Sometimes you just need to let a friendship go if it's not right anymore, but letting your pride or fears break a valued friendship … that'll haunt you," she said with a whisper of remembered regret.

We sat quietly with our own painful memories for a while. Somehow, it was better for the company. I was starting to feel a small outbreak of common sense coming on, now that I'd cleared my head.

Some of the loneliness I was feeling tonight wasn't due to Sarah, or Angela, or any one particular thing that had happened. It was the idea of the wizard clans, and everything I'd learned about their grip on the world. It made me feel small and powerless before I even started, but this woman had given me a shot of hope. She was proof that there were good people everywhere doing what they could to make the world a little kinder.

Maybe I could be that kind of person, too. If I were brave enough.

"I'm sorry I dumped all that on you," I said eventually, starting to feel a little ashamed for taking advantage of the first sympathetic stranger I ran into.

"Not at all. I'm used to it."

"Can I …" I started to ask, but I couldn't think of any practical and non-insulting way to ease out of our intense conversation.

"Just pay it forward, next time you can." She smiled.

"I will," I promised.

We chatted for a while about lighter topics—music, books, favourite TV shows—until more people started coming in with the rise of morning foot traffic. She checked the time on her phone and said she really needed to get on.

I tidied up the remnants of my meal. It was six thirty in the morning. My parents would be up and out of the house by seven. If I took a leisurely walk back, I could change my clothes, grab my bike, and head over to Angela's.

CHAPTER 22

The familiar ride from my house to Angela's cut through one of the richest neighbourhoods in the city, full of old brick-and-stone homes, and more than a few McMansion infills. It also wound through some large open green spaces. I stopped partway up a large grassy hill that was well garnished with a mix of bright-yellow and fuzzy-white dandelions. I just sat for a few minutes appreciating the cool morning air, getting my breath back after powering up the steep incline.

During my previous visit, on the last day of school, all I'd been able to think about had been my flight after our disastrous attempt at sex. This time, after last night with magic and murderous wizards looming, angsting over our sex life seemed silly.

I took my phone out of the isolation bag and turned it on to check messages. I preferred to do it here, away from anyone's house, and where I could ride out in any direction. I had no way to know if anyone was tracking my signal, but why take the chance?

There were four messages from Sarah on the Discord!

Sarah >> Please do not go back to the house. I won't be there, and to do so would put us both in danger.

Sarah >> If you are in immediate danger, and ONLY if you are in immediate danger, call the number below, and we will offer what help we can.

Sarah >> Please also stay away from the two you met last night. Associating with them will put you all in more danger.

Sarah >> There are a lot of things I wish could have been different in my life. This is another one. I hope to see you again, someday.

The message was followed by a phone number. I think. My vision was too blurred by tears to see it clearly. I had done what they wanted. Now,

I was disposable. I sank to the ground as pain knifed through my chest. I knew the pain was all emotion: that sharpness that was betrayal and abandonment from people I thought were friends was all too familiar.

I fumbled the power off and re-bagged my phone—actions that were starting to become automatic. After the first storm of emotion passed, I reminded myself that I wasn't eight years old anymore. I sat on the earth, still cold from the night, even though the sun was warming, thoughts drifting. Bees buzzed by, and the occasional mosquito whined too close, earning them a slap.

I could ride back home and let whatever was going on with Angela and Ian take its course. Of course, I'd probably never see either of them again. Wasn't that pretty much what Sarah had just said to me? Nothing about that plan sat right with me.

Or, I could ride to Angela's and attempt to stick my nose deeper into whatever they were doing. That might endanger my life, and my parents' lives, and possibly not make any difference in what happened to Angela or Ian. Everything I knew about Angela suggested she would never hurt a friend. Or stand for someone else hurting a friend. Ange's ask couldn't be part of a trap. She would never allow it.

There was no safe choice here. No good option.

I remembered the look of horror on Ian's face when he realized I'd drugged him. I remembered the incomplete swastika carved into Sarah's back, and the fear in my parents' eyes when they talked about the people hunting us.

Maybe I wasn't sure how, and I wasn't even entirely sure what side I was on yet, but I knew there were things I had to oppose and friends who needed me. I screwed up last night, big time, but if there was even a slim chance to make it right, I had to take it.

I reached the top of the hill and cruised the flat residential streets, regaining my wind. Just off the west edge of the rich neighbourhood was the almost-as-rich one Angela lived in. Houses and yards were a little bigger—and nicer—than average, but it was really the location that made it high-rent.

I parked my bike in the usual spot, and Angela opened the door shortly after I rang the bell this time. She was wearing some of her 'lying around the house' comfy outfits—blue leggings with a silver swirling pattern and an old T-shirt that hung down to mid-thigh depicting a faded wolf print on the front. I had been there when she bought it at Comic Expo years ago.

"Hi, stranger," she said with a neutral look.

"Hey. Can we talk?"

After a just long enough to be awkward pause, she said, "Sure. Come on in," and moved aside to make room.

I searched her face for any warning signs. There was definitely tension, but mainly what I expected from previous times we'd made up after a fight about something. I saw none of the inner conflict I expected if she were being coerced to turn me over to the wizards.

After taking off my shoes, I picked them up to carry downstairs.

"Leave them here." She waved dismissively. "My dad's gone all day."

"Oh, sure." I put them down again, feeling both out of place and like I was coming home at the same time.

"You know, I called you to meet at the bar last night to protect you," Angela said resignedly. "Specifically, meeting in a public place in a way that could be passed off as a chance encounter, so it wouldn't look like you're still connected to us. This probably blows that out of the water."

"I'm okay with that." I gave her a level look. "I would have liked you to include me from the beginning."

She sighed, then walked down the hall to the kitchen while I followed. She returned to her breakfast, mostly finished, but I could tell from the remnants it had been Smørrebrød—curry pickled herring on rye bread. My mouth watered, even though I was still full. She'd spent her early childhood in Denmark and had introduced me to delights like this. Sadly, while the ingredients were pretty common working-class food in Denmark, they were pricy here.

I took a glass from the cupboard and filled it at the sink, gratefully taking a big swig.

Looking at her, I still couldn't quite believe that she'd been hiding magic powers. Then again, I had been hiding my magical switches all these years. Sarah had suggested all mages were somewhat unique, but maybe Ange could help me learn how *not* to switch?

"Have a good ride?" she asked, breaking into my thoughts.

"Oh." I felt embarrassed then. "Hope you don't mind me helping myself?" I wasn't sure if I should act like the old friend of previous years, or a real guest.

"No, no. Go ahead!" Then, in a dead serious voice, she continued, "You're still welcome here, Mike." She took a deep breath. "I'm angry about what you did, but I want to talk about it and get past it, not shut you out."

"You've been doing a pretty good job of shutting me out lately," I grumped and saw her expression start to congeal. "But I'm here to apologize for last night," I continued quickly. "And I think it's time I explained some of my weird behaviour, in shutting you out, before." I stopped, a little breathless.

"I'm listening." Her tone was even, but her eyebrow quirked up. She was surprised and trying to hide it.

I'd been thinking about exactly what to say, starting at the McDonald's and throughout the whole ride over. I hoped it came out of my mouth in roughly the right order.

"I'm sorry. I let you drink something I knew was drugged. I had convinced myself I was acting in your best interests, but I should have known that was bullshit." I took a deep breath. "I can't go back and do it over, but I can promise to never, ever do something like that again, and I'll try to make up for it."

I forced another deep breath, trying to calm my jangling nerves while I waited for her response. My parents thought they were doing things in my best interest all these years as well. They figured they knew what my best interests were without asking me or without giving me the information I needed to make those decisions for myself. As a kid, that made a certain amount of sense, but they should have brought me into those discussions years ago. I repeated the same mistake with Angela, and I damn well should have known better.

"That's … actually a pretty good apology." She nodded. "What were you trying to do, anyway?"

"It was supposed to knock you and Ian out so I could get you away from him."

"Ha! And was my opinion going to matter in this?"

"I was convinced you might not be in your right mind. There's a lot you don't know about Ian, and his family …"

"No!" Anger crackled in her voice. "There's a lot you don't know about Ian, or me, but you swoop in and feed us drugs you bought off the internet?"

"It wasn't like that. I got them from someone I trusted." As soon as I said it, I felt what a weak excuse that was. "You've been so secretive and acting so weird. What was I supposed to think when I heard Ian's family was in some kind of cult?"

"I don't know …" she said sarcastically. "Maybe TALK to me?"

"I tried!" I shot back, then took a couple of deep breaths to calm down. She was stubborn and independent, but I could have tried harder to break through and talk. I let my own fear and hurt get in the way. She also could have brought me in sooner. It was a mess. "I'm sorry. I was afraid of alerting the cult and that they'd start to keep a closer eye on you. There weren't exactly safe opportunities to meet. And the few times I tried, you shut me out. I felt like I had to get you out from under their control first, then talk."

"So, you wanted to be in control," she said darkly. "Seems like both sides want that. But I'm not just some fucking pawn."

"I don't think anyone on the anti-wizard side wants to control you, just make sure you're not already being controlled by magic. For your protection and theirs." I understood that feeling of imposed helplessness better than I wanted to—the feeling that the entire world seemed to be conspiring to keep you ignorant and compliant.

Her face went dead still, her one hand leaning on the counter, gripping the edge hard. Then, she closed her eyes and visibly relaxed.

"So, you know," she said, sounding more relieved than anything.

"If I didn't know before, Ian's little display last night would have raised a lot of questions. And, to be honest, I wasn't a hundred percent sure about you. Until now."

"Right." She laughed. "Aaaaah! This is the deep stuff I've always tried my best to keep you out of."

"I've been realizing that lately. But I'm still not clear on why? I could have been a much better friend if I'd known more about what you were going through." My voice clogged with emotion at the end.

"I know," she said sadly. "I've been thinking a lot since last night. Talking this over has made me realize that you might be right. I've been living for so long with this hanging over my head, never knowing when the next slip might bring the Clan down on me."

She stepped forward and laid her hand on my arm. Her fingers were chilled, but it was a comfort. Her words were such an echo of my own struggle that I wanted to blurt out everything, but I didn't know where to start. And I definitely didn't want to intrude on her story.

"I'm realizing how much I've let my fear of the Clan control my entire life!" she said in a low, fierce voice. "Never properly learning magic, never able to properly defend myself from the shit out there that only impacts people with talent. The training I've been doing with Ian is a revelation, the kind of life I could have lived …" She sighed and said sadly, "But, of course, to have had that kind of training as a child, I would have had to live the kind of life he has."

"Oh, it hasn't been so bad." Ian's voice filled the kitchen. "I get to travel a lot."

I spun, pulling my arm from under Angela's hand, my heart thudding. Why was he here?

He stood, towelling off his hair, wearing only an old, battered pair of sweatpants, his well-defined chest and abs on full display. The sweatpants rode way too low on his hips and bulged way too enticingly for my comfort. I tried to keep my eyes on his face and think about how much trouble I was in, instead of getting distracted by his body.

"What?" Ian said, giving us an innocent look I knew had to be at least somewhat contrived. I glanced in Angela's direction and was surprised to see her face pinched in anger.

"Not the best time, Ian," she growled.

"I just finished my shower. You're not going to monopolize Mike this whole time, are you?"

"Are you … is he …" I wanted some kind of reassurance from them both, and it got all tangled in my mouth. Meanwhile, my body was stepping backward. I knew exactly where the back door was, if I could make a run for it.

"It's okay, Mike." Angela laid a hand on the back of my arm.

"It really is okay," Ian said. "Sorry I scared you last night. I was drunk. It was a shock. I did several things I absolutely should not have. The only reason I'm still in one piece this morning is because Brent screwed up so bad that my uncle probably hasn't heard anything about my flagrant violations of Clan rules against showing magic."

To my relief, but also some regret, Ian slipped a T-shirt over his head.

"At least, I don't think he's heard." Ian's face fell for a moment.

"You're not here to kill me, or to deliver me to your hired killers?" Probably a silly question, but I wanted to see his face as he answered.

"Never," he said, more serious now. "Believe me when I say I'm under as much threat from them as you are."

"Your own people?"

"I had the same choice as Angela. Be enslaved, or be killed. So, no, we're not out to get you, Mike," Ian said. "We need you, like we said last night."

"For the computer thing?"

"Yeah, and for the whole plan, really." His face relaxed and took on that subtle glow it did when he got on a favourite subject.

"Originally, Angela made me keep you out of it. She was like 'Nooo, he's my special boyyy, he can't get hurt!'"

"Ew!" he exclaimed as Angela pelted him in the face with a piece of pickled fish. Wiping it off with the help of some water from the sink, he continued, "If we're going to take down the Clan, we need as much help as we can get."

"You think you can take down the entire Clan?" My voice rose in disbelief.

"I think we'd better start at the beginning and bring him up to speed," Angela said.

"Good plan." Ian opened a cupboard and pulled out a glass. "Let's refresh drinks and retire to the living room."

CHAPTER 23

Last night, I'd been prepared to take on Ian as an enemy and deal with Angela as at least temporarily an enemy due to whatever mind-control Ian had over her. Now they wanted my help to attack the Clan?

I was overjoyed that Ian didn't want to kill me or brainwash Angela, but also angry that Angela had left me hanging while she made life-or-death plans with Ian. Then I felt like a terrible friend for worrying about that when I'd happily let her gloss over her struggles with magic all these years.

"My family got cornered into going to that wedding," Angela interrupted my whirling thoughts from her seat on the opposite end of the couch. "They pull stuff like that occasionally to get a bunch of mage-lineage families together, as a show of power and a test of our loyalties. And, of course, to sniff out any new mages they may have missed in earlier testing." She grimaced.

"Wait …" The gears clunked together in my head. "Your family is wizard-clan-related?"

"Of course," Angela said like it should have been obvious. Ian nodded from his seat in the reclining chair. "I have several relatives active in the Clan," she continued. "That's the second reason I never really wanted to tell you all about this stuff. I would have had to admit to being a supporter, however reluctantly."

"I don't think you can be blamed for not going against those bastards before," I said. "Either of you."

They both smiled, and Angela reached out and squeezed my hand. Something that had been frozen since last night finally thawed as I realized they still felt that my feelings for them meant something. Maybe

I was on the outside, looking in on their relationship, but we were still friends.

"Anyway, I selfishly brought you to the wedding as backup and because I'd look less nervous if I had a date. The very last thing you want to do is look nervous, which, of course, we were, because that hotel has been a wizard clan hangout since it was built. Since the first one was built, actually, but it was burnt down when a wizard duel got out of hand."

"I don't recall seeing that bit of history on the tourist plaque," I half-joked.

"Of course not," Angela scoffed. "You'd be appalled how much of our history is a complete fabrication." She waved a hand airily, relegating that to a side issue. "I went to the bathroom and nearly got caught in a mage trap."

I gasped. I'd known for a while now that she faced danger from the Clan, but hearing it in her own words made it all too real.

"Yeah." She nodded. "It froze me in place so the Clan could take me prisoner, but I managed to fight my way out of the spell. I was so out of it after that, though, that I don't really remember what happened next until I was in the car with you."

"I saw you wandering in the lobby and decided to just get you out of the area, as per our usual plan. I hope that was okay?"

"That was more than okay," she said gently. "It was perfect, Mike. I would still be in their hands now, waiting to be forcibly sealed to the Clan's codex if it wasn't for you."

We shared another warm glance, and my heart ached.

"I heard about it the next day," Ian said sadly. "That a budding talent was detected at my school. I knew it had to be Angela, and that meant I was out of time. I had to bring her in on my plans to break free of the Clan right away."

"Showing up at the after-grad, after that, was another way of showing my loyalty." Angela broke in. "And it allowed us to pretend to be dating, which has allowed both of us more freedom."

"When I told her my plans," Ian said. "Angela said we absolutely couldn't tell you. If we failed, the Clan could, and probably would, scan our minds and track down anyone we were working with."

"Just so you know the danger you're in," Angela interrupted.

"You are going to be out of danger, Angela," Ian said sternly. "Whether you get to the codex or not."

"That's the plan." Angela nodded. "Though I'll still be marked."

"Then we fall back to S— my contact's plan," I edited out Sarah's name at the last second. I wasn't very good at this. "She can help me get you away from the clan. I'll see to it."

"That's the one who provided the drugs for your little trick last night?" Ian asked in a very neutral voice. "Did you figure out what she was trying to accomplish? She ought to know mages, especially trained ones, are resistant to many classes of drugs."

"I think she thought I could get a higher dose into you, but she didn't anticipate Angela's immediate reaction to the drug." This was a flood of information. I wanted to get back to what Angela said about pretending to date, but I also didn't want to interrupt.

Ian nodded. "As a last resort, she might be able to help Angela hide. Not me, though. I was raised in the Clan and linked to the codex as a baby. I've heard the terrorists, ah … the anti-Clan folks, kill us when they can. To be honest, I can't quite blame them. I don't even know myself what mental conditions might be activated if I were captured."

He looked morose for a second, but recovered quickly.

"But hey! If they can get Angela out, as backup in case we fail, I'll feel a whole lot better going into this. And," he looked directly at me, speaking in a serious, measured tone, "I want you to know that I won't expose your help. I don't intend to survive the sealing. If it comes to it, and there's no other way out, I'll suicide."

"I … No!" I said, shocked. "Surely living and looking for some other escape is better than death?"

Angela didn't argue. She wasn't surprised at what he had said. She just looked grim.

"Let me tell you a story about my uncle Zach," Ian said, holding up his hand. "My mom told me this in a hushed voice when I was eleven and packing to leave for my apprenticeship. I'd been found to have a strong mage talent. My parents were like Angela's: weak talents, so not full Clan, and with minimal training. My mom said her older brother had been a warm, caring guy, even after he'd been sealed to the clan, but he was sent away one day. She was sure they'd discovered he was gay."

"They care about that?" It seemed rather petty after the evils I'd seen.

"Assuredly, they do." Ian sighed. "And with magic, they have the ability to change you. Make you straight, or at least, some version of straight."

"That's horrible!"

"I've heard they condition the women with strong mage talent, too,"

Angela said in a hollowed voice, her knees curled up to her chest. "To want to have lots of babies."

"Mom said Zack returned cold and distant. They used to be close, but after that, she barely heard from him." Ian looked at me. "I am fairly certain my uncle suspects I'm gay too, and I'll be sent for the same procedure as soon as I'm sealed to the codex. I would rather die."

I glanced quickly at Angela and back to Ian, possibilities I'd never expected exploding in my brain. Ian regarded me calmly.

"Ah … if this is not rude to ask, are you really gay?"

"As the night is long," he said with a sad grin. "I've had to hide it for so many years, but there's no point now. It's kind of freeing, actually."

A storm of emotions bubbled up in me. I wanted to deal with this in the seriousness it deserved, but my brain had other ideas.

"But, you two were kissing in the gazebo!" I blurted the first thing that jumped into my head.

"How did you …?" Ian looked confused for a second, then enlightened. "Of course, you were there, at the after-grad."

"But …" Angela jumped in. "You stayed with the car. Ravi said you stayed with the car."

"Yeah, no. That was a whole adventure I'll have to tell you about sometime, but back to the kissing part?"

"We were busy planning," Ian said. "Then, we heard people coming and needed to look busy with something else."

"I may have overdone it," Angela admitted with heavy frustration. "It hasn't been easy fake-dating the hottest gay guy in school!"

"Hey! I'm a great kisser!" Ian objected.

"True," Angela growled. "But a girl wants something else, somewhere else after a while."

"And I told you, I've tried that before, and it felt so wrong. It ended up being terrible for both of us."

"I know, and I would never ask you to do that," Angela said quickly. "But … it's been very frustrating, pretending to be infatuated, hugging and kissing, then we go to bed and … study magic." She heaved a very heavy sigh.

"You think you've been frustrated?" Ian gripped. "I've had to spend the whole school year with Mike, so, so close, but just out of reach."

"You want to talk about Mike!" Angela exclaimed. "I wouldn't be half this bad if he hadn't brought me right to the edge of having real sex for the first time, then bailed on me!"

"Sitting right here, guys!" I protested.

"We know!" they chorused, with a moderate glare from Angela and a big evil grin from Ian.

The grins and glares faded at my obvious discomfort. With a shared look, Ian leaned backward, and Ange leaned forward.

"I don't want to make this awkward," Angela said. "But what happened with us? The more I think about it, the more I think there has to be something you're not telling me. I want you to know that you can tell me anything. Not letting each other in has caused a lot more grief than any of us needed. For what it's worth, I'm sorry about my part in that."

"I …" My pulse rate spiked. We'd shared enough confidences here that it felt like the right thing to do, but I was still scared.

"Are … you maybe gay, and didn't want to tell me?" She asked curiously. Ian got very still.

"Sort of," I answered, actually trying to be honest for the first time. "Actually bi, I think, but not quite in the usual way, and there's a lot more to it."

They sported identical looks of utter confusion. I was really messing this up by being obtuse. And today, of all days, called for brutal clarity,

"I think I'm gender-fluid, but the strange thing is that when I feel like a certain gender, my body shifts to match, so I'm like, trans for a little while, then my body changes to the gender I'm feeling. Or, sometimes, in odd cases, like the gender I think I need to be." I gestured toward Ian. "I've been switching suddenly to female shape for the past few months whenever this guy made me want to jump him."

I watched their faces in trepidation. I was proud I'd managed to get all that out in a way that mostly made sense, and for all my fear of their reactions, I was relieved that I'd finally told them. One way or another, this wouldn't be hanging over my head and messing up our relationships.

"I knew it! I knew there was something I didn't know," Angela said triumphantly.

At the same time, Ian said, "Of course, a shifter! I should have known. That's how you dodged the tracker at the after-grad."

"A what?" Angela and I said together.

"A shifter. A shapeshifter," Ian explained. "People with an inborn ability to change the form of their bodies across a wide range of human variability. Their abilities are similar to mage talent in that they're inherited, come in various strengths, and usually appear shortly after puberty."

Ian gave me a considering look. "Oh, and also, all wizards are under strict instructions to capture or kill any shifters we find," he added apologetically.

Angela gave him a sharp look, and I started mentally measuring the distance to the doors while my heart raced.

"I'm not going to do it!" He held his hands up. "Just letting you know."

"Okay, I get it," I said in a conciliatory tone, trying to calm down. "I haven't slept since last night, and I'm just running on adrenaline, so be gentle with me."

"That sounds like a good idea," he said, with one of his brilliant smiles directed my way. That wasn't good for my heart rate either.

"You think I could take other forms?" I blurted the first in a long list of questions that was forming in my mind. "All I've ever done is switch back and forth along the sex scale." Though as I said it, I recalled the curvier female form I had shifted into, and the strange night vision I'd acquired. Those certainly seemed like more variability than just my gender. Maybe Ian was right.

"Yeah, though that relates to trained, adult shifters. I think when you're just starting, you might get rid of a hated birthmark, bulk out muscle when threatened, or heal wounds … anything the shifter desperately needs at that moment."

I wouldn't have described myself as needing to switch sex, certainly not at a conscious level, but it made sense. Especially if that the feeling of wrongness—the feeling of my body not fitting me that I got before a switch—was that 'need.'

"I do the wound healing, too. Sometimes," I admitted.

"Really?" Angela said, surprised.

"Only when I shift sex, though. Sometimes scratches or sprains will disappear."

"That's convenient."

"Not really, when you have to pretend to still be injured because you don't want to explain how your injury magically disappeared, and, oh yeah, you're also trying to hide that fact that you're now having your period."

"Ouch, yeah, I can see that… and, period?"

"The change is very thorough," I said grimly. I was trying to wrap my mind around these new thoughts. For me, and even for Mom, switching had been all about gender and sex. Thinking about it as a part of a more general shapeshifting ability brought out all sorts of ideas.

"Is that why you've been afraid of sex, Mike?" Angela asked. "Not just periods, but because you might shift in the middle?"

"Yes," I said. "Or, in our case, I shifted before we started. Found myself in a very different kind of form. Not male or female. It would have blown my secret wide open, so I ran, and I couldn't explain why. I'm so sorry."

She sprang across the short distance between us on the couch, only pausing for the slightest of nods from me before wrapping her arms around me.

"No, I'm sorry, Mike," she spoke into my neck. "I was only thinking about myself. I didn't realize you were going through something you couldn't talk about. I thought I was the only special one with deep, dark secrets. What a creep." I felt a wetness and realized she was crying. I hugged her to me, revelling in the feel of her body against mine, an intimacy long absent from my life.

Her comforting hug, by mutual consent, drifted into more of a cuddle, sharing a physical closeness we'd been denied for months because of the walls we'd each put up that were thoroughly demolished now. I let the weight of her body push me back onto the couch until she was lying entirely on top of me. She turned her head, her mouth found mine, and we shared a profound kiss.

I had missed this so much. Before our disastrous attempt at sex, we'd spent most of the last year reducing the physical distance between us to practically nothing. Cutting that off cold turkey had hurt, and it seemed I wasn't the only one who felt that way. This was how we were meant to be.

She made several happy noises, and, after a couple of moments, broke the kiss to speak.

"We never should have stopped cuddling," she said in low, husky tones. "The only reason I let you stay away was because I wasn't sure I could resist fondling you, and I didn't want to drive you further away. Speaking of …" She shifted her weight so she could slip a hand down between my legs. "I thought I felt something," she said with a wide grin.

The touch of her hand felt great and made me gasp. I willed aside my fear. I wasn't feeling entirely stable in male shape, but I reminded myself that it didn't matter now and tried to relax.

"Ah, hey," Ian said awkwardly, revealing a shy uncertainty I'd seen only once before, just before his uncle burst in on us and ruined the mood. "As fun as it is to be a voyeur, maybe I'll go for a walk and give you some privacy?" he said, getting up from his chair.

"Oh! I'm sorry." Angela pulled back so she wasn't right on top of me.

She did actually sound sorry. "Talk about monopolizing Mike." She laughed ruefully. "He …" She gave me a considering look. "They? should get to choose."

"That seems fair," Ian said.

"Not fair to me!" I choked. I looked back and forth between their equally lustful expressions. My girlfriend, whom I'd stood up, or the sweet guy I'd been pining after all year. It was impossible to think of disappointing either of them, and I didn't know how many chances we'd get to do this.

"Okay, who would be upset if the other joined in?"

"Are you kidding? That would be awesome," Angela enthused.

"I'm cool with that, as long as I'm not expected to touch any girl parts." Ian grinned.

Angela threw a cushion at him, which he easily deflected, laughing.

"I will attempt to keep boy parts available," I said. "But, with my body, I make no guarantees."

"It will be an adventure," Ian said, as we all headed downstairs to Angela's bedroom.

~*~

Two hours later, we lay in Angela's double bed, a tangle of naked bodies with all the blankets swept onto the floor by our prior activities.

To everyone's delight, I had managed to stay in guy form the whole time. Now that I'd stopped making assumptions about Ian, both of their obvious enjoyment of that form held back any urge to switch.

It was not the smoothest of encounters. None of us had done anything like it before. We spent as much time laughing at ourselves as we did having sex, as we tried different combinations that didn't work for one or more of us. But it was fun. Every messy, beautiful moment of it.

I knew I was a newbie at this, but three seemed like an excellent number of participants. By the time one of us was ready for a break, another was ready to go again, so we kept cycling around until we were all completely wrung out and happy.

I soaked in the unfamiliar feeling of being comfortable in my body, knowing I could switch right now, and my friends wouldn't even blink. It was the most liberated I had ever felt. Years of fear and anxiety left my body with the sweat that soaked the sheets. I felt like I might float away if it wasn't for Ange's leg over mine and Ian's arm across my stomach.

"I'm so glad we got to do this," Ian said. "I've been captivated by you all year, Mike. I dreamt of this moment many times, but never expected it to be like this."

"Sorry if I intruded on your moment," Angela said languidly, sounding not at all sorry.

Ian laughed. "Don't be. It was perfect. I think if it had been just Mike and I, we would have been so tense and afraid to screw up that it wouldn't have been nearly as fun."

"I'll second that," I said. "As much as I've wanted to get you into bed, I would have been stressed out, and Angela being here helped me relax."

We lay companionably for a while longer, talking about movies, books, and music. I was glad I stuck with the *Wheel of Time* book as long as I had; Ian was so happy he'd finally managed to get me into the books. However, we lost Angela's attention with our dissection of the differing plot points between the book and the TV show.

Midway through our discussion, we realized I'd switched to female form, without anyone, including me, noticing in the moment. They were both fascinated. Ian's interest was more technical and Angela's more sexual, though not at all urgent since we were both tired.

"I guess you're bi too?" I asked her.

"I don't know," she said easily, sounding just as curious as I was. "I'm not attracted to many people, but I'm always attracted to you."

And that was a good enough answer for both of us.

"Does it feel any different, being female? Like, inside your head?" Ian asked a little later when we were less busy.

"A little? I feel the cold more in female form, even with a very similar body shape, and I think maybe I cry more easily. In male form, it seems easier to get angry, but it's a tendency, not some major overhaul."

"I do remember Jenn mentioning the cold thing," Ian mused. "Must be hormonal."

"The big change for me is external, not internal. It's in how people treat me when they see a person they can put in a box, 'male' versus 'female'. But those expectations leak inside, too. I start pre-reacting to how other people will treat me, and so I fall into some gendered behaviours without thinking about it."

"That makes a lot of sense," Angela said from my other side, where she was lazily trailing her fingernails up and down my arm, giving me nice shivers. "We condition ourselves to fit into the space society allows for us, or the parts of us that don't fit get rubbed raw."

As much as I wanted to remain distracted, practical questions snuck back into my head and I could no longer put off seeking answers.

I confirmed with Ian that shapeshifters were not considered wizards. Our powers were completely distinct from each other. The Clan might try to kill off or control me in other ways, but no one would be trying to seal me into the codex.

Ian also thought that the anti-wizard groups would most likely welcome a shapeshifter, since we had such potent natural defences against magic. I might have been too hasty in thinking Sarah would lump my abilities in with the wizards. I felt some pangs of regret. Maybe she would have trusted me more if I'd come clean with her about my abilities.

Eventually, of course, we had to get up and clean up.

Afterward, we put together some lunch and sat around the table. Funny how a couple of hours could completely change the vibe. We were relaxed with each other now, working together in the kitchen. I could smile and laugh at accidental body touches instead of tensing up.

After lunch, Ian dragged us back to serious topics.

"We don't know for sure when the sealing will happen, but it will be within weeks, and I'm sure I know where. It will be at the Banff Springs Hotel."

"Where the wedding was?" I confirmed.

"Yes. There's a secret rooftop suite where the Clan gathers. The codex will be nearby for the sealings, and I know where it's held. Before the ceremony, I'll distract everyone while Angela leaves. She'll get the codex out of its safe and destroy it … or make a run for it if she can't."

"And I'll be there to pick you up and make a run for it, successful or not," I said.

We all avoided mentioning that Ian would be trapped, with no way to run if it didn't work.

"I don't know if the woman I was working with will still be willing to help get Angela to safety, but I'll do my best to convince her. Otherwise, we'll just try to get as much distance as possible and keep moving."

I kept it to myself for now, but Sarah had mentioned heading for Vancouver, which seemed like as good a destination as any. Maybe if we could get there, the rest of her anti-wizard org, which I'd taken to calling the 'anti-fascist-wizard' org, or antifawz, for short, would stir themselves to help us out.

I could only hope. I reached out to gently squeeze Angela's hand. She smiled sadly at me and squeezed back.

Leaving Angela was hard. Leaving Ian was worse, knowing it might be the last time we saw each other. We had all reluctantly agreed that it would be best if I didn't see them again before the operation.

I hugged Angela tightly, then hugged Ian. It was a long and comfortable hug, even though I was still in female form.

"Take care of yourselves, okay?" My eyes were already damp. "I'll be ready." I mounted my bike and sped off before I lost the will to leave, letting the wind dry my tears.

CHAPTER 24

Returning to my parents' house in the afternoon felt like defeat. Home was the same as it always was. Even my note was still on the kitchen table where I'd left it. But I felt like a stranger, like I didn't belong here anymore.

Perhaps I didn't. What if my parents took the announcement that I wasn't going to hide my switches anymore, and my note about leaving for a while, as proof that it was time for us all to move on, possibly in different directions?

A surprisingly strong wave of grief washed over me. This was what I'd been planning, but for all I disagreed with my parents on some key issues, I loved them, and I wanted to be in their lives. I could hardly believe that just twelve hours earlier, I'd been thinking about leaving my friends and family forever. And I might have done it, too, if it hadn't been for my chance encounter with an off-the-clock sex worker. The chances our paths would cross again were slim, but if they did, I wanted to let her know the impact of her kindness.

Sitting in my room in female form after a shower, the damp ends of my hair brushing my shoulders, I felt extremely out of place. This was Michael's space, not Kayla's. And certainly not Amanda's, the little girl I'd once been, who was erased to protect us from the wizard clans. I shuddered. I hadn't even let myself think of that name since I was eight.

I had texted the contact number Sarah left on my way home, in addition to leaving a note on our shared Discord, but I would have to wait for her to contact me. I couldn't see Angela or Ian again until, maybe, hopefully, the day of the sealing. Ravi's parents weren't going to want to see me for a while. I didn't have a job anymore, and I'd just blown up my relationship with my parents. My life had dropped into a liminal space, and I didn't know what to do with myself.

I had felt so confident proclaiming to my parents that I was 'going to be me,' but after Sarah dropping me and Ian's revelations about shapeshifting, I didn't know who I was anymore, or where I fit in.

In that grey moment, a new urge stirred in me. I had to figure out just how much I could do.

Shapeshifter.

Was Ian right? Could I really look like anyone? Could I learn how to change my body in ways that I wanted?

I'd never successfully willed an appearance change before, but I had focused on stopping my sex switches and had never tried to be someone else. What if I couldn't get back to my original form? That would be even more awkward to explain than a sex switch.

In cases where I had deviated from my usual form lately, developing larger hips and breasts, I hadn't had any trouble returning to my usual form. It had just happened. Returning from any other form should work the same way. In theory.

Okay. How about starting with something small? What Ian mentioned … shifters changing their muscles, or a birthmark. Sadly, neither of those motivated me. It needed to be something I cared about deeply.

I looked down at my breasts. I wondered if I should greet my parents in guy mode when they came home, to prove I was trying? Or would they clock my female form and be angry anyway? If so, what was the point?

I had made my breasts larger once, at a moment when I felt particularly insecure. Could I make them smaller? How about my hips? My hair? My voice?

I spent a while in front of the mirror visualizing myself as more boyish and trying to change myself into that image. No luck. I searched images of flat-chested, slim-hipped bodies for inspiration, but got unnaturally gaunt fashion models. Ugggh. The internet was disgusting sometimes.

I flopped on the bed, frustration eating me up. What good was being a shapeshifter if you couldn't shift into anything you actually wanted?

With my eyes closed, I let my mind drift for a few minutes. I did my best to cast off worries about my parents coming home, or what was happening with Sarah, or how much danger Angela would be in with Ian's plans. Then, I grounded myself, trying to fully inhabit my body.

I felt like Kayla. The girl who had the freedom to express herself as a girl, as a woman. The woman who had taken down the goon trying to kill her friend without a second thought. The woman who was still reeling from stupendously amazing first-time sex. I felt like my spirit actually, finally filled my skin.

What I needed to do was recapture how I felt before. Living with my parents. Dealing with school. The one who felt like I had to keep presenting as a boy, even though I was a girl sometimes. Hundreds of real-life experiences flashed through my mind. I let the familiar fear and hopelessness pervade my body. I had to accept that this was how I needed to live. At least for now. For the safety of everyone I loved.

The shift was almost imperceptible, but I'd been waiting for it. I looked down my chest and saw very little in the way of boob. I grabbed a handful of hair and was relieved to find it shorter again. I was still a woman in my head, heart, and body. I had simply adjusted my female body to take on an appearance more commonly associated with men.

I lightly wrapped my very flat boobs and put my T-shirt back on. With that taken care of, I wondered what else I could do. Could I change something I didn't feel passionate about, like my eye colour?

Watching myself in the mirror wasn't the way. I'd tried that before, and it seemed to get in the way more than help. The change had to come from my feelings.

It took about an hour of exploration, trying different kinds of thoughts to motivate my body, before I was able to open my eyes and see a clear green iris instead of the warm brown I was used to. The winning path wasn't any specific thought. It was a special kind of focus. Like how you could peer at fine details in a picture or listen closely to an intricate melody. I focused on the shape of my body with some sense I'd only vaguely been aware of before.

It was aggravating how easy it was. Years I'd spent battering at the wall of gender in my mind, and I'd completely missed all the simpler paths. It wasn't until I'd been able to let go of some of my trauma from feeling forced into switches that I could even think about consciously changing my shape.

Thumps and voices from my parents coming in interrupted my thoughts. I bounced off the bed. My small successes at shifting had given me a little boost of confidence in facing this next problem, but my gut still hurt, wondering how they would respond to my unexpected return.

Mom let out a little yelp when I came down the stairs and put her hand to her chest.

"Michael! You're home!" She didn't look angry, just shocked.

Dad stuck his head around the corner from the entryway. "Mike's home?" he called excitedly.

Well, it didn't sound like they were ready to disown me.

Mom walked over and enveloped me in a big hug. "I'm so glad you're home. We've been worried about you."

I hugged her back. Half the tension in my body dropped away immediately.

"I'm glad to be home," I mumbled.

We separated somewhat awkwardly. We hadn't shared many heartfelt hugs in the past few years. I vowed to change that.

"Let's sit down, the three of us, and have a talk, okay? We …" She glanced back at Dad, who smiled encouragingly. "Have been talking, and I realize I didn't handle our previous conversation well."

"I have some things to talk to you about, too," I admitted.

We sat around the kitchen table and talked, finally, about what it was like to have an inconsistent gender. Mom shared stories from her teen years. She'd grown up as a boy and hadn't started shifting gender until her teens. It had been really traumatic for her, first trying to hide the switches, then realizing she wanted to be a woman, being found out, and her family trying to force her back into being a boy.

The haunted look in her eyes suggested she didn't tell me all of it. As much as I felt my parents hadn't handled some things well, I had to admit they'd been better than Mom's parents, and I understood why she didn't have any contact with them.

Then, it was my turn. I talked about my constant switches, about hiding being in female-shape every week, and about finally coming to the realization that I was switching because my gender was close to the imaginary dividing line between 'man' and 'woman,' and I wandered back and forth over that line, on my own, or sometimes because of an external nudge.

"Like a hot guy," I admitted, feeling my face flush. But that embarrassment was a far better example than my life being in deadly danger from armed wizards' goons. They'd never let me leave the house again.

After a few glowing comments from my mom about Ian to my Dad, I got onto the most important topic: that I was a girl right now, even though my look was more androgynous. They were both shocked. I guess I'd managed to remove enough of the 'tells' they'd been using to know what shape I was in. Mom admitted as much, saying she could normally tell by the way I walked and sat when I forgot to camouflage it.

"So, you're willing to continue as a boy?" Mom asked.

"I think it's safest, for now," I admitted.

They seemed happy enough with that, and we all carried on with an absurdly normal evening.

I didn't mention that Kayla could be known to the wizards, so Michael offered a good cover. Especially since Sarah had deliberately avoided researching me, when it seemed likely now that she could have uncovered all my personal details if she'd wanted to. Maybe she'd been worried about the wizard mind-reading Ian mentioned? I didn't have a good enough read on her to tell whether those motives originated from a place of compassion or if she'd simply been following some protocol of her organization.

On Saturday, I went to Ravi's birthday party, which should have been a blast since it was the first time in years that I'd been able to relax about my gender, and I'd had enough money to get him a real present. However, I was so on edge wondering if Sarah would call me, and staying on my best behaviour to mollify Ravi's parents, that I couldn't really enjoy anything.

Ravi loved the game I bought him, especially because his parents had cut him off, only buying essentials, since he'd defied his dad. He'd found a second job on weekends, working at the amusement park for a little extra cash flow. One of his many cousins was in management there. It was another good example of how the wizard clans had screwed over my family. Their constant threat had cut us off from the kind of family network that provided opportunities like that.

The money I had earned from Sarah was enough to convince my parents not to worry when I said I wouldn't be working at the fictional camp job for a while. This gave me some guilt-free time to practice shifting my form. I threw myself into that and tried not to think about the future.

Eye colour became easy after a few hours. I moved on to hair colour and length, then to height and weight. Figuring out the mental trick of those first few deliberate changes had been tough, but each new type of change became easier the more I practiced.

I found that there was a limit to how often I could switch, and it was sensitive to how much of my body was changing. If I were changing a very limited area, such as my eyes, there was a high limit. Changing my height and muscles, however, I could only do a few times before each change became twice as hard as the previous one.

This led to some uncomfortable time confined to my room with my body stuck in the size of an eight-year-old while I waited for changing to become easier again. I fought down the fear that I might be stuck like that forever. I had just managed to shift back to my normal self, in male shape, when Sarah's call came in.

It was an unknown number, so I answered with a cautious hello, assuming a spam call.

"Is he really ready to make a move?" Sarah asked.

"Nice to talk to you, too. How's things?" I replied, pitching my voice back into something close to my female range.

"Don't get cute. We don't have time for cute."

"I'll always have time for my oppa, Ji Chang-Wook."

"You still on that? How anyone could pass over Yoo Ji-Tae, I don't know … Ah! Nicely done." The warm, if slightly exasperated, approval in her voice made me feel better. It didn't sound like she hated me. Maybe I still had a chance to convince her to help us.

I shook my head. I needed to keep my feelings out of this business. I had used our playful argument over whether the younger or older guy in the Korean drama we'd watched together was cuter. It made a great hook to ensure I was actually speaking to Sarah, and that she wasn't being coerced.

"Can I talk freely?" I asked.

"It's fairly safe, but don't list any specific details you don't have to."

"Got it," I said. "He's ready. He's been thinking about moving for a while. Even has some plans for how to do it and survive, but he needs help."

"Or this is all part of a plan to get me back." Her tone made it clear that 'get me back' meant revenge.

"I don't think so. He's got good reasons for wanting out. Nothing to do with you."

"Hmm." She sounded skeptical. I felt bad getting into his personal details, but if I could be sure of anything, it was that Sarah wouldn't be sharing any information she didn't have to, and certainly not with the wizards.

"He's gay," I said bluntly. "I expect you know what that means, for him."

"You're sure? He's not putting on an act?"

"He was … very convincing," I said, blushing at the memory.

Sarah chuckled, gathering the context from my tone, probably, but she still wasn't encouraging.

"I feel for him. I do," she eventually continued, "But … this is only one group, and not one of the most powerful clans. I trust you as much as I've trusted anyone, but helping guys like your friend isn't what I do, and I can't afford any mistakes. You understand, I hope?"

My heart ached. I did understand. I heard the pain in her voice, and I knew it cost her, but she was calculating on a scale I could barely imagine. My thoughts spun as my gut clenched. She was going to end this call soon. And Ian, Angela, and I would be doomed, all because I couldn't think of one little argument to persuade this deeply scarred woman to put her neck on the block for us. None of this was fair.

Try as I might, I couldn't bring myself to believe she had been cold-heartedly using me this whole time. I had been useful, for sure, but I was also certain there had been real affection and friendship between us. That made this next part hurt.

I knew there was one thing that would get her attention, enough to keep her talking at least. Ian had assured me that shifters were generally welcomed by the anti-wizard groups, even the hard-liners, but it was still difficult for me to let that information out after hiding for so long. I had to do something to help Ian and Angela, though. I wouldn't be able to live with myself if I didn't try every possible angle.

"There's something you don't know about me," I said breathlessly.

"No games, Kayla," Sarah said tiredly.

"You know how you asked if I'd been living as a guy?"

"Yes?"

"And I have been. In both mind and body."

"What?"

"Being a girl, in body, is strictly a part-time thing for me. Our friend and I both have some very good reasons to get far away from his family. You can trust that we're not working with them."

I finished breathlessly. That was as clear as I felt I could be, considering these words could be picked up by other ears.

"Hang on," she said. Then there was silence.

I waited.

I stood and paced the three steps across my room, back and forth. If she didn't get it …

"Aauughh!" Sarah's frustrated growl was loud enough that I had to pull the phone away from my ear. "That makes way too much sense. I can't believe I didn't see it before!" she wailed, then sighed heavily. "Okay, you hooked me. If you are what I think, we need to meet up."

I sagged back down onto my bed, relief flowing through me. I'd survived the first leap, and I already had a place in mind. Somewhere nicely public.

"There's a coffee shop near your place. Bistro."

"I've seen it," she said. "Yes, that's a good spot. Tomorrow. Ten in the morning?"

"Ah, sure." All I was doing these days was shapeshifting practice, other than … "Oh, crap. Can we do it a little later? I have a meeting at nine."

"Eleven, then."

"Yeah."

"Good. See you then."

My phone beeped as she ended the call.

I stared at the screen as it faded to black. I had the looming feeling I'd set something in motion with no way to control it, like rolling the first stone of a rockslide. I would just have to watch it play out.

CHAPTER 25

Dad drove the two of us to school after dropping Mom off at work in the morning, so we could meet my English teacher. I felt bad that he was taking precious time off for this. I told him I could go myself, but both he and Mom argued it was best if I had some parental backup.

I was touched, even though I had trouble feeling strongly about marks while my friends faced a potentially deadly struggle. Then Dad surprised me again while we were driving.

"I don't think I've told you how much I appreciate your hard work this summer," he said, glancing over. "You must be tired from working at camp, but you've been doing so many chores at home, too."

"Not that much," I protested, guilt rising at the unearned praise. I hadn't been working overly hard at Sarah's. She insisted on doing most of the inside chores. I couldn't watch my parents work at home after I'd spent a whole day just hanging out with Sarah, so I had been helping out as much as I could.

"It means a lot to me," he said, giving my shoulder a pat.

The gesture made me feel warm inside. I had a sudden urge to snuggle up to his side with his arm around me, the way we used to when I was a child, but fathers and seventeen-year-old sons didn't do that. At least, not in my family. *A daughter might.* I banished that thought quickly. I was in male form, which was convenient for this meeting, and an early switch would be annoying.

"I hope you know that I will always be proud of you." His voice was gruff with emotion. "It's a fine line between encouraging you to do your best and being too hard on you. I'm not sure we always get it right. Like with your grades. We know a B isn't the end of the world, especially in grade 11. It's just that we won't be able to help very much with university, so you're going to need good grades for scholarships. That's why we're on you about making money in the summer, too." He sighed heavily. "We're hard on you sometimes because life is hard, and we won't be able to shield you from that much longer, but … Don't worry about today. Let's just give it our best shot. If it doesn't work out," he shrugged and shot me a quick grin. "You don't win 'em all."

All the words I wanted to say, but was too scared to voice, piled into a lump in my throat. I reached up and put my hand on his arm and said quietly, "Thanks, Dad."

I wanted to tell him about getting caught up between a wizard clan and the anti-wizard resistance. How the world was scarier than I ever imagined it could be.

I wanted to scream at him for knowing something about who I really was and hiding it from me for so long.

But I didn't want to burst this bubble of togetherness. Especially when I didn't know when we might have a moment like this again. So, I said nothing and basked in the moment.

We were ushered into the meeting right after checking in at the school's admin office. The principal and my English teacher, Mr. James, were already there. The vibe started off icy, then Mr. James hit us with the opening salvo.

"Mr. Orea, you may have heard of students using AI to write papers for them. Well, we use a sophisticated AI detection tool here. Any paper that is determined to be significantly AI written is given a mark of zero."

"But I …" I jumped in, in hot denial, as soon as he finished speaking.

"Son!" Dad commanded.

I shut up. He didn't use 'Dad voice' often, but when he did, I listened.

My teacher and the principal sat with identical self-satisfied smiles.

"Sirs. I have indeed heard quite a bit about the use of large language models, both in the creation of text and in analyzing that text to check for hallmarks of generation. The software developers at work talk about it a lot."

Dad worked in general maintenance at a big office building downtown. He did all those little fixes that kept the doors opening and closing properly, and the thermostats working, and the electricity on. He was good friends with a number of the technical staff who knew the value of a friendly maintenance guy. He was often invited to lunch with them.

The smiles collapsed, and creases of concern appeared on their brows.

"I think, for something as important as this final grade, we should all review the report generated by the AI detection tool." Dad spoke in a calm, reasoned way, knowing from long experience, I'd guess, that these men were prepared to dismiss anything we said.

"Um ..." Mr. James said.

"Hmm, yes, that sounds reasonable." The principal replied.

I held my tongue. I knew it was more than reasonable. It was in the school rules.

A tense ten minutes followed, while Mr. James frantically tried to dig up the documentation that he was supposed to have retained from his grading. I might have felt bad for him if he hadn't come out swinging at me first.

Eventually, he turned the laptop to face us, beaming triumphantly. A report was on the screen. It had my name and class section on it. It showed clearly an AI score of 86%. As I reached out to scroll down, Mr. James started to turn the laptop away.

"Just give him a minute.'" My dad held up his hand.

Mr. James turned the laptop back toward me.

As I scrolled, I felt a tingling grow at the top of my scalp. This was too ridiculous.

"Uh, Sirs." I tried to copy my dad's even tone. "This isn't my essay." Beyond the summary, the report provided excerpts of the text it considered to be AI-generated, along with, I noticed with some bitter amusement, fulsome warnings about double-checking the results, since false-positives were possible. But in this case, the excerpts were from a completely different essay, on a different topic than mine.

"Of course it is!" Mr. James spun the laptop back around to look at the report.

"But it's on a completely different topic!" I said, getting a little heated.

Dad held up his hand again.

"Perhaps, if my son's submission is still on file, we can simply double-check it against the snippets from the detection tool?'"

This was accomplished via another five minutes of Mr. James digging through files.

The principal was visibly sweating now.

Mr. James closed the laptop, his face pale.

"Ah. It appears there may have been a misattribution of the AI scan results in this case. I will take another look at Michael's paper and will adjust his mark accordingly."

We all expressed some perfunctory goodbye pleasantries, and then

Dad and I were ushered out. The principal looked quietly furious. I normally didn't like taking pleasure in anyone else's troubles, but if there was ever a time for that, it was now. They'd both mishandled my entire future with such blatant carelessness. They probably hadn't meant to be evil, but that's where they'd ended up.

"Thanks, Dad," I said on the walk back to where we'd parked our car, my voice thick with emotion. "I'm glad you were with me." I had to resist choking up a little. I'd been avoiding my parents so much lately, thinking of them mainly as obstacles, but they always tried to be here for me in their own ways.

"I'm glad, too," he said. "You know. In my work I see a lot of really smart people making silly mistakes, mostly because of some previous step they screwed up, but thought they got right. So, they keep going, making things worse and worse because they figure it ought to work." He shook his head, grinning at memories. "Try not to get angry when they're being all arrogant and blaming you for the problem. Don't be intimidated just because they've got some fancy title. Just relax and make them explain how they got to this point. Most of the time, they'll realize their mistake."

He dropped me off in the driveway at home and immediately headed to work. I waved until our car was out of sight, then ran upstairs to get ready for my meeting with Sarah.

~*~

I wandered into Bistro, receiving a welcoming nod from Chelley on cash. A couple of other regulars glanced my way with friendly looks.

The staff, and even some customers, probably suspected something was up with this person who kept arriving as one gender and leaving as another. But I was starting to realize that I wasn't the only one who used this place for a gender-presentation swap. The gay village, at least for now, appeared to fully accept the T in LGBTQ. Everyone was used to keeping something quiet with the new laws that were starting to be enforced. We all knew that more crackdowns would be announced once the referendum passed.

I scanned the room and noticed Sarah sitting at a table with her back to the wall. She was dressed in clothes in colours more subdued than I'd ever seen her wear. Charcoal grey jeans, a dark red top, and a well-worn black leather jacket.

Her gaze swung by me with no apparent recognition, but she didn't show any surprise when I stopped at her table. She must have picked me out well before I arrived, even though I was about as masculine as I ever looked today, even having some upper lip and cheek stubble.

"Hi, stranger," she said smoothly. "Care to sit?"

"For sure." I moved the chair not quite opposite her, so she still had a good view of the room.

"Sorry for cutting you off so abruptly before, after the bar," Sarah said. "I wasn't in good shape, dealing with my own issues, and I didn't finish up properly."

"I wasn't helping," I admitted. "I think, maybe, I got up in your business when I should have let you handle things." I still wasn't comfortable with the idea of killing, even someone who'd manifestly been ready to kill her, or possibly both of us, but I had a nagging feeling I had made the wrong decision that night.

"It's okay." She sighed. "You're not trained for this. Don't take on guilt over it."

"I'll try not to," I said, and, while she seemed in a forgiving mood, I brought up my main concern. "So, what else do you need to know, in deciding whether to help Angela and Ian?"

"Can you back up to what you said, about … changing?" Her tone and expression immediately switched back to all business.

"Take a look at my eyes." I looked directly at her, closed my eyes for a few seconds and altered my eye colour to the bright green I'd been working on. When I opened them again, she nodded.

"Not bad. Though chuffed as I am to discover your abilities, it makes me even less interested in saving some boy wizard. We need to get out of here before they get wind of what really happened and decide to go all-out after us."

"No deal." I shook my head. "My best friend is also caught up in this. I can't walk away. If you or your org won't help …" I spread my hands and arms to the side.

Sarah's lips made a hard line. "It's suicide to go up against a clan like this. They have hooks everywhere: government, police, hospitals. The sealing gives them the ability to draw magic, the very life, if needed, from every member to power their magic."

"Well, yeah, that's why Ian is going after the codex."

"Impossible!" Her eyes widened.

"He seems to think he can pull it off."

"Cocky," she muttered, "Those things are the bloody life of the clan. You'd need to be a right powerful mage to get close, even, and then you'd need to get through all the electronic and physical guards. The only time the Clan is even remotely vulnerable is when they're holding a sealing ceremony, and the timing of those is a deep secret … Ahhh!" She stopped her litany as she realized the link.

"Yeah, both of them are scheduled for sealing soon," I said.

"That would give us a time and place," she mused. "Still, a lot to consider."

"Enough to meet with them to see if their plan sounds viable?"

She closed her eyes and rubbed her temples.

"I don't know." She groaned. "If we're going to lose you anyway, there's no need to throw my life away too."

I tensed. Even after all this, she could still slip away. I'd better do something extravagant to keep her attention.

"Take a close look at this." I took a deep breath and focused on that other plane that seemed to control my shape, to implement the shifts I'd practiced all day yesterday. A tweak here, a tweak there. Get rid of the facial hair, adjust the facial geometry just a little, lengthen the hair on my head, grow the chest out a little, and I made a convincing impression of my female shape. The differences were subtle, but taken all together, it made a striking change if you were close up, watching it happen. I'd taken dozens of videos to make sure I had all the nuances down.

"That's brilliant!" She sat back, genuinely shocked, then leaned forward again, speaking quietly. "How? I've been told by other shifters that you can't control the gender shifts."

"I think you're right. I learned that the hard way." I sighed. "Most of my body is still male-shaped. I'm only adjusting a few surface details to look more feminine."

"The hard way?"

"I spent years struggling with random sex shifts, obsessing about the shape of my genitals, only to realize I was tackling the wrong problem." I flicked a crumb off the table with more gusto than necessary. It landed on the thankfully untenanted table beside us.

"Ah, yes. I can see that. How long have you actually been shifting?" she asked with a penetrating look.

"Uh … like, consciously? About a week." I shrugged. "But I've been switching sex since before I can remember."

"Well, fuck." She shook her head with a pained expression.

My stomach plummeted. How had I gone wrong? Had my attempt to make myself appear more useful backfired?

"Don't worry," she said, reacting to the look on my face. "I'm not upset with you. I'm just realizing there's no way I can let a shifter as powerful as you get away."

"Powerful?" That caught my attention. I'd never thought of myself as powerful. In any way.

"Most shifters don't develop enough ability to shift until their late teens. Generally, the earlier the shift, the more powerful the shifter." She looked directly into my eyes and said, "The most powerful shifter I've ever met started shifting at eleven."

"Oh." Words failed me.

"Yeah," Sarah replied, her voice gone a little distant as she mulled over the implications. I wasn't alone in my shock. She took out her phone, and we sat in silence for a couple of minutes while she typed. Then, she abruptly looked up at me.

"Okay. Fine. I'm prepared to meet with him and at least hear what his plan is … but if it sucks, I'm out of here, with or without you."

"That's the most I can ask," I said gratefully.

Sarah nodded, then stood up abruptly. She held out a hand, palm down, when I started to rise too.

"No. Best if we don't leave at the same time," she said. "Send me the details of the next meeting as soon as you have a secure space. And don't stay here too long."

Then she was gone, striding toward the exit. I watched her head to the curb outside, and within ten seconds, a grey sedan stopped by her, she got into the passenger side, and it sped off.

I suddenly realized I'd been ignoring the need to pee. I got up and headed for the bathrooms in the back, not planning to change my clothes for once. Given the female presentation I'd put on for Sarah, I used the women's. That series of precise and related changes was nearly the most difficult shift I could manage right now, and shifting completely back to a male presentation would have to wait for about twenty minutes.

As I hurried out of the bathroom, dabbing my still-damp hands on my jeans, a hand grabbed tight on my upper arm. Adrenaline spiked. I was pulled backward and to my left. I had never specifically trained in martial arts, but you couldn't hang around a parkour den without picking up a few tricks.

I stomped my right leg down behind, my foot turned out, and threw my right elbow up and around in a short, vicious arc, keeping my captured left arm and shoulder loose to give me room to pivot.

My elbow made solid contact with something soft, yet pokey. A guy's voice cried out in pain. I turned to see Donny stumbling back, right hand cupped to the side of his face.

My fingers wrapped around the reassuring solidity of the taser in my right pocket. I quickly checked the short hallway for other assailants, but it was empty.

"Wha? Why'd you hit me?" he spluttered through his hand.

"Why'd you grab me, Dickbag?" I shot back.

"It *is* you, Mike. Don't try to deny it!" He let his hand fall to his side. There was a red mark on his cheekbone and a couple of scratches where his glasses had gouged in before flying off. His right eye was watering fiercely and starting to darken underneath.

"Oh hell," I said, remembering I'd left my body in a more feminine appearing shape. I glanced around again, happy this hallway was screened off from the main room.

"I'm really busy, Donny. What the actual fuck do you want?" I scanned the floor for his glasses, panicking. What if he called the Misinformation Tip Line on me? He knew where I lived!

"I need you to teach me" he almost shouted. Pain and passion burned in his eyes. "How do you do this?" He gestured at my body.

"Oh," I said, then more gently, "Oh, Donny." I could see the need written in every line of his body. "You can't learn this. It's just who I am. It's who I've always been. It can't be taught."

He collapsed, his face falling into his hands, his knees hitting the floor. He sobbed and rocked back and forth.

I squatted beside him. "Hey. It's okay. There are other paths you can take. If you want to be a girl, you can be a girl. I've heard hormones are pretty magical, given time. You know Jennifer … look how much she's changed!"

That got his attention. He lifted his head, scornfully. "But she's rich. I heard her parents sent her off for all sorts of surgeries and shit." His chin trembled. "Mine chucked my pills in the trash after my brother narked on me. They say they're this close to sending me off to the mental ward."

"I don't think …" I started, but Jenn wasn't the issue here. "I'm so sorry your parents are being assholes. I promise I'll do what I can to help you get the medicine you need, just … no more following me around and assaulting me, or anyone else, okay?" I added a harder edge to my voice at the end.

He agreed, looking hopeful.

"And, ah, if for any reason I'm not around for a while, find Jenn. She'll help, if you ask." It occurred to me, with the shit I was getting into with Ian, that I might not be around to help anyone.

Donny nodded jerkily.

I finally spotted his glasses. They'd nestled themselves in the soft tendrils of a mop head standing in a bucket in the corner. I extracted them and handed them to him.

"You all right for now?" I asked.

He nodded, and I held out a hand. He gripped it and pulled himself up to his feet. "Thanks, Mike. Sorry I grabbed you, and thanks." He walked quickly out of the café with his head down.

I took a couple of deep breaths to compose myself, put in the effort to switch my face and body back to the more masculine appearance I'd been wearing when I'd walked in, and hurried back to my bike.

CHAPTER 26

"You sure about the giant gorilla, Mike?" Ravi stood in the middle of the Haunted House props room, shaking his head. "That's a lot of costume for a skinny little dude. I've got a great skeleton over here."

I turned toward him, peering through the eyes of the gorilla head mask. The field of vision was pretty good. It totally screwed my peripheral, of course, but I liked the level of padding that came with this costume, in case anybody got stabby later. Which was a distinct possibility when dealing with whatever guards were following Ian and Angela everywhere.

"What? Don't I frighten you?" I hit the chin-switch to trigger the mask's recorded roar and held my hands up in a claw-like pose, advancing toward him around the cheap table and folding chairs set up in the middle of the room.

Far from showing fear, Ravi doubled over in laughter. "Oh man, you look like the world's worst Funko Pop!"

"Ha." I stripped the head off with a grunt. It was highly realistic, made of plastic and latex, and very heavy. It also smelled like stale beer. "I bet it's scarier in the dark. Besides, you'd be in here if I weren't." I couldn't easily explain that I wanted something that looked as little like my 'Mike' persona as possible, so that the evil wizards club didn't get motivated to track me down. "Just help me into the rest of this getup before you go."

"You're lucky it'll be dark." He held up the heavy, padded cloth-and-latex gorilla body as I stepped in. Its catches and zips were placed such that it really was a two-person job. Fortunately, Ravi was experienced, having worked at the new Haunted House at Calaway Park for a few weekends when it proved more popular than expected.

It had been three days since my meeting with Sarah. I'd gone out for a run with Ravi this morning, and listening to him vent about having to put on the gorilla suit tonight—because the regular gorilla guy had to go suck face with his girlfriend—had given me a sudden brainwave.

Sarah needed to meet with us before she would agree to support our strike against the local Clan and free Ian and Angela before their sealing. We'd been going in circles for two days, trying to figure out a way for Ian and Angela to shed their invisible guards without making it obvious they were trying to hide, which would draw exactly the wrong attention.

I frantically messaged Sarah and Angela, using a different Discord for each, then spent three hours unable to sit still until they'd both signalled their agreement to the plan, with Angela speaking for Ian.

Ravi had been happy to help, even when I refused to answer any of his entirely valid questions about the whole setup. He still felt like he owed me for dragging me out to the after-grad party and then abandoning me. I hated trading on that favour since I knew he'd really made the best choice, but this meeting had to happen, and this opportunity was too perfect to pass up.

"How are things with Debbie?" I asked tentatively. Thankfully, it was a happy answer today.

"Good! Hanging out at the after-grad didn't net us any contacts. But Debbie was, uh, inspired by all the sex going on, if you know what I mean." He grinned broadly.

"I think I do." I grinned back.

I hadn't told him about my afternoon of sex with Angela and Ian. It was too much bound up in everything else, but I was glad to feel like I was on the inside of the sex talk instead of outside. Finally.

"Hey, did you hear about your English mark yet?" Ravi asked as he fought with a reluctant zipper.

"Yes!" I felt a rush of pride at the memory. "Once he actually marked my essay, it brought my final mark up to an A again, so everybody's happy. Except perhaps the principal."

"Sweet!" Ravi hooked up the last part of the neck and thumped me hard on my padded shoulder. "You're good to go."

"Thanks for this," I said, adding "I mean it" when he tried to deflect. "You've always been there for me when I needed you, and I want you to know how much I appreciate it."

"Same to you, buddy." Ravi's light-hearted tone turned serious. "You're starting to worry me, like I might not see you again."

"Oh, hey, don't take it that way," I backpedalled. Crap, he was right. It sounded like I was saying goodbye. Which I guess I was. "I know you've got a lot going on with your parents right now. I don't want to add to it. I'm sorry if I did." I shook my head and accidentally set off the gorilla's roar. When it was done and Ravi had stopped giggling, I asked, "How's that going? Your dad still mad at me?"

"Yeah. He still thinks my quitting is your fault, somehow." He grimaced. "It couldn't just be that I, their dutiful son, am sick of their shit! There's got to be some kind of contagion."

"I can handle it. Don't worry about me, on any front." I glanced at the clock on the wall. It read 8:14. I had a comfortable time margin before Ian and Angela's scheduled appearance, somewhere between 8:30 and 9:00 p.m., but I would feel better if I could spend some time getting into my role.

"Okay, I got it," Ravi said, noticing my time check. He headed for the door, calling back, "Good luck! I'll be in position by half-past."

I shuffled over to take a look in the mirror after Ravi left. He was right. The rumpled suit, bulging in all the wrong places, did look ridiculous on my 5'7, 120lb frame. But he didn't know my secret.

Having learned how to minimize my feminine features when my gender shifted that way had come in handy many times lately. Today, it meant I could wear a light T-shirt and shorts into the gorilla suit without worrying I'd expose my sex switch. Adding another six inches of height and bulking out my muscles was now a simple change for me.

My mirror image looked the part now, carrying the costume the way it had been intended. I stepped forward and back, swinging my arms around. The suit felt … well, not exactly light, but a minor inconvenience compared to its previously suffocating weight.

I leapt from my flat-black painted alcove, triggering the roar sound, arms raised and spread out threateningly.

A couple of kids, a girl about ten years old and a slightly younger boy, recoiled in fright. Their expressions were clear to me, despite the red-tinted darkness of the hallway, since I'd also figured out how to replicate the night vision that I had unconsciously acquired at the after-grad party.

I shifted to more of a silly capering dance, moving back to give them room to walk past. I was here to shock, not terrify, the little ones. They laughed loudly, a healthy release of their previous fright as they edged around, hugging the far wall and holding hands.

I retreated to my alcove once more.

My next foray was less successful. I had been alternating jumping out in front of and behind visitors as they shuffled through the dark corridor. I wanted to jump as close behind Ian and Angela as I could. When I sprang out behind these two teen girls, one of them screamed. The other turned around and punched me in the face. Hard enough to rock me back.

"What the fuck?" yelled the one who punched me, wringing her hand.

There was a moment of mutual shocked silence, broken briefly by my groan. Although the latex mask had cushioned the blow, my jaw throbbed. I certainly wouldn't have wanted to take that one bare-faced. *Ouch*!

The other girl recovered and stared at her friend. "What the hell? Why'd you punch him?"

"What do you expect me to do when some asshole jumps out in a gorilla suit, hug him?" She was still glaring at me.

"He's just part of the house, you idiot. Come on." She took her friend's arm and started gently, but firmly, pulling her away. "Sorry!" she called back over her shoulder.

I waved and triggered my roar again. Ravi had told me never to break character unless someone needed medical assistance.

"Why is there a gorilla in a haunted house anyway?" I heard Punchy McPuncherton complain as they walked away.

"Because they're scary?" her friend replied tartly. "I'm never going to a haunted house with you again. I hope we don't get in trouble."

Their voices faded as they turned the next corner, and I heard the next victims approaching. It sounded like a group of kids. I positioned myself at the edge of the alcove so I could stretch a long arm out into the middle of the group. Kids seemed to love that one.

Finally, Angela and Ian showed up. My heart rate jumped. I'd been having fun, almost forgetting my deadly serious purpose tonight.

I could tell they didn't know where I was, but I saw Ian grasp and pat Angela's hand in an uncharacteristic gesture that made her face set in expectation. Angela had told me that Ian would be able to sense Ravi's presence, being familiar with him from school, and therefore the location of the utility door he'd left open for them to escape through.

As they passed, I jumped out between them and the invisible bodyguard who trailed behind. It wasn't Brent, the chief of security, but some younger guy. He, of course, was visible to me.

Angela and Ian, as pre-arranged, ran from my roar, ducking around the corner. I spread my arms, trying to fill as much space as I could, without looking obvious. The guard tried to deke around me, and I moved to cut him off, doing my silly dance in the middle of the corridor.

I tried to act exactly like before, but this time I was sweating, breathing heavily, and my legs felt like gelatin.

After about ten frustrated seconds, he shoved roughly past me and ran down the corridor. I fought the urge to follow, returning to my alcove. Either they made it through the access door, or they didn't. Either their cloaking spells worked, or they didn't. I focused on getting my breathing back to normal.

I had to look natural while scaring the next few visitors. The guard was almost certainly going to take another pass through here, in one direction or the other, and it would look very suspicious if the gorilla was suddenly gone.

~*~

I gasped in relief as Ian helped me pull the gorilla mask off, and cool air rushed into the suit. Unfortunately for Ian, in an equal and opposite reaction, the moist air of the suit with the mingled pong of all its former wearers also rushed out.

He stumbled back, waving a hand in front of his face. "Ew, that's rank."

"You're not the one who had to stew in it for over an hour. I'm gonna need a shower," I complained as I wriggled out of the partially opened suit. I had shifted back to normal size, so it wasn't too much of a struggle.

Angela, who had wisely stayed on the other side of the room, walked over, carrying a light jacket I had left on the bench before donning the suit. She encouraged me to put it on with a hint of humour in her gaze. I looked at her questioningly, and her gaze directed my attention downward, toward my chest.

I immediately realized the problem. I hadn't bothered to wear a bra because I'd flattened my chest by shifting. On my switch back, I had forgotten that detail, and the results … made it clear I was not in boy shape today. Crap.

I shrugged the jacket on and smiled at her. "Thanks, Ange!"
"Any time."
Her warm smile back made me want to wrap my arms around her and bury my face in her neck. This past week had been so busy that I hadn't had much time to miss her, but all my longing crashed in at once.

Before I could act on my impulse, the door opened abruptly. We all tensed and turned, but it was Sarah with Ravi close behind her. I sidled behind Angela, wondering what my hair had decided to do. Everything was complicated enough without having to stop and explain my current state to Ravi. Note-to-self: In the future, I would need to focus during all my shifts, not just assume I would leap back to my previous form.

Sarah was wearing the same beat-up biker jacket, as well as similar jeans and T-shirt, from our last meeting. I missed her bright colours and audacious clothes, then realized why she had always seemed so over the top. She'd essentially been on vacation, wearing all the fun clothes she didn't get to wear while working.

Fortunately, Ravi remembered my instructions and stopped at the threshold. "Your mystery woman showed up!" He looked bemused, and … envious? I had a brief moment of double vision, seeing Sarah as the vulnerable/powerful/healing/vengeful friend I knew, superimposed with how I suspected Ravi saw her—a tall, sexy woman with a beautiful face and an undeniable aura of competence. She even made suave Ian look inexperienced.

"Thank you, Ravi," Sarah said. "Do you need anything in here before you go?"

He took the hint. "Nope. Ping me when you're done, Mike." He left and closed the door.

"Well, Ian," Sarah said, after a discreet pause, "Can we speak freely?"

Ian nodded. Angela nodded too, reflexively. They were both understandably wary, meeting Sarah, though I could see Angela was intrigued as well.

"We put some wards up," he said. "They'll keep anyone from knowing we're here, let alone remote sensing."

Sarah nodded, like this made perfect sense, and pulled a plastic cylinder with a few blinking lights out of her purse. She set it in the middle of the wobbly table and turned it on. It started a series of LED flashes and beeps that didn't follow any pattern I could discern, but appeared to make sense to Sarah.

"Turn your phones off and put them in the bag." She took a large RF-blocker bag out of her jacket pocket, shook it out, and passed it around. "You can have them back after. Their signals make it harder to detect other bugs." We shuffled devices out of our pockets and obeyed, though Ian sassed about it.

"Seems unlikely someone would know we were meeting here in time to plant a bug, don't you think?"

"You never know. I've tuned into random bugs sometimes, placed for who knows what reason. And it's easy to signal sweep for existing broadcast sources."

Ian nodded, looking impressed.

Eventually, she was satisfied, and we all gathered on folding chairs around the scarred and not-too-clean table. Ian took his state-of-the-art MacBook out of his bag and opened it up, putting it in airplane mode when Sarah's monitor beeped in aggravation. His miffed expression and sharp movements would have been pricelessly hilarious, had it not been for all the tension in the air.

"There's just one thing I need to check on before we get started," Sarah announced. She took two slips of yellow paper out of her jacket pocket and placed them on the table.

"Ian, Angela. Please, each take one of these spells, and place them, with the writing facing out, against the center of your chest."

"What do they do?" Ian asked. He squinted at the characters written in red and black inks, overlapping in some cases. "I'm not familiar with this style of writing."

"Telling you would spoil the test," Sarah said. "I guarantee you won't come to any harm."

Ian and Angela looked at each other, then at me. I gave Sarah a significant look.

"I trust Sarah will be honest with me, or she knows I'll have nothing to do with her or her entire organization ever again."

"And if you won't do it, I'm cutting my losses and leaving here. I have help to give, but only if you can prove you're not compromised." She nodded at the spells.

"Okay. I'll do it," Angela said, reaching for one of the papers, but Ian snatched his up first, his hand moving toward his chest.

"No," Sarah commanded. He stopped. Her tone wasn't one to be ignored lightly. "Both together."

His look was skeptical.

"It's important for the test, folks, or I wouldn't ask." Sarah sighed.

Ian and Angela glanced at each other, came to a silent agreement, and each picked up a spell paper. Together, they placed the spells against their chests.

Ian cleared his throat a couple of times. Angela coughed. Then, their eyes widened and they gasped for breath, their throats appearing to close up, judging by the gurgling noises that escaped.

I jumped up and moved toward Sarah, yelling, "What …"

"It will pass in a second," she said to them, while holding a hand out to stop me. After a couple more steps, I saw she was correct. Another second, their struggle eased, and they could breathe normally again.

"Okay, we've taken your little test," Ian spat out. "Want to let us know what that was for?"

Sarah nodded. She started to take her laptop, paper notes, and some other mysterious equipment out of her bag.

"It proves you've both been dosed with a magically enhanced serum that induces a fatal allergic reaction to a specific kind of spell."

"Why would you?" Ian wondered out loud, then gasped in recognition. "Oh! The sealing. I thought that spell structure looked familiar."

"Yes," Sarah said with gentle bluntness. "It's for everyone else's protection. If the Clan tries to force you through the sealing, you'll have a far stronger allergic reaction and die. They won't be able to mine details about us out of your minds."

Angela's face paled, and her mouth set in a grim line.

"The number of deaths during sealing has been higher lately," Ian mused with a bitter edge, his mouth twisted down at the corners. "Uncle said it must be a sign of the weakness of the younger generation."

"The scotch," I blurted out. I barely recognized my voice. It was low and hard, but definitely not a male tone. I trembled with anger and disgust. Mostly at myself.

"Yes," Sarah admitted sadly. "I used you to get to them." She looked around at the three of us. "I used all of your trust and innocence. I'm sorry for that, but we're fighting a war. We need to be sure there's no way for you to be lured back. And a way to limit the damage if you are."

"I get it," Angela said bluntly. "I hate it, but I get it."

"Do you all want a minute before we carry on?" Sarah asked.

"No," Ian replied quickly. "Our time here is limited, and none of this really changes anything. We need to take our very best shot at destroying the codex."

I tried to put aside the sick feeling in my stomach, and I avoided looking directly at Ian and especially Angela. It was easier to lose myself in the details. We spent a good fifteen minutes just hashing out the plan. It was mostly Ian who did the planning, but there were enough questions in areas that Ian hadn't entirely made clear that it became a group effort.

Sarah's first objection was to Angela's proposed radio communication between her position in the hotel and the number-crunching laptop.

"Anyone using radio, even focused beam, is going to be a sitting duck. I'll get you laser comms. There are mountainsides around that have a line of sight to that entire side of the hotel. We'll be practically undetectable while the link is in operation, which will dramatically increase our chances of survival."

"That's awesome!" Angela said. "I looked at those, but I wasn't sure I could order them without drawing the exact attention we can't have."

The first major snag hit when Ian talked about cracking the electronic code.

"Oh, that's not good," Sarah said.

Ian looked up sharply as she scrolled through code on his computer. "What isn't good?"

"Your mock code generator is based on the PX-873A official specs, but the last time we tried to crack one, it failed miserably. We believe that either the official spec is a lie, designed to trap the unwary, or that each clan makes custom modifications to the hardware and software to protect itself from rival attacks. Possibly both."

My heart sank as Ian's whole body drooped. "I was worried about that. I've seen a hint or two about a different spec, but I wasn't able to access anything about it. My first attempt bombed, badly, and I barely covered my tracks."

Angela reached out to his hand where it lay on the table and gave it a gentle squeeze. I could see their closeness for what it was now. They came from the same world, where warring wizard clans were a fact of life. They understood each other on a level I could never reach before. Maybe someday I would … or could, if any of us had that kind of future.

"Fortunately," Sarah said, "I may be able to help with that."

Ian's head popped up.

She pulled a small USB memory stick from her purse and gave it to him. "This is a dump of files I managed to retrieve from your network."

"You retrieved …" Ian's eyes opened wide, then narrowed. "You were the hacker at our party?"

"Yes. Though if it wasn't for Mike, I wouldn't have made it out." She favoured me with a warm glance. "Did you hear anything about what the hack accessed?"

"Uncle Zach did have a rant about it, I think. He said the terrorist … " Ian stopped and winced. "Sorry, Antifawz agent, might not have accessed anything, but he was still extremely unhappy with the security team who … uh, why are you laughing?"

"What did you call me? Antifuzz?" Sarah asked, trying to control her giggles.

"Antifawz. Like 'AWZ'. Antifa plus 'WZ'. Like, Anti-Fascist Wizards. That's what Mike called your group!" Ian looked at me in confusion.

"I'm sorry! I didn't know their name, so I just made something up!" I threw myself on Sarah's mercy.

"That's brill! I think I'll use that from now on, if and when I need a name." Her voice went serious again. "Sounds like they weren't sure what I got away with, which means they probably won't be motivated to radically change the security system around the codex." She motioned to the stick Ian was holding. "I think we might have a real shot with this."

Ian copied the data to his computer, and then he and Sarah hunkered down to dig through the files together. Apparently, the wizard clans' computer systems were set up with an old language that only they used, and a strange filing system based on magic theory that only insiders could make any sense of.

I watched for a little while, but there was nothing I could do to help, so I retreated to the bench and put my head in my hands. We had all stayed focused on the planning, but I could only imagine what Angela and Ian were thinking of me now after learning I had personally poisoned them.

~*~

"Are you okay?" Angela asked gently, sitting down beside me.

"That's what I should be asking you," I said, not lifting my head.

"I'm … not really okay," she admitted. "But I haven't been okay since I got caught in that ward at the wedding. The serum … it doesn't really change much. And I don't blame you."

That got me to sit up and look at her. She seemed sincere. She could also just be saying that because she'd rather not fight on what could be the last time we'd ever see each other.

Looking into her eyes, I decided that either way, I would be smart to accept her kindness. It was a beautifully human thing—being able to pretend together and make truth out of it.

I opened my arms for a hug, and she nestled into me. We held each other in comfort, just vibing, with Ian and Sarah's voices talking in esoteric words that might as well have been a different language. Some of it, I'm pretty sure, was.

After a while, Angela spoke softly. "You didn't mention how beautiful she is."

"Who? Oh, Sarah?" I whispered back.

"Yeah."

"It didn't seem relevant," I said honestly.

Angela snort-laughed, directed at me or herself, I had no idea. Maybe both.

"Hey, you two," Ian called. "No time for necking. Get back over here."

We broke our embrace and hurried over.

"You got something?" I asked. From his excited tone, I guessed it must be something big.

"Something!" he crowed. "We got all of it. Every design and construction spec for the entire room, not just the safe. There's shit in here I never would have known about. Both physical and magical. See, there's even a ward to specifically detect the spell we would have used to pass information related to cracking the electronic lock codes." He sobered up. "I think a lot of what I uncovered before must have been planted. It was enough to make anyone thinking about going for the codex overconfident. And I ... we, would have walked right into it." He looked at Angela, his face turning greyish-green as the ramifications hit.

"That's not entirely true," Sarah spoke up. "You copied the physical key and identified most of the wards. You even deduced the most probable location of the codex safe. Which you got almost right. Don't lose faith now! I think ..." She glanced around at all of us, but paused a little longer on me. "I think this is actually possible."

CHAPTER 27

Two weeks and three days later, in the early afternoon, Sarah messaged me on Discord to say she was picking me up at 'half-eight' tomorrow morning at the coffee shop, by which she meant 8:30. The only other info provided was to 'wear something casual and pretty' which struck me as strong subtext to come looking like Kayla.

But I was pretty solidly in male shape.

Even a month ago, this would have sent me into a full-on panic, but I'd spent a lot of time refining my shapeshifting skills. One of the main goals had been to replicate, as much as possible, my 'Kayla' body when I was feeling male.

Getting all the small changes just right was a pain, but possible. For the parts I couldn't change completely, not voluntarily anyway, a pair of my tightest bike shorts and some stuffing in my bra completed the picture. It was a strange and uncomfortable feeling to look at myself in girl-mode, in my clinging sun dress, when I was actually feeling male.

It wasn't the nervous feeling of possible discovery that I'd had those first few days of going out in women's clothes, but a creeping feeling of wrongness about my body that wasn't new to me, but wasn't something I normally felt unless I was minutes from switching sex.

I quickly looked away and thrust the visual out of my head before I accidentally switched myself back to default male form and wasted all my work creating this shape.

~*~

It felt good to be on the move again the next morning, especially driving Sarah's latest car, a Nissan 370Z convertible with the top down, even if I did have to stick close to the speed limit. Anxiety and excitement coursed through my body. By tonight, it would all be over, one way or another.

I went with what I thought was a bright clothing choice—a cream coloured sundress covered in bright yellow sunflowers. However, Sarah's outfit made mine look basic. Her dress was all wide stripes of blue, orange, white, and gold. Horizontal on the top, accentuating her breasts, and vertical on the skirt. She had redone her braids at some point, this time in a swirling asymmetrical style that looked gorgeous.

With my body and hormones in a male state today, she was a little distracting, which made me uncomfortable in several ways. I hadn't forgiven her for fooling me into slipping Ian and Angela that deadly drug, even if my friends had forgiven me.

She seemed way more relaxed than she had at the planning meeting. She talked about how excited she was to see Banff and seemed enthralled by the steady approach of the mountain peaks filling the horizon, as if this was just a tourist trip and not potentially the last day of our lives.

I tried to match her mellow, but all it did was aggravate me. Even though my part in the plan was going to be easy, I ran through it again in my head, like I'd been doing compulsively for the past three weeks.

1) Ian and Angela go to the sealing ceremony, acting eager to join the Clan. And not at all like they will die in the process.

2) Sarah and I play tourist for most of the day, staying visible in public and hopefully confusing and occupying the wizard's guards since we're now known to them. Then, we disguise ourselves and split up, hopefully ducking any watchers.

3) Sarah gets into position on a hillside near Banff where she can see the hotel rooftop with one of the laser links. I head to the hotel, to a room booked by one of our ghosts, with the other laser link and a set of handy tools.

4) Angela sneaks out of the party onto the hotel roof (eight stories up, *ack!*) while Ian provides a distraction. She lets a rope down where I can grab it. Where she gets the rope, I don't know. She and Ian kept some details secret even from us. I tie the bag of tools onto the rope so she can pull it up. Then I wait.

5) Angela sets up the laser link on the roof and uses it as a hotspot to connect to Sarah's computer while Angela breaks into the Clan's safe to destroy the codex. Succeed or fail, if she survives, she climbs down the rope to me and we escape, leaving Ian on his own. With the codex broken, he should be able to escape in the confusion. If not …

"The closer we get, the more I see all the terrible risks in this plan," I said, cringing at how whiny my voice sounded even to my own ears.

Sarah took half a minute to reply. Annoyance tinged her voice. "I don't like the level of risk either, but remember, it's you who convinced me to get involved. You said you'd try it anyway, even if I didn't help."

"True. Sorry. None of that was directed at you. Is it weird that I feel guilty that I'm not taking more risks? It's mostly on Ian and Angela."

"I wouldn't underestimate the level of risk we're both in." She shot me a quick smile. "The wizard's guards may well try to kill or capture us before we can get in position to help Angela. Thankfully, they normally shy away from direct action in the public eye, and I'm hoping they won't want to risk tipping off Ian by taking us out too early. After that, things will kick off and it'll be too late for them."

I suddenly lost the feeling of freedom provided by the open road. The sick feeling that had been budding in the pit of my stomach all day burst, drenching me in nausea. I searched frantically for somewhere to pull over. Luckily, we were just about to pass a small parking area. I yanked the car over and hit the brakes hard. The car skidded as we hit a gravel patch, but the automatic braking system kicked in, and I maneuvered us safely to a shuddering stop in an open parking spot.

"Well, that was unexpected," Sarah said flatly, with a white-knuckled grip on the door handle, while I groped for the belt and door latches and hauled myself out of the car. My stomach tightened, and a drop of sweat rolled into my eye.

A couple of parents gave me dirty looks as they held their kids closer, suddenly reminded that there were vehicles moving at over a hundred kph just a few feet away. They looked extra shocked and disapproving when I proceeded to noisily throw up all over the grass.

Cool wind from the lake mingled with the smell of vomit, hot metal, and tar as I gasped for breath. Sarah appeared beside me with my drink from the car and a handful of paper napkins. I took them gratefully, wiped my mouth, and swished a mouthful of pop around before spitting it out. After a few repetitions, the vomit taste mostly subsided. Score one for acidic sugar-water.

Taking a walk down to the water's edge helped calm my stomach. Grass lightly tickled my toes and the sides of my feet in their sandals, loosening the remaining tightness in my chest.

Sarah walked with me, silently. The industrial-gothic bulk of the cement plant across the lake signalled we were close to Canmore, and the Banff Park gates were shortly after that.

With everything Sarah had just said, crossing into the park felt like a final, irrevocable step into danger. And not just danger. Responsibility. Was I ready? What if I screwed up and people, people I loved, died because of me?

"What you're feeling is perfectly natural, Kayla," Sarah said conversationally as we strolled along the water's edge. "Pre-mission nerves. Most of us get it."

"I guess it goes away after a while?" I half-stated, half-asked with a shudder. "You've been so upbeat, like we're just tourists."

"One hundred percent intentional," she replied, deadpan. "I'm keeping my mind off it so I don't work my nerves into a state where I'm the one throwing up at the side of the road." She smiled to take any sting out of her words. "It's a skill you learn after the first few times."

"Cool, cool. Nice to know." I smiled back, weakly, I'm sure. "Can we talk a little about what you said, about being attacked? What's the plan?"

"My best guess is they'll set up an ambush at our car, assuming we'll come back to it, which is why everything we'll need is either in our purses or the getaway car."

Another ghost drop-off. Sarah had arranged yet another car for us and made sure I knew where it was parked. It had Sarah's pack with the laptop and laser comms equipment she needed to support Angela's safe cracking.

"I expect they'll be curious enough about what we're doing here that they'll follow us around. Slipping their surveillance will be critical. Which is where we're betting on your shifting, and my experience, to see us through."

"And if either of us gets caught …" I said grimly.

"There's no rescue coming. We're dead," she confirmed bluntly. "Or wishing we were," she added quietly. Then, in a stronger, harder voice. "If either of us gets clocked, scarper!. Don't try to help. Don't stop. Don't look back. Angela should be able to escape, and it's of prime importance that you don't let them get their hands on you. I don't think they can compel a shifter in the same way they do their own mages, but I can't be sure. And I haven't dosed you with a fail-safe like your friends," she said pointedly. "Believe me, in many ways, that quick end is a blessing."

I recalled she had been caught before and only barely survived. Her bravery was off the charts, putting herself in this kind of situation again and again.

I still didn't like what she'd done, but I couldn't fault her personal commitment to her cause. She was only putting herself at risk here because she wanted my shifting power for antifawz. The least I could do was pretend to have a little courage myself.

"So, I pretend I'm here for the shopping, and maybe some ice cream, without a care in the world. Just two friends having a day out."

"Right," she said cheerfully. "It's a double psych. Walking around in the open makes it look like we're a decoy. They start having to look hard for the hidden threat, but even then, we're diverting attention and resources from keeping track of what the other two are up to."

"Okay, I can see that. Thanks!" Some of my panic ebbed away.

"You okay now? Think you can get into the mood for our distraction?"

"I'll do my best." Projecting happy-go-lucky girl in shopping mode while fully freaking the fuck out felt like it might be a tougher feat than sprouting wings, but hey, I'd made it through a bra fitting mostly unscathed. Maybe I shouldn't underestimate myself.

Sarah adored the mountains. And the Bow River. And, I kid you not, a squirrel she was sure she saw at the side of the road, but had vanished by the time we stopped to take its picture. I was glad we didn't see any bears. She'd probably insist we stop and take selfies!

She was also overly concerned about whether we were in the foothills or the mountains. I didn't even know where to start. I had always thought about the mountains in terms of human references: towns, park boundaries, that kind of thing. I was afraid I was a disappointing tour guide.

Sarah was practically bouncing by the time we hit the Banff exit and waited at the edge of her seat as we wound our way through the outskirts toward downtown. She was all tourist as we drove into town, rubbernecking and exclaiming at the cutesy animal-based street names—Fox, Moose, Wolf, etc.

"Carry-bough? What's a carry-bough?" she asked as we passed Caribou Street.

"It's pronounced 'Kari-boo.' They're essentially wild reindeer, but we use a First Nations name for them."

"Huh," she said thoughtfully. "Which nation?"

"I … ah, literally have no idea. Sorry."

She spent a minute on her phone. "Apparently, it comes from a Mi'kmaq word, picked up by French colonists, and then transferred to English."

"Thanks!" It was disconcerting how much of the world I 'knew' was built from layer upon layer of history that was mostly shoved into the corners, out of sight. Even something as simple as a common name. And that didn't account for the things that were actively hidden from view by powerful interests like the wizard clans.

I had already unlearned a lot of oversimplified or outright fake history in my life. How much more was there to unlearn and relearn?

I parked the car a few blocks off the main shopping street, and we quickly blended into the crowds.

We didn't have to work to stay in well-populated areas. It was the middle of the summer high season, so the streets and stores were already stuffed with visitors of every age and nationality. There were lots of kids running around and dogs outside stores taking advantage of the complimentary water bowls.

Banff's chocolate shop and ice cream store used to be the only draws for me, but being Kayla made the whole experience new and exciting. We ricocheted between corny tourist traps and high-end jewellery stores.

Sarah was all over the bear-, moose-, and beaver-themed stuff, trying on all the funny hats and mitts. I, with some real money in my purse for the first time, and comfortable in all my genders for the first time, salivated over the cool rocks and jewellery that I'd never let myself look at before.

We met in the middle when it came to cute clothing. I found a rack of fuzzy animal-themed pyjamas in the back of one store and snagged a green-and-purple dinosaur design. A ridged tail fell down the back, and it was topped with a dinosaur head hood.

"Awww, brilliant!" Sarah riffled through the rack and chose a white one with black spots, sporting a hood with cow nose and ears. There was even a zippered udder pouch.

"Like the one she wore in that K-drama we started!" I said.

"Yeah. It was so cute." She grinned and held the pyjamas up to herself to see in the mirror.

We returned to the high-end jewellery section. The prices I could see were shocking, and half of them weren't even marked. It was fun to try them on, but I guess Sarah could see I was uncomfortable. In a private moment while the sales staff were helping another customer, she asked, "Not something you're used to doing?"

"Hmm …" I considered the small mermaid pendant I was holding. It was intricately crafted in gold, with tiny rubies for the hair, emeralds for the tail, and diamonds for the seashells. "I think it's more that I can't see myself ever wearing something so small and delicate that's worth a full year's university tuition."

"Ah, makes sense." She nodded. "You're sensible. Me, I've always had expensive taste." She took it from me and handed it over to the woman behind the counter. "Please ring this up. And, ah, that chain along with it." The saleswoman whisked away before I could object.

"Sarah!" I said quietly but firmly. "I can't spend that much money!"

"Don't fret about it." She waved away my objections. "It's on me."

"I can't let you spend that much either," I hissed. We'd worked out that I should keep the ten grand she'd given me before Ian's birthday party thing until after this operation, which made sense, but I was still feeling guilty about that.

"Think about it this way." She spoke close to my ear. "In a few hours, we'll either be dead, or you'll deserve every bit of that and more."

I walked out of the shop with the mermaid on, and with very mixed feelings.

Back on the busy sidewalk, I saw the COWS Ice Cream shop ahead and convinced Sarah we should stop. We found a table outside—the inside was far too packed for Sarah—and I went to collect our ice creams. Soon, we were chilling in several senses of the word, watching the mass of people flow by. Sarah was quiet, letting her half-finished ice cream melt as she listlessly watched the crowds.

"Should we try to find a quieter place?" I asked, worried about her.

"No. It's all right." She shook her head. "We should stay in public view."

She remained half-absent for a minute, then her attention returned to me. "I'm not overwhelmed." She offered a reassuring smile that quickly crumpled. "It's all these couples, holding hands, hugging. I miss it so much."

Her cry from the heart echoed the pain in my own chest. The crowd was packed with couples. I hadn't consciously noticed until she mentioned it. They ranged from teens on awkward first dates to silver-haired life mates lovingly helping each other, and everything in between.

"Is that why you like the romance dramas?" I asked gently, hoping it wasn't a rude question.

"Maybe a little!" She laughed freely. "But mostly I think it's because so many K-dramas are really about healing, or accepting that it's okay to be a little broken." Her grim look had returned and she gazed into the middle distance. "I dragged myself back from the very edge and I'm putting myself back together, but I'm not sure I'll ever be the person I was before."

She refocused on me and continued, "I should be honest with you. That night at the bar, when I sent you to drug Ian … once I saw it was Brent on security, I lost all sight of the plan. And of you, and of Angela. All I cared about was killing him, or dying so I wouldn't have to live with the fear anymore."

"But you stopped when I got in the way." I recalled the look of frustrated rage on her face when I blocked her first strike at the goon's neck. "Don't tell me you couldn't have gone through me, if you really wanted to."

"I nearly did," she said ruefully. "But I would have hurt you, and for a second, I couldn't do it. Then we were out of time."

"I'm sorry. I didn't have any right to get in your way. It was clear he wanted you dead." I felt ashamed now of putting us both at risk like a newbie.

"You don't need to apologize." She shook her head. "You're practically a kid. I never intended to get you involved in that part, and I'm sorry I was so abrupt with you after. I should have handled that better."

"Like you said, you're still putting yourself back together. I think you're allowed some moments." I let the 'kid' comment go. She was right, I was still seventeen, and she wasn't being unkind about it, but it bugged me in a way I'd never felt before.

I could remember feeling like a kid, but I'd lost that feeling sometime in the past few weeks. When did that happen? Thinking back, it started that night in the woods when I decided to hit the guard attacking Sarah. In a split second, I'd taken responsibility for two human lives. Saved one and doomed the other. That, it hit me in a sudden revelation, was why I hadn't felt like I fit in my parents' house when I came back. They were still my family; I just wasn't their child anymore.

Huh. It was a strange feeling.

We sat in companionable peace for a while, focused on finishing our ice cream before it completely melted.

Once we were both ready to brave the crowd again, we consolidated our purchases into two bags for easy carrying … or dropping, if it came to that. Sarah checked her phone again, then showed me the screen. Ian had posted a *Star Trek* meme on Facebook.

We gave each other a relieved glance. *Star Trek* memes meant they were still on target. *Good Omens* memes would signal a problem, and *Friends* memes would signal an immediate abort and scatter.

This was likely the last we'd hear from them, good or bad. As of this evening, they would be completely out of contact until Angela made it to the roof and set up the laser tightbeam link. The wizards' hangout was apparently cut off from all electronic communication.

"It's only a quarter past four. Let's keep them guessing a little longer, then grab some supper," Sarah announced. "I could use somewhere a little less crowded, though, but still visible."

"The river?" I suggested. "There's an old bridge there. Highly visible, but less busy."

"Sounds good."

We continued walking down Bear Street, moving with dozens of other shoppers and tourists. Another three hours, and we'd be in the middle of the operation. My stomach twinged.

"There are some very good restaurants here," Sarah said. "I'm excited to try one. What do you feel like? Western food? Korean? Japanese?"

"I'm not sure it matters, I …"

The roar of an engine interrupted my thoughts. A middle-aged guy ahead of us stopped abruptly to check his shopping bag while his daughter walked on. An unmarked black van hopped the curb and hit him with a meaty thump, throwing him into a storefront hard enough to star the glass and leave a smear of red as he slumped down. Another van squealed to a stop behind us.

Screams erupted from all around. The van's sliding doors rattled open, and guys in SWAT gear were suddenly everywhere. We bolted, Sarah toward the street, while I tried for the nearest store.

Seconds stretched out like a nightmare. My legs felt like wet noodles as terror sapped my strength. Then, just as I got my hand on the door handle, a hard snap sounded behind me and I was pummelled to the ground by what felt like a thousand frenetic hammers beating every muscle.

The after-shocks were still making my flesh Jello when two guys picked me up and threw me into a van, where I lay limply, barely holding on to consciousness. There was a jab in the side of my neck, and a low buzzing filled my veins, rising to a crescendo that wiped away the world.

CHAPTER 28

I woke up in a dark, cramped, uncomfortably jolting box lined with some kind of scratchy upholstery. My wrists were painfully bound behind my back, and a warm body lay on top of me. They'd shoved us in the trunk of a car, I realized with dread.

I fought to control my breathing as panic loomed. My hands were numb from the cruelly tight bonds. I could barely move, and even if I could, I was stuck in a too-small space. Sweat slicked my body. I struggled to slide out from under the weight on top of me. I needed to get anywhere but here …

The body on me shifted and groaned. I had a moment of relief coupled with grief at recognizing Sarah's voice. She was alive, but she hadn't escaped. Then her knee hit my groin, and pain blossomed.

For a long moment, I could think about nothing else, but when it subsided, most of my panic was also gone, and I was thinking more clearly. Why was I so panicked about a small space when I could be smaller?

Easier thought than done, though. My head was fuzzy, and I felt disconnected from my body. It was hard to stay focused on that seed of chaos inside me. It kept slipping away with each jolt from the road.

No one official would transport prisoners like this. Everything I remembered about kidnapping suggested we would be dead within the next hour if we didn't find a way to get out of the trunk. Being switched to a secondary location was bad. Very bad.

Maybe I could kick out a taillight? Did that even work on modern cars? Cars were also supposed to have some kind of glow-in-the-dark trunk release handle, but I couldn't see anything like that, and didn't have a hand free to pull on it even if I did. I fought down claustrophobia again. Everything circled back to getting my hands free. The car slowed, turned, and jostled us from side to side as it traversed potholes. I heard the distinctive sound of a gravel road.

Remote rural secondary locations were the worst kind.

I forced myself to lie still and clear all distractions from my mind. It was the most difficult thing I'd ever done.

As I'd figured out from my practice sessions, switching shape was more about how I felt about myself than a pure visualization. Thinking about being smaller seemed simple, but fell apart if I started trying to keep track of all the minute details that needed to be true to scale down a living human form. I could not TRY to change form, I could only DO it.

It took forever, but finally, the only thing left in my mind was my guiding image. I'd buffed up dim memories from childhood when everything was big and small spaces were a comfy refuge. Curling up in a cardboard box just for play.

And it happened! The bonds lost their harsh grip on my wrists. The trunk seemed to expand around me, and it was easy to slip out from under Sarah.

I'd made these kinds of changes before, but only when sitting calmly in my own bedroom. I felt a moment's pure elation at my newfound skill. The situation was grim, for sure, but these fuckers had no idea who they were dealing with!

My hands slipped fairly easily from the restraints, though the sharp edges of what turned out to be plastic zip ties scraped up my skin. Once my hands were free, I was able to properly search the trunk.

The first thing I looked for was a trunk release. My hands tingled fiercely as I searched. Some of their numbness had dissipated with my switch, and strength was slowly returning. My mind felt clearer, too, like I'd shed some of the drug's influence, which didn't surprise me.

I contorted myself to get eyes on every corner of the lightless trunk. My sundress bunched up around my chest, so I slipped out of it to free up my arms. I finally found the trunk release handle … on the floor. The cut end of the wire that should have connected it to the trunk latch was dangling. Fuck.

The car slowed further and wildly jostled back and forth, slamming my head into the trunk lid. Sarah groaned and muttered, but wasn't quite conscious yet. Where the hell were they driving? Starting from Banff, we could be way out in the bush in any direction. I belatedly realized that opening the trunk now would only warn them, with nowhere to run, and no one around to help.

I switched tactics and searched for anything that I could use to free Sarah. I needed something sharp to cut the plastic. There wasn't much. The trunk was empty except for us and a window scraper, ubiquitous in Canadian vehicles. It wasn't sharp enough on its own, but maybe …

I wedged the end of the scraper into the trunk hinge and tried to pull myself up using the long handle. I tried a couple of times without success, but on the third we hit another big bump, and I heard a snap. For a second, I wasn't sure if it was my wrist or the scraper, but in feeling around, I poked myself painfully, confirming the plastic had broken into a nice sharp edge. I found the other piece, slicing myself again in the process.

Sarah was more conscious now and able to twist herself around so I could saw at the plastic cuffs. I tried to keep to the section between her wrists but nicked her a few times. Other than jerking reflexively, she didn't complain. It seemed to take forever. My arms were rubbery and my vision was hazy by the time the strap finally snapped. It was unclear which one of us was doing more whimpering.

As I helped Sarah reposition her arms and rub some feeling back into her hands, the car slowed and drove over the roughest surface yet. Plants and bushes whacked against the sides and undercarriage.

My heart pounded. Whatever was going to happen would happen quickly.

I tried to keep my mind blank, focused on survival, but rogue thoughts battered their way in. Was this it? The end of all my hopes and struggles? It seemed a cruel joke to die just when I finally understood my true nature. And I had dragged Sarah into this, a situation all her experience told her to stay away from. Now she would pay for my mistake, and Angela and Ian were truly on their own.

My breathing grew faster and more irregular as I tried to control it. I couldn't slow it down. I was amped up for fight-or-flight, but couldn't do either. I had to lie there, sweating, with my heart pounding harder and harder, waiting for it to give out.

A hand brushed my arm, then chill fingers firmly gripped my heated skin.

"Kayla. It's okay," Sarah said, her voice weak and slurred from the drugs. "This is death ground. There's no past. No future. There is only now. Only the fight. Do you understand?"

"I'm trying. I think. But you. Ange. Ian. I failed." Tears leaked down my temples.

"You tried. You're still trying." She put as much force into those words as she could, then subsided to a harsh whisper. "There's no shame in failure, Kayla. Not against this. We fight to keep our humanity, not because we expect to win, and I'm honoured to fight beside you."

Her distraction helped slow my breathing. My heart followed. I was able to shrug off some of the horrible, trapped feeling. She was right. My whole focus had to be on the next few seconds after the trunk opened. Nothing before or after mattered.

I lay as still as I could in the trunk while the car came to a bumpy stop. I was half on top of Sarah now, clutching my make-shift weapon against my side. The engine died, and the car rocked as the driver got out. The door slammed. In the silence that followed, I heard the rustle of leaves and grass as our captor approached.

The trunk popped open. Bright light flooded in, and my eyes instantly teared up. Sarah moaned. I flinched, expecting the guy to be standing over us, but he'd used the key fob button. I waited with my eyes half-lidded until his shadow occluded the light.

I jammed the splintered end of the ice scraper hard toward his throat.

Warm blood spattered over my chest, neck, and face. Some got in my mouth and I spat, trying to clear the revolting metallic taste. My vision dimmed as a hand closed around my throat like steel, and his other hand crushed my wrist. The improvised spear dropped from my numb fingers.

"Who the fuck are you?" he demanded.

My eyes were still too dazzled to see him as anything but a dark mass above me, but I knew that voice. It was him, Brent. Goon Number One from the lake. Sarah's torturer. The guy I'd tased. Man, I really wanted my taser, which was probably still in my purse somewhere far, far away.

I reached up with my free hand for something, anything. Blood pounded as it gathered in my head. Purple and black spots clouded my vision. I felt something cool, hard, metallic. The grip of a handgun in a shoulder holster.

To pull it out, I would need a distraction. A big one. But I could barely concentrate. An image popped into my head, the most bizarre form I could think of: the unfortunate 'tree man' who grew all those bark-like protrusions on his hands. I envisioned that all over my neck and arms. The spikier the better. I dug deep down and BELIEVED it.

I felt the shift.

I grasped the gun.

His panicked yell coincided with a sharp pull, launching me out of the trunk. I felt a rush of weightless flight, then excruciating pain ripped through my arm where he'd been squishing it.

The sort-of grip I'd had on the gun wasn't enough, and it was yanked from my hand.

Well-honed instincts took over, and I pulled my arms and legs toward my core. I felt light, but contact with the uneven, rocky ground was still bruising. My shoulder and hip felt like they were on fire, but I didn't feel the sickening weakness of a break or dislocation as I rolled to my feet.

We stood in the middle of a dry riverbed surrounded by coniferous forest. The spiky growths all over my body had cushioned my landing on the jumbled rocks, but they also severely limited my agility.

"Shifter." He growled the word deep in his throat, drawing a knife with a heavy, angular blade from his belt. "That explains a lot. Well, you're mine now. Your corpse might just get me out of this shit town." Blood streamed down his face from a deep gash in one cheek, making his furious snarl demonic. His dark suit and bright white shirt were liberally streaked with red.

For an instant, I was torn between fight and flight, but I saw Sarah still huddled in the trunk. I couldn't leave her. I also couldn't fight like this. Backing away across the treacherous footing of the riverbed gave me the seconds I needed to gather my thoughts and … push my body into the mould I needed.

The transition started easier than expected, in a way I hadn't felt the last time I scaled up to a larger form for the gorilla suit. But there was a disconcerting hiccup in the middle, a kind of blank space where the world ceased to exist, or I did, or something.

I felt this change in a way I'd never felt any other change. It was like a final puzzle piece clicking into place. Like the tiny little bump when a combination lock reaches the final number. There was a unique feel to this body shape that I couldn't ever confuse with any other human being.

Then, I was back—an exact copy of the guy advancing toward me, except naked. My underwear had fallen off during the switch. That was new.

His eyes widened, then narrowed in rage. He advanced, knife low, ready for a killing thrust.

I backed away at the same pace, feet skilled at finding purchase blindly on the jumbled rocks from years of parkour. I had to keep his attention on me long enough for Sarah to recover. If we both ran, one of us might get away. My new form kept him cautious. He didn't know my fighting skills were nil.

He also didn't know what else I might turn into. It occurred to me that I might have imagined myself some claws, but even that brief thought was a near-fatal distraction. A rock turned under my foot, and in the space of that slight stumble, he launched himself at me.

I threw myself into a roll again, but it tanked. I overestimated the agility of this form and fell to the ground awkwardly, only paces from the goon. He kicked me hard enough in the side to flip me over and ground his foot into my stomach until I dry-heaved.

"Enjoy the feel of my steel you fucking pervert." Bloody spittle sprayed from his lips and dripped from his chin. He held the knife in an easy underhand grip. It was enough to tell me how the killing strike would come. Under the edge of the ribcage, up through the diaphragm. Even if it missed the heart, it would still be a paralyzing blow.

He would have to come down on one knee. Years of studying movement warned me a split-second before he shifted his weight off the foot pinning me down. Years of picking myself up after falls made my body obey even while every inch ached and the world spun in my vision.

I didn't try to attack or block the descending knife. I simply rolled bruisingly across the rocks, knocking his foot aside with my hip. I heard him grunt sharply as he came down hard on a knee, but he was still poised, holding the knife. I only had a few seconds left to live.

He jerked sideways as a sharp crack echoed through the forest. The knife dropped from his limp fingers, and red blossomed through his dress shirt.

I glanced at the car. Sarah stood, leaning against the bumper. Her face was a mask of pure terror, but her two-handed grip on the gun was implacable. It bucked in her hand, and a loud crack sounded again.

Brent took another bullet to the chest. Turning toward her, he was already reaching for a holdout gun holstered at the small of his back. I lurched onto my hands and knees. I seemed to be moving in slow motion while he was inhumanly quick.

Blood spread across his shirt, front and back. He dropped to both knees, gun out. His arm swung toward Sarah.

I picked up his dropped knife and lunged, swinging its bright edge down on his wrist with all my current form's strength. Blood erupted, and the gun dropped from his suddenly nerveless fingers as the knife chopped halfway into his wrist. I heard double cracks as Sarah fired again.

He toppled, landing beside me. I rolled away, then righted myself enough to check Sarah. She'd lowered the gun slightly. I jumped up and over his body, kicked his gun away, and followed it, getting out of her line of fire.

He was still moving weakly. Squirming, really. His fast, shallow breaths were wet and bubbly. Sarah was breathing fast and shallow, too, with far too much of the whites of her eyes showing. I cautiously approached her, swinging wide. As I came closer, I understood part of her whispering.

"He's down. He's down."

I stood at her shoulder, and over the next few minutes, we watched him choke to death on his own blood. I tried to feel nothing for him. I tried to distract myself with my physical pains, but my scratches and bruises weren't enough. It was hard to watch another human being die and not help, or even just hold his hand as he went.

At least I'd been spared this with that first guard in the woods. A mix of deep sadness and grim satisfaction filled me. That it was him who was bleeding out on the rocks and not me. It wasn't nice, but feeling nothing at all would be more worrying.

About two minutes after his last gasp and the definitive stillness of death, Sarah made an odd hiccupping sound and drooped.

I sat on the bumper beside her and rubbed her shoulder. She leaned over and wrapped her arms tightly around me, sobbing uncontrollably. That twinged several deep bruises, but I held her and rocked for a long while as the indifferent forest drank up the sound and blood, leaving only the gentle rustle of wind in the pines.

CHAPTER 29

As I held Sarah, I slowly came to the realization that I was still in the goon's form and wondered if I should try shifting back to my normal form. Sarah's sobs were trailing off, and she pulled away, wiping her eyes and nose on the back of her hand.

"Sorry. I don't have any tissues," I rumbled, my voice harsh and burning in my throat. I didn't remember yelling during the fight. It was blurry, except, unfortunately, for the feeling of sticking a knife into the flesh of another human being.

Sarah gave a strangled chuckle. "Piss poor planning, really." Her voice caught at the end in a partial sob, but she pulled herself to her feet and appeared to calmly survey the scene. "What a bloody mess."

I wanted to laugh at the pun, but I was so drained of emotion that I could only nod. "Thanks for the rescue." I gestured toward the sleek 9mm handgun she was still pointing carefully at Brent's body, as she had, even in the middle of her nearly hysterical sobbing.

"That was quick thinking, grabbing one of his weapons." She said, staring at the gun, then in a very small voice, admitted, "If it wasn't for you, I'm not sure I could have lifted a gun again. If it were only me … I don't know." She took a deep, shuddering breath and continued, "Somehow, he found out about my involvement in the leak just as we were wrapping up the prison op. He came for me, and I had to shoot him." She sighed. "My first time in real action, and I botched it. Shot him just enough to really piss him off, but not enough to stop him. My scars are only the beginning of what he had planned."

She stood there, trembling, taking, or attempting to take, deep even breaths. I wished I could do something, but I knew touching her was a bad idea, and the noise and movement of even trying to look for a blanket or coat would probably be bad.

Shortly, the storm passed. She collected herself and said in a steadier voice, "What we need is some accelerant. I wonder …" She peered in the car windows. "Ah, brilliant." She opened the door and pulled out a large red gas can, dropping it beside the car. Next, she brought out a black canvas duffel bag and began searching through it. "Hmm. Interrogation drugs and spells. A change of clothes." She continued digging. "Ah! Here we go—plastic bags, bleach, gloves. Everything we need."

She seemed to be avoiding saying his name, and I was fine to go along with that. It was easier not to think of him as a person, especially with his blank eyes staring up and his bodily fluids leaking everywhere.

I carefully stood. There were some nasty scrapes and livid bruises sprouting all over, but I didn't have any serious injuries. My shifts had completely cleared the fuzzy-headed, heavy-limbed feeling of the drugs from my system.

"You want to burn the body?" I felt weird about that. I looked in the back seat and noted with relief that our shopping bags and purses had been dumped haphazardly in there, too. Hard to say if they'd been emptied yet or not. I didn't want to touch anything until I wiped the blood off myself, but I yearned to jump into the car and speed away, pretending that none of this had happened.

"And the area around it," she said absently, still searching through the bag. "It's the best way to get rid of all the evidence scattered about."

"Shouldn't we let the police take a look?" I heard myself asking, but realized how stupid that was the minute I said it. "Right, sorry. I'm still not used to this." My mind skittered on side trails, wondering if they'd planned to ditch our stuff with the car, or burn it all with our bodies, or take it apart looking for clues about Sarah's anti-wizard operation.

"You know, we're lucky in a way," Sarah said, looking around the scene. "Standard procedure is to have two agents for an interrogation and disposal op like this, to counter any chance of the kind of wild move we just pulled. And it's not a job the head of security would normally take on." She shook her head. "I'm guessing the bastard specifically took this one for himself so he could finish what he started last year."

She slipped on a pair of latex gloves from his kit, thoroughly wiped the gun with a sterile wipe, and then held it out to me.

"I don't know how you did it, but you look exactly like him now. You should probably take his gear. For now, you can just put that in the bag with the rest of his stuff. Safety's on."

I took it, and shivered at the cold weight in my hand.

She looked at me, expectantly for a moment, then sighed with a slight smile.

"Please never take anyone's word about the safety of a weapon you're handed. On or off. She showed me the switch and had me toggle it on and back to off again before I put it in the bag.

"Sorry, I've never even held a handgun before. Ange wanted me to take a gun course with her, but, cost, you know."

Sarah nodded. "No worries. Just making sure you learn it right the first time." She walked closer to the body. "We've got to get his clothes off."

"Wha … Why?" I tried but couldn't look directly at the mess we had made of a human body. The thought of touching it turned my stomach.

"Fabrics can protect the flesh so it doesn't burn properly," she said, like it should have been obvious.

"Sorry. Following your lead. Just let me know what I need to do." Her explanations weren't improving my emotional state.

Sarah handed me a clear plastic garbage bag and a pair of latex gloves like the ones she was wearing. "Look around and see if you can find any shell casings in or around the trunk and car."

I picked my way over the rocks and hunted down a couple of bright copper casings. I also found blood-tinged remnants of the snow scraper and the plastic ties that had bound our wrists, and shoved them all in the garbage bag.

While I was busy, Sarah checked his other gun, put the safety on, and handed it to me to wipe down and put in the back. I doubled-checked the safety this time.

She stripped everything from his pockets and placed all of it in another plastic bag that she handed to me. "Put these in the duffel and bring a fresh garbage bag. We'll go through them on the way back." It held a wallet, phone, an electronic key card on a lanyard, a few loose coins, scraps of paper, and, importantly, the car keys.

I wondered what had happened to Sarah's car, and whether our get-away vehicle and its cache of equipment would still be there, but I didn't want to bring it up until we had some time to breathe.

By the time I got back, Sarah was slicing up one of his pant legs with his knife. It cut through the material like tissue paper. No wonder it had just about severed his wrist. "Get his shoes, will you?" she asked as she started on the other leg.

I shuddered, but was too ashamed not to do my bit. At least I could take the shoes off without touching him. Sarah sliced open his shirt and laid the fabric aside. When she was done, she wiped her hands and the knife on a non-bloody part of his shirt. Then, she handed the knife to me, motioning for me to add it to my gear.

Stepping away from the body, she pulled her arms out of her dress and pushed it down over her hips. "Let's put all our outer clothes in this bag and take them with us."

I collected my dress from the trunk, and my bra and bike shorts from the rocks. Sarah shoved her dress in the bag while I held it open.

We brusquely cleaned each other up with the bleach wipes that had been part of the murder kit. My scrapes stung like I'd been branded, but it was good to get them disinfected. The bloodied wipes went into the same bag as our old clothes.

Sarah asked me to douse the body and the surrounding area with gasoline while she cleaned a few spots of blood on the back of the car.

The clearing he had picked was perfect for this kind of work. It was a former river loop, barren and rocky with raised banks and thick trees all around. I bet they used this area because it was unlikely anyone would spot the smoke. I felt a chill entirely unrelated to my naked state, knowing that if we'd been even a hair less lucky, it would have been our dead bodies burning here. I wondered how many times these assholes had done exactly that. How many broken bodies were part of the soil out here?

I started the car and drove it gingerly forward, lurching over the large rocks. If I got stuck in a hole or took out the oil pan, we'd be screwed. Once I reached the pebbled area nearer the former bank, I took a moment to look at my reflection in the rearview.

My stomach flipped as Brent's features glared back at me. I didn't know how Sarah took it so calmly, given their history, but the possible advantages of this form were obvious.

I got out and dressed in the spare clothes he'd brought. He had clearly expected things to get messy. There was a complete change, down to underwear, socks, and shoes. I wondered about DNA evidence. Was my DNA an exact copy of his now? Or was it some fantastic hybrid that would baffle the techs? How deep were my changes?

Sarah opened the passenger door, added her shoes to the clothes bag, tied it up, and tossed it into the back footwell. She popped the cap off a road flare and ripped the cord to light it. With a smooth over-arm throw, she launched it into the gasoline-doused area, then dropped into the passenger seat, hissing, "Go, go, go!"

I accelerated slowly and steadily up the bank, still scared of getting stuck. The flames were invisible at first in the afternoon sun, but roared into a substantial fire as they reached the body. I drove as fast as I dared down the rutted, overgrown track.

It wasn't until the urgency of putting some distance between us and the smoke receded that I started to think more about where I was going. The track leading from the river turned into a more substantial dirt road, but we were still deep in the wilderness, and it was rough enough that it might have just been a cutline.

"Uh … can you guide me?" I asked, eyeing the dipping angle of the sun. Thankfully, it was barely past the summer solstice, so we had plenty of daylight left. It just seemed darker under the closely packed trees. But it was still getting late. With a twist of worry in my gut, I wondered what Ian and Angela were facing.

Sarah retrieved her purse from the backseat and pulled out her phone. After some checking, she said, "Looks like we'll hit some kind of road soon. Carry on the way you are."

"Right."

I went as fast as the track allowed, weaving around intrusive young trees and rocks. I longed for a massive truck, but once we hit a gravel road that was actually on the map, I picked up more speed. This car stuck to the road so much better than my parents' aged car, and I didn't care if I took a few years off the life of this one's suspension.

Luckily, we reached a paved road before the shadows really started to lengthen and found ourselves not too far out from Banff. With fewer bumps and swerves, Sarah took the opportunity to unpack the cow pyjamas from her shopping bag and contorted herself into them, looking relieved to be wearing something other than underwear.

On the wider highway, our view expanded, and I noticed the sun was closer to the mountains than expected.

"How are we doing for time?" I asked worriedly. We must have lost at least a couple of hours, maybe more.

"We're not late yet," Sarah said. "Angela said the earliest she might show up on the roof was nine, but I wanted to be in position by eight to do an early scout, and it's … half-past seven now and we're still nearly an hour from the op staging point." She looked worried.

Given the form I was in and the car I was driving, I put my foot to the floor. I figured nobody would bother this guy for going twenty or thirty over. It would only save us a dozen minutes or so, but those minutes could be crucial.

Sarah inspected Brent's phone, but it was password locked, not just face or fingerprint, and we didn't have the time or tools to crack it. She left it on until we reached the Banff townsite, then turned it off and put it into a radio-blocking bag. If anyone was tracking his phone, it would look like he'd made it back to town, then went dark.

Paying closer attention to speed limits, I drove to the edge of a residential neighbourhood halfway up one of the mountainsides that surrounded Banff. I parked at the edge of the road within a short walk of where one of our ghost helpers had left another car parked at the start of a hiking trail. If anyone was tracking Brent's car, it was that best we didn't pinpoint the exact location of our getaway vehicle. I would only be here for a short time while I picked up the gear for Angela and helped Sarah set up. Then I would head to the hotel to be ready to tie the gear to the rope Angela would drop.

Sarah was still dressed in the cow pyjamas, so we picked up a couple of odd looks while we walked, but no one tried to take any pictures. Hopefully, it wouldn't create any ripples on social media. Thinking about Sarah, a question that I'd pushed aside earlier came back to me. "Sarah … you seemed surprised earlier that I'd changed to this guy's form. Why?"

"I'm not sure I should tell you." She side-eyed me.

"Well, now I have to know!" I mock-glared at her.

"You're right," she said resignedly, and the gravity of her tone buried my frivolity. "The form you're in. Him. It shouldn't be possible. That's not how shifting works. You can shift to the same general range as a target, or with sustained focus take on some specific features, but as soon as your attention wavers, you revert to some random form like, but not quite, the target. You seem to be keeping this form without even thinking about it."

"Ah, yeah. I haven't been thinking about it." Had I done something wrong? Would I be stuck looking like this guy forever now? I didn't think so, somehow. I felt uneasy in this form already, like a shift was coming, but I wasn't sure if it was my gender, the weird way I'd shifted, or my general discomfort with this shape.

"I think you need to know the wizards are not going to expect someone who looks exactly like their security chief to be a shifter, unless they catch you out some other way."

"Thanks for letting me know." I smiled. It did help calm some of my fears of being immediately interrogated when I showed my face.

"It also makes me want to knock you over the head and drag you out of here." Her tone was low and packed with frustration. "You have such enormous potential, it's frightening."

"I won't abandon my friends."

"I know," she said softly, raising a hand to lightly brush my bristly cheek, then she yanked her hands down and strode briskly ahead, not glancing back.

I stayed a couple of steps back to give her space. I had a lot to think about, too. I was barely used to being a shifter, now I was learning I had some unique talent?

Maybe.

I wondered if I'd ever be able to do it again, outside of a life-or-death struggle.

I was grateful to see our getaway car ahead. I pushed aside my doubts and tried to focus on the plan. Sarah retrieved the key from on top of the rear tire, opened the car, and, partially hidden by an open door, changed into her regular jeans and T-shirt working clothes while I grabbed our gear.

We spotted a good place for Sarah's equipment, a short walk down the forested hill from the trailhead—a rock ledge about ten feet above the path, which itself was overhung by tree branches, blocking any view from above. It took me a few minutes to work my way up the unstable, nearly vertical slope. This body felt awkward, but its height, reach, and strength more than made up for the extra weight.

Brent's clothes were less of a liability than I had feared. It looked like a cheap suit perfect for blending into the wall at a fancy party, so I had expected the usual stiff, limiting wool. Instead, it was made with stretchy fabric that offered excellent freedom of movement. Was that because the head of this clan owned a menswear chain, I wondered.

Once I was on the ledge, the custom plastic parts Sarah had 3D-printed made it easy to clip the tight-beam comms device to the telescope. Then all I had to do was open the tripod it was mounted on and point it roughly toward the hotel, sitting in clear view by the river in the valley spread out below us.

I half-climbed, half-slid my way down the slope back to where Sarah waited. We moved to a more convenient place to sit. If any late hikers happened by, we would look like two dumb tourists sitting in paradise focused on a laptop as Sarah skillfully adjusted the position of the telescope to point first at the hotel, zoom, then the roof, zoom, then … something dark flashed across the screen while Sarah was studying the printed hotel floorplan.

"Shit! What was that?" I exclaimed.

"What?" Sarah tensed, looking around.

"No. The screen. I saw someone walk past!"

"It's too early for Angela, surely." She frowned. "Let's take a look."

She zoomed out in smaller increments. Our viewpoint pulled back from the green shingled roof until we could see all of it. My gut clenched. A dark-clad figure, walking across the flat crown of the roof. After scouting around the entire area, they slipped behind a big air conditioning unit, hidden from most of the roof. Judging by the short blond hair and how they moved, it was clear that it wasn't Angela or Ian. A worker would be doing something, not just searching. It had to be a guard.

"Bugger," Sarah swore quietly, coming to the same conclusion. "Nobody mentioned rooftop sentries in the plan. Ian said they never posted anyone up there because the invisibility trick doesn't work at long range."

"They shouldn't have any reason to suspect Ange, right?" My hands clenched into fists.

"Shouldn't have had." Sarah sighed. "This could be a perfectly normal security measure that Ian didn't know about. Either way, it cuts Angela off from both the codex and her getaway route."

And there was no way we could contact her before she was exposed on the rooftop.

"I have to get on that roof," I said, not really expecting the words until they were out of my mouth. My mind raced with plans. I would have to find some way to reach the roof without drawing suspicion …"

"I don't think you want to take on …" Sarah looked at me. At my current form. At the determination in my eye., She changed her mind with a brief flicker of pain across her face. "You'd better move fast. It's nearly nine."

~*~

I parked in the lot closest to the hotel as if I had a right to it. For all I knew, this guy did. His remaining gear weighed down my pockets, except for his gun. That went into the duffle. Partially because he hadn't provided a spare shoulder holster, but also because I didn't have enough experience with guns to start waving one around.

My purple dino pyjamas also went in. They were the only thing we could dig up as replacement clothes for Angela, and she'd need something warm after her rooftop excursion. I fiercely told my churning gut that I *would* get there in time. I *would* deal with the guard. She *would* escape from the sealing ritual party and *would* still be in a state where warm clothes would help her after tackling the codex room.

My initial entry to the hotel went smoothly. I strode across the grand marble of the hotel lobby like I belonged there and found the right elevator with only a little backtracking. I passed at least two wizard guards at their posts, who fortunately didn't look surprised or suspicious, nor did they try to ask me anything.

The Clan guards and staff members used this one elevator to get to the reserved, second-to-top-most floor of the hotel. We'd discussed trying this route in our planning, but Ian felt it was too risky for him to try stealing a keycard. They were tied to specific identities and strictly guarded.

When I presented the chief of security's shiny black, but otherwise unmarked, keycard to the elevator sensor, it started automatically and took me all the way up past the topmost floor on the panel, showing R2 as the floor number.

There weren't many rooms on this level—just three doors on what had to be the outer wall. I was relieved that it matched my expectations. I had studied the floor plans intently, just in case. The first and second doors would be rooms where the wizard guards relaxed or slept when off-duty. Muffled voices came from the second room as I passed. I sweated, expecting a patrol of goons to pop out at any moment and pummel me with questions I couldn't answer.

I made it to the third room without incident. It had been listed as a briefing room. Summoning all of my bravado, I opened the door with a jerk and strolled in. The room showed some recent use—dirty disposable coffee cups, napkins, and crumbs on a conference table that dominated the room. Rows of chairs along its sides pointed every which way. But, to my great relief, it was empty of people.

Brent was probably the one who called the meetings in here, and he wouldn't be scheduling any more. Ever.

My stomach hurt, and I felt queasy at the thought, experiencing again the feel of my blade slicing through barely resisting flesh and crunching into bone. I shoved all security chief-related thoughts out of my head and focused on my task. I locked the door and moved to the windows. The view outside in the fading light confirmed I was in the right spot. More or less.

The room's larger window had been replaced with a double pane at some point, but one of the smaller ones to the side was still an older single pane. I took my first present from Sarah's bag of tricks: a spray bottle of quick-drying plastic coating.

I sprayed it on the window and did some warm-up stretches and exercises while waiting the few minutes for it to dry. Each passing second increased the risk of Angela to walking into an ambush, but I was not going to make the same mistake I had in the parkour test. I gave each step the time it needed, no more, no less.

When the spray film was dry, I smashed the window with the gun butt, making only a dull thud, not the telltale tinkling of shattering glass. It was a tight fit, wriggling through. I kept underestimating the size of this body and almost didn't make it.

Standing on the narrow ledge outside the window, I pulled the duffel bag out and looped the long strap across my chest, so it dangled behind me. I was well conditioned to heights, but nothing this high. I had to forcibly put any thought of the seven-story fall behind my heels out of my mind.

The ledge ran from here to an inside corner where the body of the hotel jutted out another ten feet. The edge of the steeply slanted roof was tantalizingly close, low enough that it was only a few inches above my bald head. Its overhang meant I would need to lean impossibly far back to grab hold.

The corner had jumped out at me immediately when I scanned the plans. This section of the solid metal gutter running at 90 degrees would be in easy reach of a leap, with the corner itself providing purchase to haul myself up onto the roof.

I studied the gutter where I'd need to land a solid grip for several minutes while the sun edged behind the mountain peaks. There was still enough light to tell that the gutters were solid. Hopefully, solid enough to take this guy's weight. I had to reconcile myself to the fact that I couldn't know until I tried.

I could still run away from this. The poisonous thought wiggled into my head. Sarah wouldn't ask any questions. She'd made it clear she wanted my talents. She would happily drive out of here, taking me away to people would not only accept my shifting as normal but help train my abilities.

It sounded beautiful.

But I would have to sacrifice Angela. And Ian. And everyone else these wizards hurt from now on. Likely the same people who could offer me that training. People like Sarah. What was the point of a beautiful future if I would never be at peace again?

I had to jump.

CHAPTER 30

I centred myself, visualized the jump, made it real in my mind, and then leapt off the roof into open space. Nothing below me for seven stories down …

… and caught! One hand slipped, but I quickly replaced it with a firm grip. The gutter flexed alarmingly but held!

Breathing harshly, pulse hammering, I worked myself over a couple of feet to the corner where the gutter would be strongest and I could get extra leverage. I swung my body back and forth, then muscled up. Putting all my willpower into it, I pushed up until my arms were straight and locked again. I leaned forward and managed to hook my toes into the gutter beside me and push myself up onto the steep incline of the rough-shingled roof.

I rested for a minute to calm my racing heart, and more importantly to stretch out my triceps and biceps. I took special care with my left shoulder. It felt like someone had stabbed me, but a couple of careful stretches helped head off a complete muscle spasm. This guy was strong, but really heavy.

The lights in the valley spread out below me. A very long vertical drop awaited the slightest slip in the deepening darkness. I kept a firm grip on the smooth lead flashing moulded around the roof peak.

After a few more calming breaths, I reached inside and adjusted my eyes to be more sensitive to light. The town lights became almost painful to look at, while the dim light shining from the odd trapezoidal windows of the wizard's penthouse above me blazed, giving me more than enough light to navigate the rooftops.

The second I had my wind back, and my muscles felt a little less like jelly, I went hand-over-hand as quietly as I could along the peak until it joined the higher peak of the penthouse where Ian said they would be holding the party. It was eerily quiet up here. Either the wizards' idea of a party was pretty dull or, more likely, some kind of magic kept the noise from leaking out.

I was in the middle of working my way carefully across the very steep and convoluted roof toward the flat top of the main wing where Angela said she'd show up, and where Sarah and I had seen the guard, when I heard Angela's voice cry out. A short, sharp sound of pain. A bright, blue-tinted light, like misplaced lightning, flashed from around the corner of the penthouse.

Sacrificing safety for speed, I leapt across the gaps between the last two dormer window rooflets and swung around the corner. My dark-adjusted, shapeshifter eyes had no trouble seeing Angela, who was wearing a sparkly black curve-hugging evening dress, and the blond goon standing over her. He had an extendable baton raised, poised to crash brutally down on her bare, upheld arm.

But, as I swung down at my best speed, finding handholds and footholds in wires clipped to the old brick, I saw Angela was hardly defenceless. She'd blocked the guard's swing and appeared to be holding his arm in place with some force I couldn't see. He reached across his body with his other hand, trying to draw his gun from its holster on his opposite hip.

I reached into the duffle bag slung across my chest for Brent's gun, the one Sarah used to kill him, and clubbed the guard in the head with the butt, using all the force of my oversized muscles. The goon dropped without uttering a sound.

The despair in Angela's eyes shifted to confusion.

"Sorry to interrupt, Ange," I grinned. "But we don't have time to play around with these assholes."

Her eyes shifted from confusion to relieved understanding.

"Mike!" she breathed, then grimaced. "Please don't smile at me with that face. It's creepy."

I had no trouble losing my smile as I checked the felled goon. He was still breathing. I had mixed feelings about that.

"You get started doing your thing." I handed her the duffel bag. And the gun. "I'll check this guy."

Angela nodded. She quickly checked the safety and the clip, mostly by feel, in what for her was near darkness, then set it down within easy reach. I handed her the small red light flashlight Sarah had included with the prepared gear, and the tightbeam laser comms unit with its little tripod. She squeezed my hand in thanks and started setting it up.

I took the goon's baton, radio, and keycard. He didn't have a gun stashed anywhere I could find. Then, I carried his limp body and dumped it behind the air conditioner box where he'd been hiding. With his dark clothes, he could probably go undisturbed until morning.

On my way back to Angela, I saw the comms gear was tucked beside another one of the air vents that dotted this section of roof. The Wi-Fi access point was connected to the tightbeam receiver and both were plugged into a battery backup. The receiver was pointed roughly toward the mountainside where Sarah waited.

I wondered if she'd noticed that I left the guard alive. I knew it was a risk, but I wasn't ready to kill someone who couldn't fight back. I had a crazy temptation to give Sarah a wave, but what if someone else was watching? I keenly felt how exposed we were.

I caught up with Angela. She was contemplating a window in the penthouse section, part of which I'd just clambered over to reach her.

"Didn't you just get out of there?" I whispered.

"No. I got out of the bubble. This will get us into the real-world section."

"The what now?"

"The wizard's gathering is in a bubble, a pocket dimension tethered to the hotel here, but not part of it. The working offices, containing the codex, are in the real hotel. This setup has the interesting property of keeping the codex close to the sealing victims but also safely removed from any physical attack they might make."

"Oh." That sounded brain-melting to contemplate, so I pretended it made sense.

She used the same spray on this window that I'd used below, then while it was drying, she traced several glyphs on the window glass in the corners with a marker, and in a perfect circle around the sprayed area.

Once she gave me the go-ahead, I used the guard's knife to break and hack out the circular section. Her spells seemed to strengthen or protect the glass around the edges, so the middle broke off neatly, leaving a large circular hole.

"That's cool," I whispered.

"Yeah. Should prevent mechanical alarms," she said, distracted. "Now for the ward."

She reached out and delicately drew more glyphs, but directly in the air this time. They glowed a cool green as she wrote them, slowly fading from my sight. The runes didn't look quite the same as what I'd seen on Sarah's yellow papers, but the structure seemed similar. After nearly a minute of focused drawing, Angela took her hand back and waited tensely, breath held.

A bright spark of green lit up the center and quickly expanded out to a radius larger than the hole in the glass. Angela blew out her breath in a long, relieved sigh.

"You're good at this," I said in awe and with pride .

"A lot of practice with Ian," Angela replied tersely, but with an upward quirk of her lips showing she appreciated the compliment. "Okay. Follow me."

She climbed gingerly over the edge of the glass, not touching it or the still-glimmering edge of the ward. Her legs were a little too short to fully straddle it. I held out one hand to give her a boost so she could clear the bottom of the window frame. My legs were long enough that I could step right over, though getting my head and shoulders through was a tight fit. It was awkward being this big.

Angela prowled across the room, what looked like an office, alert to dangers I couldn't see. I tried to follow exactly where she stepped. Maybe the wards wouldn't stick to me for long, but they could still warn any watchers that we were here.

We reached the door without incident.

"Let me go first," I whispered, gesturing to my altered body. She nodded.

I opened the door and stepped out. It looked like any other well-decorated hall in the hotel. It was empty, for now. I waved Angela out. She pointed out the right direction. We took that hall a short distance to a corner. I was starting to recall the quick map Ian had drawn. The outer hallway made up three sides of a square, then there was one secure door to an inner hall, which led to several high-security rooms, one of which held the codex in its safe.

We reached the security door without seeing any other goons. Angela took some electronic gadgets out of the duffel, but I put my hand on her arm and took out Brent's shiny black card. She shrugged in tentative agreement. I laid the card against the sensor. Would the security chief have access? If he didn't, would this ring alarms?

The lock beeped and lit solid green. I pulled open the door and walked in, trying to pretend like I belonged.

I was two steps away from the door when a rail-thin old white guy in robes stepped out of one of the rooms along the plush-carpeted hall. The purple fabric draped elegantly from his shoulders to ankles and was covered in intricate embroidery in darker purple, red, and black. He recognized me, for sure, and didn't tense up. Maybe I could keep him occupied? The security door clunked closed behind me. Angela must have ducked back before he saw her.

"You've dealt with that little problem that followed you from Arizona?" he said in a weak, creaky voice, dripping with condescension.

I tried to speak in the same cadence I remembered Brent using at the after-grad. The guards worked for the wizards, so I assumed he'd probably ignore the insulting tone of voice.

"Yeah. Her and the sidekick she picked up, too."

"Hmm. Indeed. They're always recruiting impressionable young minds. Best to remove them before they become a problem." He looked a little unfocused as he approached. I stepped aside to let him pass. I desperately wanted to glance back to check on Angela but didn't want to raise any suspicions. Maybe getting rid of this guy would be easier than I …

The bare twitch of his fingers was my only warning. A rope of flame lashed out from his hand to coil around my body. Everywhere it touched erupted in searing pain. The old guy had a skull-like grin on his hollow-cheeked face, his eyes wide. He was enjoying this.

"Your usefulness has reached its end, you insolent buffoon!" he screamed.

I struggled to reach him, but all the strength had been sucked from my body by the agony. If the ropes of fire hadn't held me in place I would have collapsed. All I could do was writhe in place, howling while they stripped my flesh.

Two shots hammered my eardrums and the fire flickered out. The old guy's chin dropped in shock. His lips moved but no words came out. Two dark stains spread down the front of his robe. His eyes closed slowly like he felt a sudden need for a nap, and he crumpled to the carpet.

I stayed on my feet only because I was scared falling would hurt more. The fire was gone, but the burns were still stripes of agony across my chest, arms, and back. Angela hurried past, her face a blank mask. She pointed the gun down and put another bullet in the wizard's head at point-blank range. Then, she turned to me, gun pointed to the floor. She must have slipped through the security door after me and hidden from the old wizard using some kind of magic. Or maybe she'd been hidden the whole time.

My mind was wandering. Shock, probably. Damn.

"Mike! Oh, shit, shit. Can you walk? We have to get out of here!"

An alarm was wailing now. We heard it, muffled, from outside the security door.

"Hurts," I groaned through gritted teeth. Moving would be agony. I had to send Angela away at least. Ian would die, but what else could we do?

I had one chance. A switch might heal my burns enough for me to escape with Angela. I tried to push aside the pain and look inside myself, to that place where I'd found control over my body.

Though, at the same time, I couldn't help but envision Ian waiting for the power of the codex to break. Hoping desperately. Terrified that Angela would be captured. He would die never knowing what had happened to her.

Captured. Angela.

An idea blossomed in my mind, all at once, like a 3D puzzle.

Ian's uncle was a smart guy. Probably a lot of these wizards were. But what if I could make them assume they knew where all the pieces were, when they really didn't? Like my dad had said, often the smarter they were, the easier it was to trick them with what they wanted to be true.

I turned to Angela and gazed deep into her eyes, while looking inside myself at the same time. I pushed aside the pain, pushed aside my panic, and tried to capture the same feeling I had in switching to this form. *Please*, I begged to I don't know who, *just one more change*. I felt the need to change. I was as unsettled in this body as I'd ever been, but it was stubbornly resistant. After all the changes I'd been through earlier today, my flesh felt like cold clay. I brought up all the memories I could of Angela, but I couldn't recapture that feeling of a dial clicking into place.

"Mike. We have to go." Angela's voice rose in panic. She wanted to flee but she wouldn't leave me behind.

"Blood!" I gasped, realizing the missing piece. "I need to taste your blood!"

She spared me a quizzical look, but she trusted me. She quickly nicked her finger and stuck it in my mouth. The coppery taste flooded over my tongue. I closed my eyes. Yes! This was it. All my impressions of Angela came together, given focus by DNA, or her magical essence, or whatever.

The change came in a surge. Slow enough that I felt each distinct step that was normally over in an instant. Even at this slow pace, I didn't feel my meat and bone rearranging. It was more like an undoing, a separation from the ordered world where my physical form dissolved and I dangled over an abyss of pure chaos for a few agonizing moments until I was jerked up and into my new shape.

Angela stared at me, alarmed now. "You … faded out for a few seconds there." She touched my arm, tentatively at first, and then with a firm grip.

She was right. The goon's clothes lay in a pile at my feet. I was completely naked. That had only ever happened when I changed into Brent's form earlier today. What if I dissolved and never reformed?

I shook myself out of that new terror. That wasn't my most pressing concern. My wounds were gone. My head was clear. Now I just needed …

Angela had already pulled her stretchy, sparkly, black dress over her head and was pushing it into my hands. Then, she wriggled out of her bra and stepped out of her shoes. Wearing only her underwear, she picked up Brent's clothes and carried them into one of the rooms. By the time she returned, I her clothes and shoes on. Smoothing the dress down made me realize I wasn't feeling any disconnect to being fully in female form, including my crotch. Much of the discomfort with Brent's form that had been growing in me was gone now. Either because I was feeling more female or, I was a lot happier shaped like Angela than that murderous asshole.

"Your hair is a mess," she said, shaking her head. There was no way we could replicate her complex up-do. She thumbed my earlobe. "And your ears aren't pierced. Details, Mike!" She said chidingly, flashing a half-hearted grin. Taking two of the little gold clasps out of her hair, she used them to pin my hair back. "That's some continuity, anyway."

"Can you still get the codex, if I give you time?" I asked urgently.

She brought her electronic gadgets out of the duffel again and checked a status.

"Our Wi-Fi is still up. Sarah's still there. I'm good for an attempt, at least." She looked nervous, but determined.

"And if it doesn't work, get out. Please." I captured her eyes.

She nodded reluctantly.

"Good luck." I leaned forward and laid a brief kiss on her lips. "I love you."

"I love you, too." She hugged me and I squeezed her back, trying to imprint this moment on my memory. It was different, being in a twin of Angela's body right now, but that barely registered with either of us.

I pulled myself away and ran, refusing to give in to the temptation to look back. They had to find me wandering the halls, not in this secure area where they might be tempted to search further. This was still a long shot, but it was the best chance we had at rescuing Ian and hurting the Clan.

I heard the guards coming as soon as I closed the card-locked door behind me. I could even hear them over the wailing alarm, which was trying to split my skull now that it wasn't muffled by the thick walls and door.

I ran, but they boxed me in. I struggled, but two of the guards quickly overwhelmed me. The jump from the heavily-muscled goon to Angela's body had been quite a shock. It was a good thing I didn't actually want to get away.

CHAPTER 31

The guards escorted me down the hall with brutal grips on my slender arms. It was a short walk to an imposing dark-oak door. It had a dull metal frame engraved with hundreds of arcane symbols.

I tried not to cringe away. Would some built-in magic here reveal me as a shifter? Ian said there was some kind of shifter-detector on the only door between the main part of the hotel and the wizard's area. I hoped we were already inside that permitter.

One of the guards behind me twisted my arm up higher for no reason, wrenching my shoulder until I gasped in pain.

"Golden boy sure picked a shitty girlfriend," he muttered.

"I don't think he's the best judge of girls, Andrew." The other guard replied, and several others laughed crudely.

"At least we caught up with her," Andrew said, and I belatedly placed the wildness in his tone as fear. "The chief's in a bad enough mood as it is. I'd hate to see what he'd do if he came back to find we'd screwed up bad enough to lose her."

We stepped through the doorway. I felt nothing and no alarms went off.

Beyond the doorway was an even-more-lavishly-decorated hall. It looked like pictures I'd seen of royal palaces—all dark, carved wood with carved ivory statuettes in niches and coffered ceilings with gilded pictures of fantastical creatures.

We walked at least twice the width of the entire hotel penthouse in one straight hall alone, never mind the shorter cross halls. If that hadn't convinced me we were somewhere else, the room we entered would have confirmed it. It was bigger than the entire penthouse and its ceiling rose to at least three stories. A mezzanine balcony ringed the room, showing hints of full bookcases and more oil paintings in its shadowed depths.

The atmosphere of the room enveloped me like a drunk grandpa's hug as I was pushed in. Tobacco smoke and scotch hung heavy in the air, with a virulent mix of colognes and perfumes. The crowd was mostly old, white, and male, though I saw a few white women in dresses. Even the guards and the few serving staff were all white.

A few of the men wore robes of varying colours, like the old guy Angela and I ran into by the codex. Others wore fancy scarves of the same colours folded around their shoulders with the ends trailing down their chests. Most of the crowd were wearing black or navy suits, looking more like executives or politicians than wizards. In fact, I thought I recognised a few faces from the international news.

The attendees, both in the gallery and on the floor, were watching something happening in the center of the room, but Angela's body was too short for me to see. Many in the crowd were chanting something that sounded like nonsense syllables. Fortunately for my curiosity, I was being led through the crowd, my guards politely but firmly nudging their way past the collected clan members. Most of the comments as we edged by were in English, but I caught some French, German, and what I suspected was Russian.

As we reached the front, I noticed Ian's uncle first. Dressed in an impeccable black suit, he wore a purple scarf with a wide metallic gold border. It wasn't until I followed his gaze that I realized Ian was one of the two young men standing in the cleared circle in the centre of the room.

They seemed to be simply staring at each other, though as I watched, the other guy flinched, taking an involuntary half-step back. Ian closed in with a half-step of his own, but, catching the disturbance in the crowd, he glanced over. His face went dead the instant he saw me. I desperately wanted to shout "It's all good! I'm not Angela!" to wipe the despair from his eyes.

His opponent took advantage of his lapse in concentration. Ian jerked as if from several quick blows and staggered back several steps. Shouts of surprise and dismay rippled through the crowd. The guy quickly closed the gap and drove Ian two more reluctant steps back to where his heel nearly touched a circle of dull metal inlaid in the hardwood floor. From the gasps, I guessed stepping over the line wasn't a good thing.

Then, Ian rallied. Holding up his hands, fingers spread, he appeared to deflect the worst his opponent could hurl at him. He looked over at me again, then to his uncle, whose expression had taken on a particularly smug, gloating vibe.

"Enough, Connor," Ian said. "I yield."

"No!" The guy snarled. "I refuse! Take your beating like a man."

"There's no point," he said, sounding defeated. "It's over."

"You coward," Connor hurled at him. "Guess I shouldn't have expected you to be real man."

Ian's face hardened.

"Fine, let's do this." Ian brought his hands up further and slowly began to spread them apart. Connor continued to hurl something at Ian, with increasing frustration at its lack of effect. The crowd was muttering now, disturbed.

Then Ian brought his hands together in a loud clap, and Connor's body flew like a ragdoll across the entire circle to land, tumbling, while spectators scrambled out of the way, in a heap against one of the elegant settees that lined the walls. A girl about our age shrieked and ran over to check on him.

A single slow clap started. The muttering crowd cut off abruptly. It was Ian's uncle, Zachary. He strode into the ring.

"I have long maintained that Ian is the brightest star of this generation. Impetuous, as you've seen tonight with his brash challenge of Connor, ending in an uncouth display of unnecessary violence marring our celebration." He paused to collect himself, or at least that was what he wanted to project. You could almost buy his 'more in sadness than anger routine' if you didn't see the cruel anticipation in his eyes.

No longer distracted by the fight, I could see that Ian looked terrible. He was ashen-faced and swayed slightly on his feet. A trickle of blood ran from inside his sleeve down the back of one hand.

"And this very brashness has been used against him." Zachary pointed an accusing finger at me. "This woman is no humble petitioner. No innocent girl. She has been corrupted, trained by terrorists to take advantage of our Ian's faults and infiltrate our Clan to destroy us. Found and forestalled only by my vigilance."

My gods, the guy was politicking. If I wasn't so terrified, I'd be bored.

"We will deal with this threat now." He looked around the crowd with a self-satisfied smile. "Let this traitor no longer pollute our sacred gathering." He looked directly at me, eyes like gun barrels. "Bring her."

Andrew pulled me forward with an iron grip. I decided to play meek for the moment, resisting just enough to slow him down. Ian and I were the floor show. Angela was doing the real work. I sincerely hoped.

"What is this, Uncle?" Ian called out, stepping in the way of my captors. "By ancient tradition, those who gather for sealing are under the protection of our clan, as if they were already members." Murmuring broke out in the crowd. Most of it sounded unhappy, but I didn't know if that meant support for Ian, or his uncle. I was way out of my depth.

"You've raised suspicions," Ian said, then yelled, "Where is your proof?" He had no idea about the switch. No idea how closely I could mimic a specific person. As far as he knew, the entire plan was in ruins. I was newly terrified of what he might do in his despair.

"A certain level of youthful rebellion is acceptable, even commendable," Zachary began in a mild tone, talking directly to Ian, then finished with a roar. "But there are limits!" His voice softened again. "You need to know your place. You will learn that tonight."

He waved a hand in a sinuous fashion, ending with a clenched fist, and Ian cried out in pain. Holding his stomach, he stumbled back. The watching crowd gasped. "She will be sealed now. And then we'll hear her confession from her own mouth." He raised his hands in front of him in a prayer-like gesture, palms facing towards me. Quite a few people in the crowd took up the same posture. It should have looked ridiculous, but I wasn't finding any humour.

Ian's face went waxen, his expression slackened and his head drooped as he brought all his focus to bear on what I feared was something entirely self-destructive.

"Ian!" I cried. "Don't sheathe the sword, you muttonhead"

His head popped up, staring at me, wild, hopeful suspicion in his eyes. Angela had never watched the show or read the books.

Alerted to the possibility that Ian wasn't as cowed as he looked, a couple of the guards grabbed him, forcing him to his knees. In his weakened state he couldn't break free. The look on his face was pure misery, with fear and hope warring for control. My muscles clenched and I felt a sudden desperate need to pee.

Ian's jerk warned me a split second ahead. His uncle hadn't moved. I felt a tingle on my skin, and a deep hummm all through my body. It felt like a thousand bees burrowing into my soul—not painful, just very, very odd. The buzzing reached deep inside and … passed through me, dissipating into nothing.

This time, most of the crowd gasped. Zachary slumped, looking physically drained. All the others who had taken the same pose looked the same, except for the ones that had fallen to their knees. "But ..." he said, sounding truly confused. "How?"

I tried to retain my shocked and concerned look, inwardly gloating. *Surprise, sucka!*

Ian's eyes closed, and a single tear trailed down his cheek. When he opened them again, they were shining with renewed joy. Hope ascendant over fear, for now. He understood what Angela and I had done. Whatever spell had been tearing at his guts before was gone. He rose from his knees and called out in clear, ringing tones. "You have attacked my guest, in direct violation of Clan law. I demand satisfaction!"

Silence descended like a lead blanket. Then, voices rose from the crowd, the majority sounding more approving this time. Zachary surveyed the room. Many who had supported him in the attempted sealing looked away. His face took on harder lines. He seemed to realize he'd been suckered.

"Very well. This won't take more than a few minutes." He waved in my direction. "Hold her! She's hiding something." Then, he advanced on Ian, who backed away cautiously, his face blank in concentration.

Andrew's grip tightened on my arm, and from the corner of my eye, I saw another guard approaching. Should I make a break for it or lie low? I shifted my weight, sizing up my chances of breaking free, when a shockingly cold gun barrel pressed lightly against the nape of my neck. "On your knees," a cold voice said.

I dropped to my knees, not entirely of my own will.

The crowd was edging back now, some of them pushing toward that long hallway and exit.

Zachary pitched his voice loud enough to be heard from one end of the hall to the other. "Let me remind you: the sealing has begun. No one may leave until the ritual is complete." And in an aside to one of the guards, "Lock down the inner citadel. No one enters or leaves."

The guard turned and spoke urgently into his wrist-mounted radio. Clan members who'd started to leave shuffled back into the room. A couple of the famous faces in my field of view were filled with repressed anger, but they didn't complain.

"Family," Ian said in a clear, loud voice with an undertone of desperation. "You know this is between Uncle and me. If he wants to beat me before the bidding to show his control, fine, but let my girlfriend go first. Please. She's no threat to us."

He wasn't acting anymore. He was scared. The bottom of my stomach dropped out. The best time to make a break for it had definitely been a few minutes ago.

"And I say this is Clan business," his uncle snarled. "First, I'll deal with you, then we'll see what your whore is hiding." He advanced on Ian, who grunted and jerked back a couple of steps. His uncle must have launched some kind of attack, though he made no outward sign. A half-smile quirked Zachary's lip.

The remaining crowd lost some of its tension and began chanting again. It picked up raggedly, and I could tell that many stayed silent. A few still drifted toward the back edge of the crowd with worried expressions, but a fair number were rabidly focused on the fight.

It wasn't a fair fight. Once Zachary really launched in, he pummelled Ian. It hadn't been over-confident bravado when he said it should only take a few minutes. The difference between a young, partially trained wizard like Ian and the head of the Clan was ridiculously apparent. It was like an adult beating a child.

But Ian kept getting up. Again and again, until there was blood streaming from his nose and mouth, his normally smooth movements reduced to a jerky stumble.

His uncle could have ended it sooner, but it was clear he revelled in Ian's pain. Several more in the crowd looked embarrassed and stopped chanting. Connor, whom Ian had beaten unconscious before, was sitting on the settee now, propped up by his girlfriend, both of them watching the beating with smug satisfaction.

I knew at some point he'd get tired of playing with Ian and kill him, or seal him, which would amount to the same thing. I put myself in the zone, like my previous jump on the roof. I meticulously constructed the sequence in my mind before I tensed a muscle.

The gun was still in contact with the back of my skull, but it was an empty threat where it was placed. Zachary wanted me alive for questioning. That might give me enough of an edge to survive this stunt, and maybe give Ian a few more minutes.

Come on, Angela. I deeply hoped she was still alive. There was no way for us to know whether she'd managed to reach the codex or not until she broke it.

As Ian groggily attempted to return to his feet once again, I sensed the shift in his uncle's mood. A subtle stiffening of movement from enjoyment to business. Ian was doomed. The crowd knew it, too. Zachary lifted his hand—

I dropped to the side, throwing my body at the ground with no thought of a soft landing. This yanked my arm from Andrew's surprised clutch, his nails scoring my skin. My shoulder hit hard, my head a little less hard, but enough that I saw bright sparks in my vision for a second.

I kicked up into the space my head had been a split-second earlier. The low heel of my shoe connected with something hard, transmitting a shock all the way to my hip bone, and the gun that was previously pointed at my head went off.

Aimed directly at Zachary.

A bright point of searing blue light, like a welding arc, blossomed in front of Zachary. Then, like a striking snake, a beam of similar light flickered briefly between him and the guard.

The guard screamed. There was a grapefruit-sized divot out of his chest, exposing charred muscle and bone. Smoke rose from his eyes. Andrew, the guard who'd had a grip on my arm, was flung away. He landed on his back, unmoving.

I rolled out of the way as fast as I could, not relishing the idea of the smoking guard landing on me. I only made it one revolution before three guards subdued me, flat on my stomach with my hands zip-tied behind me.

The crowd went silent.

"Well, that was exciting," Zachary drawled.

Ian was still on his knees, head bowed.

The Clan chief lifted his hand again.

Then Zachary staggered. Half the crowd slumped to the floor, immobile. Many others clutched their heads, screaming and gagging.

Ian staggered to his feet, wobbly, but chuckling, and then all-out laughing. "Oh yeah! You're fucked," he yelled joyfully.

A wave of elation ran through me. Angela must have done it! Whatever happened here, at least she could probably get away … if destroying the codex hadn't hurt or killed her.

His uncle's head whipped up. "You insolent—"

Ian closed the distance between them in two quick strides and snap-kicked his uncle in the crotch. As his uncle's head went down, Ian placed his hands on either side and held tight for a few seconds as his uncle struggled ineffectually.

The guards had their guns out, looking uncertain, but kept them carefully pointed away from any of the wizards, including Ian. I stayed very still.

Some of the wizards recovered their senses, but the few who tried to interfere with the fight were blocked by others who wanted it left alone. Their bickering was stilled by a high, keening scream pouring from Zachary's wide-open mouth. He pulled free and backed away from Ian, rubbing at his arms, tugging at his collar, screaming with barely a pause for breath. Even though I hated him, the look of absolute horror on his face sickened me.

Ian strode quickly to where I lay on the floor, taking only a second to release my hands from the zip tie. I felt a moment of pure envy for magical talent, recalling my struggles in the trunk. He took my hand as if helping me to my feet, but I quickly realized I was the one keeping him from falling down.

"Time to go!" he gasped.

Unfortunately, the guards had not forgotten about us.

"Sir, you're not permitted to leave," one of the guards from the group that had been holding me down said. His gun was out, but pointed at the floor. Two other guards flanked him. Andrew was still on the floor, glancing between us and the smoking body of his former comrade.

"You served the Clan. I get it," Ian said in a low voice. "But this clan is finished. The codex is broken. So, you're no longer a security team. You're just a bunch of thugs with guns facing a very, very pissed off wizard."

He looked from guard to guard with an air of total confidence. I pushed up against his shoulder, clasping his hand hard, taking as much of his weight as possible without making it look too obvious.

The guards looked around the room for support. The people who weren't already stumbling toward the main corridor gathered into groups at the edges of the room, carrying or dragging wizards that were still unconscious and trying desperately to wake them. The gatherings appeared random for a moment, until I realized I only saw robes or scarves of a single colour in each group.

The hard-faced guards looked like they might make a fight of it any-way, until Andrew got to his feet in abrupt, jerky motions. He turned toward us with a stiff, unnatural posture. His face was slack, expres-sionless, except for his eyes, which radiated pure terror. He strode stiffly toward the middle of the lounge. The same thing was happening to other guards spread through the crowd.

The guards backed off, terror on their faces, and headed for the main hallway themselves, perhaps deciding it was time to make their own retreat. I saw flickers of light at the boundaries of each group, and even saw one guy's pant leg burst into flame, though it vanished as quickly and mysteriously as it had started.

Ian urgently pointed me toward a narrow hallway that opened in the corner of the hall. We both did our best to shuffle there quickly. This room was absurdly large. Fortunately, the former Clan members seemed too busy fighting each other to target us.

"Your form," Ian said breathlessly. "It's an amazing replica. I didn't think shifters could do that!"

"We can't. Apparently, I'm special."

"You are, you know." He said, with earnest, admiring honesty in his voice.

"What?" I looked up at him.

"Special, in so many ways. I hope you realize it."

"I'll make time to reflect on it once we're very far from here," I said, too flippantly, but I couldn't handle the emotions he brought up just now. "What did you do to your uncle back there?"

"Oh, I took the chance while he was still dazed by the codex destruction and released all the forced heterosexual conditioning in his mind." He frowned. "It worked better than I expected."

We arrived at a narrow hall. It turned out to be a small nook with only one door. It was labelled 'Cleaning Supplies.'

"Ian?" I shot him a skeptical look.

"Uncle was so busy congratulating himself, he never thought to ask the key question: How did Angela slip out of the gathering?" Ian opened the door. It was, indeed, a set of shelves filled with cleaning supplies. He closed the door again. He reached into an alcove beside the door with a small statue of ibis-headed Thoth and produced a small silver key. He locked, then unlocked the door and re-opened it. A bracing waft of night-chilled fresh air blew in, and we looked out onto the hotel roof where I'd met Angela a bare hour before.

"I found this years ago, poking around. A secret escape hatch. I'm not sure anyone else remembers it's here." He was practically giddy, showing off his power to help someone else. It was so perfectly Ian, it brought tears to my eyes.

Glancing back into the hall, I saw Andrew the guard still walking stiffly. He was covered in blood from slashes all over his body, and gentle curls of smoke rose from his shoulders.

"It's disgusting," Ian said, pure loathing in his voice. "We've put the Clan in shambles for now, but soon enough one faction's going to win, they'll regroup, and get right back to screwing over everyone with less power. See?"

As we watched, the blue faction, the smallest one in the room, stripped off their robes and vests, then hurried over to swell the ranks of the orange group.

"We've done what we can. Let's bounce!" I stepped halfway through the doorway, but stopped when Ian resisted.

"No, I really haven't," he said lightly. "Thank you. For everything, Mike. I felt more alive this year than I have for a long time, and it was all because of you." He stroked my cheek once with his gentle fingers.

While my brain was still catching up, he shoved me, hard. As I stumbled away from the doorway, he said, "I'm sorry. Get as far away as you can, as fast as you can. I don't know how much damage this will cause when it implodes." With unshed tears glinting in his eyes, he slammed the door a second before I reached it and I ran into a bare stone wall.

CHAPTER 32

"Mike!"

Angela's desperate call brought me back to myself. My bloodied knuckles throbbed painfully from punching the wall. It was a whisper compared the to the scream of grief inside, but finally, fear for Angela gave me the strength to turn away from Ian's tomb. If I forced her to save me, the delay could kill us both.

She crouched by a ventilation fan midway down the roof. As I stumbled over, I saw dimly that she'd tied the knotted climbing rope from the duffle bag to the vent pipe. The tightbeam and other gear were gone, probably in the duffel she now carried. Right on the plan we'd discussed a month ago, in another world where Ian's smile still existed.

Angela wearing dinosaur pyjamas had not been part of the plan, but you could never anticipate everything.

I heard myself shout, "Go! Go! I'm right behind you."

"Ian?" She asked with an anguished look.

"Not coming."

She nodded solemnly, and with a very deep breath, backed over the side, walking down the very steep, but not quite vertical, roof. We didn't have far to go. The dormer window of the room booked for us by a ghost helper was just twenty feet down, but we were both frazzled and exhausted.

I waited, lying on the gravelled rooftop. Not wanting to look but unable to look away. I no longer had the armour of naivety that my friends wouldn't be ripped from me without notice.

She reached the window without falling, smashed through the glass with a gun butt, and vanished inside.

I gripped the now slack rope and stood up, prepared to back down the roof in the same way Angela just did, when crunching gravel gave me a split second warning. The blond guard I'd left on the rooftop, his face blood-streaked, ran toward me. I knew instantly I wouldn't be able to climb down fast enough. His outstretched hands would snatch me back onto the roof, layering new bruises over the latest ones. Whatever he did to me, it would matter less than the time running out on the implosion.

I let go of the rope and dropped, letting gravity move me faster than my muscles could. Angela's low-heeled pumps didn't offer any purchase on the shingles. I half-slid, half-bounded down the steep slope until the first projecting dormer roof. I hit hard, flexing my knees and curling up to take as much of the shock as possible. I still rolled, but I was moving slowly enough as I hit the edge of the tiny rooflet that I managed to get a solid grip on the edge and, just barely, hang on.

The guard rolled by, screaming. His mad rush to snag me before I fell out of reach must have carried him over the edge. He reached the end of the steep shingled roof and launched into empty air. Next stop, the pavement seven stories down.

Angela's face poked out of the window below, terror masking her features. It lessened only slightly when she saw me hanging. Waving was out of the question. The climbing rope was too far to grab unless I made a jump for it, and I was feeling like I'd used up all my luck for tonight.

Then a big guy appeared suddenly at the window I was dangling in front of. A middle-aged man with East-Asian features.

"Are you all right, Miss?" He called in heavily Korean accented English, looking highly concerned.

"Sorry ahjussi! Could I come through your window?" I yelled, the honorific springing to my lips. An echo of happier evenings watching K-Drama with Sarah.

I expected some argument. Instead, he immediately stepped back, picked up the hotel chair and drove one leg through the glass, knocking most of it out of the frame. He cleared the remaining shards and easily helped pull me inside with one thick arm.

My parents had always said a little politeness went a long way.

"Thank you so much," I tossed out as I hurried toward the door, ignoring his urgent questions. As I hauled the door open, I called back. "Um, I've heard there's a bomb in the hotel, please leave as soon as you can!"

The look of alarm on his face confirmed he'd understood enough. He was hurriedly stuffing his laptop into its bag as I left. I pulled the fire alarm on the way to the emergency stairs. It didn't do anything immediately, but seconds later, while I was running down the stairs, I heard the bells start.

Angela was waiting for me on the landing, two floors below. I waved her on, annoyed. She was going to get herself killed if she kept waiting for me! A few other people, fast reactors, were already entering the narrow emergency stairwell. It would get crowded, fast.

We were down past the fourth floor when the whole stairwell shook, dust suddenly hanging in the air. People started screaming. Angela and I shared a worried glance and hurried as much as we could, but we couldn't go faster than the people below us.

A few steps later, a startled yell sounded behind me, and a heavy body crashed into my back. I clamped down on the handrails with both hands, but it had caught me already leaning forward. I was slipping. I either had to dump this guy on Angela, or I was going to fall and take her with me! Angela turned to face me. Her hand shot up, and just as I passed the tipping point, the weight on my back disappeared with a grunt and startled gasps from behind me. I was able to pivot on one hand and hug the railing. The guy who'd tripped lay on the stairs beside me, uninjured.

We ran on and left them all startled behind us. What explanation could we give?

We were past the second floor before the stairwell in front of us really started to choke up, and we were all stuck, nearly stopped, for a few minutes. A few people were yelling, others crying. Angela and I held hands tightly.

I took advantage of the wait to get the small first aid kit from a side pocket of the duffle, though Angela took it from me and insisted on cleaning and bandaging the torn skin of my right knuckles herself.

"Can I ask what happened?" she whispered close to my ear.

I closed my eyes at the swell of pain. I wasn't ready, but she deserved to know in case we didn't make it out.

"He could have escaped with me," I choked out. "He said they would just start over if we left them like that, so he stayed behind to collapse the bubble, I think."

"That sounds like him." She sighed and scrubbed her face with her hands, pushing her hair back. "He mentioned that he fantasized about taking them all out every time they had a Clan gathering, but that the bubble was untouchable, tied to the codex. I hadn't thought ..." she trailed off.

"He felt responsible, I think. He was always helping people." I blinked to clear my eyes. I didn't want to rub dust into them.

"Yeah," Angela agreed.

There didn't seem like much more to say. Not yet. Not here.

Eventually, we burst out into the blessedly chill air of the late-summer night. We pushed our fatigued, bruised bodies just a little more and jogged, threading our way through the crowd stalled outside the emergency exit before stopping for a rest.

Looking back, I saw the wizard's penthouse was gone. The now uppermost floor of the of the hotel's centre block was engulfed in flames. The screaming sirens of firetrucks raced closer.

Some hotel staff were trying to get people to move away from the building, while others were running by with armloads of blankets. I snagged one to cover my distinctive coppery-red hair. I felt bad because some people had fled their rooms in nothing but underwear, or nothing at all, while other people had phones out already capturing the fire. Some of them were panning the crowd too.

Angela and I walked away quickly, not wanting to be in the way, and definitely not wanting to be recorded. Ange had the hood of her dino pyjamas up, hiding her own distinctive hair. The rescue blanket was long enough on Angela's frame for me to also cover most my dress, which would be familiar to any surviving wizards or guards.

"I hope all the guests get out okay," Angela said.

"Me too." I thought about the guy who'd let me use his window. My reply was partially drowned out by the fire department's arrival. Their engines and horns were so loud that we had to cover our ears until they cut the sirens.

We wended our way through parking lots and walking paths, staying away from the main road. I noticed Angela wincing after stepping on a pebble.

"Oh, here, my turn to carry the duffel," I offered, holding out a hand. "And wear these shoes for a while. They're starting to give me blisters anyway."

"Ha! I guess your shift didn't inherit my callouses," she said with a fleeting grin. She accepted the shoes, though she was reluctant to pass me the duffel.

"There's something I have to show you, before we go on." She looked nervous.

"What?" Any trace of relaxation I had acquired on our jaunt vanished. I really needed to be done with shocks for today.

She put the bag down on the grass beside the path and opened it up. Its lumpiness wasn't only the comms gear and weapons I remembered. It was the soft sheen of small gold bars and packets of cash, a riot of dollars (both Canadian and US), pounds, and euros.

"It seemed a shame to just leave it there," she said, with only slight embarrassment.

"More than fair, I think," I choked out. My brain stalled trying to estimate the value of her haul.

"I don't see any tracking spells on it," she said, "But I wanted to let you know. It's a potential risk."

"Worth it, I think. We'll let Sarah know when we see her." And if we didn't see her again, it would be a huge help in staying ahead of any vengeful Clan survivors.

"There's one other thing." She pointed to a separate plastic bag in the duffel, with what looked like magical symbols painted on it. We'd used it to transport some ingredients Angela had prepared ahead of time to support the spells she needed to unlock the codex safe.

"There was some kind of artifact in the safe too. Definitely magic. I stuck it in here and wrapped a magic-dampening spell of my own around it. Again, it's a risk, but I figure anything they locked away like that has to be important, right?"

"I'm willing to roll with it, but if someone starts chasing us, we're dumping this entire duffel, okay?" I shuddered in memory of my desperate run through the woods at the after-grad.

"For sure!" Angela agreed.

I hefted the duffel. Not only was it heavier than it had been, but I was also a lot smaller and weaker now. I had new admiration for Angela's endurance and persistence, lugging this all the way down the emergency stairs and from the hotel.

We walked in silence for a little while longer, down the road toward the river and its bridge to the town centre. If Sarah was still okay, we would find her at our meetup point there. If she didn't show up, we would need to find our own way.

"How long can you stay in this shape?" Angela asked.

"I'm feeling female for now, but I expect that will change tomorrow, or maybe next week. I won't be able to resist the change to some kind of male form, but I think I should shift to some other form as soon as I can, probably by morning. We stand out as twins."

"That's good." She sighed. "I'm probably going to have to cut and dye my hair. This part of the Clan has been severely pruned, thanks to Ian." She paused briefly, and I reached out and squeezed her hand. She drew in a deep breath and continued, "But I expect that might just motivate the remaining branches to search even harder for us."

"For sure. They'll be afraid we'll do the same thing to them!" I said fiercely, surprising myself with how deeply I wanted every wizard clan member wiped off the face of the earth.

Angela nodded, though she looked too exhausted for rage. That she could produce force from thin air and manipulate wards seemed, well, magical, but I had to remember it had a physical cost too.

"How was it, getting the codex?" I asked gently.

"Easy enough," she said plainly. A hardness in her tone suggested otherwise. She went silent for some time while we walked. We were nearing the foot of the bridge, and I was starting to miss the shoes. I wondered if Angela was tired of them yet.

"You don't have to talk about …" I started.

"No, it's okay. I probably should." She laid her hand on my arm, briefly, and smiled. "Sarah's code-breaking was fast. Taking down the wards was exhausting but not tricky. The physical key Ian copied worked perfectly. It was all very anticlimactic, really. Except for the body out in the hall, with the smell of blood and brains and shit, and the constant fear that any second I was going to die in agony too." Her voice cut off, choked in incipient tears. Her hands squeezed into fists. "I've never shot at a person before. I don't think I'll ever forget the look in his eyes, laying there, knowing the bullet was coming."

We were crossing the bridge now. Her breathing was harsh, coming in small gasps. I wanted to comfort her, but I knew touch was right out.

"I had to stab a guy today. That guard who was at the bar for Ian's birthday." Grief rose again and I ruthlessly pushed it down. It was too soon, too raw. "I heard him take his last breath. I don't think I'll ever forget that sound."

"What? Today?" Angela said, shocked.

"Sarah figured we'd be safe in public, but they grabbed us right off the street, knocked us out, and drove us out into the bush to finish the job."

"Gods!" she said, wide-eyed. "I didn't … why didn't you …" She pressed her hands to her forehead, regaining control. "Sorry. I get it. We've been busy. How did you …?"

"Sarah shot him. With his own gun that I got away from him. It was chaos."

"Yeah." She turned and drew me into a hug. We'd reached the other side of the bridge and could take a moment cloaked in shadow behind one of the pillars. I returned her embrace tightly. We were, of course, exactly the same height now, which made for a surprisingly ungainly hug experience, but we managed. We hung onto each other for a solid minute while I cried into her shoulder. From the way her body shuddered, she was equally soaking the rescue blanket.

The gritty crunch and suspension rattle of a truck stopping suddenly nearby lit up all my nerves. I flung myself back from Angela, ready to fight or bolt. Sarah waved from the driver's seat of our getaway SUV, an entirely unremarkable grey RAV4, not body-armoured goons bursting from a black van. My heart still tried to escape from my chest, and I crossed my legs to hold in my pee.

Angela and I each took one strap of the duffel and jogged to the car, shoving it into the backseat footwell.

"You want me to drive?" I asked, more from concern for her than feeling up to it.

To my relief she shook her head. "I'm all right. Just get in."

We did, hurriedly, and Sarah pulled a tight U-turn as Angela and I buckled up in the back. She drove in a strictly controlled manner until we were out of town.

Angela told Sarah about the cash and artifact. She wasn't entirely happy about it, I could tell, but she didn't tell us to ditch the bag. And she didn't ask about Ian. Thankfully. I didn't have the strength right now to explain to someone who hadn't been there. Angela and I leaned together, not talking, just taking comfort from each other's presence.

"Is it weird," I asked, "Cuddling with your twin?"

"Not quite as weird as kissing my own face was," she said sleepily.

I was glad she was able to drift off, but my heart didn't stop racing until we were on Highway One after leaving Banff, well on our way to Vancouver. It was probably illusionary, this feeling of safety increasing with distance, but I was willing to accept it if it made my stomach stop hurting.

Angela lay limp against me, breathing softly in sleep. I ached with exhaustion, but I couldn't imagine closing my eyes.

"He saved us," I said, just loud enough for Sarah to hear. "Ian. He trapped all the wizards inside their secret magic hangout. Then he kicked me out, closed the door, and destroyed it."

"I saw," she said gently. "I guessed as much when I saw the top of the hotel explode. I didn't know if any of you got out until I saw you two at the side of the road, and knew it must have been Ian who collapsed the bubble. Brave kid!" She shook her head.

"Braver than me," I said, my throat constricting and hot tears welling up.

"No," she said with gentle weight. "It takes just as much courage to live with the loss and keep fighting. And I think you will. Keep fighting?"

She left the question hanging between us, but we both knew the answer even before I spoke. "Yeah. I'm with you."

"I'm glad," she said warmly. "Welcome to the resistance."

"Do you know …" I started, but I couldn't finish. Sarah knew what I meant.

"What it would feel like, in the bubble?" she said sadly. "No. I've never heard of anyone coming back to tell."

"Yeah, that's what I thought," I said and sat back in the seat. I appreciated that she didn't make up some crap about it being instant and painless. "I'm going to sleep. Wake me up when you need me to drive."

That's what I said, but really, I turned my head to the side and let the tears fall. Sleep was a long time coming.

CHAPTER 33

Forgive me for the delay,
I wrote. In pen. On paper.

To avoid leaving an electronic trail, we would mail this, with some ghost help, from a post office in another part of the country. My parents would appreciate something in my own writing, as messy as it still was. Even writing it, I felt a sense of closeness knowing they would hold this piece of paper, read these strokes of ink.

I rubbed my hands vigorously up and down my bare arms, goose-bumped from cold more than emotion. I wished I had remembered my hoodie. I still wasn't used to Vancouver weather. It didn't seem that cold for late September, but when the temperature dropped even a little out here on the coast, the damp chill cut right to the bone.

I picked up the pen and started copying the lines I'd agonized over from my phone screen to the paper once more.

I trust you received my earlier note and didn't worry too much.

Of course they worried. A postcard supposedly from Utah with 'I'm fine, will write soon' scrawled on it couldn't have been reassuring.

I'm sorry for leaving with no notice. In helping my friends, I may have drawn the eye of those we tried to leave in the past. I would hate to lead that attention back to you, or force you to move. Again.

I'm sharing a house with friends and am in school and enjoying it.

That was a massive understatement. My classes were hard, but I loved them. Between my shifting sex, and lack of money, I'd long ago given up any dream of attending university. In following Sarah, I'd thought if I were very lucky, I could apprentice to another shifter and practice changing forms. What I got went beyond anything I'd dreamed.

Apparently, a successful shifter needed to be fluent in several languages, trained in martial arts, and know dozens of other skills. With my unique talent for taking on someone else's exact form, my instructors wanted to cram as much knowledge into my head as they possibly could. As they described it, there was no point in looking exactly like someone else if I was exposed the minute I opened my mouth.

I'm learning what I need to work against those we've been hiding from, so maybe in the future, we, and people like us, won't need to hide any more.

Ian's sacrifice had already saved so many from suffering. Key figures from right-wing groups all around the world had disappeared. I'd remembered seeing some of them at the sealing gathering. It couldn't be a coincidence that that many popular conservative influencers had either gone silent or pivoted their content away from politics.

The 'bombing' of the Banff Springs had been front-page news in Canada for a few days, though Sarah had confirmed that the only people reported to have lost their lives had been working for the wizards. None of the public figures who'd mysteriously died or disappeared the same night had been linked to it. Not even the ones from Alberta.

It was of some relief to Angela and I that no innocents had died as a result of our actions, though several people had been injured in the blast or the evacuation. Although everyone, including my therapist, asked me not to, I still felt responsible for the father who'd been murdered, rammed by the van when the goons pulled Sarah and I off the street.

I won't go into detail, but you've likely seen the impact of our work around the world, and in Alberta recently.

The referendum that would have replaced the federal RCMP with provincial sheriffs, and shifted a load of powers from city police to the sheriffs, had been resoundingly defeated last week after the ruling Conservative government had fallen into complete disarray. Half of their sitting MLAs, feeling the political winds changing, or perhaps feeling their future rewards less certain, had come out strongly critical of the plan.

I want you to know I'm happy and healthy, and I will see you again in person someday. I love you both so much.

I blinked and had to quickly wipe away a tear before it fell on the cream paper. We'd had our disagreements, but I missed them.

A warm weight of fabric draped over my shoulders. I tensed to spring, heart racing, before realizing it was Angela.

"I saw you left your hoodie at home," she said, sitting down in the free chair beside me at the table. At this hour of the morning, the university library was thinly populated. Most students were in class or sleeping.

"Thanks, Ange." I put down my pen and stuffed my arms in the hoodie sleeves.

When we'd arrived in Vancouver, Sarah had found and bought another fixer-upper that was a reasonable (well, my idea of reasonable) bike ride away from the university. When I wasn't busy with classes, I helped her plan the upgrades and keep an eye on the contractors. She told my instructors to give me credit for it as one of my skill paths.

Sarah visited the university hospital often, receiving treatments to reduce or eliminate the scars the Clan had left on her body. Angela and I lived with her, handling meals and stuff when she had trouble moving around after treatments. It seemed that killing that wizard guard, Brent, had helped give her some closure.

Angela was even busier with classes than I was. Apparently, learning to be a mage involved far, far too much math. She said the only thing keeping her sane was that most of it was immediately useful in spell work, which she threw herself into with a passion after having been restricted from using her magic for so many years.

As part of our cover identities, she'd changed her look. Her hair was straightened and dyed black. She said it was a pain to upkeep, but she was taking advantage of it to wear all the shades of red that had clashed with her hair before, like her current fuzzy sweater.

I still missed her beautiful coppery hair, but I kept quiet about it., I didn't want to rub salt in the wound in case she missed it too, or to make her think her appearance affected my feelings for her. My look had shifted, too. I practiced until I could consistently reproduce a different face, one that matched my new identity, with light brown hair and green eyes.

I kept the androgynous look, and with the control I'd gained, I was able to keep the gendered changes to a minimum, so my body was roughly consistent no matter what gender I was feeling. Everyone here knew me as non-binary, and no one was rude enough to ask about my genitals. Angela was the only person who needed to know about that!

And did she ever know! We kept our own rooms in the house for studying, and any time we felt like sleeping alone, but that wasn't very often.

"You know you could work on that at home," she said, glancing at my letter.

"Yeah, but it's a little quieter here," I said neutrally. Mostly, I didn't want her or Sarah concerned by my sadness. They meant well, but they would make a big deal of taking care of me again, and they had their own challenges to deal with.

The letter to my parents was an easy job I was getting out of the way so that I could focus on the hard one—my eulogy for Ian. Sarah thought it was time we held a wake for him to help in our grieving. While on some level I knew she was right, I dreaded returning to those emotions. I had put them out of my mind in the rush to get used to our new home and attending university a year earlier than expected.

"Well, in that case, I'll leave you to it." She smiled gently. "I have to get to the lab anyway. I have a wards class this afternoon and I'd like to suck less than I did last week."

"You'll get it," I encouraged. "You don't have to learn it all in a month."

"This from the person who was freaking out about their Korean class?" she needled me.

"Yeah, I guess. It turns out watching lots of TV with subtitles doesn't help as much as I hoped it would." I grimaced.

"Especially when you're taking advanced French and Spanish at the same time," she said in amused tones. "I never know what language you and Sarah are going to be speaking. It's exhausting."

She leaned forward and we shared a lingering goodbye kiss, then she was off with a wave. I watched her go. Of course.

As Sarah said, feeling the weight of the world was on your shoulders was the exact time to indulge yourself in the simple joys of being alive and free.

ACKNOWLEDGMENTS

When I started this book in 2014, it soon became clear that there was no way to write this sex/gender shifting story without trans perspectives. I owe a debt of gratitude to the many transgender people who shared their lived experiences online. It helped me understand why I needed to write this book—that I was trans!

I am thankful, as always, for my partner Rebecca Brae. For her constant encouragement, her reading and re-reading of multiple drafts, and her patience with many, many questions about what it's like to move through the world as a teen girl. And of course, for her active support of my transition journey that was sparked by this book's development.

And finally, this book would never have reached its full potential without the invaluable assistance of editor Molly Desson and the team at Renaissance Press.

ABOUT THE AUTHOR

Adriaan has been writing since 2010, working happily with their wife who is also an author. They come up with five story ideas a day but alas are unable to write that fast! The esteemed title of 'daddy' was bestowed upon Adriaan some years ago and they still take those duties as their highest calling. Adriaan came out as nonbinary in 2020 and started a transition journey for which there is no defined end goal. Links to all their books and socials can be found at braevitae.com.

ABOUT RENAISSANCE

Renaissance was founded in May 2013 by a group of authors and designers who wanted to publish and market those stories which don't always fit neatly in a genre, or a niche, or a demographic. Like the happy panbibliophiles we are, we opened our submissions, with no other guideline than finding a Canadian book we would fall in love with.

Today, this is still very true; however, we've also noticed an interesting trend in what we like to publish. It turns out that we are naturally drawn to the voices of those who are members of a marginalized group, and these are the voices we want to continue to uplift.

At Renaissance, we do things differently. We are passionate about books, and we care as much about our authors enjoying the publishing process as we do about our readers enjoying a great Canadian read on the platform they prefer.

pressesrenaissancepress.ca

pressesrenaissancepress@gmail.com